Under the
ENDLESS MOON

CW01064396

Copyright © 2025 A.L. Jackson Books Inc.
First Edition

All rights reserved. Except as permitted under the U.S. Copyright Act of 1976, no part of this publication may be reproduced, distributed, transmitted in any form or by any means, or stored in a database or retrieval system, without prior permission of the publisher. Please protect this art form by not pirating.

A.L. Jackson
www.aljacksonauthor.com
Cover Design by Qamber Designs
Cover Image by Michelle Lancaster
Editing by SS Stylistic Editing
Proofreading by Julia Griffis, The Romance Bibliophile
Formatting by Champagne Book Design

The characters and events in this book are fictitious. Names, characters, places, and plots are a product of the author's imagination. Any similarity to real persons, living or dead, is coincidental and not intended by the author.

MORE FROM

A.L. Jackson

NEW YORK TIMES BESTSELLING AUTHOR

Moonlit Ridge
From Here to Eternity
Under an Endless Moon
At the Edge of Surrender
Beyond the Blue Horizon
On the Brink of Bliss

Time River
Love Me Today
Don't Forget Me Tomorrow
Claim Me Forever
Hold Me Until Morning

Redemption Hills
Give Me a Reason
Say It's Forever
Never Look Back
Promise Me Always

The Falling Stars Series
Kiss the Stars
Catch Me When I Fall
Falling into You
Beneath the Stars

Confessions of the Heart
More of You
All of Me
Pieces of Us

Fight for Me
Show Me the Way
Follow Me Back
Lead Me Home
Hold on to Hope

Bleeding Stars
A Stone in the Sea
Drowning to Breathe
Where Lightning Strikes
Wait
Stay
Stand

The Regret Series
Lost to You
Take This Regret
If Forever Comes

The Closer to You Series
Come to Me Quietly
Come to Me Softly
Come to Me Recklessly

Stand-Alone Novels
Pulled
When We Collide

Hollywood Chronicles, a collaboration with USA Today Bestselling
Author, Rebecca Shea
One Wild Night
One Wild Ride

Under an
ENDLESS MOON

NEW YORK TIMES BESTSELLING AUTHOR
A.L. JACKSON

Chapter

ONE

OTTO

"THIS ONE SHOULD BE EASY," RIVER SAID, THOUGH IT SOUNDED almost like a question as he glanced around at our crew.

We were down in the hidden basement at Kane's, which was the most popular club in our small town of Moonlit Ridge.

The heavy thud of music seeped through the cracks, vibrating the ceiling and walls.

Down here where we were secreted away, the small space was dim and dingy, the single bulb that hung from the ceiling the only light in the room.

Five of us sat around the big circular table beneath it. My attention bounced around at every member of Sovereign Sanctum:

River, our leader.

Kane, our money launderer.

Theo, the protector.

Cash, our hacker.

Then there was me, the deliverer.

Tension was always tight whenever we met like this. You'd think that after doing this for close to ten years and the lives we led, it would have abated by now. But no, I could taste the apprehension that would forever leak from our spirits.

"No. I don't foresee any problems," I told him. "Everything is set."

River shifted his attention to Theo. "You're sure they're ready for transport?"

He kept his voice low like someone was going to overhear when we were buried thirty feet below.

Angie and her two sons had been hidden away at The Sanctuary for two months. It was the motel Theo owned and ran, a cover since we used it as a transition house. A temporary place to shelter those who we were helping to give new lives while we figured out their permanent accommodations.

Theo gave a tight nod as he roughed a tatted hand through his shock of black hair.

"Yeah. Angie is still skittish, but I'm not sure that's going to change any time soon," he said.

"She's been through it," Kane agreed.

River turned his dark gaze to me. "Then it's a go for you. Are you ready?"

Every one of us had a specific job. A task in our organization. Mine was to get them to their new homes. The one who was there when they went on their own.

I gave my crew a giant grin, playing light the way I did. "Always ready for it."

Kane laughed with a shake of his head. Dude was covered in tats like the rest of us. But he still somehow came off a little more polished.

"You always take it on like you're running a game," he tossed at me.

"Only way to live life, isn't it?" Especially when we never knew when it was going to come to an end. Had never had the illusion that I was going to make it to be an old man.

Might as well live fast and hard and to the extreme while I had the chance. Use up every second that I was given. I could almost feel the end coming up fast. A roil of hatred burned through me when I thought of what I'd discovered. Finally picking up the scent of the motherfuckers I'd been hunting for the last seven years.

I glanced at my left hand where two stacked Ss were tattooed with an eye in the middle of them. A broken, mangled heart sat atop the dagger that ran it through. I flexed my hand, trying to quell the rage, to tamp it down and save it for when I could use it.

Vengeance was coming and it was coming soon.

I forced myself back into my typical casualness when River grunted at me. My best friend was nothing but a grumpy asshole, though he'd softened a bit since his girl, Charleigh, had come into his life.

"Want you to be careful," he warned.

I rocked my massive frame back in the wooden chair. "When have I not been careful?"

Kane scoffed a mocking sound. "Says the guy who runs straight into danger like he's looking for it."

I shrugged with a smirk. "When duty calls."

Everyone else was grinning, too.

All except for Cash who basically glared at me from across the table. Dude never said much, anyway, so it wasn't like it set off any alarm bells for the rest of the crew, but I knew exactly what he was thinking.

I beat down the rash of unease and instead glanced around at the rest. "Are we good, then? This boy is ready to get back upstairs and have a little bit of fun."

Theo chuckled. "Not sure *a little bit* is in your vocabulary."

"He's going to have to play it cool tonight. He has a big job ahead of him tomorrow night," River said like he was my mother telling me not to stay up too late because I had a test in the morning.

"I'll be sure to be in bed by midnight, Mommy," I razzed.

It was already twelve-thirty, but what the hell ever.

His annoyance couldn't blot out the amusement, but then he was sobering as he said, "Be safe, brother."

My head dipped, and I tried to beat back the guilt that wanted to surface. "Always."

He gave a nod of acceptance before he stuck out his fist that was tattooed with the same stacked Ss as the rest of us, though his dagger was topped with a crown. Each of ours varied a bit, though the oath it represented remained the same.

We all stretched out our fists to meet in the middle of the table.

"Our oath to the afflicted. Our oath to the forsaken. Our oath to Sovereign Sanctum," River chanted.

We all repeated it, the vow we had made years ago to stand for the abused and neglected. By any means necessary. Our good deeds were usually done dirty. All our hands were blood-stained and tainted, but it wasn't like we didn't start our lives out as criminals when we'd first met.

The five of us on the streets of LA.

None of us were related, but we were brothers. Through and through. And this oath? It ran deep.

Chair legs screeched as we all pushed out from the table, and in an instant, the mood changed to light as we started up the narrow staircase that led to the main floor.

I wasn't the only one here who liked to have a good time.

All except for Cash who would slink right out and head to his cabin that was secluded in the mountains. Last place he'd want to be was in a packed club.

River was at the helm, moving faster than the rest of us since the sappy motherfucker couldn't wait to get upstairs to Charleigh and his little sister Raven.

Raven.

I did my best to ignore the bolt of greed that slammed me at just the thought of her. That was not the place I needed to let my brain go.

We wound to the top, and River opened the door that led from the basement and into Kane's office at the back of the building.

We all piled into the room, then he closed the door behind us, making sure it was secure and concealed behind the façade of bookshelves that covered the entire back wall. It made it impossible to locate if you didn't already know it was there.

Everyone trudged for the main door of his office, and Kane unlocked it and let everyone out. The decibel of the music grew tenfold as we stepped into the dimly lit hall, my crew laughing and joking as we slipped through the swinging door at the end and out into the main area of the club.

In an instant, I was caught in the frenetic energy that seethed in the cavernous space.

The band had already played, and the DJ had taken over. A throng of people were crushed on the dance floor, writhing as they danced their cares away.

Kane's was housed in an enormous old church, and above, the ceiling seemed to disappear into eternity. Long, vertical stained-glass windows were situated way up high on the walls. Strobe lights struck against them, and it sent glittering flashes of every color through the entire place.

Off to my right was a bar that ran the length of that wall, and there were at least five bartenders slinging drinks behind it as a ton of people vied to get close enough to catch their attention.

But my attention? It immediately swept to the left.

To the private, secluded booth at the very back of the club that was always reserved for our family. River asked Kane to keep it roped off because he was a protective bastard like that, not that I was going to fault him for it when I was one hundred percent on board.

Because there she was.

Raven. Fucking. Tayte.

My best friend's little sister.

Sweetest girl on the face of the planet.

And to my great misfortune, the sexiest one, too.

She was behind the rope with Charleigh, and the two of them were giggling and laughing. Raven's arm was slung over Charleigh's shoulder as they shared what looked to be some sordid secret.

Leave it to Raven to be dressed completely in black, wearing the shortest fuckin' skirt I'd ever seen and a black leather corset that smushed her tits up at the top. Then she had to go and pair it with these thigh-high boots with a five-inch stiletto heel.

Looking like the only place she belonged was on the back of my bike.

Lush, black hair was done half up and half down, showing off the sharp angles of her stunning face. Makeup thick the way she always wore it, lips stained red.

But it was those inky eyes that nailed me to the spot.

So dark and mesmerizing they held me like a trap.

A thunderbolt of lust gripped me by the guts, but I sucked it down and pinned on a giant grin as I sauntered her way, reminding myself with each step of who she was and who she would always be to me.

When she saw me coming, she squealed and lifted her frilly drink over her head.

"Otto! It's about time you got your cute butt over here! I thought you guys forgot all about us."

Highly fucking unlikely.

Especially with the way River went straight for Charleigh and pulled her into his arms so he could kiss the fuck out of her.

"Hey, way to steal my bestie!" Raven shouted at her brother's back. He only slanted her a grin from over his shoulder as he backed Charleigh deeper into a dark corner.

"Can you believe him?" she asked in feigned offense.

The rest of our crew, sans Cash, of course, slipped into the big horseshoe booth.

I went for where Raven stood, playing it casual the way I always did because what else was I supposed to do, and I slung my arm over her shoulders and gave her a squeeze. "Now don't go and get jealous, Raven. You have your older, even better big brother to hang out with."

Yup. I'd dubbed myself her big brother. Way fuckin' safer that way, putting her into that box when I could never have her the way I really wanted.

"It's not the brother part I'm worried about, Otto. He stole my bestie. Stole her right out from under me. Just like he did from the beginning. He keeps saying he saw her first, but I beg to differ. I'm the one who invited her to come hang out with us the first time, and since my brother is nothing but a big oaf, he never would have taken it upon himself to do it. Where would he be without me? And there he goes, whisking her away from me again when he should be kissing the ground I walk on."

She gave me the most ridiculous faked pout I'd ever seen. Wasn't sure how one woman could be so adorable and sexy at the same time.

A rough chuckle scraped up my throat, and I hugged her a little closer. "Think you're just going to have to share that bestie of yours. One look at Charleigh, and your brother goes feral."

Her nose scrunched. "I don't need that vision in my head, thank you very much."

I laughed, and she nestled into my side like it was what she was meant to do.

Her aura invaded my senses.

She smelled like a vineyard of honeysuckle.

A sweet fucking moonflower.

I was almost used to disregarding the urge I had to tuck her all the way into me. Press my nose into the thick black locks of her hair. Breathe her sweetness right down into my lungs. Drown myself on her intoxicating floral scent.

Would never do that, though.

Raven was pure. Good right down to the marrow.

This world might have made me a vile beast, but I at least had the conscience to be sure of that. Had almost made that mistake once, and it'd proven to me exactly why I could never deserve someone like her.

How I only failed the ones I loved most.

Besides, River would straight-up gut me if I even considered pushing past those barriers with his sister. Hell, he'd do it now if he had half the inclination of the fantasies she conjured in me every time I looked at her. If he knew how I'd felt that time when he'd confronted me about it, and I'd lied through my teeth.

So, I shoved it down into the deepest parts of me and pretended like it didn't exist, ignored that ravenous desire, and guided her over to the booth.

Theo pushed into the middle, and Raven slipped in with me right behind her.

I slung my arm right back over her shoulder.

Our server immediately showed, balancing a bunch of drinks on a tray. "Here we are. Another round for my favorite table."

"Ahh, Tiff, you are always two steps ahead of the game," Kane told her. Dude was rocked back in the plush, high-backed booth like he was some kind of king, but I guessed around here, he was. The owner of his namesake, which we used to cover all the funds that we had rolling through.

"Gotta keep the boss happy," she said, her tone light.

Didn't miss the way she looked at me when she set my whiskey in front of me.

A candid invitation.

Had gone back to her place a couple times. The woman was crazy hot and more than a good time, but I got the sense that maybe her thoughts had started slanting in a direction they shouldn't.

Thinking she might rein me, when I'd promised her from the get-go that was not gonna happen.

"Thank you," I told her, jutting my chin at her before she reluctantly walked away.

I felt the force of Raven's scowl.

"What?" I asked her, my stomach unsettled but my voice full of a tease.

"I don't know how you get away with it."

"And what's that?"

"Come on, Otto, you know exactly what I'm talking about. You're such a player."

"Well, of course, I am, darlin'. And you know exactly how I do it." I jostled her a little.

"Ugh," Raven groaned. "So arrogant."

"Like you don't know you're the fuckin' hottest thing in this club," I tossed back.

Shit.

Maybe I was pushing it too far because Theo arched a speculative brow as he took a sip of his scotch, clearly thinking he should deliver me a warning.

Kane let go of a low chuckle.

"Well, I *am* pretty hard to look away from," Raven said. "Have you seen this top?"

Top?

I would hardly call it that.

She shimmied her shoulders.

Taunting me the way she liked to do. As if I hadn't noticed. As if I didn't see her face every damned time I blinked.

Sometimes I thought she was purposefully trying to drive me to the edge.

"Honestly, I can't believe River let you out of the house dressed like that," Kane said with a disbelieving shake of his head.

"Yeah, my baby sister is a fuckin' stunner. I'm going to have to look after you tonight to make sure the pervs stay away," I said as casually as I could.

Calling her that was nothing but a bucket of ice water dumped directly onto my head. A wedge driven between us. A reminder of every reason I could never go there.

I mean, fuck, I'd known her since she was just a little kid. Since she was nine years old.

Back when River had shown up with her in LA after he'd gotten her away from the abuse of their piece of shit father.

Would never forget the first time I saw her. This terrified little thing who'd been wrapped in a blanket and shaking in the corner of the abandoned building where we'd lived.

A shiver of old fury rolled through me. The knowledge of what she had gone through. Both then and later.

A flash of annoyance took hold of her expression, making me sure she hated when I called her that, before she pinned on a saucy smirk that was nothing but a challenge. "Maybe that's exactly what I'm looking for tonight…some hot guy who wants to take me home."

I had to restrain the growl from getting loose of my chest. I knew she'd been dating some little douchewad a month or so back. Couldn't handle the vile image of the bastard wrapped up in that lush, gorgeous body.

I'd overheard her telling Charleigh that she'd ended things. They'd gone to whispering when they realized I was eavesdropping, so I hadn't been able to get the full story. The only thing I'd known for sure was the fuckin' punch of relief I'd felt at the news.

If she hooked up tonight with some other loser, I was going to go off the rails.

"You know, someone who's rough and dirty," she continued, driving the needle in. "Maybe one of your biker friends."

She looked around the table like she was asking one of us to set her up.

That time, I did growl. "Watch yourself, Raven, or any prick you decide to grace with your presence tonight is going to end up missin'."

"Second that," Theo said, lifting his glass like we were making a pact.

She laughed like it was absurd. She should have known better. She pointed around the table. "All of you, including my brother, are going to have to stop that nonsense." She hooked her thumb toward her chest. "I'm twenty-five. TWENTY-FIVE. I'm not a little girl anymore. Time to accept it because this girl is ready to spread her wings."

Was pretty sure the spreading of her wings would be the death of me.

The song changed and Raven gasped, and immediately her attention was on me, her black tipped nails digging into my right bicep. "It's my jam! Out you go. We're dancing. You know, since my bestie is otherwise occupied."

She shooed me out to standing and slipped from the booth. There was nothing I could do but trail behind her as she strutted that fine, leather-clad ass out onto the dance floor. Heels so goddamn high I couldn't breathe.

Then she turned to me and grinned as she started to swivel those hips.

Maybe I should have accepted it as my fate. That it was already over. Maybe I should have known Raven Tayte was really going to be the end of me.

Chapter

TWO

Raven

"I T'S DECIDED, OTTO. I'M GOING TO FIND ME ONE OF THOSE BIKERS tonight." I winked at my brother's best friend as I swiveled my hips to the dark beat that thrummed in the club. Lights strobed in time, colored flashes striking over the throbbing crowd packed on the dance floor.

My claim was hysterical considering I couldn't look at a single other person right then.

Could anyone blame me, though?

Otto Hudson was so hot it was unfair.

So hot it was physically painful.

Staring at him was like standing in the sun and knowing you were going to get burned, but you did it anyway because it felt so good while you baked in the blistering rays.

The man was a mountain hewn of rugged stone.

A beast barely contained.

My burly bear covered in tats.

There was no questioning it with the way the ground shook with every step he took. A rolling thunder that moved through me in battering waves.

He'd cut his hair, one side cropped short and the other a little longer, and a day of scruff covered his strong, brutal jaw.

But what made my insides quake were his eyes. A piercing, entrancing blue that always made me feel as if I'd been speared to the spot. As if they could carve and cut and see right down to the depths of me.

The man would be wholly terrifying if it wasn't for the constant smirk he wore at the edge of his mouth and the tease that was never far from his tongue, though I knew well enough he was as deadly as the rest of my brother's crew.

Only I was pretty sure the smirk currently sitting on his striking face was forged right then. "Ah, playin' with fire tonight, are we?" he grumbled, his voice coarse and just loud enough to be heard over the deafening decibel of the music.

Otto stepped forward and snaked an arm around my waist, moving in time the way we always did.

Fire raced beneath the surface of my skin.

I'd been almost nineteen when he'd taught me to dance. It was after he'd been sent away to prison and then had been released. When everything had changed for me. When the feelings I'd always felt for him had amassed into something bigger, and I'd fully understood what they meant.

I knew for him, it had been innocent, but it'd never felt that way for me. It'd felt salacious. Like stolen touches that weren't meant for me, but I wanted to take them for myself, anyway.

He dragged me closer and leaned in close to my ear. "You keep it up, and I'm going to have to haul you out of here over my shoulder."

My spirit throbbed against his threat.

A very foolish part of me begged him to do it.

"You wouldn't dare," I told him instead.

"Try me, darlin'." His smirk spread. "It seems you're looking for a whole lot of trouble...dressed like that. Every man here has to be losing his damned mind."

God, he was impossible. Warning me over the truths that I gave him, as if I didn't have the right to my own needs—to my own desires—and then turning around and drawing me right back into them.

But it'd always been like that with him. Since I was eighteen and I'd been ignorant enough to believe there was a chance that he would look at me the same way I'd always looked at him. The only thing I'd ever wanted was for him to *look* at me, and when he did, for the void I knew lived inside him to pulse and glow. For him to feel it. For him to know I was supposed to be something so much more than his friend.

So much more than his baby sister.

Just the thought of that title icked me out.

But this was the relationship we'd slipped into. This man who felt like a piece of my fabric, but our stitching had never quite come together.

"I'm here to blow a few minds." I twisted my voice into a tease, my belly trembled at his proximity.

"Just like I thought. Nothing but trouble," he murmured. "What am I supposed to do with you?"

"Dance with me?"

"One of my favorite things to do," he said, and he tucked me even closer.

His aura surrounded me.

Patchouli and warm apple pie. No man should smell that good.

I wanted to sink into it.

Disappear.

"Think I might keep you…just like this." His words were a warm vibration that slithered across my flesh.

What I wouldn't give to fully fall into it. Have him wrap me completely in those massive arms. Hold me the way I'd always dreamed of him doing.

But I knew better than getting my hopes up for that. The only thing it'd ever done was set me up to get my heart crushed. It was time I grew beyond it.

I'd been trying. Trying to escape the cage where I'd been trapped.

The problem was, every time I attempted it, I freaked out. My exterior might come across as bold, but it was the inside that shuddered at moving on.

But Otto didn't need to know that.

"I'm not that great, am I?" I went for light as I peeked up at his rugged face.

A deep chuckle rolled through his chest. "I think you know exactly how great you are, Raven Tayte."

"How great?" I pressed through the razzing.

"Oh, the greatest."

"Is that so?"

"Mmhmm..."

I was sinking, melding into his form as we moved to the rhythm. "We're out of here."

When the voice hit us from the side, Otto jerked back like he'd been caught committing a mortal sin.

My brother was there, wrapped around my bestie from behind.

I did my best to clear the need from my being and pinned on an affront of disbelief. "What? You can't leave already. We're just getting started."

I reached out, took Charleigh's hand and swung it between us. "I promised that you were going to have a blast tonight, and hello, I am a blast. Look no further, a good time is standing right in front of you."

"Think she's going to have a good time with me. Nolan is with the sitter tonight, so it's just us," River rumbled.

I tried not to gag at what he was implying. It was hard when your best friend was dating your brother.

I scrunched my nose at him. "Thief. You stole her right out from under me."

Charleigh giggled as she leaned back against him. "Let it be said that I belong to both of you. Equally."

"Nah, Little Runner, you're mine," River grumbled at her cheek.

She turned red, her love for him shining in her expression.

I might give them a hard time, but they were perfect for each other. I loved them together so much.

But I also was kind of starting to feel like a third wheel.

"I'll give Raven a lift home." Otto's voice was easy as he issued it, and he slung an arm over my shoulders the way he always did.

A shiver rolled down my spine.

I wanted to turn and press my nose into his thick throat. Inhale him into all the secret places inside me where I wanted to keep him.

"You sure you don't mind?" River asked.

"You know I've got her covered."

River reached out and squeezed Otto's shoulder. "Appreciate it, man. You always looking out for her."

"Always."

I would have argued that I could get myself home, but riding on the back of Otto's bike was kind of my thing.

"See you in the morning then," River said, and he stepped forward and pecked a kiss to my temple. "Be safe."

"You don't have to worry about her when she's with me."

Charleigh edged forward and hugged me. "Sorry I'm bailing. It's just…"

She trailed off, leaving no question what the *it's just* meant.

I playfully waved her away. "Go on and be with your man. I'll be fine. I have Otto here to keep me company."

I hip checked him, except he was so tall that even in my heels, my hip barely made it to his upper thigh.

"That's right," he rumbled in his rough way, that grin perched on his distracting, delicious mouth.

"All right, then, see you later." Then River's expression darkened when he turned his focus on Otto. "Be safe tomorrow. Text me when the package is delivered and you're on your way back."

My stomach clutched.

This was the part of their lives that sent dread spiraling through the middle of me. I knew it was worth it. What they did. But that didn't mean I didn't worry every time one of them left on a mission. I rarely knew the details. It was a Sovereign Sanctum rule. The less someone knew, the better. The safer it was for everyone.

But sometimes I hated being left in the dark.

"You know I will." Otto's promise was solemn.

With a tight nod, River took Charleigh's hand and they disappeared into the fray.

I turned to look up at Otto. I knew my worry was written in every line on my face.

Bodies writhed around us, while I just stood there, staring up at him.

Finally, I found my voice. "You have a job?"

A thousand emotions raced through Otto's eyes, so many that I didn't know what to make of them. His mouth hitched on one side as he reached out and traced the pad of his thumb over the edge of my lip.

I nearly came apart at the sensation.

"You don't need to worry about me, Raven."

"You think I don't? You think I could stop?"

Regret spilled into his features before arrogance came riding back. "You think anyone could get at me? Don't worry, darlin'. I'm as safe as could be."

Disquiet gusted through my being. I didn't know what it was, but his words hit me like a lie.

"We need you here, you know that." A bit of despair colored my voice.

"Wouldn't leave you, Raven."

Energy swelled between us. Our connection that we'd shared for so long flaming in the space. It was so intense and consuming that sometimes I swore it had to mean more than what we'd been labeled.

I nearly scoffed at myself.

I'd been thinking that for so long that it was becoming pathetic.

Clearing my throat, I cocked my head, covering the emotion and tossing it in light. "Good because I would have to hunt you down and kick your stubborn ass if you let yourself get hurt."

Otto chuckled as his gaze swept over me. Something dark pulsed in the depths of that sapphire gaze. "Stubborn? Think you need to look in the mirror."

My heart fisted when he said it, a thousand memories slamming me at his words. They shouldn't mean much of anything. But to me? They'd meant everything.

"I just know what I want, Otto, and I'm finally going to go after it. Now, if you'll excuse me, I'm going to use the restroom, grab another tasty drink, and then take a little whirl around the club to see if anything catches my eye. Maybe I won't require a ride home, after all."

I tossed my hair over my shoulder, giving him as much sass as I could muster, acting like every interaction I had with him didn't make my very untrustworthy legs quake.

Irritation buzzed through his demeanor, though he cracked a grin. "Just make sure he's not a biker. Or a douchewad with a tiny prick who thinks he's God's gift to women. Or wearing a goddamned suit, for that matter. Last thing I need is for you to go breaking my heart."

I had to hold back a scowl. I didn't think he had the first clue about breaking hearts.

"You pretty much just whittled my options down to nothing."

He tugged on a lock of my hair. "Exactly the point."

Ugh. I wanted to stamp my foot and scream. Instead, I strutted off the dance floor, and I lifted my hand above my head and gave him a middle finger as I went.

I could feel the ripple of his chuckle follow after me.

Frustrating, infuriating man.

Still, a smile threatened as I wound through the horde of people packed in Kane's and headed down the hall to the left of the dance floor toward the restrooms. I pushed into the women's and went straight to the sink, trying to gather the disorder of thoughts that whirled around me.

This need to let go. To set myself free.

All mixed up with the bindings that had always tied me to Otto.

Blowing out a sigh, I washed my hands and dried them with a paper towel, then I blotted it against my face before I stepped back out into the hall.

I came to a halt when I saw who was standing directly on the other side.

Tanner.

Unease twisted my stomach.

"Tanner, hey. What are you doing here?"

A frown pinched his brow, and I saw the hurt and frustration spin through his green eyes. "Was out with a friend and saw you come this way."

The twist in my stomach lessened. "Oh…well…"

I trailed off, not even sure what I was supposed to say.

"I haven't heard from you," he said.

Okay, so he was just going to toss it out there. Make an awkward situation even more uncomfortable.

Tanner was another failed attempt at me trying to spread my wings. To break out and fly. He was definitely good looking. Not quite a biker, but he was a mechanic and was covered in tats which I was pretty sure was my thing.

I'd truly given dating him a shot, but it couldn't be helped that I'd wanted to vomit when he'd set his hand on my thigh when he'd kissed me.

He'd tried to talk me into giving it another try, but I didn't see the sense in dragging it out when we'd clearly hit our end.

He and I were just not it.

I didn't want to hurt his feelings, but also, I'd been totally clear, and he'd still texted me a bunch of times trying to pressure me into changing my mind.

I was not about that.

"Um…that's because we broke up."

He took a step forward, and there was something about it that made me take one back. "I thought we were going to talk about that?"

"And I told you that would only prolong the inevitable."

I gasped when he snatched me by the wrist. "Come on, Raven…I don't understand what happened."

A tiny shock of fear thrummed through my spirit, and I wrangled my arm free of his hold. "I told you that it didn't feel right to me. Let's leave it at that."

I tried to keep the tremble from my voice, but my breaths bottomed out when he pushed in closer and backed me into the wall.

Panic started to well. Old fears rising up at someone touching me when I didn't want them to. Ringing blared in my ears, and his voice was garbled when he said, "But we could be so good—"

Except he didn't make it to the end of the sentence before the shockwave of aggression rocketed through the air. A fiery ferocity that froze him to the spot.

"I'd think twice about touching her when she made it plenty clear that she doesn't want you to." The words coming out of Otto's mouth were daggers.

Sharp and impaling.

Tanner glanced over his shoulder at Otto who raged behind him. A beast that vibrated malice. So tall he nearly touched the ceiling. Shoulders so wide I thought they might be brushing each side.

The colors and innuendos written on his flesh writhed over his muscles that flexed and bowed with barely held restraint.

You'd think Tanner would be smart enough to back away, but instead, he sneered, "This is none of your concern. Think you've been in the way enough."

It was the wrong thing to say.

Okay, the worst thing to say.

Because Otto had grabbed him and had him pinned to the opposite wall before any of us could make sense of the movement.

The man might have been a giant, but damn, he was fast.

Otto's arm pressed up under Tanner's chin, tight against his throat. "Ah, see, now that is where you're wrong. Raven is very much a concern of mine, and if some little twat comes around, pushing her in a direction she doesn't want to go, then things aren't gonna end well for him. Do you understand what I'm telling you?"

"Otto." I tried to get his attention, but he was too busy scaring the crap out of Tanner for me to break through to him.

He cracked a menacing grin as he pulled Tanner from the wall then slammed him back against it. "Now get the fuck out of here before I break your fuckin' legs."

He shoved him off.

Tanner stumbled to the side, and he raked the back of his hand over his mouth as if he was trying to wipe off a bad taste. He turned his attention to me. Disgust pulled all over his face. "Yeah, he's like a brother to you, my ass."

"Just leave, Tanner," I told him, praying he wouldn't be an idiot and push this any farther.

He stared at me for a beat before a harsh breath jutted from his lungs, and he turned on his heel and strode out like he hadn't just been pinned to the wall by a mammoth.

Otto stood there fuming as he watched him disappear around the corner before he spun back to me.

My heart was jackhammering at the interaction, at both the confusion of the way Tanner had acted and the ridiculous show of force that Otto had issued. My offense rushed out before Otto got the chance to say anything. "That was unnecessary, don't you think? I don't need you coming around here tossing all your brute around. I was just fine."

Burly. Freaking. Bear.

Only right then, Otto wasn't the cuddly teddy bear he sometimes was with me.

He absolutely fumed with fury.

It was these moments when I knew he wasn't the happy-go-lucky guy that everyone thought he was. When I knew he was violent and dangerous underneath all those smirks and grins. Hell, I knew Otto Hudson better than anyone.

"I think it was very necessary," he growled.

"I can handle myself."

Otto pressed forward, his big body covering me in shadow, a tall tower that loomed with all that dark intimidation. But his hand was soft when he reached out and set it on my cheek, and he leaned in close when he said, "Told you I would never let anyone hurt you again, and I meant it."

Chapter

THREE

OTTO

River used to razz me that I was a pretty nice guy unless I was murdering someone. Let it be known that I was not feeling so *nice* right then. Was inclined to chase the bastard down and show him exactly what the warning meant.

But Raven was staring up at me, her brow pinched and those inky eyes churning with so much emotion that I didn't know how to make sense of it.

A vixen mixed with fragile vulnerability.

Didn't know what to make of her half the time.

How to handle her.

What to do with the insanity that she conjured inside me.

One thing for sure, I needed her to understand the lengths I would go.

I thought she might argue with me, but instead she whispered, "I'm ready to go home."

Yeah, it was probably a damned good idea since the only thing I wanted was to toss her over my shoulder the way I'd warned her and get her out of the sight of all these motherfuckers who'd been eye-fucking her since the second she'd stepped out onto the dance floor.

Get her away from the prick who'd been pressing in on her like he had the right.

Just get her the hell out of here before I did something stupid and snapped in front of everyone.

Before I did some of that murdering or got really reckless and told her she belonged to me. Maybe push her fully against the wall and make that sexpot mouth mine. God knew all the fucked-up ways I wanted it on me.

I roughed a hand through my hair, just realizing then I was covered in a sheen of sweat. Fiery possession singeing me through. "Sounds like a good plan."

What I really should do was put her in an Uber and send her on her way, seek out Tiff so I could burn off some of this aggression. Distract myself with a hot body like I normally did when this woman spun me up so tight that I couldn't see.

Wasn't sure what the fuck was wrong with me, but I didn't think I could stomach the thought of it tonight. Didn't think there was a chance of letting her out of my sight until I had her tucked safely behind a locked door.

Raven angled around me, her stride quick on those wicked heels, like part of her wanted to get away from me as fast as she could.

She should.

She should stay far the fuck away from me.

But I was right behind her, acting as a fortress as we pushed through the club. Didn't bother to give Theo or Kane a text since they were likely on the prowl, letting loose the way I was a firm believer we all should do.

Except the only person I wanted to *let loose* with right then was a thousand times forbidden. The last fucking person I could take.

She was family.

I guided her through the thrumming throng of Kane's and out into the night.

This late, there was the slightest chill to the air as fall approached. The door swinging closed behind us cut the noise level in half, the quiet of the night butting against the roar from within.

I gave a jut of my chin to Ty and Jonah who were manning the door, and I stayed one step behind Raven as she strode out into the parking lot that was still packed.

My palm barely made contact with the small of her back as we went.

Didn't matter.

The connection still burned me through.

Which meant I needed to get this shit under lock and key considering she was about to be wrapped around me on my bike.

Never said I wasn't a masochist.

Her heels crunched on the loose gravel as we treaded to the line of bikes that were parked along the exterior wall at the front of the club. Mine was right between Theo and Kane's, and Raven strutted right for it, like she was drawn to the metal, though tonight, her energy was all off.

Normally, she was excited as hell to get on the back of my bike.

She was facing away when I rumbled, "You okay?"

Raven barely shook her head as she turned back toward me, and a long sigh pilfered from those red-painted lips. "I just…I need to know that I can handle myself, Otto. *For myself.* I need to know that I don't need you or my brother to sweep in and fix everything that goes wrong for me."

My chest panged.

I got it. I got it. But our lives came with a certain danger, and I'd seen firsthand the depravities that people succumbed to. The atrocities inflicted.

"I know you need your independence, Raven. But the world we live in…"

She blinked those inky eyes. "We all live in that world, Otto, and yeah, it's fucked up and bad things happen, and I know you want to keep me from that, but I need to be able to make mistakes for myself. Fall in love and out of love and deal with douchebags and get my heart broken. I need all of that so *I* can discover what I want and who I want to be."

She fisted her hand over her heart.

Air heaved from my lungs, and I scrubbed a hand over my face. "I know. And I'm sorry if I was being overzealous. But when I came around the corner and found that bastard had you against a wall? There wasn't a speck inside me that would allow me to ignore it. That asshole was pressing you."

He was lucky he wasn't floating face down in the lake.

Frustration billowed out of her, and she tossed an arm out like she was gesturing at him. "Tanner is harmless."

I couldn't do anything but reach out and take her by that wrist. I tugged her forward a step so she was right in front of me. Her presence hit me like a landslide. "Maybe. But I didn't like what was comin' off him. Like you owed him something."

"He's…fine."

Wasn't satisfied with the way she said it. With the uncertainty that flashed through her expression, like maybe she'd felt exactly what I'd felt oozing from him, too.

"I want you to tell me if he's harassing you. That's all I'm asking."

Energy pulsed around us, that thing that I'd been ignoring for years, pretending it only meant I cared about her as a part of my family.

Complete bullshit.

"Promise me," I urged. "Can't stand the idea of someone trying to get you under their thumb."

Emphasis tightened her brow. "You know I would never get myself in a situation like that."

That was the thing, though. No one ever intended on succumbing to an abusive relationship. It was just that they got blindsided along the way and they found themselves in that situation before they knew they were there.

Shucking off the intensity, I canted her a grin. "Good. Just so we're clear."

She rolled those mesmerizing eyes. "Yes, Otto, we're clear. Like you and River would ever let me forget."

"Let you forget how much we care about you? I think not." I wound as much lightness as I could into my voice, and I swung my leg over my bike and kicked it over.

The powerful engine roared to life.

It was a restored 1960s chopper and basically the love of my life since it was the only thing I could ever truly give my heart to. Jud Lawson over in Redemption Hills, one of our friends and the king of restorations out here in the West, had restored it for me.

It was nothing but smoky grays and black matte metals. Its beauty was only second to the girl who was standing to the side of it. The sole reason I'd had him install a fourteen-inch backrest on the rear was so she'd be comfortable whenever she took her spot.

I revved the throttle twice as I widened my grin at her. "Now are you going to get on the back of my bike or are you going to stand out here all night?"

She was still a little annoyed, which I took full responsibility for but still wouldn't change. It seemed her love for riding was close to mine, though, and it took her all of two seconds before she stamped that little foot and grumbled, "Fine."

Shifting, I dug her helmet out of the saddlebag and handed it to her. She was quick to put it on, then I reached out to help her, and she had to swing her leg up to get over the saddle. It gave me a quick flash of the black lace under that short as fuck skirt.

Tried not to take a peep like some kind of creeper, but damn, she didn't even try to hide it. She just climbed on like she wasn't shy, and it wasn't the first time she'd done it.

I wondered if she did it on purpose. Wondered if she had full intentions of driving me out of my ever-lovin'-mind.

No doubt about it as she tucked herself up close to my back and wrapped herself around me.

Heat singed me through.

That lust-inducing body igniting me in her flames.

Revving the engine again, I shouted, "Ready?"

She gave me a squeeze as she hooked her chin on my shoulder, her seductive voice in my ear. "I was born ready, Otto."

I took to the street, and there was no missing the thrill that ran through her being. This girl who fit me like a glove who I forever had to keep at arm's length.

Chapter
FOUR

Raven

WIND LASHED AT MY FACE AND THE STARS TWINKLED AND shined overhead as I clung to Otto as we rode through Moonlit Ridge. The howl of the engine was the only sound in our ears.

The small town was pretty much closed down for the night except for the few bars that remained open. The windows of the trendy stores and shops on Culberry Street were darkened and the streets were close to barren.

It felt as if we were completely isolated and alone as Otto took to the road.

His massive body at the helm of the heavy metal, tattooed arms stretched out as he commanded the vibrating, rumbling machine. Our hair whipped around us, and my heart thundered in time, my blood racing through my veins as we traveled beneath the glinting heavens above.

There was nothing in the world as exhilarating as being on the back of Otto's bike.

I knew he kept our speed safe and controlled whenever I was with him, but that didn't mean adrenaline didn't buzz through me like an electric charge. My spirit nothing but a live wire plugged directly into the man.

This was when I felt the closest to him. When all the intricacies of our lives seemed whittled away, pared down to nothing, and this wordless, perfect moment was the only thing that counted.

We traveled all the way through the main part of town until Culberry Street curved and came to a T at Vista View. He made a right onto the two-lane road that followed along the side of the lake.

I never failed to lose my breath at the stunning view.

It was gorgeous. The expanse of lake was smooth as glass beneath the night. It was surrounded by lush woods, and the mountains rose up high behind it in the distance, their jagged peaks silhouettes where the moon sat proud halfway down the horizon.

Silvery rays glinted over the water, and the few lights of the houses and cabins tucked around the lake glowed their peace.

On the far side of the lake, I could barely make out the neon sign for The Sanctuary, the motel that Theo owned and ran.

I thought of what would be hidden there under the guise of vacationers.

A woman.

Possibly with children.

I didn't want to fathom the horrors that might have brought them there, but ignoring it was impossible.

The pain and danger they'd endured.

The hope that began right there, beneath those bright, shining lights.

I hugged Otto a little tighter as worry infiltrated my being because I knew getting them to safety didn't come without risk.

The lives my brother and his crew led were riddled with peril, though it seemed a little safer than when all of them used to ride with Iron Owls MC back in LA.

That was when it felt like every step they'd taken might be their last.

It didn't mean they were immune now. Look at what had happened to River, Charleigh, and their little boy, Nolan, at the beginning of the summer. How their lives had intersected in a beautiful, horrible way. Charleigh's ex trying to destroy them.

I still thanked God every day that they were safe. They'd made it through, and now they had each other forever.

It was worth it. Of course, it was worth it. For everyone they helped.

But that didn't mean I wasn't terrified any time one of them stepped out the door.

Otto set a big hand on my arms that were linked around his waist. I had to wonder if he had direct access to my thoughts and it was a silent promise that everything was going to be okay.

He slowed as he took a right into the neighborhood where I lived with River and his family, then the next left onto the long drive that led to our house.

A modern cabin tucked deep beneath soaring trees.

Two stories with a pitched roof, made of stones and dark brown woods.

Otto pulled his bike around the circular drive and stopped at the front. He killed the engine, and in an instant, the silence consumed. The night all around and the energy that'd been freed suddenly locked and held tight.

A stark tension that surrounded.

He reached around and took me by the hand. That simple touch was always enough to annihilate me.

"Off you go, darlin'," he said as he helped me stand, which was all kinds of awkward considering the skirt and boots that I was wearing, but I never let that stop me.

No way when I loved how Otto's gaze fired when I dressed like this, his eyes raking over me as if he couldn't help himself.

Once I was steady on my feet, he climbed off, too.

The man a stronghold that towered in the night. So fierce and brutal, though he still wore that smirk on the edge of his decadent mouth as he reached out and carefully undid the straps of my helmet.

Sapphire eyes never looked away as he worked, the air thin and shimmery between us.

When he had it freed, he rested it on the bike's seat then said, "Let's get you inside."

I forced all the need down and rolled my eyes the way I'd done back at Kane's.

"I'm perfectly capable of walking to the door by myself, Otto. Look at me, such a big girl with my own keys and everything."

It was pure sarcasm as I dug into my tiny bag that hung on my hip and pulled my keys out as proof, dangling them between us.

A rough chuckle skated out of him. "And what happens if you slip on those ridiculous heels and break your neck?"

I huffed as I started up the walkway toward the front door. "Then I guess River will find me in the morning when he wakes up. And ridiculous? I don't know what nonsense you speak of. I look amazing in these heels."

I started up the three steps to the wraparound porch that circled the entire house. Otto was right behind. Every step he took was an earthquake that reverberated through me.

"That you do, darlin', but they look about as dangerous as the lives we lead, and since I promised your brother that I'd get you home safely, that means I'm going to get you all the way. Not going anywhere until you're locked tight behind that door."

"Yeah, yeah, yeah," I grumbled. "The promises you make my brother. I see where your loyalties lay and how little I have to say about any of it."

I tried to force the teasing into my words and keep the hurt out, and I turned away from him and started to put the key into the lock.

A short gasp rocked out of me when he took me by the wrist and spun me toward him. Rays of moonlight rippled in behind him, his giant frame covering me like a shield. The breath was ripped out of my lungs when he reached out and ran his fingertips down my cheek.

"You fuckin' count, Raven. Count more than anyone else."

My stomach twisted and my heart careened. God, why did he have to say things like that? Make me feel like I was the most important person in his life before he turned around and broke my heart when he would leave some bar with another woman?

But it was times like these when I thought…

I blinked to stop the stupid train of thought. I was moving beyond that. Beyond him. It was time. I just had to figure out exactly what direction I was going to go.

I turned back around and finished unlocking the door, and I pushed it open to the darkness radiating from inside. I stepped through before I shifted to look at him from over my shoulder.

"Here I am. All safe and sound."

"Only way I want you." There was a softness to his voice when he said it.

"Goodnight, Otto. Thanks for giving me a ride home."

He wore that easy, casual grin, though I swore there was a storm brewing in the depths of his blue, blue eyes. "It's my pleasure, darlin'. I'll see you soon."

I paused, unable to let him go before I whispered, "Be safe."

My chest clutched when he reached out and hooked his pinky with mine. He swung it between us, his voice low when he murmured, "Promise."

It felt like a full minute passed before he released me and rocked back on the heels of his boots as he shoved big, tatted hands into the pockets of his jeans. He remained planted, just wearing that grin, until I shut the door and locked it between us.

With the separation, I breathed out a strained breath and attempted to pull all the frayed edges he always left me with back together. To stitch myself up and mend the pieces he always left undone.

When I heard his motorcycle kick over, I crossed the foyer to the curved staircase that led to the second floor. I kept my footsteps quieted as I went. The landing was dark when I hit the top, and I crept to my bedroom that was down the hall on the left.

I slipped inside, closed the door, and moved across my room as I wound the strap of my bag off my shoulder and tossed it onto my bed. I peeled myself out of the heels that I had to admit were kind of ridiculous but in the best way, then slinked out of my skirt and corset before I pulled on a tank top and sleep shorts.

I stole back out into the bathroom that was next to Nolan's room, brushed my teeth and washed my face, then padded back into my room and crawled into bed.

The second I climbed under the covers, my phone buzzed from my purse. I grinned when I saw who it was from, the nickname I'd given him long ago saved in my phone.

> Burly Bear: You all snug and tucked in?

Talk about ridiculous.

I wavered, unsure if I should answer him directly or taunt him a little. Taunting him seemed the prudent way to go.

> Me: Wouldn't you like to know...

> Burly Bear: Exactly why I'm texting...because I want to know.

I bit down on my bottom lip as my fingers flew across the screen.

> Me: I sent out a booty call, and I'm currently waiting for one of those bikers to crawl through my window.

If only I had the courage to make that happen, but the last thing I wanted was for Otto to think I didn't possess it. For him to know that I'd never recovered.

It took him two minutes before he finally responded.

> Burly Bear: Don't make me turn this bike around.

I hesitated, knowing I was doing nothing but *poking the bear*, but loving the power a little too much.

> Me: Why? You want to watch?

Okay, maybe I had taken the inappropriateness too far. Maybe the margaritas I'd been slinging back at Kane's had gone to my head. Maybe I was playing with fire. Because I might not have been able to hear his voice, but I knew the words he shot back were rabid.

> Burly Bear: Don't push me, Raven. You don't want to see what it looks like when I come unhinged. Think it's best if you keep your conquests to yourself. Don't want to think of you with another man, and I sure as fuck don't want to watch you with one.

I reread it four times.

Another man.

Another man.

Maybe I was looking too much into the phrasing. Conjuring that hope I needed to stamp out.

A seed of guilt sprouted. I shouldn't toy with him like this. Lead him to believe something that wasn't true. But I couldn't bring myself to confess to him what it really meant. How I was stuck, and I wasn't sure I would ever get out of the quicksand that forever dragged me under.

Still, I tapped out a reply, hoping to assuage some of what I'd done.

> Me: I'm only playing with you, Otto.

> Burly Bear: Go to sleep, Raven, before I turn this bike around, anyway.

There was the tease. A promise that I was off the hook. Besides, I doubted that Otto would ever truly be angry with me.

A heavy sigh pilfered from my lips.

I knew I had to end all of this if I was ever truly going to get over him. Just stop it. Stop the teasing and the playing and the pathetic eagerness to always be in his space. That endeavor wasn't looking too great when another text blipped through and a rush of anticipation stampeded through my body.

Only this one wasn't from Otto.

Disquiet thudded through my veins.

> Tanner: Tonight was bullshit, Raven. I at least deserve for you to talk to me.

I wavered, unsure of what to say or if I should even respond. Finally, I decided to tap out a quick message.

A firm, final ending.

> Me: Like I said, Tanner...we don't have anything to talk about. Please don't try to contact me again.

I blocked his number before I gave him the chance to reply, and I leaned over so I could plug my phone into the charger on my dresser. I started to pull my hand away, though I slowed when my attention caught on the relic that sat on a decorative box beneath my lamp. My chest tightened as I gave in and picked up the small hand mirror.

All the lightness floated away, and in its place were the memories that both comforted and haunted.

The mirror was antique, patinaed, ornate metal. The glass hazed and distorted and cracked down the middle.

The faintest light glowed through my window, and I held it up and gazed at my reflection.

"Look at you, Raven. Look at who you are. If you could only see the way I see you. You are brave and strong. So goddamn beautiful. A bloom in the middle of the darkest night."

The old whisper of Otto's voice wisped through my brain and threatened to drip down into my soul. Hell, who was I kidding? He'd been there all along. And I had no idea how to get him out.

Chapter
FIVE

OTTO

Eighteen Years Old

OTTO STUFFED THE THICK WAD OF CASH INTO HIS POCKET AND waltzed down the destitute, indigent street. The sidewalks were littered with garbage and the buildings were covered in graffiti. Sirens wailed as three police cruisers flew by, though Otto kept his cool and his head held high as he strolled along, like he didn't have a care in the world when the weight of it would forever be on his shoulders.

Acting like he wasn't every bit as guilty as whoever those cruisers were gunning for.

He took the right down the narrow, dingy alley between the backside of two crummy apartment buildings. He ignored everything around him—the handful of kids who were running amok in the back parking lot on the other side of a chain-link fence, arguing as they played with a flat basketball, the blare of music as a car whizzed by, some dickbag shouting at his wife from one of the apartment balconies.

None of it was his concern.

You didn't survive this place by putting your nose somewhere it didn't belong. It was a surefire way to get yourself dead.

He took a long drag of his cigarette as he ambled past the

apartment complexes. Though his gaze was furtive, peeking around to make sure no one was paying him any mind as he approached the rotted wooden fence on his right. When he was sure it was clear, he ducked through a hole in one of the planks and pushed through to the other side.

He kept his footsteps quiet as he slunk along the side of the abandoned building that was three stories high and basically as decayed and shoddy as the fence he'd come through. He crept to the broken back door, peering around before he opened it, slipped through, then quickly shut it behind him.

It might have been shitty, but at least it had walls and a roof.

Inside, rays of sunlight managed to break through the grease and dirt-caked windows, casting hazy spikes of light through the rambling room.

His attention rushed to take in the scene. A brand-new dose of adrenaline pounded through him when he found a ton of shit out of place considering only his crew should be in there.

Kane, Theo, and Cash.

They were the three people in this world he could trust. Their survival staked on each other.

Except they weren't alone.

Some guy who wasn't more than a kid was standing all kinds of antsy where the three of them surrounded him.

Otto started in that direction, and it was Theo who heard him. The tall, lanky motherfucker turning around and cutting him off midway as Otto aggressively crossed the floor.

"The fuck is going on here?" Otto demanded below his breath.

Theo roughed a hand through his black hair, his voice just as low. "Don't freak out, man. Dude is in trouble. He's got his little sister with him. Both of them are hungry and clearly without a clue how to handle themselves on the street. Couldn't turn an eye."

"Fuck," Otto spat.

He wanted to be a dick. Tell Theo to get them the fuck out of there before things went bad. Instead, he met the eye of the kid across the room. Probably fifteen or sixteen.

Hopelessness radiated from him, the kind of desperation Otto had seen a million times on these streets. But it was undercut in ferocity. In a severity that promised this guy was going to do whatever it took to make it.

But what really got him was when his attention traveled, and he caught sight of the little girl who was sitting on one of the dingy mattresses in the corner.

Wrapped in a blanket and rocking.

Scared as all fuck.

Fuck. Fuck. Fuck.

Otto scrubbed a palm over his face. None of them could afford to get sentimental or soft. But God, had he devolved so far that he'd become a monster? Gone so depraved that he'd been stricken of his humanity?

What if it was *his* little sister sitting over there?

His chest fisted, and he supposed that was when Theo felt the shift because he reached out and squeezed his shoulder. "Somethin' tells me we can trust this guy."

Otto gave him the slightest nod before he followed Theo over to the group. Otto sized up the kid who was wearing expensive clothes that were dirty as shit.

Instantly, he pegged him as a runaway.

"Name's Otto," he said, still gauging.

The kid lifted his chin. "I'm River."

"And what are you doing here, River?" He wasn't pressing him to be an asshole. He just needed him to be straight.

River's throat bobbed as he peeked at his sister. "I'm making sure her piece of shit father never gets to her again. Whatever it takes."

Otto's stomach bottomed out, sickness pulsing. It was easier to ignore those around you when you kept walking right on by. Their business none of your concern. Not so easy when it was right in your face.

Otto blew the strain from his nose as he looked at his crew. "We need to vote."

Otto slowly edged up to the little girl who still rocked in the corner, curled into the blanket with her face completely concealed. He could feel the fear roll through her when he got close.

Bile prowled his throat, rage rolling through him at the truth that someone could hurt a child this way. The things that River had told them, the horrors he'd confessed.

Vote had been unanimous.

"Hey there." He kept his voice as soft as he could as he carefully knelt in front of her.

She flinched, still keeping her face hidden.

"I'm Otto."

"I'm Raven." Her voice was tiny and tremulous.

"It's nice to meet you, Raven. It sounds like you're going to be staying here for a bit if that's all right with you?"

"Okay," she whispered.

"I have a little sister who is about your age."

"Really?" She perked up, lifting her head and peeking out at him. There was no missing the fear that lingered in her dark eyes, but there was a light in them he was surprised to see there.

"Yeah, her name is Haddie. She's ten." Affection pulsed through him. He loved that little girl like mad. Worried about her ceaselessly. She wasn't living the best life, either, since his mom was a pathetic piece of shit junkie.

Nah, he didn't like much that Haddie lived with their mother, but he paid the bills and kept the refrigerator stocked and chased off any creeps his mom thought she was gonna drag home.

He saw to it that no one touched her. That she was safe.

"I'm only nine," Raven said with a puff of disappointment.

"Well, that's still pretty close."

"Do you think she'd like me?"

Well, fuck.

"I bet she would. Maybe you can meet her sometime."

"That would be nice."

"Yeah, it would."

A little dent furrowed her brow as she looked at him, timid again. "You're really big like a bear."

Soft amusement huffed from his nose, though in his words was a promise. "Might be as big as a bear, but that's just so I can make sure no one can get in here. So, I can make sure it's safe. And I promise you, no one will ever hurt you here. You don't have to be afraid anymore."

He stuck out his pinky finger, and she wavered for one second before she hooked hers with his, and he murmured, "Promise."

Chapter

SIX

OTTO

IT WAS NEARING EVENING WHEN I ROLLED MY MOTORCYCLE TO A stop in front of Cash's cabin which was about twelve miles farther up the mountain than my place. I had the job to do tonight, and I needed the information he had to go along with it.

Our homes were on the opposite side of Moonlit Ridge. Sitting on the far south end of the lake where another range of mountains hugged the town in a deep valley.

Cash's place was so secluded and remote that you couldn't see it by road or air since it was two miles off the main drag and covered by the foliage of the deep, dense woods.

The road to get here was nothing but a bumpy dirt trail carved of tires, forever overgrown since there wasn't a whole lot of traffic that took the winding path.

His cabin was as rugged as the man.

He was already sitting out on the porch, and he stood from the rocker with a file folder in his hands, his dog, Duke, right at his side.

He ambled down the four steps to the ground while Duke came bounding my way, wagging his golden tail in the air.

I swung off my bike and leaned down to give Duke a scratch behind his ears, though my attention was on Cash as he approached.

Wavy brown hair and keen brown eyes and dressed more like a cowboy than a biker, though he sported just as much ink as the rest of us.

"Hey, man, how's it goin'?" I asked.

"Decent," he told me in his rough grumble. Dude was as surly as they came. More suspicious and suspecting than anyone I'd ever met. Probably had a lot to do with the fact he knew firsthand how to undercut. How easy it was to twist and manipulate.

As Sovereign Sanctum's hacker, he could break into about anything and reconfigure it into whatever he wanted it to be.

He was mostly in charge of creating new identities, but he also had a knack of wiping out histories that we never wanted to be found.

As a little bonus? He did a whole ton of stealing, too. Wiping out the accounts of the pricks who thought their money and position gave them the right to beat their wives into submission. The ones who held them so under their thumbs they couldn't breathe. The ones who wielded their power with cruelty and inhumanity.

It was how we funded what we did. How we supported ourselves and the families that we set up, though the cover businesses we'd started here in Moonlit Ridge had all begun to flourish, which only gave us the opportunity to help more victims.

But what I'd asked of him was entirely different, and he gave me a look that warned he knew exactly what I was up to, just like he had last night at Kane's.

Sure my request was less than honorable.

As far as I was concerned? Justice *was* honorable. Justice for the innocent. Justice for the one person I'd loved more than anyone who'd been stolen from me.

I had sworn him to secrecy. The last thing I needed was the rest of our crew getting a whiff of this, which I was certain he counted that as confirmation that I was up to some shady shit.

"Did you get me an address?" I asked.

I'd been hunting for years and had never picked up a trace. And finally—fucking finally—I'd had a lead. I'd come to Cash with it because he was the only one who had the skills to crack it.

He arched a brow. "Did you think I wouldn't?"

I let go of a low chuckle to cover the rage that boiled inside me. "Was sure that you would. Why do you think I came to you?"

"Because you want to put me in a bad position with the rest of our crew?"

"Nah, man. This is just something no one else needs to worry about. Something I have to handle myself."

"And it's the way you plan on handlin' it that concerns me."

"Don't need you to be worried about me." I said it as easy and as cocky as I could muster. Like this was no big deal when I was heading toward the depraved.

I reached for the file that held the information I'd asked for.

He ripped it out of my reach before I could grab it. "You think I'm not gonna worry? You think I don't know exactly what you're thinkin'?"

Anxiety had me shifting on my boots.

Cash's brown eyes dimmed with concern. "It was a long fuckin' time ago, Otto. You need to let it go."

Let it go?

After what they'd done?

I forced a casual grin. "Just checkin' on things, Cash. Seeing what the old crew is up to."

Such bullshit.

Cash knew it.

"Just be careful, man. Know what it's like to want revenge, but you gotta know what you mean to this family. To all of us."

Without saying anything else, he slammed the folder against my chest. "Mean it, Otto. Be careful. Know you think you need to go this alone, but we're a family. We've always fuckin' been. You get in too deep? You come to us. Everyone will understand."

A hot blade of grief cut through my being.

I knew they would. But this was on me. Something I had to do. The risk I had to take. Wasn't about to drag any of them into it.

The nod I gave him was reticent as I took the folder. "Know it. But I'll be fine."

Without saying anything else, Cash turned around and bounded up his steps, Duke right at his side as they disappeared into the cabin.

It was probably the most he'd said to me in two years, though I knew that didn't mean he cared any less. It was just his way.

Which I hoped to fuck meant he wouldn't say anything to the rest of the crew. That he'd keep it between us the way I'd asked him to.

I got his concern, but like I'd said, it was on me to handle it.

And this revenge was going to be so fuckin' sweet.

Bittersweet, yeah, because there was nothing I could do to bring my sister back.

But the motherfuckers who'd stolen her from me? They were finally going to pay, and it was going to start tonight.

Chapter

SEVEN

OTTO

It was just past midnight when I took a final look at Angie and her two little boys. They were all buckled in the trailer of the truck, huddled together and dripping fear, which I fucking hated with every ounce of my being.

"You okay?"

Angie gave a shaky nod as she curled her arms around both her boys. "Yeah. I think we're definitely going to be."

Even though I could tell she was terrified, I could still hear the hope and gratitude in her voice.

"Gonna get you there safe. Trust in that," I told them. "I'll be right in front."

I pulled down the partition that kept them concealed in the trailer. It'd been fitted with seats and buckles. The space hidden by a façade that we then covered with pallets. Plus, the actual trailer itself had been fortified so it was safe for someone to ride back there.

All of it was compliments of Jud Lawson who'd done the work pro bono, saying it was an honor to get to participate in what we did in some small way.

Once we had them locked inside, Theo and I loaded the pallets of soda cans in front of the partition before we shut the double doors, making sure it was locked and secure.

My part of the job was often considered the easy part—the best part because I got to drive the chariot that took them to their final destinations.

To the new starting line where they got to begin their lives anew.

But it was tough seeing them like this. When they came to the realization that everything they'd known was gone. They were no longer who they'd been born, their identities completely erased, their brand-new path unfamiliar and terrifying.

No doubt, that detail alone could fuck with the mind, not to mention what they'd been through to get them to this point. I just hoped with all of me that where I was taking them would be so much better than the turmoil they were coming out of.

That they'd find peace and joy and life.

That all of this would be worth it.

"Be careful with them," Theo said, his face cast in shadows where we were hidden behind The Sanctuary in a giant storage unit, closed off and concealed from the rest of the guests.

"You know I always am."

We were actually settling them in Sacramento, which was only a couple hour drive from here, far away from Georgia where they'd come from. I always drove straight through, no matter where we were taking them, but tonight's delivery would be short.

My mind turned to the file folder I had in the front cab, my guts churning with the knowledge of the little detour I'd be taking on my way back.

"House is furnished and stocked. Documents have been delivered and accounts have been set up. They should have everything they need." Theo rambled it like he was checking off a list, recalculating everything in his head as he stared at his boots and ran an anxious hand through his hair, his stacked Ss tattoo writhing in the night.

He always got antsy at this point of the process. Worried that something had been missed along the way, dude growing attached since they stayed here at the motel for up to two months while everything was put in order.

"Yeah, everything's been triple checked. We have it handled. I'm going to get them to their new home safely, and they can start their new lives. Just like we always do. There's no need to worry."

He scoffed as he peered up at me, his dark gaze tormented. Demons playing in their depths. "Always worry, brother. Always fuckin' worry that something's going to go wrong. That they're gonna be discovered or go…"

He gave a harsh shake of his head to cut off the train of thought. We'd had a couple instances when one of the victims had gone back to their abuser. We put in a lot of work to make sure that didn't happen, but we couldn't control everything, and we sure as shit didn't try to lord supreme over the decisions they made once they moved on from here.

We set them up and let them go, making sure they had the resources they needed to keep them secure for the rest of their lives.

Reaching out, I squeezed his shoulder and dipped down to make sure I got into his line of sight. "Angie is strong, and she wants to give those boys the best life she can. She's not going to go back on that."

His nod was reticent, and I slanted him a grin, trying to inject some lightness into the mood. "Your job is done here, brother. Why don't you go and find yourself a little fun? Grab a beer or two and find someone sweet to put a smile on your face. No need for you to be moping around. Tonight should be a fucking celebration."

He grunted though he smirked. "You act like you need to twist my arm."

I clapped him on the back. "That's what I thought."

He gave a low chuckle before he sobered. "Be safe out there. Text me and let me know when it's done."

"I will."

I strode to the cab and climbed inside. It was a newer truck we had painted to look exactly like one of the soda distributors' trucks. The cover was perfect for traveling at night. I even had a part-time job with the company to make this shit halfway legit, delivering to some of the businesses around town, though this truck was always hidden until I had a job.

I buckled, then I picked up my phone to make sure I had the correct address inputted.

My guts tangled when I saw the texts waiting for me. My insides an instant riot when her face slammed into my mind. The way she'd had me so spun up last night I hadn't been able to sleep, thoughts consumed with that fucked-up image she had put in my head.

But any teasing and tempting she'd been doin' last night had been eradicated. Gone with her concern and affection.

> Raven: Please be careful out there. We need you here.

> Raven: I need you here.

For one second, I gave myself over to wishing I was different. To wishing I could have done it all differently and it hadn't come to this. To wishing I could be something better for Raven.

To wishing that I could have stopped it. Saved her. Saved them *both*.

I'd failed.

And Raven?

I wanted so much more for her than *this*.

Chapter
EIGHT

OTTO

THE NEXT MORNING, I STOOD BENEATH THE HOT SPRAY OF MY shower, the water close to scalding. My head was slumped between my shoulders, and I supported myself with both hands against the wall, trying to breathe through the turmoil that ravaged.

The careening of thoughts and the disorder of senses.

The fall pounded against my head, shoulders, and back, the water gliding over my body and swirling at my feet a blood-tinged pink.

Washing away the evidence of what I'd done, but there was no chance of it erasing what had been written on me.

This revenge both sickening and sweet.

The thing I'd wanted for so long but still didn't come close to making me feel complete. The grief no less. No reconciliation for her broken body that had been left like garbage on the floor.

Because of me. Because of me.

Rage and regret coiled deep down in my soul, an ugly red glow that clouded all sight.

Last night when I'd broken into his house, the fucker had laughed in my face when I'd given him the chance to repent. His grin smug when he'd spat at my boots and told me he'd enjoyed it.

So, I gave him no mercy—the same as they'd given her.

One monster down. Six feet underground.

Two more to go.

Gasping for breath, I forced myself to wash, to stand, to remember exactly why I was doing what I was doing. I had to get my shit together.

It wasn't like this was the first life I'd taken.

It was just the first I'd sought out since I'd ridden with Iron Owls MC. Back when we'd fully devolved into corruption. A stupid piece of me had thought that part of my life was over, but the truth was, it was what had caused this tragedy in the first place.

I rinsed, turned off the faucet, and stepped out, grabbing the towel hanging on the hook and drying myself off.

I roamed out into my bedroom.

Sunlight poured in through the floor-to-ceiling windows that sat behind the massive bed that was covered in black. The entire place was cool as fuck. Everything I'd ever imagined my dream home would be.

Was struck with the truth that I didn't deserve it.

That I shouldn't be here when she'd never made it through.

Still roughing the towel through my hair, I wandered up to where I'd tossed my phone to my nightstand when I'd come in an hour ago.

The morning more than half over.

> River: How did it go last night? Are you back? Been worried about you.

I fought the swelling wave of guilt that nearly inundated me as I looked at the text. Like I might look down and there'd still be blood covering my hands and splattered on my clothes. But even though soap and water had washed it away, that didn't mean I wasn't stained.

> Me: Delivered safe and secure, like I'd have it any other way. She fucking cried and hugged me before I left her there, telling me how thankful she was for what we've done. Heroes, all of us.

I tacked on a bunch of winky faces at the end like this was all a big fucking joke.

River: You think she'll stick?

It was the most dangerous part of what we did. Someone going back. Exposing who we were. It'd only happened twice.

First one had somehow kept her oath and hadn't thrown us under the bus. Other had ended up dead, and her piece of shit husband had come after us. That choice hadn't exactly landed in his favor.

Me: Yeah. Like I told Theo—she wants the best for those boys. Could see it in her eyes. The flickers of joy and the hope that had sprouted.

River: Never gets easier, does it?

My spirit thrashed.

Me: Never, brother. Which means we have to take the opportunity to enjoy ourselves in the moments we can. Take a bit of the finer things in life…like your ugly ass has been doing since Charleigh walked through your door. You know I'm going to.

Nah, I was gonna wallow for the whole fuckin' day. Try to make penance for my sins when they could never be forgiven.

River: Never thought I'd get this.

Me: You deserve it more than anyone I know.

I meant it.

River: Hardly, but I'm not gonna be the prick who swindles what he's been given. Speaking of, she just came into the shop. Wants another tat. I'd better run.

Me: Yeah, know exactly what you're running to.

I chuckled when he only replied with a bunch of winky faces, the asshole tossing them right back at me when they were typically my favorite way to give him shit. Didn't think the guy had even known what an emoji was before he'd met Charleigh who'd come into town about six months ago and had changed everything for him and Nolan. Wondered if he realized his grumpy ass was going soft.

Made me damned happy, though, that he was happy.

I pulled on a fresh pair of underwear and flopped onto my back, picking up my phone and staring at the text thread from Raven.

Thumb hovering over the text that I'd left unanswered.

Should leave well enough alone.

But I was never so good at that.

So I tapped out a message like the selfish fucker I was, never able to fully let her go.

> Me: Don't worry, darlin'. I'm home safe and sound. Like I'd ever dream of leaving you.

Chapter
NINE

Raven

"YOU'RE AN ANGEL ON EARTH, MILLIE." I SCOOPED UP THE GIANT bundle of fresh-cut flowers and grinned at the woman across the counter from me.

She'd been a total savior since she'd started working on the weekends here at Moonflower. I loved owning the quaint little floral shop that was my pride and joy. Loved putting together bouquets and making people's days brighter. But I also loved to be able to take some time off to spend with my family, as well.

Millie only wanted to work on the weekends, so it was a win-win.

She arched a penciled-in brow. "It is my job, and you're here on a Sunday morning just after dawn taking care of a big part of it."

"I have to pick up some treats for our family picnic today, so I was already in town. It's no bother."

Her scowl was full of affection. "I think you're the one who's the angel on earth."

My chest expanded. God, I loved this woman. She was so kind and gentle and caring. The type of person I wished my mother would have been, which was probably why I'd adored her the second she'd walked through Moonflower's door two months ago and I'd hired her on the spot.

She was in her sixties and had retired from her job at the bank. She'd said she needed something to keep her hands busy so she didn't go stir crazy.

"Angel?" I would have waved her off if my arms weren't loaded down with blooming stems. "Ha, you should have seen what I was wearing last weekend at Kane's."

I waggled my brows at her.

Her chuckle was low. "Oh, I can only imagine. I bet you were knocking them boys off their feet."

Too bad there was only one *boy* that I wanted there.

Still, I played it up. "You should have seen it…men just falling all over the dance floor. Boom, boom, boom. One right after another. On their hands and knees as they crawled to me."

She laughed outright. "Now that is a picture I would pay to see."

I giggled. "All right, I need to get these over to the café so I can go home to get ready. Let me know if you have any issues today."

"I'll be just fine. You go on and have yourself some fun."

"I plan to." I gave her a little curtsy before I turned and started through my shop.

Happiness brimmed in my heart.

My store was adorable. Total country chic with a dash of whimsy. The floors were rustic wood, the same as the reclaimed countertops.

The middle was filled with two rows of every sort of fresh-cut flower, buckets holding each variety slotted into custom wooden frames that Otto had built for me.

Running the sides were refrigerated cases where we kept the pre-made bouquets, and the front was spinning card displays and a few racks for special gifts that sat in front of the windows that overlooked 9th Street.

Pride swelled. Sometimes I still couldn't believe that I'd brought it to fruition.

It'd always been a dream, and for once, I'd gone for it.

Made something my own.

My spirit flailed and expanded, a need lighting inside me to finally claim that for other aspects in my life, too.

It was time.

I pushed open the glass door framed in white wood, and I crossed to the edge of the sidewalk. I glanced both ways before I darted across the street.

A brand-new café had opened directly on the other side, and they'd contracted with me to bring them fresh flowers to decorate their tables with every day.

I loved that a bit of Moonflower was getting splashed all over this town.

I whipped the door open to Sunrise to Sunset Café.

Inside, it was posh and trendy while somehow still managing to be comfy. The walls were done in rustic red bricks, and the floors were a dark-stained concrete. Booths that looked more like leather couches ran the length of the front windows and the back wall. Tables fronted them and regular chairs sat on the opposite side.

In the middle of the restaurant were high-top tables surrounded by stools.

A long counter ran the right side, and the kitchen was to the back.

I headed for the counter, grinning wide when I saw Sienna working the espresso machine with her back to me.

"Um, excuse me, can someone get a little service around here?" I had to lift my voice over the whirring of the machine, my words fully a tease, though she whipped around like she thought someone was actually complaining.

The irritation drained when she saw it was me, and she wadded up a hand towel and threw it at me.

I laughed as I dodged it.

"You brat. I thought I was going to have to deal with a disgruntled customer at six-thirty in the morning. On a Sunday, mind you." She kept her voice low so the few tables already in the restaurant wouldn't overhear, her brown ponytail swishing around her shoulders as she shook her head at my antics.

Sienna had moved to town about a month ago and had gotten a job here soon after the café had opened.

I was all about welcoming new friends.

I'd struggled with it for a long time.

Friends.

Being confident enough to open myself up to new people.

Terrified of trusting.

A pang of grief nearly consumed me when I thought of what I'd lost. How closed off I'd been after I'd lost the first true friend I'd ever had. The one person I could confide in. Dream with and laugh with.

It'd all started when I'd taken a leap when Charleigh had come to town and had moved into the apartment above Moonflower. There'd been something about her that had made me do everything in my power to befriend her. It was the best thing I'd ever done, and now that I'd started, I didn't intend on stopping.

"I'm sorry," I said around my laughter.

"You are not." Sienna gave me a death glare that was completely faked.

I shrugged. "I couldn't help myself. You were ripe for the picking."

"And here I thought you were one of the nice ones, and it turns out you are just plain mean." She went back to prepping the gourmet coffee she'd been making, her voice light with the jest.

"What do you expect when I hang out with my brother and his friends all the time? Giving someone shit is our love language."

"Aww, you love me?" Touching her chest, she set the cup on the counter so the server could pick it up.

"Of course, I do. Just like you love me. Adore me. Can't live without me."

I let my voice get more outrageous with each word that fell from my mouth.

"I told you that I was the best around and you absolutely had to be friends with me, didn't I?" I laid it on thick.

"Only about thirteen times," she deadpanned.

I laughed before I asked, "Speaking of, when are we hanging out next?"

We'd met a couple times, once to get coffee and another to grab a cocktail. She's been super nice, and it was fun. She wasn't afraid of getting giggly and goofy with me. It wasn't like she was going to replace my Charleigh or anything. No one could slide into the spot reserved for my best friend who'd basically become my sister, but it was cool to have someone else to hang out with since Charleigh spent so much of her time with River and Nolan now.

I moved to the nook at the end of the counter where the owner, Neena, asked me to leave the flowers each day.

"Whenever it is, let's make it soon. This girl needs a little bit of fun," Sienna said.

"Then you've come to the right place," I told her with a shimmy of my shoulders. Then my eyes went wide when the awesome idea occurred to me. "You should totally come to Otto's birthday party in two weeks. It's going to be at Kane's, and everyone will be there. I've been wanting you to meet my family and friends."

Excitement toppled around in my stomach. It was going to be a big bash. Dancing and drinking and celebrating the man who'd come to mean the most to me. Even our friends from Redemption Hills were going to be there.

Her expression turned conspiratorial. "If that means Theo is going to be there, then you can count me in."

Theo had apparently come in one morning to have breakfast. She hadn't stopped talking about him since.

"He'll absolutely be there, but you probably shouldn't count that as a bonus. That boy will chew you up and he won't bother to spit you out...he'll just swallow you whole," I warned her, only half joking.

Because Theo would.

He totally would.

"I think I'll be the one to swallow...especially with someone that looks like that." She bit down on the tip of her tongue, obviously really proud of herself for making me choke and heave over the innuendo. "Eww."

She cracked up, and I held up both hands in surrender. "Fine, I will gladly facilitate, but I cannot be held responsible for any breaking that comes your way."

"Maybe I'm the one who'll be doing the breaking."

"I think I'm getting the picture that's the way it's going to be. And as long as you and I remain friends on the other side, then go for it."

"You never know…I just might."

"It's a date, then." I situated the flowers then brushed off my shirt where a few leaves had gotten stuck to it. "Before I go, I need to grab one of those chocolate lava cakes, and throw in a dozen lemon bars, too."

So what if chocolate just so happened to be Otto's favorite.

"Big family gathering?"

"We get together almost every Sunday," I told her.

Sienna moved over to the display case where the treats were kept, and she loaded a big white box with the cake and another full of the treats. I paid, then she passed them over the counter. "Here you go."

"Thanks so much, Sienna. Hope you have the best day." I started toward the door, hollering over my shoulder, "Can't wait to hang out."

"Me, too! Have fun today."

"I will!" I walked out of the café and into the breaking day, feeling light.

Because I could feel it.

My wings stretching. This chance of soaring free.

Chapter

TEN

OTTO

I PULLED MY RESTORED FORD INTO THE CLEARING. THE REST OF the family was already there, smiles on their faces, everything for our barbecue set in a pile behind River's SUV. Theo and Kane's bikes were parked to the right of it, and I pulled into the spot beside them. I hopped out and grabbed the cooler I'd packed from the bed of my truck.

"Yo, brother," Kane shouted from where he, River, Charleigh, and Theo were chatting under the shade of a tree in the distance.

"What's up?"

"Just waiting on your sorry ass," Kane punted back.

River and Theo laughed, no one really minding.

All except for maybe my sweet little tot who came bounding my way. Nolan was growing too fast. It blew my mind the kid was already five.

"Uncle Otto, Uncle Otto! Sheesh, it's about time you finally got here. I thought we were gonna have to leave you behind and you were gonna have to find your way all the way to the lake by yourself because we can't be late."

I set the cooler down so I could sweep him up and into my arms the second he was within reach.

Affection squeezed my chest. His cherub face shining all its glee. His tender spirit so damned sweet. The kid had me wrapped around every single one of his little fingers.

"Looks like I made it just in time," I told him.

"Whew." Nolan dragged the back of his hand across his brow, wiping up nonexistent sweat.

Except my skin was instantly slick with it when I caught sight of Raven. She was across the clearing, bent over and leaning into the rear of the SUV as she dug around for something, wearing a pair of black shorts that hugged her splendid ass in the best of ways.

Did my best to rip my attention away and not stand there ogling her like some kind of perverted asshole, but it was damned hard to look away.

She straightened as she turned around, slinging a reusable grocery bag over her shoulder. A grin spread across her gorgeous face when she saw me standing there.

"Thank God you're here. We need all the hands we can get."

I looked at the giant pile of shit that we needed to carry.

"At your service." I ambled that way with Nolan still in my arms, kid wrestling around like he was trying to take me to the ground while my focus remained on Raven. She had on an oversized white tee with a unicorn printed on the front. The neck was stretched out and it draped over one shoulder, and she had the loose hem of it tucked into her shorts.

That buzz intensified the closer I got to her. "You think we have enough stuff for one afternoon?" I asked, arching a cynical brow.

She gave me an innocent look. "Don't judge me, Otto."

Couldn't judge her. Not ever. Not when I sure as hell didn't have the right.

A week had passed since I'd stepped out of Sanctum's bounds. Wasn't sure if I'd even really processed it yet. What I'd done or the consequences it might bring. The only thing I could do was press on. Act like nothing had changed when I knew I'd taken a sharp turn toward destruction. When I knew there was no way I could stop until it was finished.

"No judgement here. Just making sure you didn't need me to run into town to grab something else." I let the razzing wind into the words.

Nolan wiggled around to get in my line of sight. "Don't worry, Uncle Otto. I helped my auntie pack everything we needed, and we got so many lots of things there's no way we're gonna starve."

"Well then, it sounds like a picnic."

I set him on his feet and he went running back for the rest. "Come on, guys! Our whole family is here except for Uncle Cash because he's a really big grump, but that's okay because I like him a lot anyway, and now we gotta go to the lake and eat the best food ever," he shouted as he flew that way, a torrent of words spilling out of him nonstop.

They were all grins as they headed over to load themselves up with supplies. River had the portable grill and a bunch of bags, and Theo and Kane weighed themselves down with the rest.

I trudged back to where I'd left my cooler next to my truck, heaved it up, and started toward the narrow trail that ran through the woods toward our favorite spot by the lake.

It was tucked in a little cove where there was an actual beach plus a big area where wild grasses grew. Massive trees hugged the meadow, offering shade and making it extra beautiful, but it was a hard enough hike through the woods to get to it that there were never a whole lot of other people around.

We all started up the incline. We had to get to the top of a small hill and then back down on the other side to make it to the secluded spot. In two-point-five seconds, Raven was huffing behind me. "Guys, why can't we just go to the beach that has an actual parking lot and picnic spots in front of it?"

"Because then there'd be a ton of assholes around us," River grumbled.

"A little walk never hurt anyone," Theo hollered from way up ahead.

"Speak for yourself, Theo. What kind of masochist goes on a hike for fun?" she tossed out as she clomped along behind me.

Funny since she was the one who always suggested it.

I supposed it was because once she complained enough, she didn't have to keep up with the tromping through the woods. Because just like I always did, I stopped, leaned down, and muttered, "Hop on, darlin'."

She giggled, but she didn't hesitate, since at this point it was basically protocol. She wrapped her legs around my waist and her arms around my neck, and I straightened, balancing her and the cooler.

"Hey, no fair, you always get a piggyback ride, Auntie!" Nolan cried from where he trotted behind his mother up ahead.

"That's only because your uncle Otto is putting us all out of our misery and stopping us from having to listen to your aunt Raven complain." River tossed an annoyed look over his shoulder at his sister.

I could feel Raven's smile at the side of my neck, could taste her breath, that sweet moonflower scent, and her words were whispered, meant only for me. "I think it's just because Otto likes me most."

I grunted and heaved us up the hill, not even able to deny it.

"What the hell is wrong with you, man? Are you trying to burn these burgers to a crisp? There are enough goddamn rocks around here without you making my lunch another of them."

Couldn't help but give River shit as he manned the grill. The asshole clearly didn't understand the intricacies of barbecuing.

He sent me a scowl as he flipped a charred to fuck burger. "Not gonna have my family gettin' sick off a burger if it isn't cooked long enough."

I gave him the most exaggerated lift of my brow. "Don't you know your meat is supposed to be *moist* and full of flavor? Like biting into a ripe, juicy ass."

River shook his head like he thought I was the most obnoxious guy around while Kane cracked up. "You do realize how wrong that sounds? I hope you aren't actually taking chunks out of the women you somehow convince to climb into your bed?"

"My dear, poor, ignorant Kane. You can rest assured that anyone who climbs into my bed is not complaining." I dramatically touched my chest, playing it up. "Only thing I do is leave them begging for more."

Kane knew I'd never hurt a woman. Loved women. Respected the hell out of them, and I made sure to give them as much pleasure as they gave me. It ended there, though.

Tinkling laughter rolled through the fall air, and my attention immediately was drawn to where Raven was playing at the edge of the lake with Nolan and Charleigh. All three of them were barefoot and splashing around in the cool water.

"Auntie, Auntie, watch this one!" Nolan shouted as he jumped and splashed in the water. He had a giant rock that he tossed from the side like he thought he was going to skip it.

It was his favorite game at the lake, though he hadn't quite gotten the hang of it, and the rock sank straight to the bottom.

Not a shocker that Raven gave him a giant high five. "That one was amazing! Did you see the big splash it made? I think it was the biggest one yet."

Yeah, someone made a big splash, that was for sure.

"Sure, sure, you just keep telling yourself whatever you need to." Kane's razzing jolted me back to the conversation.

"Oh, what matters is what they tell *me*, brother," I told him. "Maybe someday you'll do it right and you'll know what that's like."

I reached out and patted his shoulder in mock sympathy.

He flicked off my hand. "Fuck you, man. I always have them chanting my name."

Theo grunted from where he sat lounged in a folding chair, nursing a beer. "Only the assholes who don't know what they're doing need to brag about it."

Our conversation clipped off when Nolan suddenly came running up the shore toward us, flapping his hands over his head as he sang, "Is the food almost ready yet? I'm starving, so I gotta eat."

"If your dad here wasn't trying to burn the burgers, it would already be ready." Couldn't help but toss out the taunt.

River grunted before he turned a smile at his son. I wasn't the only one the kid had completely smitten. "Yup, just finishing up. Why don't you tell your mom and auntie that we're about ready."

"Yes!" He punched a fist in the air, and he gave me a high five as he blazed a path back toward where Raven and Charleigh were whispering something to each other, two of them always giggling and keeping secrets.

"Hey, hey, my best Mommy and Auntie!" Nolan shouted as he jumped, his blond hair bouncing in the wind, rallying the crowd. "Hurry up! It's time to eat."

Spinning again, he beelined for the big cooler that sat next to the portable picnic table we'd set up. "Uncle Otto, get over here and help me get everything because you know it's really good to help out our family because family takes care of each other."

Wasn't about to argue with that.

A low chuckle rumbled free as I ambled his direction. He was on his knees, grunting as he tried to pry open the lid.

"Here, let me help." I acted like it took a whole lot of effort to get it free.

"Woowee, Uncle Otto, that was a rough one, but I guess because you got the really big muscles, you got it."

I ruffled a hand through his hair. "Don't worry, Little Dude. Soon your muscles will be big enough, and you'll be so strong that you'll have to be careful not to rip the lid clean off."

He giggled like mad. "Like the Hulk?" Then his blue eyes went wide as he curled up his nose. "Except I don't want to be green."

"Nah, you don't have to be green."

I helped him load everything from the cooler onto the table. Sliced tomatoes and onions and lettuce. Ketchup, mustard, and mayonnaise. A fucking delicious looking potato salad.

I'd done up a fruit salad, and I went to my cooler to grab it. I was setting it onto the table just as Raven placed a hot dish that looked like some kind of casserole onto the table across from me.

She leaned over so she could reach an open spot. A lock of midnight hair caressed her sun-kissed cheek, and those inky eyes did desperate, stupid things to me when she angled her gaze up in my direction.

Fuck, wasn't sure why I couldn't keep it tamped of late. Why it felt like I was losing my damned mind anytime I was around her. But maybe I did know. Maybe it was because I couldn't stop thinking about that time. Wounds ripped wide open. The truth that this vengeance wasn't just for Haddie.

It was also for her.

She peeled the foil from the dish.

I sucked all the chaos down and forced a casual grin to my mouth. "Smells good."

"Don't get your hopes up too much. It was just something I threw together super-fast this morning." Raven leaned farther across the table, her voice dropping to a secret. "But what you really should get your hopes up for is the chocolate cake I brought for dessert."

A groan rumbled through my chest.

Fuck. She knew it was my favorite. I probably shouldn't take so much pleasure in it.

"Don't tease me, darlin'."

"You eat your food like a good boy, and I might save you an extra piece." She winked as she straightened, and I had to fist my hands to quell the smack of lust that slammed me.

Woman acting the tease as she strutted off to help River transfer the burgers from the grill to a platter.

Baby sister. Baby sister. Baby sister.

Yeah, chanting it didn't do anything to make me feel like that designation was true.

Five minutes later, we'd all gathered at the table, filling our plates.

Everyone gave themselves over to the airy, relaxed mood. Was easy to put your cares behind you when your surroundings were like this.

The placid lake that barely rippled with the cool breeze that whispered through the trees. The laughter of the ones you held dearest babbling in your ear. Nolan on his knees next to me as he took a humungous bite out of his burger.

It left a glob of ketchup on his cheek.

"How is it?" I asked as I used a napkin to clean the mess off his face.

"Deeeeelicious." He rubbed his belly.

"And here someone was questioning my cooking skills," River grumbled from where he sat on the other side of Nolan.

"Well, Daddy-O, I have had better, but it would be rude manners if I said that you did a terrible job and it was burnt since you did so much work," Nolan said, so nonchalant.

A howl of laughter ripped out of my chest, and River was laughing too as he curled an arm around his son and pressed a kiss to his temple. "Guess your poor dad had better stick to the things he's good at."

"Like loving me and Mommy so much?"

Adoration rolled out of my best friend. A fuckin' landslide of it. He slung his other arm around Charleigh on his opposite side and gathered his little family tight. "That's right. Like loving you both."

"I have to say, you're pretty good at it," Charleigh said.

Swore, she cherished these two more than I'd ever seen anyone do before. She'd been separated from her son for so long, and getting to have him back in her life? She wasn't about to waste a single second.

Nolan leaned around so he could look at her. "And you love me a whole lot, too, right, Mommy?"

"There aren't words that have been created to express how much I love you, Nolan."

The kid beamed, and I could feel the love rolling out of Raven as she looked at them from where she sat across from me.

Nolan took another giant bite of his burger, words garbled around it. "I got the best family in the whole world...so many uncles and my auntie *and* a mom and dad. I think I got really lucky and got a really big family. Gotta remember family is who you love most, and I love you all the most, so don't you forget it."

It was funny looking at my crew who were all hard as stone and vicious to their cores turn to mush.

But it was always the way Nolan had us. Mush. The kid an actualization of what we did. Proof that it was right and good.

Theo reached a fist across the table to bump it against Nolan's. "That's right. Family is who you love most. And this family will always take care of each other."

Nolan fist-bumped him back. "You got that right, Uncle Theo."

Kane reached out, too, mumbling, "No question about it, Little Dude. Family is who you love most."

We'd started saying that years ago since most all our actual families were jacked. Fucked-up, appalling examples of what a family should be. We came to the swift conclusion that blood didn't necessarily matter. It was about the loyalty you shared.

A rumble of agreement went up, but it was Raven peeking over at me that sent the blood thundering through my veins.

That gaze said too many things.

Her own promises and some kind of plea.

Every oath I had made spiraled through me.

Love. Protect. Never cause harm to the innocent.

But it was the one I'd made her brother that shouted loudest right then.

The one thing I had to remember most. To accept.

She deserved so much better than this life. So much better than what I had to offer.

My thoughts drifted to what still had to be done, and my stomach knotted in shame.

Guilt rising high as I sat here bumping fists like I wasn't betraying every single one of them.

Chapter
ELEVEN

OTTO

It was early evening the next day when I was driving my truck down the main drag through Moonlit Ridge. I wasn't sure if I was a sadist or a masochist, which one of us I was hurting most, but I couldn't stay away.

She was always the balm.

The one who could soothe the sting that forever lived in me.

I made a right onto Broadway then the left onto 9th Street. Moonflower was on the opposite side of the road, so I flipped a U-turn so I could pull up at the curb in front.

My chest panged, heart beating errant as I hopped out of the front seat and strode for the door that'd been propped open by a small A-frame chalkboard sign.

Today it read in Raven's swirly font: *Snip, sniff, smile, repeat. All stems 25% off.*

Swore, the woman spread those smiles all over town, and mine probably came a little too easy when I strode inside to find her standing facing away at the long work counter that ran the back wall, the customer counter separating us.

Since she hadn't noticed I'd walked in, I took a second to admire her where she was doing a little of that snipping as she put together a bouquet.

Taylor Swift played from the speakers, and she was bouncing to the beat, totally different than the way she always danced at Kane's. This was sweet and innocent as she bobbed along, those lush hips barely swaying, completely oblivious that anyone had even walked through the door.

Which had her whirling around on a gasp when I rumbled, "Sign me up for a sniff or two."

But it was her own floral scent that I was interested in.

Those dark, dark eyes gaped open wide, completely caught off guard, before she narrowed them at me. "Otto Hudson, what do you think you're doing, sneaking up on me like that? Are you trying to give me a heart attack at twenty-five? That would just be embarrassing."

"The question we really should be askin' is why you didn't even notice that I came through the door. Place is wide open. I could have been a murderer, for all you knew."

I was not going to delve into the irony of the statement. Only thing that mattered was I'd never harm a hair on this woman's head.

"Um, hello, Otto, that is not going to happen. Are you even standing inside my shop right now? This is a place of happiness." She spun around and acted like she was tossing fairy dust into the air.

Of course, because she loved to drive me out of my mind, she was dressed in a white dress with black polka dots, cinched at the waist and flared at her hips, and sky-high black stilettos.

My dick kicked.

Yeah, this definitely was a place of happiness.

"Some creeper steps through the door and all ill intentions go scadoosh!" She did some crazy wild flare of her fingers. "Right out the window."

A slight chuckle rolled out of me as I edged forward and rested my forearms on the counter that separated us.

"Is that how that works?"

"Yep. That's exactly how it works."

For someone who'd been through the most brutal shit, she had a beautiful way of looking at the world. Fuck, how I wanted to protect that. Make sure she never suffered any pain again.

"Just do me a favor and watch out for these assholes around here? Someone could get obsessed watching you through the window dancing around in that dress."

I tried to play it a tease, but my mind was back on that bastard who'd been bugging her the weekend before last at Kane's. I still wanted to hunt the prick down and squeeze the life out of him.

She rolled those pretty eyes that were rimmed in black liner with the lashes coated thick. "No one is obsessed with me, and from where I'm standing, you're the one who should be listening to his own advice. You're the one running around doing dangerous things." She dropped the last like we might have an audience when we were the only two in the store.

I didn't want her to know just how dangerous they were.

I lifted my arms out to the sides. "Look at me. Do you really think anyone would mess with me? You've got nothing to worry about."

Those eyes took me in, and a roll of heat shattered the air, before she seemed to yank herself out of whatever thoughts she'd drifted into and scoffed. "The only thing I do *is* worry about you boys. Every single one of you is a boatload of trouble."

"Doubt you'd have us any other way."

Her laughter was soft as she went back to trimming some stems, though I could see the intensity she peered back at me with from the side. There was absolutely no teasing to her voice when she whispered, "And I doubt I'd be alive if you weren't."

A blade of pain cut through the middle of me. I knew exactly what she was referring to. As if I had stopped it? As if I'd been the reason she was still standing?

Old rage wound through me, though now, it was fresh. The blood on my hands still wet.

The mood must have gotten too deep because she smiled a bright, enchanting smile. "What are you doing here, anyway?"

Needed to see your face because you're the only thing in this world that keeps me sane. Only thing that grounds me to reality when I feel it slipping.

"Just had run an errand and was in the area. Thought I'd stop in and say hi." Would anyone fault me for the tiny fib?

She placed the stems she'd been trimming into a bucket. "I'm glad you did. It's been quiet around here this afternoon."

She rounded the counter and moved to place the bucket into an open slot in the middle section of the shop, then she ran her hands down the front of her dress to dry them.

Leave it to Raven to use her sexy as fuck dress as a hand towel.

"All right, I think I'm pretty much finished for the day. I need to shoot River a text to come pick me up."

A frown instantly dented my brow. "Where's your car?"

On a groan, she tipped her face toward the ceiling. "I dropped it off to get the oil changed this morning and they found like ten different things wrong with it, so they're going to be keeping it overnight. River said to send him a text when I was ready, and he'd come pick me up."

I shook my head. "No need for that. I can give you a lift."

Wasn't about to pass up a few more minutes with her.

"I don't want to put you out."

"Not a big thing, Raven."

"Are you sure you aren't the one who's obsessed with me?" Her perfectly shaped eyebrow arched with the ribbing, though there was something in it that had me straightening and moving her direction.

This girl a lure. No way to resist.

I was nothin' but a fool who reached out to take her by the chin. Those mesmerizing eyes grew so wide I was sure I could topple right into their depths. I leaned down as I murmured what I was pretty sure amounted to a threat. "You wouldn't want to see me obsessed, Raven."

Wouldn't want to see me letting go. Giving into the insanity she conjured inside me.

Before I let myself delve any farther into the treachery, I released her and stepped back. "Now let's get this place locked up and get you home."

She seemed to be stuck in that spot for a moment, dazed, before she jumped into action. She went around the counter and tidied up a couple things before she headed into the back and returned with a small purse that she secured across her body. "Ready."

I followed her out, and I grabbed the little sign, folded it, and set it inside before she locked the door behind us.

On instinct, my hand moved to the small of her back, not quite touching, though I still felt like I was being scorched as I guided her to the passenger door of my truck. I opened it and she climbed in, and I was quick to round to the driver's side.

I took to the streets of Moonlit Ridge, making the few turns that would lead us in the direction of her house. The radio played some old country rock that I preferred, and the sun was just beginning to set, the sky a toil of blazing pinks and blues that whispered over Culberry Street.

Raven chatted about her day as we traveled, telling me about the different people who'd come into her shop, so casual and right where she sat in the passenger seat. The mood between us was easy the way it usually was, though there was always an undercurrent that was impossible to miss.

Five minutes later, I pulled into the drive and stopped at the front walkway.

We both hopped out and started for the house. Raven was pulling her keys out of her purse as she asked, "Do you want to stay for dinner? I was thinking I'd make a quick spaghetti. That and open a bottle of wine. My feet are killing me, and this girl is ready to relax."

I chuckled as I ambled up the three steps onto the wraparound porch behind her. "Of course, your feet are hurting…wearing those heels around like they're made for hiking."

"Beauty hurts, Otto," she tossed out with a grin as she slipped her key into the lock. That stunning face flitting toward me for a beat. Vision of it squeezed my chest in a fist.

Yeah, it sure fuckin' did.

She tossed the door open and stepped inside without care.

Then she screamed.

Screamed this blood-curdling scream.

Protectiveness ripped through me with the force of a hurricane.

In a flash, I was in front of her, pushing her back toward the door, ready to tackle any danger waiting inside. Terror ricocheted through me like fiery bullets. I wouldn't make it if something had happened to River and his family. It wasn't like we hadn't made a slew of enemies, and with the lives we led, it would forever be a risk. The threat always lingering at the back of my mind.

Only I came to a grinding halt when I found the reason for Raven's screaming.

Ah, shit.

It was a whole ton less dangerous than I'd thought but apparently just as traumatic for her.

Because River had Charleigh bent over the side of the couch, both of them in varying states of undress, though they'd frozen, their eyes fucking wide as saucers, shocked at being caught with their pants down.

I whipped back around, rising high to make sure I was completely shielding Raven from the sight. Not that she could see a whole lot of anything, considering she had both hands pressed so tight over her face I figured there was a chance she was suffocating.

"Oh my God, oh my God, oh my God," she mumbled against her palms, and I grabbed her by the outside of the arms and guided her back out the door. I slammed it shut behind us to give River and Charleigh the chance to right themselves.

The second the wood rattled, Raven spun away and went storming back toward my truck.

"Where are you going?" I shouted at her.

"Well, I'm not staying here, that's for sure," she shot back as she yanked open the door. "Like I'm ever going to be able to look at my brother again."

Chapter

TWELVE

OTTO

YOU NEVER KNEW WHEN A DAY WAS GOING TO ALTER YOUR fabric. The framework of your life. I'd carefully built mine around the person that I'd become. Made boundaries that I'd driven like rebar into concrete to shore up the treasonous greed that I'd felt for my best friend's sister for too many years.

Maybe I knew in that moment that I was getting ready to cross a line because I hesitated for a beat where I stood on River's porch before I tugged my phone out of my pocket and shot him a text.

> Me: Think your sister is a bit on the embarrassed side. She needs a minute. Your ugly ass might have traumatized her.

Dude should expect I was going to drag him through the mud on this one. I mean, seriously, didn't he realize Raven would likely be home soon? And where the hell was Nolan?

I tucked my phone back into my pocket, jogged to my truck, and hopped in. I had it started and was taking the circular drive back out to the main road before I finally glanced in Raven's direction.

As pretty as could fuckin' be and as fuckin' red as a beet. She was still scrubbing at her eyes as she looked toward the ceiling of my truck.

"You okay?"

She spun on me with those eyes wide. "Am I okay? No, I am not okay. I just walked in on my brother and Charleigh going at it. It's bad enough I have to hear them from the end of the hall. But to see it? Do you have any idea how disturbing that is?" She flapped her hands like she might manage to shake off the memory. "Gah…I'm scarred for life."

A rough chuckle skated out of me. It was a good thing that for the most part River had kept her from the club back when we'd ridden with Iron Owls MC. That kind of shit went down in broad daylight all the damned time. "Think he wasn't expecting you."

She groaned. "Obviously. I mean, I was supposed to text him to come pick me up. He probably thought I was still busy, so he decided to *get busy.*"

She said the last like she was testing out her first curse word.

My brow arched as I took the left onto Vista View, glancing both ways before I pulled out. "Busy?"

"Um, yeah. Busy. Knocking boots. Doing the dirty deed." She said it all kinds of exasperated.

"What, are you eighty?"

"What do you want me to call *it?*"

For someone who was full of sass and snark and tossing out claims that she was on the prowl for someone dirty all over the place, she sure dipped into shyness an awful lot. Never fuckin' knew what to make of her, even though I felt like I knew her better than anyone else.

The woman a dichotomy.

One moment this seductive siren and the next blushing all over the place.

"I usually call it fuckin', but feel free to call it whatever you want. You know, something along the lines of taking a roll in the hay. Shagging. Bonin', baby." I deepened my voice on the last.

She choked over a laugh.

There. That's what I was looking for.

Her amusement. Couldn't stand for her to be upset.

I took a left onto Culberry Street and headed back toward town. "And where exactly are we going?"

She sighed. "Just take me back to my shop. I'll spend the night in the back."

"Have you lost your mind?" The words whipped out of my mouth.

"What?" she defended.

"You're not going to spend the night at your shop."

"And why not?"

"For starters, there is not a bed."

For second…just fuckin' no.

"Well, it's a whole lot better than having to walk back into that house. Talk about awkward."

"It's not that big of a deal. You think kids don't walk in on their parents going at it all the time?"

A sigh pilfered from her lips, and she stared out the side window as we hit the main part of town. "I know. It's just…I think it's time I find my own place. So much has changed since Charleigh came into the picture."

Surprise tore through my consciousness.

"I thought you loved Charleigh?"

Raven turned toward me. Sincerity was written in every line of her face. "I adore her. She's the best thing that ever could have happened to River and Nolan. The best friend and sister I ever could have asked for. But they're a family and they need their space, and I need to be able to walk into my house without being worried I'm walking in on them. It isn't fair to any of us."

River wasn't gonna fucking have it. Wasn't sure I could stomach it, either. The idea of Raven out on her own. Living by herself. Vulnerable.

But shit. She was right. She wasn't a kid any longer.

"How about you come stay at my place for a while before you make any big decisions?"

The reckless idea was out of my mouth before I could think through the repercussions.

Raven at my house. Under my roof. What kind of idiot was I?

"Hello, Otto, but you don't have an extra bed, either."

"I can sleep on the couch." I kept right along like this might actually be a prudent idea.

She sighed when her phone rang from her purse, and she undid the zipper and pulled it out. I peeked that way, able to see it was River. She rejected the call, and instead, she tapped out a text that I didn't even bother trying to stop myself from reading because I was a nosy fucker like that.

Raven: You're gross. I don't want to talk to you.

Amusement rolled out of me. "You're really going to bust his balls over this, aren't you?"

She pitched me a disgusted look. "Can we please not talk about my brother's balls?"

I cracked up. "Fine. Fine."

Then she sobered and whispered, "It really is time for this girl to spread her wings, Otto."

Emotion gathered heavy in my chest. I got it, her need to break free of the boundaries it'd felt like a duty for us to keep her under.

"Well, I guess you can start stretching them at my place until you figure out exactly what you want to do."

It was a terrible fuckin' idea, and maybe I should have known it was the moment that my framework was going to shift. Should have known that things would start to bend, giving way to the breaking. That the second Raven stepped through my door, everything was going to change. Every oath I'd ever made obliterated.

But there seemed to be no stopping myself right then.

Chapter
THIRTEEN

Raven

WAS HE SERIOUS? IT HAD TO BE A JOKE. AN OFFHANDED OFFER that he would never see through. But he actually made the right that would lead us into the woods on the southern side of Moonlit Ridge.

"Where are we going?" I demanded.

Because staying with Otto?

It was hard enough loving him the way I did on a daily basis. Interacting with him and acting like he didn't affect me. But I always had the reprieve of going home. Staying at his house, even if it was only for a night or two, sounded like torture.

Sublime, beautiful torture.

But still torture.

That smirk played all over his delicious mouth as he glanced between me and the road, the man so ridiculously hot, slung back in the seat of his truck.

It truly was unfair.

"Thought we already discussed that?" he said in that grumbly, low voice that rolled through me like a tease.

A total tease because I'd always imagined that voice saying dirty, dirty things to me. It was never going to happen, but a girl could dream.

"I wouldn't call it a discussion if you're the only one who came to the decision."

"Fine, I can take you back to your house if you'd prefer." He acted like he was going to flip a U-turn in the middle of the road.

My hand flew out to grab him by the arm. "You will not."

"Then I guess this discussion is settled then."

"I've obviously been cramping River's style enough. I don't want to be cramping yours, too."

Otto scowled, his thick brow curling in disbelief. "You know I don't bring women back to my place."

"In case you missed it, Otto, I *am* a woman."

That piercing blue gaze swept over me. I would have gotten all flustered by it except he said, "You don't count."

I narrowed my eyes at him. "Flattered."

He laughed that sexy sound that flooded through me like a wash of warmth. Like I was being hugged by the sound and his scent. The man was mayhem to my senses.

"Don't get your britches in a twist. You know my only exception is this family," he defended.

"Britches? Now who's eighty?" I tossed back.

He reached over and squeezed my thigh. I almost came out of my skin. Not the way I'd done when Tanner had done it.

No.

This was out of the riot of desire that smacked through my body. I tried to inhale, but it was unsteady.

One second later, that hand was back on the wheel as he maneuvered up the winding road that led to his cabin tucked deep in the forest.

Baby sister.

Baby sister.

I did my best to remind myself that was what he thought of me. That this didn't mean anything.

I sobered a little as I stared over at him. At the vicious strength of his profile. The line of his nose and brow. His lips that were forever curled with his grin. "I don't want to be in your way, Otto."

Intensity filled his expression when he swept his attention toward me. "You're my favorite fuckin' person in the world, Raven. What makes you think I wouldn't want you at my house?"

Tingles scattered.

It was moments like these when I became a fool who believed.

A fool who thought he might actually see me the way I wanted him to.

But I knew better than that.

Two minutes later, Otto made the right onto the dirt lane that dipped down the side of a ridge and then rose back on the other side. His house sat on the upper portion of it.

I called it a cabin since it was completely surrounded by soaring pines and a swath of leafy oaks, though his place was as modern as they came.

A tall rectangle made of metal and glass. The bottom floor was a huge garage where he kept his motorcycles and restored cars and trucks, and the upper floor was the living area. A balcony ran along the sides, overlooking the break in the trees that gave a view to the southern part of the lake low in the distance.

I was sure there wasn't a more beautiful view in all of Moonlit Ridge.

He tapped into his app and turned off the security system, then pushed the button to open the garage. The big metal door slowly wound up, and he eased his truck inside and parked it next to the motorcycle he normally rode.

There were at least four more scattered inside, along with two cars and three more trucks.

He called them his babies. His only loves. The only things he could truly give his heart to.

Was it wrong I was a little jealous?

He glanced over at me as he pressed the button to drop the garage door behind us, and he was grinning that grin when he said, "Welcome home, darlin.'"

My heart sped an extra beat.

"I won't be in your hair for long. I just need to find a place of my own, and I'll be on my way."

It was too bad Charleigh's apartment that was directly above Moonflower had already been leased once she'd moved out. It would have been perfect.

But I was sure there would be a place that would be equally as perfect. I didn't need much. Just a place that I could call my own.

Excitement blazed through me at the thought.

I'd felt this coming for a while now. The need to…do something. Make a change. Like Otto had said, walking in on Charleigh and River wasn't that big of a deal.

But it'd made me feel…like an intrusion.

A burden.

In their way.

And also, really freaking embarrassed and wishing for a way to purge the vision from my mind.

I was going to use it as the motivation I needed to take the jump.

Concern played through Otto's severe features, though I could tell he was trying to maintain the lightness he normally wore. "You can stay for as long as you need."

"Thank you, Otto. I truly appreciate it."

"Like I'd leave my girl out on the street." He reached over and tugged a lock of my hair like he was my big brother trying to annoy me before he tossed open his door. "Come on, let's get upstairs."

He and I got out of the truck, and I went directly for the interior stairs that led to his house above. I climbed the metal steps, my hand on the railing.

Otto's presence swarmed me from behind.

We got to the top, and he reached around me and pushed open the door. When I stepped inside, I was hit with his overpowering aura.

Magnified a thousand times.

That patchouli scent mixed with what smelled like warm, cinnamon apples, as if there might have actually been a pie baking in the oven.

No man should smell that good.

The interior of Otto's house was just as industrial as the exterior. Everything metal and black and sleek, though his furniture was oversized and comfortable.

The left side of the great room was the kitchen, and the living area was to the right.

A dining table sat on the far opposite side of the door, overlooking the gorgeous view through the floor-to-ceiling windows.

Just left of the kitchen were three wide steps that led to a low loft where framed artwork was displayed on the walls and a few sculptures were positioned around a lounging couch.

Situated in the middle of the loft were double doors leading to the single bedroom beyond.

"Are you hungry?" he asked as he rounded me and tossed his keys to a bowl that sat on the entry table.

Right.

I hadn't even had dinner yet, and it was just then I realized that I'd run out of my house without any of my things.

Just awesome.

But it was a whole lot better than showing my face when I'd screamed like I'd walked in on a murder scene rather than the very natural thing my brother and his fiancée were doing.

"Starving. And please tell me you have a bottle of wine. Okay, after today, make it two."

He chuckled as he strode into the kitchen and headed for the liquor cabinet. "Not sure about the wine, but I have vodka."

He waved a giant bottle at me.

I sighed as I tossed my purse onto the black granite island. "That will just have to do."

"When did you get so fancy?" he asked with a quirk of his brow. "My vodka's not good enough for you?"

A soft giggle rolled out as I headed deeper into the kitchen and opened the pantry where I knew he kept his mixers. I grabbed two bottles of ginger beer. "I don't know what you're talking about, Otto. I've always been fancy. Have you even met me?"

Lifting the bottles overhead, I did a little shimmy.

Air huffed out of Otto's nose as he pulled two crystal low-ball tumblers from a glass cabinet.

Talk about fancy.

"Guess I always did know you were a whole ton better than the rest of us." He said it over the clinking of ice from the dispenser in the fridge.

I popped the caps off the bottles as he poured the vodka over ice.

"Better than the rest of you? I think not," I said.

Moving to his side, I peeked up at him as I poured the ginger beer into the glasses.

Something dark passed through his features.

"We aren't exactly good people," he said, his thick, tatted throat bobbing as he swallowed. The owl wings that he'd had forever painted there seemed to flutter as he did.

I handed him a glass then took the other, and I whispered as I brought it to my lips, "No, you're the best people."

He stared at me for the longest time before he mumbled, "Think you might have the meaning backward."

"No, Otto, I know the meaning just fine, just like I've always known with my brother. What you do is the most honorable thing I could imagine."

That time, what passed through his expression was unmistakable.

Guilt.

Then he donned a smile that was far too casual for the conversation.

"I'm the last person you should think is a good guy. You could scrape me right out of the bottom of the barrel."

That was Otto's way. He acted like everything in his life was fun and games, as easy as they came, when I knew what was concealed underneath.

I knew what had sparked it in the first place.

I guessed we were a match that way. So many times, I reacted the same.

"Do you regret it?" I asked him.

"Sanctum?" he asked.

"Yes."

He wavered, then said, "Have a million regrets in my life, Raven. But this? What we do? It's not one of them."

"Then I guess this is to knowing what is important to us."

We were so close when I reached out and clinked my glass with his. So close as we both took a sip of our drinks. So close as he watched me like he wasn't sure what to do with me standing in the middle of his kitchen.

I spilled half my drink on the floor when my phone suddenly started ringing from my purse, and Otto jumped back a step as if he'd been caught doing something salacious.

He cleared his throat as he roughed one of those giant paws through the longer pieces of his hair. "Why don't you go into the bedroom and give your brother a call because you know he's freaking out, and I'll get this cleaned up and make us something to eat?"

I managed to shuck the moment into the secret spot inside me reserved for him.

"Do I have to?"

He stretched out one of those enormous hands and touched the little freckle I had to the side of my left lip. Heat spiraled through the middle of me. "Yeah, Raven, I think you do."

Chapter
FOURTEEN

Raven

I DIDN'T HAVE TIME TO MAKE IT INTO OTTO'S BEDROOM BEFORE my phone pinged a bunch of times.

I stepped inside and shut the door behind me, blowing out a sigh as I read the messages that had come through.

River: Raven, answer your phone.

River: Where are you?

River: Come on, Raven, I'm sorry, but I don't think you need to ignore me over this.

It wasn't like he'd given me any time to even respond between the call and the texts that kept blipping through.

Still, my stomach twisted.

I could feel his worry woven in the words, though he should have known I was with Otto and was completely safe.

Okay, maybe safe wasn't the best definition.

Because my heart definitely wasn't safe. Not when the man shredded it without even knowing it.

But my body was at least.

Me: Sorry, can't come to the phone. Busy bleaching my eyes.

A tweak of mischief pulled at the edge of my lips as I sent it.

Yeah, I was so going to bust his balls about this.

I lifted my head as I stepped deeper into Otto's bedroom.

My stomach twisted in an entirely different way.

I'd never been in here before, and my gaze jumped around to take stock.

It mimicked the rest of the house. Everything black and steel. His bed was enormous like the man. Fit for a king except he hadn't made it. The heavy black comforter and gray sheets were a rumpled pile on top. The bedframe itself was black, and the headboard butted up against the far wall that was also made completely of glass.

A buzz glowed in my belly at the thought of him there, naked and bound in the fabrics, all those colorful tats rolling over his flesh.

I blinked the vision away.

Dangerous, dangerous thinking, Raven. Do not go there.

I let my attention drift.

He had more artwork on the walls, and a massive dresser sat on the right side of the room.

Old pain clutched my spirit when I saw what was sitting on top.

I eased over and picked up the picture.

Haddie was there. Her head tipped back as she laughed toward the sky.

Always, always laughing.

I ran my fingertips down her face like I could reach out and touch her. Remember. My first true friend.

Grief splintered through me as I thought to the way it'd spiraled. The way we'd lost control. I'd tried to stop it, but I couldn't break through. Couldn't do anything before it was too late. Before the insurmountable pain had come.

I squeezed my eyes closed when the memory raked through my consciousness like a blade. A ghost. A specter. My own depravity that I'd kept shored and secreted. The one thing I could do. A victory that still felt as if it'd stolen a piece of my soul that I could never get back.

The tattoo on my side burned like a branding.

I will make it to the sunrise.

I startled when my phone started ringing in my hand, and I nearly dropped the picture, though I managed to right it and set it back onto the dresser. Then I couldn't stop my smile when I saw who was calling.

Blowing out the strain, I accepted the call as I moved toward Otto's bed.

"Well, if it isn't my recently estranged bestie." I went ahead and dug it in deep.

From the other end of the line, Charleigh groaned in mortification. "Oh my God, I am so sorry, Raven. I can't believe we let that happen. I'm so embarrassed."

"You should be," I teased.

"You can be sure I am sufficiently humiliated."

"Honestly, it wasn't that big of a deal. I just was…caught off guard."

There. I'd be pragmatic. Let her off the hook.

"Caught off guard? You screamed so loud the neighbors came over to check if everything was okay."

A disbelieving giggle erupted from my throat. "They did not."

"Oh, they did. I had to let them come into the house to make sure nothing was awry before they'd go away. I told them I'd seen a spider."

"Oh my God." Once I started laughing, Charleigh started laughing, too, and in a second, we were both cracking up, me bent over while she giggled like crazy.

I was wiping moisture from under my eyes, unsure if they were tears of amusement or if they were actually bleeding. "I know my bestie is a sexy bitch, but I didn't need to see that much of her."

She choked over a snicker before she sobered and whispered, "I really am sorry."

"It's fine. But you should know I'm never going to be able to look at you or my brother again. You ruined everything."

"River said you were going to text when you were finished at the shop, and Nolan was at the park with his friend Mitchell and his parents, so we thought we were alone. We got…carried away."

I sighed. "It's your house. You two should be able to get naked wherever you want."

"But it's your house, too."

I hesitated before I admitted what I was sure was going to come with a ton of resistance. "And I think it's time that it's not."

She paused, and when she spoke again, her voice dampened with hesitancy. "What do you mean?"

"I think it's time I find my own place."

"Raven—"

"I know what you're going to say, Charleigh, and I know you love me and love living with me because, yeah, I'm pretty amazing and great, and like, what crazy person wouldn't want to live with me? Best roommate ever, am I right?"

I threw as much humor into it as I could before I softened, "But you and River are past the point of needing a roommate. You're a family now, and it's time you have the space to be able to build your lives the way you want to."

"You are our family."

"I know…but not like that. You, River, and Nolan need to grow together, and you don't need me standing in the middle of it all the time."

"You're never in the way," she argued.

"I think you really just want easy access to my shoes," I teased her.

I could feel her grin. "What masochist wouldn't want easy access to your shoes? Have you seen your collection?"

"Obviously. I am the curator."

"And a really great one." With the way her tone went soft, I knew she was talking about more than just my taste in shoes. "I love living here with you," she added, the words barely a wisp.

I rubbed the heel of my hand at my temple like it could massage away the sting. "I know. I love living with you, too. But it's time that you have your privacy, and it's also time that I learn how to live on my own. I've lived with River my entire life, and I haven't had the space to have experiences on my own. The freedom to make mistakes under my own roof. To make decisions without someone looking over my shoulder. I'm ready for that."

Anxious nerves rolled through my being. This would be a huge step for me.

I'd always lived with my brother. All the way back to when I was a little girl, and he'd stolen me away from the abuse of my father and had hidden me on the streets of LA. All the way through my teenage years and into adulthood.

It hadn't been a traditional upbringing, that was for sure.

And when Nolan had come into his life, it'd made sense that I would continue to live with them so I could help take care of the tiny baby boy.

But I'd be a liar if I said it wasn't more than that. A liar if I denied that my fears had held me back. I'd used River's overprotectiveness as an excuse, acting as if I was the one who submitted to it because it was easier than dealing with him getting all surly and bossy rather than the truth that I'd hidden under it.

Used it as a shield.

As a way to keep from having to face the traumas of my past and stand on my own.

It was time.

Charleigh hesitated, her empathy and intuition kicking in when she asked, "Is this…something you've been thinking about?"

"I suppose I've been thinking about it for a long, long time. But now with you there? I can't ignore it any longer."

"This kind of breaks my heart," she whispered, sadness and concern seeping into her tone.

"It doesn't change anything between us."

"But I won't see you as much."

Some of that sorrow invaded my spirit, too. "It just means when we do see each other, it will be a party. A time to celebrate."

"What are you talking about? Every day with you living here is a party."

"I know. I know. I am basically a blast, aren't I?" I choked over it as I said it.

Charleigh let go of a soggy laugh. "The best kind of blast." Then her voice dropped in affection. "The best kind of friend. The best kind of sister."

Love pressed full. The first time I'd seen her walking past Moonflower, I'd known there was something about her. Something that had pulled me to her, like my heart had known she was going to become an integral part of our family.

"And you know I feel exactly the same about you."

"I know, Raven. I know." She paused for a second, then asked, "Are you still with Otto?"

"Yeah, I'm going to stay here with him for a couple days until I find a place of my own."

"Okay, good." Silence passed between us before she whispered again, "Are you sure about moving out?"

"Yeah. I think I am." I fiddled with a loose thread on Otto's comforter, contemplating before I asked, "Can you not say anything about this to my brother? I'd rather be the one to break it to him."

"Of course, but you know the second I get off the phone, he's going to demand to know how you are."

"Tell him I'm officially blind."

She giggled. "Can't you just strike that memory from your mind?"

"Well, I'm still hoping the bleach helps."

"Oh my God, stop," she choked.

"I will never let you live this down," I goaded, then softened. "Seriously, I'm so happy my brother has you and you have him. Please don't feel bad or worry about me. I'm actually...excited about this."

Also terrified, but I didn't need to tell her that.

"I'm glad." Her voice was full of support.

"Don't get too comfortable, payback is coming, bestie. You're the one who's going to have to figure out a way to distract my brother once I tell him I'm moving out."

"Impossible."

"Oh, I'm pretty sure you can work your magic." I let the innuendo wind its way into my voice.

"I might have a few tricks up my sleeve."

"Clearly, you do." I chuckled before sincerity weaved into my voice. "I love you."

"I love you, too."

"I'll talk to you tomorrow, okay?"

"Yeah, talk to you tomorrow."

I ended the call and let my phone drop to my lap. I sat there for a couple seconds, absorbing the events of the day.

Finally, I exhaled the tension, stood, and headed back out into the main room.

I wondered if there would ever be a time in my life when I didn't lose my breath when I looked at him.

Otto was in the kitchen, larger than life, stirring something in a pot.

A pillar in the middle of the room.

Powerful to the extreme.

As if he could single-handedly hold up the roof.

Conquer every threat.

When he felt me hovering on the elevated platform, he tossed me one of his sexy, casual grins from the side. "How'd it go?"

"That was Charleigh. I didn't talk to River."

Amusement tugged the edge of his mouth up higher. "Chicken."

"I am not a chicken," I scoffed. Okay, I was totally, one hundred percent a chicken.

I might have been twenty-five, but River had never stopped treating me as if I was twelve. It was going to take a lot to break free of that.

Maybe I'd just write my brother a note.

Then he could tear it to shreds and toss it in the air and stomp around like the hothead he was, blow off some of his overprotective steam, then we could have a rational conversation about me moving out.

"You sure about that?" Otto asked as I angled down the three steps.

I headed for where I'd left my drink on the island, and I picked it up and took a sip of the spicy concoction.

"What are you talking about? You know I'm as confident as they come." I popped out a hip, and Otto turned from where he was at the stove.

Mischief ridged those lips that never failed to make my thighs quake, and he started edging for me with a gleam in his eye.

I could already see what was written all over him, and a vat of excitement dumped into my stomach as he approached.

Still, I was backing away, ready to play, setting my drink aside and pushing my hands out in front of me. "Don't you dare, Otto Hudson."

I wasn't fast enough to dodge him when one of those tatted hands darted out and he poked me in the side. "Chicken."

Squealing, I turned on my heel and started to run around the island.

The jerk knew I was crazy ticklish.

He was right behind me. My heels were definitely not working in my favor, and I wobbled and tried to stay upright as I skidded around the other side of the island.

Otto's heavy footfalls echoed behind me, and one second later, he was wrapping both arms around me and lifting me off my feet before I could prepare myself.

He pinned my back to his chest.

To his hard, packed, chiseled chest.

Those massive arms locked tight around me.

I squirmed and kicked like I wanted to get away when I would have preferred to stay right there for the rest of my life. "Put me down, you big brute."

He held me with one arm and started tickling me with the other. I shrieked and thrashed, and one of my heels went flying off my foot and toppled to the floor.

He had the nerve to *bock* at me like he might have been playing around with Nolan.

"Put me down!" I screeched.

"Only if you admit that you're totally a chicken, and you don't want to tell your brother the way you really feel."

"What? That he's gross and he should have taken his activities elsewhere?"

Otto chuckled. "You could probably also tell him that." Then he slowed as his arms tightened around me, his words soft encouragement as he murmured them at my ear. "But you have to be honest with him, too. Tell him what you want. Otherwise, it's gonna be a fight. And you deserve everything in this world that might bring you happiness."

I stopped my fighting, too, and I just let him hold me there. I wanted to sink into it. Fall into the strength of who he was. Turn around in his arms and press myself against him. Confess to him what it was that I *really* wanted.

But I'd never do that. Would never lay myself bare. The one time I'd tried, it'd left me devastated, and I wasn't ready for another round of that.

"I'm not afraid of my brother, Otto," I murmured into the dense air. "I just understand the sacrifice he's made for me. Understand the things he's done to protect me, and I know how difficult it will be for him to shift the dynamics of our relationship. Especially after so many years of him thinking he's had to take care of me."

Heavy emotion rolled from him. "It's goin' to be good, Raven. Good for the both of you."

"I hope so."

He pulled me even closer, and his lips brushed the shell of my ear. "I know so."

"You have a lot of faith in me."

"I have all the faith in you."

Energy bound. So intense. Deep and profound. Pulling around us in a force so severe it felt impossible to resist.

But apparently that force only applied to me since I could feel the easy grin that he pressed to the side of my neck, and his words rumbled through me when he said, "All right, then, Moonflower, you win. You talk to your brother when you're ready, and I'll be here to support you through it. Thick and thin."

Moonflower.

My heart panged.

"You've always been there to support me."

"You keep forgetting that you're my favorite person in the world."

I wanted to be more than his favorite. I wanted to be his everything. But I didn't say anything when he gave me a tight squeeze then settled me onto the floor. "All right, let's get my girl something to eat."

My girl.

He really was trying to wreck me tonight. I sucked it down and turned with what I hoped looked like an effortless smile on my face, snagging off the single heel that remained and landing myself on bare feet.

"What are we having?"

"I didn't see the point in diverging from a solid plan...so spaghetti it is."

I grinned. "Well, then, feed me, you big brute."

He grinned his cocky grin. "It'd be my pleasure."

Chapter

FIFTEEN

OTTO

Listening to Raven moan around the forkful of spaghetti she put into her mouth was some kind of special torture. The sound wasn't close to ladylike, and my dick was straining so painfully in my jeans I thought I might black out.

She slurped up the last bite and pushed her empty plate away with a satisfied sigh. She was sitting across from me at the square table under the windows that overlooked the lake in the distance.

Twilight weaved through the heavens, and the last rays of the sun slanted in over the soaring pines and through the panes of glass. They cast her in this glittering glow that made her appear ethereal.

Impossible.

Too beautiful to be real.

She'd undone those locks of lush black hair and had let them cascade around her shoulders. The ends dipped down to mingle with the black polka dots of the dress that threatened to knock me senseless.

She'd fully ditched those sky-high heels, which would have been a travesty if it weren't for the fact those dainty bare feet kept brushing my leg from under the table.

Raven could have hailed from the 40s. A perfect pinup with the sole purpose of enticing the lesser sex. This girl so high above she might as well have been propped on a pedestal where she could never be reached.

Except I had a hunch that was not the way she wanted it. She wanted to be *reached*. She wanted to be *touched*. She wanted to be adored.

Exactly the way she deserved to be.

Too bad I was the sorry fucker who would never be good enough for the likes of her.

What made it worse was she kept looking at me like I might be worthy. Like I was some fucking hero with a cape when I was bred of nothing but corruption and calamity.

"Okay, I'm never making spaghetti again. Tonight proved I'm nothing but a hack," she said as she sat back and patted her belly.

I pushed to standing and grabbed our plates. "It's just spaghetti."

"Says the man who just knocked my socks off."

If she only knew the way I really wanted to knock her socks off.

"Used to make it back in the day when I was a prospect for the MC. Pretty sure it was the only thing that got me patched in." I gave her a wink.

She rolled those mesmerizing raven eyes. "I'm sure you had plenty of other attributions that made you a shoe-in."

Yeah. Like killing and maiming.

She sure as shit didn't need to know that, either.

Raven had a romanticized idea of what me and my crew really were. We kept it that way to protect her from the horrors of our truth. Of course, she had a clue, no question about it. She was far too intuitive and intelligent to be completely in the dark. But until you saw what was going down in real time? Firsthand? You could never truly grasp the barbarity.

She stood, too, and reached for the dishes. "Here, let me do those since you cooked."

"Not gonna happen, darlin'. You go sit on the couch and relax, and I'll do these dishes up real quick. It will only take me a second."

She scowled at me. "You keep spoiling me this way, and I'm never going to want to leave."

She really shouldn't fuckin' tempt me.

Raven roamed into the living area and flipped on the television while I loaded the dishes into the dishwasher and wiped down the counters, then I sauntered over to where she was lounged across the length of the couch. Her head was propped on a pillow on one end and her legs were stretched out to the other.

I could tell she'd gotten sleepy by the way her gorgeous face had gone laden and soft. That dark gaze lax, her long, long lashes fluttering slowly as she tossed a lazy smile up my direction where I hovered at the edge of the couch looking down at all the beauty set before me.

I wavered, unsure of what to do.

Fuck it.

I picked her legs up by the ankles, sat down, then rested her feet on my lap.

"What are you watching?" I asked, my attention drifting to the giant television that hung on the wall. She had on some show where all the chicks were dressed up in these massive, frilly outfits. Hell, the dudes pretty much were, too.

"*Bridgerton.*"

"Never heard of it."

Giggling, she shook her head. "Have you even turned on Netflix recently?"

Nah. Didn't watch TV much. Spent most of my time out in the shop, tinkering with my bikes and trucks. Doing those bogus deliveries that didn't mean much.

"Only time I ever turn on the TV is when I'm watching Disney Junior with Nolan."

It was good shit.

She laughed. "You're missing out on the best things in life, Otto."

I gazed over at her laid out on my couch.

No fuckin' question.

She wiggled her black-painted toes as she sighed and shifted and turned her attention back to the couple who were arguing on the screen.

God help me, but I was only a man, so I started kneading my fingers into the soles of her feet.

The most delicious sound rolled up Raven's throat. "Oh God, you've done it. Now there is no getting rid of me."

"Told you that you could stay for as long as you want."

"Forever," she mumbled.

I dug deeper into the soles of her feet. "How the hell are your feet so soft?"

She giggled as I massaged her cute fucking toes. So damned ticklish. "It's called self-care, Otto."

My dick perked up at her words, though my eyes lifted in question because I was pretty sure she and I were not envisioning the same thing.

Hers did the same, though it was only because I was clearly clueless. "Pedicures?" She drew it out, nice and slow, like I was dense.

I quirked a teasing brow. "There's only one type of self-care that I'm familiar with."

Redness flamed her sharp cheeks, and she picked up a throw pillow and chucked it at me. An *oomph* left me when it hit me in the chest.

"I did not need that vision in my head, thank you very much. I've already been traumatized enough for one day."

A rough chuckle rumbled out of me, and I dug around in my head for the correct kind of quip that would say playful and not *the only time I do it is when I'm thinkin' of you*, except the couple on the screen were suddenly no longer arguing because the blonde chick was moaning loud while some dude ate her out.

Holy fuck.

I was off the couch in a flash because there was no chance in hell I could remain sitting next to Raven and act like a gentleman after that. Because the show was way hotter than it should have been, and I was suddenly all too eager to sit there and *enjoy* it with her.

Since doing that sort of enjoying was nothing but blasphemy, a line I could never cross, my frustrations were bubbling out, instead. I gestured wildly at the television. "What the hell are you watching?"

She scowled like I was ridiculous, but I could see the redness on her face had ratcheted by a thousand. Sitting up, she pointed the remote at the television and clicked it off. "Seriously, Otto, I think you might be worse than my brother. Twenty-five, remember?"

Good, let her think I was freaking out because I thought it was inappropriate she was watching it. Not because I was pummeled by the vision of getting on my knees, pushing up that dress, and doing the same.

Getting to all the sweetness underneath and sending her soaring.

"It's not your delicate sensitivities I'm worried about. It's mine. Disney Junior, remember?" I said it a tease.

She shook her head as she stood. "You're ridiculous, do you know that?"

"Oh, darlin', you don't have the first clue." I let as much coyness as I could muster coast into my voice.

She stretched those arms overhead, her back curving in the most delectable way. "I guess I'd better get to sleep, anyway. It's been a really long day." She glanced at the couch. "I'll sleep here."

"You know that's not going to happen."

"I don't want to take your bed, Otto."

There was no stopping myself from reaching out and brushing the pad of my thumb over the tiny, dark freckle on the edge of her upper lip. That spot that I never ceased wanting to dip in and lick.

She froze at the contact, shocked by my touch. I didn't even try to go for light. "Want you in my bed, Raven."

She didn't need to know what that really meant.

She seemed to sway though, caught off guard by my words, before she slowly nodded. "I'll find a place soon."

Clearing my throat, I stepped back. "Come on, I'll find you something to sleep in."

She followed me into my bedroom, her bare feet padding up the steps behind me. Even though I could easily toss the girl over my shoulder, I still felt the weight of her like a riptide. Pulling fierce and strong, threatening to drag me under.

I crossed to my dresser, and my attention caught on the picture that I kept on display. A constant reminder of my purpose. The reason I could never give or take.

My teeth gritted, and I pulled open the top left drawer and dug around for a white tee. I turned to find Raven near my bed. Nerves ricocheted from that tight little body and battered into me.

I gulped my reaction down and took the four steps required to be standing in front of her. "Here you go. I'll grab some fresh sheets."

Before I could walk out, she reached out to stop me. "That's not necessary."

My brow furrowed. "You don't want clean sheets?"

That lust-inducing mouth quirked, rippling with temptation. "I'm wrapped around you on your bike all the time, Otto. I think I can handle being wrapped in your sheets."

Swore to God, the woman knew exactly what she was doing to me. She had to know the way my guts twined with a greed unlike anything I'd ever known with the suggestion that was clear in her voice.

But I knew better. *She* knew better.

I forced myself to take a step away before I did something I couldn't take back. "Goodnight, Raven. Let me know if you need anything."

I headed for the door, and her voice stopped me before I made it out. "Otto?"

I turned to look back at her from over my shoulder. "Yeah?"

"Just so you know, you're my favorite person, too."

Chapter
SIXTEEN

OTTO

Eighteen Years Old

OTTO HUSTLED UP THE SIDEWALK THAT CUT THROUGH THE yard that was nothing but dead grass toward the small, tattered house. Its white paint peeling and the screen on the front window dislodged and barely hanging on at the corner.

He didn't pause to knock. He didn't want to give his pathetic excuse of a mother the chance to prepare for him.

He wanted to be sure what he was walking in on was legitimate and not fabricated. Not a result of more of her stellar manipulation.

The door complained against its hinges when he threw it open. The television was on, tuned too loud to some soap opera, though he could actually hear his sister's laughter rising over it from somewhere in the kitchen.

He closed the door behind him and strode through the living room filled with worn furniture and old pictures, though for once, it was actually tidy and not littered with garbage. He edged right up to the small square arch and peered inside, gaze sweeping the surroundings.

Shock nearly knocked him flat when he found his mother stirring something at the stove. But it was Haddie laughing where she sat at the round table in the nook, clearly cackling at whatever wild story their mother was telling, that had him reeling.

His little sister squealed when she noticed him, a bright smile filling her face. "Otto!"

The chair legs screeched against the floor when she threw herself out of it to get to him. The angst he'd carried like a millstone around his neck lessened a fraction when she threw her arms around him and pressed her cheek to his chest. "I missed you."

Devotion tugged at every cell inside him, and he curled his arms around her, mumbling, "Missed you, too," to the top of her head before his attention lifted to his mother who'd turned with the commotion.

Annoyance colored her features, and she lifted her chin as she stared him down. "What are you doin' here?"

There wasn't a whole lot of love lost between the two of them. He'd been subject to her bullshit for too many years, her selfishness and greed, way she always came before anyone else.

Well, herself or whatever prick she decided to drag home to share both her bed and her needle.

She'd kicked him out when he was just fourteen after he'd called the cops because some dickbag had been beatin' on her, like *he* was the one to blame, like it was his duty to keep her dirty secrets.

He'd been living on the streets since. Starving and scared until he'd figured out what it took to survive.

He'd basically run alone until he'd met Cash, Theo, and Kane, and they'd decided that things would go better if they teamed up. If they made a pact to forever have each other's backs. It was only the four of them until River and Raven had come to them a week before.

"Wanted to come check on things."

His mother scoffed and went back to stirring the pot. Even though the life she led had frayed her edges, she was still beautiful. Stunning, really.

His baby sister was starting to look so much like her it was painful.

Tall and willowy. Warm brown hair and these big brown eyes.

"You don't need to come around here checkin' on me. I'm just fine," his mother grumbled.

Funny, she never had a problem with him stopping by when he was bringing her money.

Otto angled back and turned his focus down to his sister. "Well, someone had her first ballet class, so I had to stop in to see how that went."

Yeah, he was paying for that, too.

Not that he was complaining. Only issue was where that money was coming from. How he just got deeper and deeper. He guessed he'd been a fool that he'd thought by now he'd have shucked this life-style like a bad skin.

Moved beyond it to bigger and better things.

He was beginning to believe once you were there, you were trapped.

Which was why he was going to make sure Haddie got out of it before it had the chance of ruining her.

Excitement blazed in her demeanor. "It was amazing," she drew out, tipping her face toward the ceiling. "And the dance bag I got with the money you gave me is so cute! You have to see it." She grabbed his hand to tow him back through the arch and to the hallway that led to the three rooms on that side.

She dragged him into her room that was decorated frilly and pink.

She had her ballet stuff out on her bed like she couldn't wait for her next class in a week.

"See!"

It was a big pink duffel bag that had *Born to Dance* embroidered on the front.

"Now that looks right up your alley to me."

"Because it's pink, right?!" she enthused.

A big grin pulled to his mouth. "That's right."

She was so damned cute. Her joy still true.

Disquiet buzzed through him when he thought about Raven back at the abandoned house. How shy and timid she was. How she'd been stilted. He hated it for her, and he hoped to God that she was able to come out of it.

Haddie scrambled onto her bed and crisscrossed her legs, and he settled himself on the floor, which was pretty much their routine when he came to visit. "So, how's everything else going?" he asked.

He tried to keep the edge out of it, but he couldn't help it. Way he was always waiting for things to go south.

"Well, I got an A on my math test, and we're learning long division, which is bleh, but I still totally aced it." She rolled her eyes dramatically before she threaded her fingers together and sat forward. "And oh my gosh, guess what?"

"What?" he asked, his worry fading since it was clear his sister was doing just fine.

"I got invited to have a sleepover at Stephanie's this weekend. Mom said it was totally fine."

"She nice?"

Haddie groaned like he was impossible. "Why would I want to be friends with her if she isn't nice?"

Well, that was pretty simple and plain, but he also knew girls could be mean as fuck. Probably making her wear pink on Wednesdays or some shit.

"Just checkin'."

Haddie giggled. "You're always checking on everything, and I already promised that I would tell you if anyone was mean to me."

"That's my girl."

She beamed.

Otto roughed a hand through his hair, wondering how to broach it. "Speaking of friends…I met a new friend who has a little sister about the same age as you."

Her brows rose. "Really?"

"Yeah…they're staying with us for a bit."

Haddie's brows that had been high in exhalation knitted in worry. She knew where he lived only because he'd had to take her there once when their mom had disappeared for three days. He'd had half a mind to keep her, but in the end, he'd decided it was better for her here.

Where she had a real house.

He made sure she had a phone so she could reach him at any time, though, and she knew to use it if she needed him.

"She doesn't have a house?" she whispered.

Air rushed from his nose. "Not a good one, Haddie, and she's kind of sad and scared, so I thought it might be cool if she had a friend."

"Like me?" She perked right back up.

"Yeah. She's shy, though, so it might take her a bit to warm up."

Hell, he didn't even know how to facilitate it.

Haddie squealed as she tossed herself from her bed. "I have the perfect idea. I'll write her so she can get to know me, and then we'll totally hang out, and if she has a phone then we can text."

She marched for her little desk against the wall and dug through the bottom drawer. She pulled out a pink notebook with a buckle, and she immediately went to work, her head down for at least five minutes before she passed it to him. "Here. But you can't look at it. Girls only."

Otto's chuckle was low. "Fine. Fine." Then he blew out a sigh. "All right. I'd better go. Need to talk to Mom really quick before I head out. Give me a minute with her, yeah?"

Her nod was slight and tinged in disappointment. "Okay."

He tipped up her chin. "I'll take you to get ice cream soon. How's that sound?"

"That sounds nice."

He dropped a kiss to her forehead before he headed back out and into the kitchen where his mother was smacking dollops of mashed potatoes onto plates.

He leaned against the arch and said, "Hey."

"I'm not in the mood for a lecture from you, Otto, so you can save it. Like you're livin' your life so much better than I'm livin' mine."

A splinter of pain jabbed at his spirit.

Sometimes he wondered why the hell she hated him so much. But the feeling was pretty much mutual.

He figured he'd cut to the chase. "Brought you money."

Her eyes flicked to the cash that he pulled out of his pocket. "Good. Groceries are runnin' low."

He tucked the notepad under his arm as he crossed to her, his voice a low gruff of indignation as he leaned in closer to her and passed her the thick wad of cash and gritted, "Only reason I live that life is so I can take care of my sister. So I can put a roof over your heads. Make sure those *groceries aren't runnin' low*. I didn't pick this life. You picked it for me."

And he walked out without saying anything else.

Chapter

SEVENTEEN

OTTO

MY EYES SPRANG OPEN TO THE SHADOWS THAT PLAYED LIKE ghosts in the room. Moonlight spilled in through the bank of windows on the east side of the house, the night rippling with a calm that somehow felt forged.

Disoriented, I blinked, trying to discern what had ripped me from sleep.

A cold dread slipped through my senses when I heard it again.

A low, mournful cry. The same kind of cry that used to pull me from sleep all those years ago. A devastating whimper that billowed through me like a plea.

A hook straight in my soul.

Tossing off the blanket, I slowly rose from the couch and onto my feet. My heart thundered, a battering so loud I could almost hear the reverberation of it against the walls.

Or maybe…maybe it was just her fear.

This thing that came alive in the room. A haunting that proclaimed.

Throat closing in, I edged across the floor and toward the steps that led up to my room.

Part of me shouted that I should ignore the call. Pretend I hadn't heard. I'd learned the hard way that I shouldn't intrude. I'd get wrapped up so fast I wouldn't know what hit me.

But there was no chance I could disregard her pain. Especially when I heard another whimper echo through the door.

A dark energy roiled from within and bashed at the wood.

A thrashing of grief and a convulsing of horror.

Could barely swallow around the dread as I reached out a shaky hand and set it on the knob. I hesitated for a prolonged, uncertain beat, before I clicked open the door to the duskiness of my bedroom.

The huge windows on the far wall right behind the bed offered just as awesome a view as the ones in the main room, though this side overlooked the woods beyond. Moonlight fell through the panes and lit her in a milky incandescence.

That smooth, soft skin aglow where she was in the middle of my bed.

Would have stared at the vision for my whole goddamned life if it wouldn't have been for the fact that she wasn't shrouded in the peace I'd always prayed she'd have.

No.

She was writhing, her head thrashing from side to side as she flailed her legs, so hard that the blankets and sheets had been pushed to the floor.

Raven's gorgeous face was pinched and twisted in distress. Like she was fighting off a demon wherever she was lost to the night.

I wanted to chalk it up to a simple nightmare.

But I couldn't do that when I knew firsthand that Raven's demons had been real.

When I knew the way those demons haunted her. Ones she kept hidden behind those teasing smiles and that bright, shining belief.

I crept across the floor, knowing I wasn't anything but a demon, too.

It didn't matter.

There wasn't one fuckin' thing in this world that could have kept me away from her right then.

Coming up to the side of the bed, I leaned over and murmured her name. "Raven."

I kept it soft, praying she would be comforted by the sound. Praying it would be enough to draw her out of the dark, dark place she had gone.

Only she thrashed harder, and a long cry rolled up her throat. The sound was so fucking devastating that it nearly dropped me to my knees.

I wavered, standing there wearing only my briefs, sure that I was crossing so many lines that it was going to come back and bite me in the ass.

But the only thing that mattered right then was her.

Comforting her.

Letting her know she wasn't alone in her suffering.

So I gave, helpless but to climb all the way onto the bed.

Carefully, I reached out and I brushed my fingertips down her cheek. "Raven, wake up, it's me."

"Please, no, stop," she begged from the depths of her misery.

My spirit screamed and my pulse careened. My arms trembled like a bitch when I snaked them under her back and pulled her to my bare chest.

A flashfire ripped through my body at the contact.

"I've got you, Raven. I've got you. You're safe. You don't have to be afraid." I muttered the promises to the top of her head.

"Otto." Nails raked down my back as she clawed at me.

I wasn't sure if she issued it within her dreams, but I let my lips drift down her head to her temple where I whispered across her soft skin, "I'm right here, Raven. I'm right here."

I felt it the moment she came to coherency, and she gasped as she pulled back an inch. Enough that those inky eyes were blinking up at me. Saturated with surprise and uncertainty before they softened with this gutting relief that tore through me like a knife.

Moonlight danced within the endless pools, dragging me right down to their depths.

I could fucking drown in this woman. Float in who she was for eternity.

"Otto." It was a quiet, haggard whimper.

I brushed my fingers through her hair. "I'm right here. Right here."

A shuddering breath left her, and I could physically feel the tension drain from her as she shifted to curl herself around me.

Nearly came apart when she climbed right onto my lap.

Long, luscious legs wrapped around my waist.

Like as if on instinct, she knew that was exactly where she belonged.

I became painfully aware that my white tee she'd gone to sleep in had ridden up around her waist, and her lace-covered pussy was pressed up tight to my cock that I was trying to will into submission.

I could not fuckin' get hard right then. Not when she needed my comfort. Not when she needed to feel safe.

Wasn't sure that I was that strong, though, so I shifted us, unwinding her legs from my waist and lying us down so we were facing each other.

Keeping her close.

But not that fuckin' close.

I stared at her, fingers gentling through her hair as if it could chase away her fear, soothe the sting of wherever her mind had forced her to go. Those eyes were on me.

Fierce.

Wounded.

Bright and still so fucking sad.

"It's okay," I muttered, trying to tamp the rage that blistered through me.

Unsure which bastard she'd been taken back to.

Wishing I'd been the one to wipe out every single one of them.

"Nightmares are still plaguing you?" I finally asked once she seemed to have caught her breath. I kept brushing my fingers through her hair. Unable to stop touching her. Hoping it would be enough to pull her all the way back to the here and now.

Would give anything to be able to end them permanently. But the only power I had left was to end the few that remained.

Her hair swished across my pillow as she gave me a slight nod. "Sometimes."

"How often?" I pressed. Couldn't stomach the idea of her waking up like this.

Alone.

Guilt tugged at my conscience at the thought that I'd abandoned her when she'd needed me most. But I'd had to put an end to it. Draw a line when my loyalties had become blurred.

Raven warred, teeth clamping down on her red bottom lip like she wasn't sure she wanted to admit it. "Maybe once a week."

My chest squeezed in a fist. "Fuck, Raven."

"It's not that bad," she whispered.

My thumb brushed the apple of her cheek. "It sounded pretty bad to me."

Her gaze drifted away before she blinked back my direction. "You were the only one who could ever keep them away."

It sounded of a confession.

My guts turned over in a tidal wave of protectiveness.

Taken back to that time.

When I'd hear her crying in the night and go to her.

A wraith climbing into her bed at night.

Somehow, I'd managed not to fully push through the boundaries I'd set, but that didn't mean I hadn't wanted to.

Didn't mean that I hadn't wanted to wrap her whole and keep her.

But I'd known I'd only hurt her in the end. Burn a thousand bridges that would ruin us all.

Still, I was murmuring, "I hate that I haven't been there for you."

She was about twenty when we'd moved here to Moonlit Ridge. It'd been the year before that when things had gotten skewed between us.

My loyalties.

My devotions.

The way I looked at her.

That was all right before every good thing in my life had been ripped out from under me. When I'd failed my sister.

Once we'd come here, the crew had all split up and no longer lived together.

That separation had been for the best. Putting up physical walls and miles between me and Raven. It wasn't like we hadn't remained close, but it was easier to ignore the wicked thoughts that invaded when I wasn't sleeping under the same roof as her night after night.

But that also meant I couldn't hear her when she needed me.

"Does River know?" I asked.

I hated that I thought I saw a glimpse of shame play through her features when she shook her head. "No."

Goddamn it.

She had been alone, and my own shame gripped me by the throat. I pulled her a little closer and whispered against her forehead, "So fuckin' sorry, Raven. Can't stand it if you felt abandoned."

She peeled herself back enough to look at my face, her voice wishing for a lightness neither of us could seem to find. "You couldn't drive all the way across town and climb in through my window every time I had a nightmare, Otto."

My thumb stroked along her jaw. "Maybe I should have."

A thousand emotions arced in a wave through her gorgeous features.

Sorrow.

Belief.

Loss.

Love.

Did my best to tuck back what all of them really meant as she snuggled closer to me. "I want to be brave, Otto, but sometimes I think…"

She trailed off, going silent, her breaths long and choppy in the quiet night that billowed around us.

My arms curled tighter around her to bring her flush.

Heat flamed at the connection, but I ignored it, focused on what was important and not the distorted need I didn't think I'd ever get free of.

"You are brave. So goddamn brave. Look at you, the way you smile and shine all your beauty into this world. Spreading joy like it's gushing out of you. It's a better fuckin' place because of you, Raven Tayte."

I could feel her long blink, the girl pressed so tight into me her lashes brushed my chest. "Sometimes I wonder if it will ever go away. The pain. If I'll ever truly heal."

I exhaled a weighty breath. "No, Raven, I doubt the things we go through ever fully go away. They scar us and mark us forever. It's how we handle those scars that define us."

Mine had festered under the callused surface. Fermented until the best parts of me had become spoiled.

But not Raven.

"And you, Moonflower, through all the horrible shit you've had to endure. Through the abuse. Through living on the streets. Through…" I croaked off the last. I was unable to give it voice—that moment that had crushed us both. Still, I managed, "In the darkest night, you bloomed."

I could feel her sinking into me.

Giving me her trust.

Except I knew that I'd always had it.

Knew she'd always thought of me as her safe place.

I'd made an oath to myself that's what I'd always be. I'd always be there for her. Her support. A promise that I'd never fucking hurt her, and I'd crush anyone who did.

Which meant I damned sure shouldn't be allowing myself to get this close, but I found I couldn't tear myself away.

Not when I could feel that she needed me to hold her up right then.

Not because she was weak.

But because we all needed someone sometimes. Needed the support and the belief.

Raven edged back enough so that she could peek up at me, so

goddamn pretty she ripped the breath straight out of my lungs. "You've lost so much, too, Otto, and look at you."

She saw the exterior, though. The parts that remained unscathed. My loyalty for this family. My devotion. The way I joked and teased and didn't hide the fact that I was all about the pleasure.

But that was surface. What I let everyone see.

It was all the vile bits that I kept hidden. But I had a hunch she wasn't ignorant of those ugly pieces inside me.

"You want to tell me about that dream?" I asked, diverting the subject back to her where it belonged, though I was unsure if I could handle knowing what monsters followed her into the night. If I was responsible for them. If she saw the same damned thing I did whenever I closed my eyes.

She chewed at her bottom lip, and her gaze darkened as she was taken back to that place. The words were carved in harrowing secrets. "It's always the same, and I'm always right back in that room where my father terrorized me. Just a little girl who had no strength. No voice."

A skitter of rage ripped through my being. I wondered if she could feel it. The pulse of it where our flesh was pressed together.

It was the same dream she'd been having all that time.

Since she was little.

"What I wouldn't give to be able to go back and rewrite that history for you. Give you a different start. A better start. The one you should have had all along," I told her.

End that fucker before he'd ever had the chance.

River had taken care of that problem years ago. Put the fucker six feet under because fiends like him didn't deserve the oxygen they were stealing.

Made sure the deviant never had the chance again.

She blinked, dark eyes glinting beneath the moonlight. "None of us have that power, and I hate that my brother carries the guilt that he couldn't stop it. He was a child, too."

He was older than her by seven years, though, so I understood how he'd taken on that burden.

"I hate that all these years later he still carries it. Hate that he still worries about me so much," she admitted.

Knew firsthand that he did. And I understood both sides—his innate need to protect her and Raven's need to find herself outside the gilded cage all of us had taken a part in keeping her in.

"That why you're afraid of telling him you're moving out?" I asked.

She wavered before she said, "I just don't want to cause him more worry than he already has. Don't want to put more of a burden on him. Don't want to upset him."

"He's gonna get that you need this, Raven. He's going to put your needs in front of his. It's what people who care most about each other do. They take care of each other. Support their goals and dreams. And it might take him a minute to wrap his hard head around it, but I know he always has your best interests at heart."

My insides shriveled at the thought of her out on her own. But there was no question that she needed it. Deserved it. Last thing she needed was all of us trying to stifle her spirit.

"And here I'd thought you were going to take River's side and try to convince me to stay with him?" It was almost a tease from those seductive lips.

"The only thing I want is for you to be happy, Raven."

Safe and fuckin' happy.

Glowing all her light.

"I feel happy...right now," she whispered.

"After that dream?" Didn't seem possible.

"With you...right here. I missed this."

Something pulsed through her distinct features, her face flushed with things she should never feel. Things neither of us should contemplate. Which was why I should haul myself out of this bed and plant my ass back on the couch.

Only she nestled herself closer. I could tell she didn't have on a bra as she pressed those tits against my chest, only the fabric of my tee separating us. Her heat all around. This need saturating the air in some kind of greed that made me lightheaded.

Stupid and reckless.

Because I curled her closer, too, and tucked her head under my chin. "It's where I want to be, Raven. Right here with you whenever you need me."

"Then stay. You make it better, Otto."

I swallowed down the lust that bolted through me, my voice haggard when I muttered, "Sleep."

Because there was no chance in hell I was going anywhere.

Chapter
EIGHTEEN

Raven

A PALE GRAY GLOWED THROUGH THE BANK OF WINDOWS AS THE earliest hours of the morning nudged me from sleep.

Warmth covered me whole, a blanket of comfort that soaked me through.

Any of the fear I'd felt last night had been eradicated by the presence of Otto who I was currently plastered against.

His enormous body wrapped around mine as he slept.

Protectively.

Possessively.

And there was no question within me that lying in their strength was exactly where I was supposed to be.

Sometime during the night, we'd kicked off the covers. Apparently being in this bed with him had ignited a fire, and now I burned at a thousand degrees.

My skin flaming in every spot we touched.

A hazy, filmy light filled his room. Through it, I gazed across at his handsome face where he rested his cheek on the pillow. A face that stirred a riot inside me. The longer pieces of his cropped hair were a mess, and his stubble had grown thick.

His eyes were closed, and the sharp curve of his jaw had softened with his sleep. Plush lips barely parted as he breathed.

His scent swamped me.

Patchouli and warm apple pie.

His aura was the only thing I could breathe.

I wanted to sink into it.

Inhale and imbibe.

Disappear.

No question, even thinking about it was dangerous. But I didn't know how to stop myself when I would likely never have another chance.

I gave into the compulsion and allowed my eyes to caress over his bare flesh.

A tremble flash-fired through my body. Desire burning through me in a quivering of need. I hadn't seen him without a shirt in quite a few years. Whenever we went to the lake, he rarely played in the water, which was a complete injustice because, oh my God, this man was beautiful.

My gaze roamed over his thick, muscled arms and the swirling art that River had tattooed on him.

Otto's ink was a mix of dark and light. Skulls and crosses and spirits that crawled up his flesh.

Though flowers were woven in between, as if hope had braided itself into his grief.

My fingers itched with the need to trace the designs. Memorize each one. Commit him to memory in a way he'd never allowed me.

I lost my breath when I shifted and the top of my thigh grazed his front. I froze as a firestorm of heat swept through my entire being.

My stomach tight and my heart battering.

Was that his...cock? And was he...hard?

I gulped around the jagged rocks that had suddenly lodged in my throat.

Crap, what was I supposed to do?

A dark, deep sound rolled through Otto's chest, and he started to press himself harder against the top of my thigh where one of my legs was pinned between both of his.

Definitely his cock.

I didn't know if I should hold really still and let him go about his business because interrupting him seemed like an injustice itself, or if it would be more considerate to wake him up from whatever dream he was having the way he'd done with me last night.

Only that fire blazed into a complete inferno when he rumbled in a gruff, sleep laced voice…

"Raven."

I swore, he moaned it, and I felt the reverberation of it all the way down to my toes. The spot between my thighs became heavy and achy.

I had the intense urge to shift and wrap my legs around him so he could rub his hard length against my throbbing center.

Only his eyes popped open.

Those deep endless pools of blue stared back.

For one, perfect second, our connection screamed between us. That invisible thing that I'd sworn had been there all along.

Fierce, desperate desire.

Agonizing want.

A longing that went so deep there would be no way to crawl out from under it.

Our breaths harsh and our hearts thundering.

I felt it like a life-beat pounding against the walls.

Did he?

Did he feel it?

Or was he immune?

He couldn't be. This was too—

Whatever it was demolished the next second. That second when recognition at what was happening slammed him.

Shocked horror took to his features, and he reeled away.

He tried to cover his reaction with that mischievous, easy grin. As if all of this was normal.

Still, he reached out and took me by both arms to separate us.

"Sorry about that, darlin'. Dangers of sleeping with a man in his bed. Can't be helped."

I wanted to tell him there might be a way I *could* help him. That I really wanted to. Just go right ahead and confess that I wanted to experience everything with him.

But I knew what would happen.

He'd reject me. Like he'd done then. And I'd feel small and ignorant and vulnerable all over again.

So rather than suffering all of that again, I forced a coy tease. "Don't worry. I barely felt it."

His grin turned into a playful scowl as he peeled himself farther back. "Barely felt it, huh?"

"That's right. I'm not sure what all those women are falling over themselves about."

Amusement played across his face as he chuckled low. Maybe he really was immune.

"Wow, way to demolish a man's ego first thing in the mornin'. And after I stayed with you the whole night."

"I'm just speaking the truth." I let my lips quirk up at the side.

Lies. All lies.

He was the only thing I could feel.

"Besides, you act like you were doing me a favor. Who wouldn't want me in their bed?"

A low sound rumbled in his chest, and his eyes dipped to my mouth.

His tongue stroked out, and a shiver ripped through my body.

Intensity climbed between us again, and I nearly came apart when he lifted his hand and stroked his fingers through my hair. "You're right, Raven. Who wouldn't want you in their bed?"

His gaze drifted, then I felt him stiffen. I realized that his tee that swallowed me had bunched up and was cinched around my waist.

My black lace underwear on full display.

But that wasn't what he was looking at.

He was looking at the scars that covered my abdomen. The

hundreds of burns that covered all of my front, hips, and back. Strategically placed so they would be hidden under my clothes.

Inflicted by a monster who fed on my pain.

A sick sadist who'd traumatized me for so many years.

For one beat I was back in the nightmare I'd suffered last night.

My *father* in my room, a man who was supposed to protect me but instead had used me as some twisted plaything.

It was never sexual. He'd just loved to hear me scream. But that didn't mean I hadn't spent my life terrified of someone touching me.

Everyone except for Otto.

His gaze roamed, going to the newer scar, the one that had been left on my side when I was eighteen. I felt him flinch, the rage that he tried to contain, the hate that blazed as hot in his eyes as the intensity between us did.

This scar was the deepest. The one that had been driven all the way into my soul.

A tattoo now covered it. One that hadn't been there the last time he'd seen my marred, disfigured flesh since I'd only been brave enough to ask one of the artists at River's shop to do it for me two months ago.

The wings inked on his throat fluttered as he swallowed hard, his eyes so clearly tracing the script.

I will make it to the sunrise.

Except Haddie hadn't been able to.

I didn't let my stare waver when he looked up to my face, his own pain stark in his expression. I could see the war go down in his features, could feel the tremor that rocked through him as he let his fingertips whisper over the inscription.

Need careened through my senses at his touch, though it was a touch that felt too much like an apology.

"Would do anything to erase them, Raven. All of them." His voice was gravel.

I let my fingertips caress down the sharp edge of his brutal face. "But you can't. None of us can. And like you told me last night, it's how I live with them. And I intend to live, Otto. I intend to live every day of my life with everything I have."

I wouldn't let any of them steal it. Not my father. Not the bastards who'd laughed and mocked as they destroyed. Not the ones who'd wanted to hurt him.

Something flashed through that blue, depthless gaze. Something that looked like determination and guilt. "I want them to suffer the same." The words were shards. "I want to go back and end every single one of them."

My spirit flailed. The confession trapped in the abyss where I kept it locked.

"And I don't want to ever go back."

It was time for me to rise above it.

Agony filled his long stare before adoration replaced it. He let his hand glide up the words on my side then lifted it to cup the side of my face. Tingles raced as the pad of his thumb traced the apple of my cheek. "Sweet fuckin' moonflower."

Desire weaved through me like a giant thread. Knitting me in a desperation I hadn't felt in a long, long time.

"Otto." I murmured his name, hoping he would understand what I was asking of him.

We hovered there, connected in a way we hadn't been for a long time. And I guessed it was too much for him because he suddenly flew off the bed.

He stood at the side staring down at me.

Hands clenched in fists, his big body rippling with explicit, untamed strength. With him towering over me, there was more of him on display than I'd been able to explore when I'd been plastered against him.

And now, I couldn't stop from gobbling up the sight. This man the brute force of a bull. Obscenely tall and shoulders intrusively broad.

A pillar that covered me in shadow where he towered at the edge of the bed.

Pure muscle and brawn.

He wore these tight, tight black briefs, and I gulped when I saw he was still hard. Huge and hard and vibrating with need.

Flames consumed, and I was sure I was being burned alive.

A witch at the stake.

Because it had to be wicked and wrong, what I was doing. Ogling this man who'd reiterated a thousand times that he only thought of me as his family.

But I was only human, and he was…something else entirely.

A dark avenger. Carved of stone and hewn in gold.

Adorned in all those tats that covered every exposed inch of skin.

My mouth watered as I devoured every inch.

Only I froze when I saw it.

I wasn't the only one who had gotten new ink in the last few years.

The stunning piece took up the entirety of his left lower abdomen and hip.

A tortured moon that hung in an ominous sky. Disfigured and misshapen. The earth was barren beneath it.

All except for the single moonflower that cracked the dirt and blossomed beneath the pale, murky light.

His jaw clenched when he realized what I was gaping at, my breaths coming short and my spirit spinning with possibility.

I looked back up at his beautifully brutal face, and my heart clattered in my chest as I struggled to get the air into my lungs.

Something tortured twisted through his expression. "You shouldn't be lookin' at me like that, Raven."

"And what am I looking at you like?"

"Like you want me to crawl back into that bed with you."

I exhaled a shocked breath. Unable to believe the way he'd given it voice.

Like…like maybe he wanted to.

A crash of confidence rolled through me, and I moved up to sitting, shifting around until I was on my hands and knees. Angling his way like an offering. "Maybe that's exactly what I want you to do."

Otto growled this low sound that trembled through the room.

My world canted to the side as he came forward to lean over me. Dizziness rushed me with this dream.

Because, oh my God, was Otto Hudson actually going to touch me?

He did, but not in the way I was dying for him to.

He set one of those giant hands on my cheek, so big it covered the whole right side of my face. His voice scraped the dense air. "Would be the luckiest man alive, getting to touch you. But I swore to myself a long time ago that I would never hurt you, and I fuckin' meant it."

The butterflies flapping in my belly tumbled and sagged, and my heart hurt at his confession. At the shame that littered his face.

"You'd never hurt me."

He grazed his thumb over my lips, and that intense blue gaze dipped to the action before he forced his eyes back to mine. "That's right. You're too fuckin' good for what I have to offer, Raven."

Then he straightened to his full, imposing height. Severity lashed between us, and his jaw clenched in sharp restraint. "I'm going to go take a shower, then we're going to go about our day like this never happened."

I couldn't say anything as he turned and strode across the room and into the en suite bathroom.

He clicked the door shut behind him, cutting off the energy that banged the walls of his room.

I flopped onto my back and stared at the ceiling. "Otto, what are you doing to me?" I mumbled, quiet enough that he could never hear.

Because I wanted it. I wanted to experience the things I'd never been brave enough to experience before.

I wanted to fly.

I wanted to *rise*.

And I knew, all the way down to the deepest parts of me, that I wanted to rise with him.

Chapter

NINETEEN

OTTO

WHAT IN THE EVER-LOVIN'-FUCK DID I THINK I WAS DOING? Jacking myself when she was just on the other side of the door and doing it with her face imprinted behind my squeezed eyes, no less?

Motherfuckin' treachery.

But this solution was a whole ton better than giving into what I'd really wanted to do. I had never been so tempted in my life than when she'd been on her hands and knees on my bed.

Nearly crawling to me, desire carved into every crease of that gorgeous, stunning face.

The bare morning shining around her, that black hair a tumbled mess, the outline of her nipples just showing through the thin fabric of my tee.

She looked like a fuckin' goddess.

A moonflower.

A morning glory.

No better sight to ever behold.

I knew she'd been drenched, girl giving off this floral scent that was doused in arousal.

But it was the plea in those dark, dark eyes that had nearly been my undoing.

And it was the memory of those eyes that had me tightening my grip around my cock, pumping myself hard and fast as I replayed the need that had thrummed between us as if it was music rather than utter blasphemous temptation.

Because that's exactly what this was.

Blasphemous.

I had to support myself with my free hand on the shower wall as I came so fuckin' hard that I bent in two. Thinking about her this way. Wanting to say fuck it and walk straight back out to that bed and crawl back into it with her.

It'd make me nothing but a liar and a traitor.

I'd promised River.

And I'd promised myself.

Groaning through the blissful agony, I let myself relish in the ecstasy for one second more before I forced myself to tuck it back in the tight box where I kept it locked.

I blamed my weakness on the fact I'd had to sleep tangled with her last night. The way protectiveness had bound me in a fist when I'd heard those cries. The way old rage wanted to come barreling back at the sight of her scars this morning.

And that tat. Fuck. It did too many things to me all at once. Gutted me and lifted me, pride swelling so high all while I'd felt like I was on my knees.

Baby sister.

Baby sister.

Chanting it never seemed to make it any truer, though. But I couldn't give into this. Only thing I could do was go back out there and act like it'd never happened like I'd told her we had to do.

I washed myself then turned off the spray, climbing from the shower as I grabbed a towel and dried off.

Clicking open the door, I peeked back out into my room to find the bed was empty.

I didn't know if I was disappointed or relieved.

I tossed the towel to the floor, then pulled on clean underwear, jeans, and a tee.

Then I cracked open the door to the scent of fresh-brewed coffee filling the air.

It was still early, the morning just beginning to fully take to the sky, the sound of the woods coming alive around us.

But the real light was in my kitchen. The woman was still wearing my tee like a dress. That black mass of hair piled up high on her head.

Legs and feet bare.

Fuck me.

She was nothing but a fantasy. A wicked, tormenting fantasy because I couldn't allow myself to go having thoughts like this. It was hard enough on the daily. But with her staying under my roof? It was already proving to be torture.

The best kind of torture because she didn't act shy or weird after what'd happened.

She just tossed me one of those mischievous grins as she poured a mug of coffee. "Thank God you have fresh beans from Morning Dew Brewhouse." She groaned. "This girlie cannot be expected to start her day without it. How did you know it's my favorite?"

I took the three steps down to the main floor, my feet bare on the cool tile. "Know most of your favorites, Raven. It's my job."

I tugged at an errant piece of her hair as I passed, and I casually strode for the refrigerator like I hadn't told her fifteen minutes ago that I'd be the luckiest bastard alive if I got to touch her.

I opened it and pulled out the Italian Sweet Cream creamer and waved it between us. "Like this."

Letting go of a feigned gasp, she touched her chest. "You really do know me, Otto Hudson. I'm honored."

"That's right, I do." I set it down in front of her.

"But why do you have it?" she asked with a quirk of her brow. "I thought you take your coffee black?"

Like a fool, I reached out and touched that little freckle near her left lip. "Keep it in case you drop by."

I wondered how much that revealed. Because softness instantly infiltrated the playfulness, affection ridging that stunning, striking face as she gazed up at me.

Clearing my throat, I stepped back. "You heard from your brother?"

She rolled her eyes. "He only texted me twenty-five times."

A light chuckle rolled out of me as I drove my fingers through my still damp hair. "Think I'm going to go have a chat with him. Let him know you might be staying with me for a bit."

She doused her coffee with the cream and stirred it as she glanced my way. "I want to be the one who tells him I'm moving out."

"Ah, I see your chicken tendencies are waning."

With a giggle, she swatted at me. "What are you talking about? I'm as brave as they come."

Yeah, she was.

"What time do you need to get to the shop? I'll be sure to get back in time to give you a ride."

"I need to be there for my morning delivery at eight."

"That works. I'll be back in a split," I promised her.

"I'll be ready."

Chapter
TWENTY

OTTO

The second I killed the engine on my bike, Nolan came running out the front door. No doubt, he'd heard me coming.

My smile was a mile fuckin' wide when I swung off and he barreled down the steps and came bounding toward me.

Blond curls bouncing around his freckled, cherub face.

"Uncle Otto! Did you come to see me?"

"I sure did," I told him as I swooped him off his feet and tossed him into the air. He howled with laughter as he flew, and I caught him and pulled him into a tight hug against me.

Love went skittering through. My adoration for this kid so fierce he made my damned heart ache. River was a lucky motherfucker that he got to have this kid in his life. That he got to have a love this great.

None of that shit was meant for me, but that didn't mean I couldn't appreciate it for my brother.

"I've been missing my favorite little tot," I told him.

He gave me a confused scowl. "I'm not a tater tot, Uncle!"

Rough amusement rolled through me as I set him on his feet and ruffled my fingers through his hair. "Nah, you're pretty much a man these days, aren't you?"

"That's right. I'm going to be starting kindergarten next week."

"What?" I asked him aghast, like I'd completely missed him going on about it for the entire summer.

Giggles erupted from him as he trotted along at my side as we headed toward the house. "You're just teasin', Uncle Otto. I already showed you my new backpack and lunch pail. They both have got Jake and the Neverland Pirates on them...our favorite show, remember?"

"Course, I remember. Just teasin' you. Think it means I might be jealous you got all that cool new stuff."

"Don't worry, I can tell my mommy we need to get you some, too."

Affection pulsed as we climbed the steps. "You're too good to me, Little Dude."

"No way, I could never be too good to you. We gotta give all our good to the people we love the most."

"Well, you sure are good at that."

He beamed, then I felt the air shift when we stepped through the door. Immediately, I could feel the cagey concern that radiated from River where he stood at the edge of the kitchen to the left of the great room.

"Dad! Uncle Otto is here!"

"Thanks, bud. Why don't you run upstairs and get changed for the day?"

"Okay!" he shouted before he went scampering off for the curved staircase that led to the second story.

River stood behind the long counter that sectioned off the kitchen and living space, face haggard and looking like he hadn't slept a wink.

Striding that way, I let a smirk hitch on the corner of my mouth. "Glad to find you fully dressed."

He grunted at me. "Fuck off, man. This shit isn't funny."

"Oh, I beg to differ. It's fuckin' hysterical. Gonna be laughing about it for the rest of my life."

"Great," he grumbled. "You could have rung the doorbell or something," he added with a huff.

My brow arched for the ceiling as I rounded the counter. "Raven needs to ring the doorbell at her own damned house? I think not, brother. And besides, you should have heard my old truck rolling up the drive. It's not exactly quiet."

"I was otherwise occupied."

"Obviously. House could have come down around you, and I don't think you would have noticed."

Sighing, he roughed a tatted hand through his black hair. "Think the house might *have* come down around me. Felt like that when Raven took off and then refused to come back or talk to me."

"She's fine, River."

True concern pulled through his features. "Is she?"

I hooked my hip to the edge of the counter and crossed my arms over my chest. "Yeah, think she's gonna be. She was just embarrassed, is all. Feeling like she was intruding."

He squeezed his eyes closed for a second. "Don't ever want her to feel that way. She'll always be one of the most important people in my life."

But it was clear some of his focus had turned from Raven to Charleigh.

There was no blame to be made.

It was just the way it was. When new people came into our lives? Into our hearts? Things always had to move and shift to make room.

"She knows that."

"Then why won't she talk to me?"

"She'll talk to you when she's ready. Think she's just sorting through some things in her head right now."

His nod was slow. "That's what Charleigh said, but fuck, about went out of my mind last night, sitting there waiting for her to call me back."

"Told you I had her."

Air blew from his nose. "Yeah. Hope you know how much that means to me. Knowing she couldn't be in better hands when I fucked up."

Guilt flared. He sure as shit wouldn't be saying that if he knew what'd gone down this morning. At least I'd resisted. Maintained the oath. The promise I'd made him.

"Not a problem. I'm always there for her just like I'm always there for you. She can stay with me for as long as she wants," I told him.

He scrubbed a hand over his face before he was staring me down. "And did she say how long that was gonna be?"

I didn't tell him what she'd confessed. That she was ready to move out and spread those beautiful wings.

"I'm sure she'll talk to you about that when she's ready."

Footsteps thudding on the staircase stole my attention, and I shifted that way to find Charleigh coming downstairs with a big duffel bag slung over her shoulder.

Charleigh was gorgeous to the extreme. This knockout who'd let her hair go back to its natural blonde once she no longer had a reason to be hiding her identity.

Once she'd found her place. Her home and her family.

Was so fucking happy she was here, exactly where she belonged. I knew Raven felt the exact same way.

"Hey, Otto," she said as she took the last step onto the bottom landing. Her head was cast a little lower than usual and a bit of timidity colored her voice.

Unlike with River, there was no way I was going to give this sweet girl shit. She clearly was mortified enough.

"Hey there, darlin'. How are you this morning?"

Her gaze dipped to the ground. "I'm okay." Then she lifted her attention back to me. A concerned frown was carved into her brow. "How is Raven?"

Gorgeous.

Infuriating.

Driving me out of my mind.

Still having those damned dreams that have haunted her for her whole life.

How did they not know it? Why was she going it alone?

"She's good."

Charleigh set the duffel on the counter. "I thought maybe you could take some things to her. I know she must be beside herself that she doesn't have her makeup and a change of clothes." A tinge of lightness infiltrated her voice.

My laughter was knowing. "I'm sure she would appreciate that."

"It should tide her over—" Charleigh clipped off, reeling back in whatever she was going to say, which I was pretty sure was going to be *until she gets the rest of her stuff.*

River would have lost it.

"That's great. She needs to be at the shop at eight, so I better run so I can get this to her. Don't want her to be late. I'll be sure we get her car picked up after it's finished this afternoon, too."

"Thank you, Otto. Mean it. Would have been worried sick had she been with anyone else but you," River said.

"You know I will always be there for her. Whatever she needs." My throat felt itchy when I said it.

"Know it. You've always been. Not sure what she would have done without you."

He just kept driving that dull knife in deeper and deeper and he didn't even know it. Showering me with praise when the only thing I deserved was condemnation.

Knew it'd be coming…when he and the rest of the crew found out what I'd been doing. What I still had to do. But this was on me.

Clearing my throat, I tossed the duffel onto my back and tossed on a massive grin to cover the guilt clinging to my guts. "You know I'm the fun brother. She doesn't have to deal with your grumpy ass when she's hanging out with me."

River scoffed. "Whatever, asshole, I'm plenty of fun."

Charleigh looked at him like he'd grown another head.

"What?" he defended.

"You tried to give her a curfew the last time she went on a date," Charleigh accused.

I cracked up, though part of me wanted to clap him on the back and tell him good job. Warn him about what I'd walked in on at Kane's the weekend before last.

But Raven would hate that. Was over us treating her like a child.

I wouldn't do that to her.

"Loads of fun," I told him before I moved to Charleigh and pecked a kiss to her cheek. "Take care of this one, yeah?"

"Always," she said as she sent a soft gaze toward him.

Two were fucking mad over each other. Was happy for it. Happy he'd broken free of the rule he'd made for Sanctum years ago. An oath we'd taken to never fully give ourselves to a woman.

It was too dangerous for all parties involved.

Mainly, it was to protect her from getting chained to the life.

But also, it was a liability for the club since the more people who knew what we did, the more likely someone was to divulge our secrets.

But sometimes, laws couldn't contain hearts, and his had busted right through it.

The crew still hadn't come to a decision on how to handle it. If that clause was being permanently redacted or if he and Charleigh got a pass.

"All right, gotta get out of here." I started for the door when Nolan came banging down the steps at warp speed.

"Nolan, you know you're not supposed to be running on those stairs," River warned. "You remember the last time you took a tumble."

"That's right, I do. We met my mommy at the doctor's office. Totally worth it, Daddy-O!" the kid shouted as he hopped down onto the bottom floor.

How the heck were you supposed to argue with that?

I could feel the adoration permeate the air, and I let my attention sweep to Charleigh. Charleigh, who was watching him with so much love it kicked a tiny pang of pain right in the center of my chest.

"Think it was worth it, wasn't it, Little Dude?" I agreed as I turned my focus back on Nolan.

"Family is always worth it," he said with his adorable face tipped up to me.

It hit me profoundly.

He was absolutely right.

Family was always worth it.

"Gotta run, Nolan. I need to get some things to your auntie Raven, but I hope you have the best day."

He wrapped himself around one of my legs and squeezed. "Okay, give this hug to my auntie for me."

Too bad he had no idea how badly I wanted to wrap my arms around her and never let go.

I murmured an easy, "How about you give her an extra giant one the next time you see her?"

"Smart plan, Uncle!"

Nah. There wasn't a thing in this plan that was smart. Because I'd turned down the most reckless path, and I wasn't sure there was a way to make it back.

Chapter
TWENTY-ONE

Raven

"**O**H MY GOD, YOU'RE A LIFESAVER, OTTO," I SQUEALED AS I tossed my Louis Vuitton duffel onto his massive bed. While he was gone, I'd showered, and I'd found a black robe that I was currently wrapped in.

I was in desperate need of my necessities so I could finish getting ready. "Please tell me my red lipstick is in here."

"Not sure about that, and I sure can't take credit for this. It was all Charleigh."

Pleasure rolled through me as I unzipped my baby.

Okay, fine…my bag, but I kind of wanted to cuddle it like an infant.

My heart stretched tight as I opened it.

Charleigh truly was the best bestie ever. She knew exactly what I needed. I dug through, finding at least three changes of clothes, clean underwear, shoes, and my toiletries bag tucked inside.

Tears nearly sprang to my eyes when I saw the notebook stuffed inside at the bottom. The journal that was covered in fake pink fur and held the greatest treasures. The memories that had been branded inside and had printed a seal on me.

Plus, the mirror that I always kept at my bedside was carefully wrapped in a hand towel to keep it safe.

Best bestie ever.

Sucking the emotion down, I focused on squealing over the two pairs of shoes she had packed. I grabbed my favorite red Valentino flats and hugged them to my chest.

"She really loves me, doesn't she?" I sang.

Otto leaned casually against the doorframe of his bedroom, staring over at me. So massive it felt like he was filling up the entire room.

So damned hot in the jeans that clung to his thick, muscled thighs, another plain white tee stretched thin across his mercilessly wide chest.

Grin kissing his delicious lips but that fiery intensity boiling in the depths of that unrelenting gaze.

It was strange looking at him like this after what had happened last night and this morning.

It felt…normal. How we ususally were. Though there was an undercurrent that had carved itself deeper. As if a new channel had formed. A new conduit of understanding.

"Don't think it's possible for someone not to love you, Raven Tayte."

I got stuck there.

Gazing at him.

Why did he have to say those things to me? But I swore there was something different about him as he watched me, except I had a bad habit of believing my wildest fantasies would come true. Imagining things were there that were not.

Silence stretched between us. This strange awareness rippled on the waves. Then he suddenly pushed from the jamb. "You'd better get dressed or you're going to be late."

He didn't say anything else before he turned on his heel and headed back out. His heavy boots echoed on the stairs as he ambled down to the main floor, and I quickly changed into a pair of black cropped jeans, a red, frilly sleeveless blouse, and the red Valentinos. I'd already dried my hair and Otto had set out an extra toothbrush for me, so I quickly applied a little makeup before I grabbed my hand-bag and walked out.

"Ready."

Blue eyes the color of a toiling sea raked over me. A heat wave that blasted through me.

I felt lightheaded.

God, I really was losing it.

Letting myself drift.

I had to tamp whatever had been loosed inside me.

Whatever?

I knew exactly what it was.

I mean, how was I ever supposed to forget him saying that he'd be the luckiest man alive if he got to touch me?

And on all things holy, I wanted to make him lucky.

He tucked his phone into his back pocket and headed for the in-terior door. "Let's get out of here."

I followed him downstairs, and he jabbed at the button to lift the garage door. Light poured in from outside, and he went directly to the motorcycle that he usually rode.

The one that was painted a misty, haunting gray, the metal black matte.

Low and wide.

Both menacing and screaming of freedom uncontained.

The perfect accessory to the man.

"Come here," he said as he grabbed the black helmet he'd specially ordered for me. I crept forward, losing my breath all over again when he carefully placed it on my head, his watch intent as he buckled the strap under my chin.

Those fingers adept.

A chill rolled through me as he let them drag down the side of my neck once he had the helmet secure, then he reached out and took my hand to guide me to the bike. He slung himself over first, never releasing me, before he helped me onto the back.

He kicked it over. The loud engine grumbled, and my stomach rolled. Anticipation lighting me through.

I wondered if he had any clue how much I loved being on the back of his bike. I tucked my front right up to his back, my thighs wrapped around the outside of his legs.

Flames sparked, and I could hardly breathe.

His muscles flexed along his back as I fully pressed myself against him, my arms wrapped tight around his waist.

I guessed I was feeling reckless. Bold. Because I splayed my hands out over his abdomen, making sure one of them was directly on the spot where I'd discovered the tattoo this morning.

The one that made me question everything.

He flinched against my touch before I felt him release a heavy exhalation, some of the tension bleeding away, then he used his boots to back us out. He tapped the button on his phone to close the garage door and set the alarm, before he turned the bike around and took to the road.

There was nothing like being with Otto this way. When he was at his freest. When I could feel the strain melt away and the joy of the endless expanse of road set out ahead of us.

The wind in our hair and the sun on our faces.

Okay, fine. I didn't mind the part where I was completely plastered against him, either.

His heat blistered into me. His big body so strong and sure as he took the winding road. Trees whipped by on either side before we got to the bottom of the hill where it opened to our small town.

He took the couple turns required to get us onto 9th Street where my shop was located, and he made a U-turn so he could pull up to the curb in front of Moonflower. His booted feet stretched out to support us as we came to a stop.

In an instant, all the easiness we'd been riding on shattered.

My fluttering heart dropped like a rock to the pit of my stomach.

Written in white spray paint across the big windows fronting Moonflower was *Little bitches bleed red.*

I knew that Otto had seen it at the exact same time as I did because every muscle in his body went rigid.

Rage billowed from his being as his attention raced to take in the area.

Fury streaked like a lightning strike across his flesh as he searched for any lingering threat.

There was quite a bit of traffic at this time, people rushing around to start their days. A few loitered on the sidewalk in front of my shop, taking in the spectacle.

My stomach roiled in a vat of nausea, and my head spun with dizziness.

Oh God, I thought I might be sick.

Otto put a hand on my leg and slowly turned to me.

Rage colored every inch of his face. "Stay right there."

"Otto—"

"Mean it, Raven. You stay right there and do not move."

He killed the engine and kicked the stand, and he managed to shift off the bike while leaving me sitting on it.

He stepped onto the sidewalk, his attention darting every direction as he scanned the area, the man a fiery blaze as he stormed toward Moonflower's door.

There were five people standing near it, but only two that I recognized.

Pete, a kid who couldn't be more than sixteen who was working next door at the coffee shop for the summer, and Sienna. Sienna who'd had her arms crossed over her chest, hugging herself. I saw the outrage and disgust lining her face when she shifted to look behind her as Otto prowled that way.

"Anyone see anything?" he demanded as he approached.

Pete shook his head. "No, I got here an hour ago and it was like that."

Sienna ran her hands up her arms as if she was trying to chase away shivers. "No. I just got here for my shift and heard what happened. I wanted to come and check if Raven was okay."

The others rumbled their *nos* as Sienna's gaze drifted my direction. Sympathy rippled through her features.

"*It's okay,*" I mouthed.

If only saying it made it true.

Because it was one hundred percent *not* okay. Not when some prick, asshole, dickface had done this. And for what reason other than to be mean and rude? To scare me?

A sticky sensation crawled over me. Those old chains that had bound, held me in terror, and the determination to never let someone bully me again.

Never to let them hurt me or intimidate me.

Otto stormed across the sidewalk and pressed his face to the window.

He cupped his hands on either side of his eyes so he could see inside. When he obviously didn't find anything, he went stalking around the side of the building in search of anything amiss.

That burly bear who could be so tender nowhere to be found.

He was a grizzly ready for attack.

A beast that raved.

While I sat there itching, not sure if I wanted to hide or get off the bike and hunt this jerk down, too.

Disquiet gusted as my brain shifted through who might be responsible.

Dread pooled in my chest when my thoughts immediately went to Tanner.

I blinked to cut the idea off. He wouldn't. He'd been nothing but kind to me. Well, until he wasn't.

I didn't have time to contemplate it any farther before Otto rounded back around the side of the building, his expression grim. "Couldn't find a damned thing. Let me have your key. I'm going to check to make sure no one has been inside."

"I'm sure it's just—"

He'd leaned down to get in my face, his proximity cutting me off before I could say anything. "Please, just let me check. Won't take the chance of some fucker hiding out to get at you."

I swallowed around the thickness in my throat, and I unzipped my bag and pulled out the keys. He already knew the security code, and he disappeared inside.

Frustrated, I undid the buckle on my helmet and pulled it off, while Sienna moved toward me, her brown ponytail falling over her shoulder. When she got close enough, she reached out and squeezed my arm. "God, Raven. I'm so sorry this happened. Who would do this?"

Both our gazes drifted to the window.

Something about it felt...ominous. Like it wasn't a threat but a harbinger of what was to come.

Apprehension rolled through me, but I swallowed it because no way.

This was ridiculous.

I wasn't going to let some creep ruin my day.

I forced a tight smile. "I'm sure it was just some punk coming around here being stupid in the middle of the night."

That's what it had to be, right?

There was no chance I'd been targeted.

I turned back to Sienna. "Do you know if any other stores were vandalized last night?"

Pete ambled up to Sienna's side as I asked it. The shake of his head was regretful when he said, "I think it was just yours. I walked around a little and it was the only one I saw, at least."

Awesome.

Just freaking great.

A tidal wave of volatility ripped through the air when Otto tossed the door open and came thundering back out. "Nothing. Not a fuckin' trace."

"It was probably some random kid with his first can of spray paint." I gave him a version of what I'd given Sienna.

It made the most sense. No one would actually be that stupid to paint this on my store's window and actually mean it.

Did they have any clue who I was affiliated with?

Otto glowered. "Don't fuckin' care who did it. He's dead. I'm sure the security camera will tell us something."

Surprise blanched Sienna's expression, as if she'd felt the violence skating out of the man and she was worried he was actually serious.

I wondered what she'd think if she knew he likely was.

I giggled like Otto was exaggerating his anger, and I climbed off the bike, voice going soft in an attempt to assuage the situation. "It's probably not a big deal. I'll get it cleaned off before anyone even comes in."

"You can't be serious? You think you're going to work today?" Otto's voice was full of disbelief. Somehow, he appeared even taller than usual as he towered over me. A vibrating hedge of protection and animosity.

I gulped down the intensity. "Um, yes, I am."

"Yeah, no," he said as he took a step forward.

My voice lowered in hopes of keeping it from Sienna and Pete, but they were standing right there, so they were going to get a first-row seat to this showdown.

But it had to be said.

"You don't get to come here bossing me around, Otto."

I had enough of that from my brother.

Pete and Sienna looked between each other in discomfort before Pete mumbled, "I need to get back to work. Hope you figure out who it was."

It'd be better for whoever this poor idiot was if we didn't. He had no idea what he was dealing with. Stupid kids.

"I'd better get back, too. I'm supposed to be clocked in." Sienna hesitated, like she wasn't sure she should leave me.

"It's okay. You don't need to worry."

Otto standing next to me guaranteed I was in no danger.

Her nod was reticent, definitely seeing it, too, and she took a step forward and pulled me into a tight hug. "I'm sure it's nothing. Text me if you need me, though, okay?"

"I will," I told her, then asked, "I'll see you at Otto's party, right?"

Sienna's brow lifted. "Is it still on?"

"Um, yes, it is still on. No chance we're letting whoever this asshole is get in our way of a good time." My voice was emphatic. Then I grinned. "Tell me you ordered something hot to wear."

Her eyes widened in excitement, and she lifted her index finger. "Oh, good call. I'll get right on it."

"Your girl will always look out for you," I teased.

Otto grunted, annoyed that I'd turned to happy topics rather than the one he looked like he was going to go ballistic over.

"We don't need to be thinkin' about my birthday right now, Raven," he grunted low.

"Sure we do…how else am I going to remind Sienna that she has someone to seduce?" I said it completely innocent.

Sienna giggled a scandalous sound. "That I do. Okay, gotta go!"

She gave a tiny wave before she looked both ways then jogged back across the street. I watched her go, trying to ignore the heat wave that blasted me from the side.

When she disappeared into the café, there was nothing I could do but turn my attention back to Otto.

Otto who was nothing but a ball of hostility. Rays of sunlight blazed around him, making him appear an orb of fire.

That unease spun in my belly, but I tried to hide it behind an easy grin.

"This isn't a big deal, Otto. People get vandalized all the time. You don't need to get all surly and grumpy."

"Oh, I can assure you I'm a whole lot more than *grumpy*, Raven."

I rolled my eyes as I started for the door. "I'm sure it was some thirteen-year-old boy going around tagging things."

Little bitches bleed red.

Okay, maybe it wasn't a typical tag.

But I couldn't believe it was anything else. Couldn't believe Tanner would be so petty.

I tossed open the door and stepped inside.

Moonflower was my happy place. The place where I could be completely me. A place that was mine and only mine. A place where my brother and his friends didn't get to intervene.

Only there was Otto stalking in behind me, radiating anger, his big body a hurricane that swept into the space.

Apparently, my claim that the second someone stepped inside their aggression would go poof was completely incorrect.

"Bet you a million bucks it was that fucker Tanner. Saw exactly what he was thinking at Kane's. He thinks you owe him somethin'."

"Tanner is harmless."

He had to be.

"No man is harmless, Raven. You know that."

I blew out a sigh. "I don't want to start laying blame on anyone when there is absolutely no proof against them. For now, I'm going to chalk it up to vandals, clean the mess, and get back to business."

I rounded the counter, and Otto followed, his enormous frame covering me from behind.

Energy surged and shook. Darker than normal. "Don't like this, Raven."

I turned to him. He was so close, it ripped the breath from my lungs. I played off the reaction like I was only frustrated. "I get that you worry about me, Otto. That you all worry about me. But I refuse to be that girl who caves or shutters. I won't be the girl who hides behind my fears. This is my store. The thing that brings me joy. And I won't let anyone stand in the way of that."

Worry pulled tight through Otto's features. "I get that. Just—"

"There's no *just*. I mean it. I won't cower. Especially when it's probably some random kid running the streets."

He sighed before I felt him give. "Stubborn girl."

"Burly Bear," I retorted.

He grinned at his nickname. I called it a win.

"I'm just looking out for my favorite person," he muttered before he scrubbed a hand over his face then dropped it. "Gonna need to look at that footage on the camera."

I nodded and moved over to the computer, brought it to life. There was nothing all night until there was the ghosting of movement just after 4:00 a.m. A figure dressed all in black and completely concealed that was barely captured. His features hidden. The only thing we could make out was that he was medium height and slim. Way too thin to be Tanner.

"Fuck," Otto grumbled.

Unease rolled through me, but I forced it down and clicked out of the program. "I need to get to work."

Otto let go of a pained sigh, then said, "Fine. Then I guess we'd better get this mess cleaned up." He turned on his heel and moved into the back of the shop, going directly to the big basin. He grabbed a bucket and set it inside, turning the water to high as he squeezed a giant stream of soap into the container.

He tossed in a sponge and started for the front door.

"You don't need to do that. I'll take care of it," I told him as I attempted to catch up to his long strides.

Standing in the open doorway, he tossed an easy look back in my direction. As if the worry from five seconds ago had been eradicated. "Nah, I've got this, darlin'. You go meet your delivery guy and continue on with your day. Business as usual. Just like you said."

Gratitude flooded my spirit. "You're too good to me, Otto."

Reaching out, he hooked his pinky finger with mine. "My favorite person, remember?"

Every element in my being fluttered.

Body and soul and mind.

My favorite person.

I only wished that meant what I really wanted it to.

"Okay," I relented.

"Good. Now get to work. No more slacking."

Levity pulled between us, that easiness we normally wore. "Fine, but if you need help, let me know."

"Got it covered," he said as he let the door drop behind him.

I wandered deeper back into the store, though I slowed, peeking over my shoulder to watch as Otto leaned down to dip the sponge into the water then started scrubbing off the offensive words.

Like maybe in doing it, he could erase some of my scars.

"The fuck happened?"

Oh, here we go.

From where I sat on the high stool behind the counter, I scowled at my brother who stormed in through Moonflower's door.

"Whatever are you talking about, dear brother?"

I was going to make him work for this one a little bit.

He scowled right back. "Don't act like you don't know exactly what I'm talking about. You think I wasn't goin' to hear about it?"

"What, that someone got super clever with their spray paint on my window?" I injected as much sarcasm into the words as I could muster.

"Someone fuckin' with my baby sister, that's what. Motherfucker is dead."

I rolled my eyes. "Do you and Otto share scripts?"

"Otto loves you like a sister, too, so yeah, can assure you he and I are on the same page."

I tried to ignore the jab of discomfort his statement elicited. "Both of you are ridiculous, the way you worry."

River's sharp brow arched. "Says the girl who thinks I'm dead in a ditch somewhere any time I'm runnin' five minutes late."

I shrugged a shoulder. "There are creepers out there."

"Exactly my point."

Crap. I walked right into that.

"Well…you have enemies. I'm just as innocent as can be over here. No one has any reason to take issue with me."

"Plenty of sick bastards hurt people for no reason at all or because they think they're justified in some way. Worried this is some asshole who got his feelings hurt when you realized he wasn't good enough for you."

"You don't think anyone is good enough for me."

"Pretty much, yeah," River said. "Half the time, all it takes to drive a man out of his mind is for him to get some twisted notion that he's been wronged."

I shook my head. "I don't think I've been driving any man out of his mind lately."

"Except for me." He mumbled his exasperation.

I narrowed my eyes. "You don't count. Besides, you're the one who's on trial here."

There. Change the subject. But it really wasn't a subject I wanted to tackle all that much. But it was going to have to be someday, so it might as well be right now.

Rip the Band-Aid off while the wound was still stinging.

River flinched, and he dropped his gaze as he roughed a tattooed hand over the top of his head. "Sorry about that. Thought you were gonna text, and Nolan was at the park with the neighbor kid, so…" He trailed off in discomfort.

I couldn't even keep up the affront. "It's fine, River. I'm not mad. You should be able to do whatever you want in your own house."

"Your house, too."

And there goes that Band-Aid.

Rip. Rip. Rip.

"It's not anymore."

The snarl that tore out of River was no less than terrifying. "What the hell are you talking about?"

"I'm moving out. Getting my own place."

"Are you fuckin—"

I put out my hand. "I know what you're going to say, but I've already decided."

"You've already decided?"

I inhaled a steeling breath. "Yes, I have."

"Raven—"

"It's already done, River. I'm going to stay with Otto until I find a place to rent."

Hurt carved his brow, and I slipped off my stool and rounded the counter. Slowly, I approached him, my voice soft. "I want you to know how much I appreciate everything you've ever done for me. I know your sacrifice, and I will never pretend as if it didn't come at the greatest cost. I will never forget the way you cared for me when I was young. The way you nurtured me. You were only a kid yourself, and you took on this terrified little girl and protected her. Raised her and showed her what *family* really meant. I could never express how much that means to me."

I inhaled a shaky breath and pushed on. "But it's time, River. It's time for me to live my life as an adult, and not one who's barely figuring out who she is under your roof."

"Raven…" That time when he said my name, it was wistful. Sorrowful.

"I love you so much," I whispered.

Soggy affection rose up from the depths of me.

I'd been prepared for a fight, but that's not what this was. This was me being honest.

"I am so thankful for you, and I'm so thankful for Charleigh and Nolan and this amazing life and the experiences we've had. But it's time for both of us to begin a new era."

River sighed. "Knew this day would come. Was always scared of it, though."

"You don't have to be scared, River. It's not like I'm moving out of state. I'm going to find a little place here in town, so I'll be nearby."

"But I won't be able to watch out for you all the time."

In emphasis, I tipped my head to the side. "Which is basically the point."

He scrubbed a palm over his face. "Right." Then he peeked up at me with a half grin. "That's going to take some gettin' used to."

He looked around my shop. "But it's good you're staying with Otto right now…'til we get this thing sorted out."

I knew what *get this thing sorted out* meant.

Someone was going to sorely regret making the mistake of picking my store to vandalize.

"Try not to go too hard on whatever poor kid was out having a little fun."

"Never go too hard."

My brow arched in disbelief, and River let go of a guilty chuckle before he reached out and squeezed my hand. "Just want you happy and safe, Raven, and if that's what moving out makes you, then I support you. I'll always support you. Will always love you. And I want you to know how damned proud I am of everything you've accomplished."

"I couldn't have done it without you."

Eyes that were the same color as mine creased at the corners. "Pretty sure you would have. Pretty sure there isn't a damned thing in the world that could stop my baby sister from soaring."

Love filled me so full I wasn't sure my ribs could contain it.

"Thank you," I whispered.

"Mean it," he said. Then he curled me in his arms and kissed the top of my head. "Just need you to promise that if anyone bugs you… if you get that sense…the intuition that something is off, don't ignore it. Don't take the chance. Especially after what happened this morning. Trust your gut, and you call us."

Pulling back, I gave him a shaky nod. "I will."

Mischief tweaked his mouth. "You gotta know we'll still be watching over you."

Clearing the roughness from my throat, I stepped back and tried to shake off the emotion, my voice wrenching with the ribbing. "As if I expect anything less. I'm sure you're going to post one of the guys outside my door for the rest of my life."

"Obviously."

I could only hope he was teasing.

"All right, I'll let you get back to it," he said. "Just needed to make sure you were okay. Be careful, Raven. Don't think you know what you mean to all of us."

Emotion swept me in a soft, undulating wave. "I actually think I do."

A puff of satisfied air heaved from his nose. "Good."

When there was movement out front, our attention swiveled to the big window that was now squeaky clean to find Otto whipping my little white BMW into an open spot at the curb. He climbed out, looking as if he'd barely been able to squish himself behind the wheel.

Obliterating reason and sight as he drove the fingers of both hands through the crop of his hair as he came striding for the door.

Right then he was all grins.

The casual, easygoing guy back in full force.

A teddy bear rather than a grizzly bear. I wasn't sure which version of him I liked best.

He pulled open the door with that smirk tacked to his face and did some bow with a flourish of his hand. "My lady, your chariot awaits. As good as fuckin' new. Took it upon myself to pay the mechanic a little visit to make sure of it."

He wagged his brows.

Crap. I bet he worked out some of his worry from earlier by busting some balls. Throwing around his massive weight. I was never going to be able to show my face in there again.

"Always going the extra mile for our baby sister," River rumbled.

Otto glanced at me. My knees knocked with the sudden storm that raged in his sea-blue eyes.

"That's right. No one is going to take advantage of her." He didn't look away from me when he said it.

Silence weighed heavy before River shifted on his heavy boots. "All right, I need to go pick up Nolan and get home."

Broken out of the severity, I gave my brother a soft nod. "I'll be by this evening to get some more things."

"You better. Nolan was about to lose his mind when you didn't come home last night. Mostly because he was jealous that you got to have a sleepover at *Uncle Otto's,* and he didn't. He might stage a revolt when he finds out you're going to be staying there for a while."

Wistfulness tugged hard at my heart. "It's going to be so hard not living with my little man."

"And not with me?" River razzed.

I let go of a soft laugh. "Don't fool yourself, big brother. Nolan is the life of my party."

He chuckled, too. "Kid is going to miss you." He hesitated then said, "And I'm gonna miss you, too."

Chapter
TWENTY-TWO

Raven

Nine Years Old

RAVEN WAS HAVING ANOTHER NIGHTMARE. THE SAME ONE THAT came every night.

"No, no, no. Daddy, please, no." She used her heels to slide across the carpeted floor, trying to get away from him. But she couldn't. She never could, no matter how hard she tried. No matter how quiet she tried to be. No matter if she hid beneath her covers or at the back of her closet.

He always found her when he was mad.

And he was mad right then. She could see it even though his face was twisted in a grin.

"Told you that you'd be punished if you left the light on again."

"I didn't, Daddy. I didn't."

He flicked the lighter and she screamed.

Screamed and screamed.

Her scream echoed through the dark room as she awoke, so small in her tiny bed, and she flailed her arms as she tried to get away. She had to get away.

"Shh, Raven, it's okay. It's okay. It's me. Otto. You're safe."

Her breaths kept heaving out of her, and her heart beat so hard that it hurt, her chest squeezing tight as she tried to process where she was.

She blinked through the shadows that covered the room, and it took her a minute to be able to make out who was there.

It was Otto.

His face was pinched up like he was mad, and his breaths were hard, too, but his blue eyes that shined in the dark chased away the feeling in her stomach that she might be sick. She felt sick a lot, a yucky sense inside her that made her feel like something was always wrong.

But it'd always been wrong, at least most of the time.

But it didn't feel wrong right then.

"You're safe," he murmured again, his voice low. "You're safe."

She nodded to tell him that she understood since she couldn't make any words come up her throat.

He nodded, too. "Okay."

Then he plopped down on his butt beside the little bed that Theo and Kane had brought for her and put in this room because they'd said a princess needed her own special space. "Bad dream?" Otto finally asked.

She nodded again.

He roughed a hand through his brown hair that was kinda shaggy and long. "I'm sorry."

"It's okay," she whispered.

He sighed. "Hate it for you...that you feel scared here. Mean it when I tell you that none of us will let anyone get to you here."

She nodded again.

He seemed to waver then stood as he mumbled, "Wait right there."

He was gone for a minute before he returned, and he knelt with two different things in his hands.

Interest sparked in Raven, and she sat up a little bit as he passed her a mirror with a handle. In the dark she could tell it was silver and looked old, a crack through the mirror that cut her in two.

"That used to be my grandmother's, and I've kept it for a long, long time," Otto said quietly. "And now I want you to have it."

With a frown, she stared at her murky reflection. "Why?" she whispered.

"Because when you look at it, I want you to see the way I see you. I want you to see this brave, strong, smart girl who's amazing. Who's a fighter. Who even when she's scared, she knows that she's going to rise above it."

Her heart felt too big as she looked at herself in the night.

"You think I'm brave?" she asked.

"Yeah, Raven, I think you're really, really brave."

A long sigh puffed from his nose, then he shifted and handed her the other thing he'd brought in with him.

"And I want you to have this, too." He passed her a notebook that was covered in pink fur.

"What is it?" Her voice was quiet.

"It's a note from my sister. I told her about you today, and she thought it'd be a good idea if you two were friends, too."

The sickness in her stomach shifted to something else.

Excitement, though she also felt nervous. She'd never had a friend before. Her mom wouldn't let her.

"Really?" she asked.

He pointed at the notebook. "See for yourself."

She set it on her lap, unsure, though Otto passed her a pen and said, "You don't have to write back, but if you end up wanting to, I can take your message back to her."

"Okay." The single word sounded small.

Otto eased toward the door that was broken and didn't shut all the way. "Try to go back to sleep and know I'm in the room right there."

He pointed behind him.

She nodded, and he walked out.

There was only a tiny sliver of light that cut into her room, the moon coming through a crack in the piece of wood that was nailed to the window on the other side. She opened the notebook and peered down at the words.

Hi, Raven!

I'm Haddie, and I'm Otto's little sister. We should totally be friends since you live with my brother now. I'm ten, and I just started ballet, and it's my favorite thing ever. Also pink is my favorite color so I hope you like it, too, and the thing I hate most is spinach because it's gross. Do you want to go get ice cream? I bet Otto will take us! write me back!

Haddie ♡

Hi, Haddie,

Thank you for wanting to be my friend. I'm nine, but your brother said he didn't think you'd mind too much. I haven't ever done ballet, but I think learning to dance would probably be my favorite thing ever, too. I like pink and ice cream. I think my brother won't mind if I go with you to get some.

Raven ☺

Hi, Raven,

I loved that we finally got to meet, and oh my gosh, can you believe I dumped my whole cone on the ground? And bubblegum is my favorite. Wahhhh. Of course, Otto got me another one, but still, I was so embarrassed. But you were really nice. My other friends would have laughed and told me I deserved it. They pretend that they like me, but I don't really think they do. Ugh, they're dumb. I'm really glad I met you.

Haddie ♡

Haddie,

Well at least you have friends.

Raven

Raven,

Um, hello, you have me. You totally have a friend. And also my brother's friends because my brother told me you're a part of the family now. And all of them are so cool and always bring me stuff. You're so lucky you get to live with them. My mom sucks sometimes, but she's been cool lately, so that's good. Okay, I have dance class. Gotta go!

Haddie ♡

Haddie,

I'm sorry I didn't write for a while. My brother thought I should have a better place to live, and I went to stay with my grandma for a little bit. She was supposed to keep it a secret, but she told my DAD. I hate him and I hate her now, too. But I got back here, and River promised I would never have to leave again. I hope we are still friends.

Raven ☺

Raven,

Of course we're still friends. What do you think BFF means? It means best friends forever. No matter what. And my brother was so mad River took you there. He wouldn't tell me at first, but then I made him because he was being so grumpy when he came to visit. I'm really glad you're back! Haddie ♡

Haddie,

So guess what? We are getting a new house. A real house!! I mean, not that I don't like it here, but it's kind of gross and we always have to sneak in, and my brother is always worried we're going to get caught and I'm going to get taken away. And my brother got a motorcycle, almost like Otto's and Theo's, but his is black.

Raven ☺

Raven,

I'll see you Friday! Otto said I can come spend the night at your new house!

Haddie ♡

Chapter
TWENTY-THREE

OTTO

MORE THAN A WEEK HAD PASSED SINCE RAVEN HAD BEEN staying here, and I was about to fuckin' lose it.

The woman under my roof. Her laughter all around. That sweet, moonflower scent invading.

The woman was constantly underfoot, driving me halfway to unhinged. I wasn't sure if I wanted to hurry to help her pack her things to get the hell out of there or beg her to stay forever.

The problem was, I fuckin' liked it.

Liked walking in my door and finding her in the kitchen sipping from a glass of wine or stretched out on the couch watching TV or reading a book.

Liked her girly shit strewn all over my bathroom counter.

Liked her sleeping in my bed, even though I'd made sure to stay out of it considering what'd happened the last time I'd woken with her curled in my arms.

She hadn't had a nightmare since. I'd been more than thankful—both because I couldn't stand her being tormented by her ghosts and because I was beginning to question my morals.

Guilt clamped down on my chest, my conscience flailing behind its bounds, tendrils reaching out to remind me of what I'd done.

Morals?

What a fuckin' joke.

It was all right there below the surface. The truth of what I'd cost. The truth of what I had to do. The truth of what would go down tonight.

And there I was, a twisted fuck who was so close to reaching out and taking what he knew he should never touch.

Raven had found one apartment that she'd really liked, but it'd already been leased by the time she'd decided to take a leap on it.

I should have known I was in trouble when I was pummeled with a rush of relief. Should have known I was already half gone when my insides had buzzed with the knowledge that I got to keep her here for a little while longer.

Hell, I should have known it right then when I came bounding upstairs from the garage and swung open the door late that evening to find her standing in the kitchen, making dinner.

Should have known it when my chest squeezed in a fit of pleasure so severe it nearly knocked me from my feet.

She had a bottle of red wine open and a glass sitting next to her on the counter. Taylor Swift was blaring from the speakers.

My stomach twisted at the sight. The whole setting so much Raven Tayte that it stole my damned breath.

"What do you think you're doin'?" I asked as I stepped inside and tossed my keys to the high table next to the door.

She canted me one of those saucy grins as she swayed from side to side, swishing those lush hips, the girl wearing another one of those pinup dresses that she loved to torment me with. This one was fully black and sleeveless, the neckline high and wrapped with a frill around her neck.

Makeup done thick, red painted lips and her eyes drawn in a sharp cat eye. Lashes long as fuck.

Only Raven would still be wearing those sky-high heels, as comfortable as if she were barefoot.

"What does it look like I'm doing? Making dinner." She was all coy grins. Completely light and playful tonight.

"Ah, trying to spoil me, huh?" I asked, a stupid grin hugging my mouth since clearly, I was a self-indulgent moron when it came to her.

"Well, you're always spoiling me, so I thought it was only fair that I returned the favor."

"You know you don't owe me anything."

"You've been letting me stay here and feeding me for more than a week. I'm pretty sure I do."

"I like having you here." Couldn't keep the honesty out of my words.

That raven gaze dipped for a second before she whispered, "I like being here, too."

"Ah, thought you were gonna be sick of me by now," I told her as I wandered deeper into the kitchen, drawn to her.

A motherfuckin' magnet that I couldn't resist.

She had her hair piled on her head, and I had the urge to walk up behind her, lean in, and press my nose to the delicate slope at the back of her neck.

"Sick of you?" She playfully rolled her eyes. "My favorite person ever? I think not."

"Well, that's good to hear since you're never getting rid of me." Of all the terrible ideas I could have, this one was probably the worst, but even knowing it, I still reached out and took her hand.

Raven squealed when I gave her an impromptu spin.

Her gaze went wild with that infectious glee as I pulled her back to me then hooked an arm around her waist.

I'd always danced with her. Since I could remember. It'd always been safe. Fun. A way for us to goof around. But in the last few years, it'd become something else entirely.

It'd become gluttonous, the feeling that swept through me when I was touching her like this, acting like it was as innocent as ever when the only thing I wanted to do was splay my hand over her soft, soft skin.

Explore and taste and devastate.

Raven knew exactly what was up, and she spun out of my hold and moved to her phone on the counter so she could change the music. She switched it to one of those old swing songs I used to teach her to dance to years ago, all the way back to when we'd been living in that abandoned house.

The second the quick beat hit the air, she shimmied back in my direction. Pure fuckin' sass. So goddamn sexy as she strutted in those heels.

I might have been the one leading her, but she was the one who compelled it all. The one who guided me as I spun her and dipped her, both of us giggling as we gave ourselves over to the freedom of the moment.

I spun her in one direction, then the other, before I tossed her out wide. Releasing my hand, she kept going, spinning and spinning across the kitchen floor before she turned to grin at me, standing about six feet away.

"Are you ready for it?" I asked.

"I was born ready for it," she said with a curve of those distracting red lips.

She moved for me, gliding across the space. When she got within reach, I took her hand, pulling her toward me fast and flipping her over my arm. She squealed as she flew, then she was landing right back on those heels, forever steady on her feet.

It was me who was losing ground.

Me who couldn't find his footing when I curled her into me, bringing her back to my chest as I swayed us side to side. The next step would have been spinning her back out.

But what did I do?

I banded a greedy arm all the way around her front and tucked her back tight against my chest.

My mouth went to her ear as lust smacked me in the face. "You were born for this, Raven. Fuckin' perfect on those feet."

"Born to dance with you." It was a breathy murmur from her mouth.

I tried to play off our words with a laugh, though I doubted I was pulling off casual, since I pressed my nose to her neck, breathing in the soft flesh at the sensitive spot behind her ear.

Inhaling the overwhelming scent of moonflowers.

As sweet and fragrant as honeysuckle.

Before my urges got away from me, I forced myself to spin her back out, thanking fuck that something on the stove was starting to spit and sizzle. "Looks like we have a bit of an issue on the stove."

A shaky giggle slipped out of Raven as she turned back to quickly stir the vegetables. "You're distracting. Get out of here before you make me burn the place down."

She waved the spoon at me.

I rumbled a chuckle, though it was half in pain. "You know you love it."

"Of course I do." Her voice was softer than it should have been.

I cleared my throat, the levity squashed when my thoughts moved to the reality of what was coming. What I was about to do.

"Going to take a shower really quick before we eat. Have a job I have to run tonight." Could barely force the words off my tongue. "Gotta leave after dinner, and I probably won't be back until sometime tomorrow night."

Sticky shame engulfed me when I said it.

It toiled with the dread.

Confusion bound her brow when she looked at me. "For the club?"

I rubbed my palms together like it could wipe away the guilt. The very indignant part of myself screamed that I was doing it for her, too.

That they deserved this.

Revenge.

Justice.

The part of me that wished I would have been the one who got to end them all that night when they'd come for me.

But I couldn't quell the disquiet that whispered like ghosts in my senses.

"Nah. Have a job for the distributor."

Her frown deepened. "Oh."

That guilt amped so high it was suffocating.

Hated lying to her.

But I couldn't lay it straight. I had to do this on my own.

"Going to have Jonah keep a lookout."

Jonah was one of the bouncers at Kane's. One of the few who had the inside of what we did. I trusted him to watch over her while I was gone.

Raven scowled. "That's not necessary."

"I think you know it is."

She huffed a small sound with a shake of her head. "And just when I think I'm getting my freedom…"

I was an idiot, across the space separating us in a flash, the woman a magnet that I couldn't resist. I took her by the chin and forced her to look up at me. "Want you to have that, Raven. A normal life…"

One outside of Sanctum so she wouldn't have to constantly be looking over her shoulder. A life where we didn't have to post guards any time we left. But after we still hadn't picked up a trace on whoever had spray painted her window at Moonflower?

I wasn't going to take that chance.

"I love this life," she whispered.

My head shook and I forced myself to step away. "Only because you haven't known anything else."

Disappointment filled her expression. "Don't ever tell me how I feel, Otto."

Fuck.

I kept messing everything up. Pushing into the spaces I couldn't go while trying to dredge up a mountain between us.

I gestured toward the room behind me. "Going to hit the shower."

In an instant, her eyes went molten. Her gaze dark.

Like she was immediately picturing me naked beneath the fall.

Fuck me.

She was nothing but a temptress.

She had no fucking clue what she was doing to me.

My need for her might have been easier to ignore if I couldn't feel what radiated from her.

If I didn't know.

If I didn't recognize the way her heart sped whenever I was near.

The way the energy shifted and intensified. Desire distinct in the depths of those ink-kissed eyes.

This attraction that blazed.

But it wasn't quite that simple.

It was deep and earnest.

Easy and light with the familiarity we'd always shared.

Sweet with the friendship we'd forged.

Bruised with the grief and pain we'd suffered.

It was close to two decades of history.

But I could never go there.

Could never take my best friend's little sister, the one woman I'd been forbidden to touch.

Swear it.

Could still hear the finality of those two whispered words bang in that closed-in hall where River had had me backed against the wall.

Could still feel the rattle of the oath I'd made.

Nine years older than her, the guy who'd sworn to be nothing more than her protector.

But more than that? It was who I was. Who I'd become in that grief and contempt that would forever rage inside me.

I was the last fuckin' guy to deserve Raven Tayte.

Hell, that cum-stain Tanner was better than me, even though I wanted to tear my hair from my head when I thought of him touching her.

When I thought of anyone touching her.

Thoughts spiraling, I forced myself to head into my room. I didn't know if it was any safer in there with all of Raven's things around. My bed made to perfection with a giant fluffy white pillow in the shape of a heart sitting against the headboard. The old mirror I'd given her years ago safely stowed on the nightstand.

Her shoes in my closet.

Her fuckin' birth control pills sitting on the counter in the bathroom.

Nearly came unglued when I saw a pair of black lace undies just sitting on the floor.

I tried to block the visions but it was impossible as I stepped into the spray.

And I gave myself over.

Letting the fantasies of her invade.

Her spread out on my bed, all naked curves and delicate flesh. Me exploring every damned inch of that beautiful body.

Adoring and devouring.

Fuck. The ways I would have her.

I gripped my cock with my hand, stroking myself hard and fast as I thought of her out in the kitchen. What it'd be like to go up behind her the way I'd always wanted, toss the skirt of that dress up around her waist and pull her underwear aside.

Drive into her deep and desperately.

Take her the way I was dying to.

But I couldn't have her.

I wanted so much more for her than this. A good, simple life. Someone to adore her the way she deserved to be adored. Someone who wouldn't keep her chained to the darkness. Someone who didn't devolve into depravity.

Leave it to me to be the fool who wished I could be every single one of those things as I ate dinner with her.

Except I knew I could never be when I walked out the door and into the wickedness that was waiting in the night.

Chapter
TWENTY-FOUR

OTTO

I DROVE THE ENTIRE FUCKING NIGHT. GUTS IN A TANGLE AS I traveled beneath the stars that blinked like beacons from above, guiding me to my disgraceful destination, giving way to the cover of darkened clouds that sagged over the earth like a shroud the closer I got to my target.

Eight hours to the slum buried deep in the city.

I'd ditched my truck a mile away, taking the rest of the distance on foot. Adrenaline rushed as I crept along the run-down street, keeping my footsteps light as I slinked through the shadows, dodging motion lights as I ducked between the forlorn, weathered houses, half of them barely standing.

My heart thudded at high speed as I eased up to the side of the derelict house at the end, breaths scraping like barbs from my lungs as I hopped over the short chain-link fence without making a sound and slipped unseen along the wall to the door in the back.

Daylight would be coming in less than thirty minutes, and I pressed my back to the peeling white wood, my spirit screaming and coating my tongue with vengeance as I searched the threadbare night for any movement.

When I was sure I was in the clear, I inhaled a tremulous breath before I spun toward the door and quickly picked the lock.

Bastard without a clue that I was coming for him as I felled the single deadbolt in less than thirty seconds.

The hinges creaked as I slowly pushed open the door, boots squeaking on the sticky linoleum floor as I crept through the kitchen that was rank as fuck, dirty dishes caked with rotted food piled in the sink.

Sickness coiled, hitting me on all levels as I craned my ear to make sure I remained undetected.

Silence echoed back.

Thick and tacky.

I made sure the fucker lived alone. My wrath only meant for him.

I leaned my back up against the wall and peeked around the entryway and into the living room on the other side.

I froze when I heard the rattling breaths coming from somewhere close.

It was just this side of pitch, a single wedge of light from the moon coming in through a crack in the drapes and illuminating the space.

Holding my breath, I scanned, taking it in.

Bottles littered a coffee table and the lid to a pizza box was left open to the half-eaten pizza inside.

The monster hadn't even hauled his ass to his bed. He was passed out on the couch, shirtless but wearing jeans. One arm was lifted over his head and one leg had fallen off the side where he was sprawled out.

Lost to the world.

Rage spiraled through my consciousness, my sister's face so clear in my mind.

Laughing.

Always laughing.

Wanting to take on the world. Live it big and beautiful and free.

I crept forward until I was standing right over him, staring down at the pathetic fuck who had no idea justice was coming for him.

I had my knife out with the tip pressed to his throat before he even knew I was there, then his eyes were popping open to the darkness where I stood over him like a wraith.

A reaper who'd come to collect.

The dark storm of my words a fulfilled prophecy.

"Did you think I'd let you get away? Did you think I wouldn't make you suffer for what you did? Did you think I would forget?"

Hate spun me into disorder as bile prowled up and down my throat. Seven years had passed. Seven years since the three of them had disappeared. Seven years that I'd been hunting. Seven years of this motherfucker thinking he'd gotten away.

"There is no place you could have run that I wouldn't have found you."

Because I'd sworn over Haddie's grave none of them would get away with what they'd done. They would atone for their sins. And that atonement had come due.

It was past midnight the next night when I pulled my truck up to my cabin that glowed like a lantern hung in the woods. The gold haze spilling from the windows whispered of peace and sanctuary.

Funny since I'd never felt a chaos so severe than right then.

Jonah leaned against the exterior wall, pulling in a deep drag of a cigarette as he gazed at the endless sky, though he lifted a hand in hello as I approached.

I pressed the button to lift the garage door, and I eased my truck inside. I killed the engine and stepped out to Jonah coming around my truck to greet me.

"Hey, man, how'd it go?"

I'd given him the same faulty excuse that I was running a legit trip.

"Good. Wiped, but good." Guilt nearly swallowed me, my head spinning as I attempted to keep myself together.

"All quiet around here?" I forced out, angling my head to indicate the house.

"Yup. Bedroom light went out about two hours ago. Think she's out for the night. Of course, she insisted on feeding me every meal for the last twenty-four hours since *I was the poor bastard who got assigned to keep the grizzly bears away.*" He chuckled when he said it.

"Shocker," I said, almost hearing her voice verbatim.

"She's a sweet one," Jonah mused.

"The best," I said low, glancing at the interior door like I might be able to see her form through it. Like I might be able to feel her warmth radiating out. Fall into its comfort.

I looked back at him. "Thanks for hanging out."

"Any time." Then he hesitated, his eyes narrowed. "You sure you're good?"

My spirit rumbled, and I managed a half-cocked grin. "Yeah. Just a long trip."

"All right, man. Get some rest."

I gave him a jut of my chin then closed the garage door behind him as he walked to his bike off to the side of the drive. He turned it over, the low grumble echoing through as he took off.

Only I couldn't bring myself to go upstairs. I grabbed a bottle of Jack that I had left half drunk on one of the worktables, spun off its cap, and tipped it up so I could take a giant gulp.

I rambled back to my truck and slunk down in the driver's seat, every few minutes guzzling at that bottle like I was going to find the answer at the bottom of it.

It burned as I gulped it down, hitting my stomach in a liquid fire that toiled and tumbled like the pits of hell.

I rocked my head back on the headrest, eyes going closed as I struggled through the emotions that gripped me.

Guilt.

Shame.

Determination.

A war of confusion that raged.

Every time I closed my eyes, I kept seeing the blood spilled across the floor and across my hands.

Halfway back to Moonlit Ridge, I'd stopped at a dingy motel and rented a room so I could take a shower and get a few hours' sleep.

Thinking it would be enough to wash the evidence away, only the dishonor had hunted me right back to this place.

I lifted the bottle again and swallowed a mouthful.

It left a path of fire, flames in my guts and ashes in my spirit.

I forced the jagged puffs of air through my nose as I sat there searching for everything I was missing.

Like I was going to find redemption.

Forgiveness.

Like I could ever make amends when my crew found out what I'd done behind their backs.

The lies I'd been telling.

I squeezed my eyes closed as visions flashed, but I was unable to block the horror of them out.

Running into that room that night so long ago. Blood splattered everywhere. The two people I loved most in this world mangled. Discarded like trash where they'd been left on the floor.

Raven barely breathing.

And Haddie...

Haddie...

I gasped through the blade of agony that speared through my chest, and I pulled the bottle back to my lips, sucked it down before I muttered, "One left, Haddie. One monster left."

I'd wanted to be the one who'd taken out all seven of them. Wanted to be the one who'd enacted this revenge.

The first four had gotten lucky and had been taken out by a rival MC back in LA. I still wanted to rage when I thought about the way it'd gone down. The night I'd hunted all seven of them. The night they all should've died but it'd been me who'd ended up with a gun pointed to my head.

The raid that had happened at exactly the right moment, the spray of bullets that had come from out of nowhere.

But this...this would have to suffice. Would have to be enough to fill the void that had been carved out in the middle of me.

"One more, Haddie. One more and you rest." The words were garbled as I repeated them into the cab of my truck.

But it was the face of Raven gliding behind my closed lids that had me finally getting out of my truck, no clue how much time had passed while I'd been sitting there. She'd be long asleep, but I wanted to be close to her. Let the beauty that she exuded seep through the bedroom wall to wrap me in a disordered embrace.

I staggered for the interior stairs.

My brain was fuzzy. The torment dulled but distinct.

I was as quiet as possible as I let myself into the weeping shadows of the living area. The moon was just bright enough to toss glittering silver dust through the room, and I shuffled across the floor to the couch, barely able to remain upright with the amount of alcohol that slugged through my veins.

I prayed to God that I'd just pass out.

Be taken away from this day.

Given a reprieve from the horrors and the atrocities.

The ones committed then and the ones I was committing now.

No choice left but to see this through.

I was just getting ready to faceplant onto the cushions when a cold slick of ice slithered down my spine when I heard it.

A moan.

It whipped through my head and tugged at my spirit.

I turned and fumbled that way just as I heard a low whimper as I climbed the steps. One followed by my name.

"Otto."

I hurried forward and tore the door open so I could get to her. So I could erase her pain. Hold a small piece of what had been perpetuated against her.

Only I skidded to a stop, throwing my back against the wall as I tried to process what I was seeing.

I blinked through the intoxication.

Thinking I had to be imagining things.

This fantasy too fuckin' real.

Raven laid out in the middle of my bed with her legs spread as she drove a toy into her pussy.

She moaned again, lifting her hips from the bed as she fucked herself with the vibrator.

I was slammed by a rogue wave of lust.

An avalanche that knocked me upside down.

"Fuck," I hissed as I pressed myself harder against the wall like I might be able to hook myself to it.

A gasp raked out of Raven and her head popped up. Inky eyes went wide when she saw me standing there gaping at her like a deranged, sick fuck.

But I couldn't move.

Couldn't move when her tongue swept over her lips. She paused for only a moment before she started thrusting that toy deep into that sweet cunt again.

She was completely bare from the waist down, though she had on one of my tees that basically swallowed her except for where she was spread wide.

Moonlight poured in through the window and lit her like a dream.

She'd shifted enough that I could see the toy had a nub that hit her clit with each plunge, and she was making all these breathy sounds as she kept stroking it between her thighs as she watched me.

"Otto," she whimpered, but she still didn't stop, and she was tweaking at her fabric-covered nipple as she kept working herself into a writhing, messy pile. Clearly, she was racing toward an orgasm that I could see glimmering all around her.

"Fuck, Raven..." I scrubbed a palm over my face to break up the disorder. To give myself some clarity. To fucking come back down to this godforsaken plane where I didn't get to do this. Where I didn't get to watch this goddess come undone in the middle of my bed.

It snapped me back enough that I wheezed, "Fuck, didn't mean to barge in like this. I thought...I thought you were having a dream."

"Maybe that's what I'm doing...dreaming." She whispered it in a seductive tone as she kept driving that toy into all her slick heat.

I'd never wanted to cross a room more than I did right then.

Had never wanted to give in so badly.

Had never wanted to steal the goodness. Feed on it until it filled my empty soul.

Somehow, I found the willpower to force myself back out the door, and I slammed it shut behind me at the same second as she cried out, an orgasm tearing so violently through her that I swore I could feel it reverberate through the door and ripple through me.

I chugged for the nonexistent air as I forced my ass back to the couch, still fucking staggering and lumbering my way across the floor, wondering if I was truly hallucinating.

Wouldn't be surprising since I had just downed half a bottle of Jack.

But I could still feel it. The energy she emitted. The pleasure that seeped beneath the door and crawled across the floor like a vapor tracking me.

"Fuck." I flopped onto the couch, trying to catch my damned breath. To make sense of what the fuck had just gone down. My cock so fucking hard there was nothing I could do but free myself from my jeans and jack myself right on the couch.

I came hard and fast and with a groan, and I cleaned myself up with my tee that I ripped over my head.

"You fuckin' sick bastard," I muttered as I tossed it to the floor, still disoriented, head spinning with dizziness, heart hammering with need.

I fumbled into my pocket and pulled out my phone, eyes squinting as I tapped out an apology there was no way I could issue to her face.

> Me: So fuckin' sorry, Raven. Didn't mean to barge in. Thought you were having a nightmare, and you needed me.

I faceplanted onto the couch. I squeezed my eyes closed, and I was right there, on the cusp of passing out, when my phone buzzed in my hand.

I barely shifted so I could peek at it through the night, the words blurred in the haze of my mind.

> Raven: I did need you.

Chapter
TWENTY-FIVE

OTTO

I WOKE TO THE SUNLIGHT BLAZING THROUGH THE WINDOWS AND groggy as fuck. That and the scent of coffee riding on the air and the patter of bare feet.

That was all it took for it all to come back to me in a barrage of visions flash-firing through my mind, and my heart fucking seized as my mind spiraled back to last night.

Fuck. Fuck. Fuck.

I sat up on the couch, facing away from the kitchen as I scrubbed both palms over my face in an attempt to squash the anxiety that rolled through me. Throat thick and head pounding like a bitch as I sat there trying to figure out what the hell the protocol was after I'd walked in on her practicing the type of self-care I'd been idiot enough to tease her about when she'd first started staying here.

Turmoil swamped me as I sat there, itching like a fiend.

Raven's soft voice hit me from behind. "Please don't feel uncomfortable around me, Otto. Don't tiptoe or treat me differently. That would kill me."

I stood, slowly turning around to face her, not really prepared to see her in the morning light after the way I'd seen her last night.

So goddamn beautiful that looking at her felt like a kick to the gut. Body hidden beneath another one of those dresses. But somehow, I managed an easy grin when I told her, "It's already forgotten, darlin'."

She flinched like that wasn't the response she'd been hoping for, though she pinned on a smile as she gestured to the coffee maker. "Coffee's ready. I'm going to finish getting ready and I need to hurry to Moonflower. I'll see you later tonight?"

"Yeah. I'll be here. My turn to make dinner."

Not that I wouldn't be keeping an eye outside of Moonflower, though we'd scaled off, deciding that the incident with her window had been random.

That time, her smile was genuine. "That sounds nice."

I blew out some of the strain and murmured, "Good," hoping that by the time I saw her tonight, I'd have gotten myself together.

That I'd truly forget it like I'd promised.

Because standing there right then? I was afraid nothing was ever going to be the same.

"It's almost ready," I told her when she came down from the bedroom.

Raven inhaled, easiness on her face when she sighed and murmured, "Smells good."

"We should eat outside tonight. It's really gorgeous out."

Easiness rippled between us, thank God. Maybe the incident hadn't been forgotten, but at least it'd been reined, and the elephant was no longer loose and tearing through the room.

"Sounds great," she said.

I opened a bottle of wine and poured two glasses, and she was all grins as she came padding barefoot to my side and picked one up. "Ugh, you know exactly what I need, don't you, Otto Hudson?"

My stomach tightened as I thought of what she really needed, but I ignored it as I clinked my glass to hers and said, "Just taking care of my favorite girl."

I piled food onto our plates, and she grabbed the silverware and our drinks before we headed out the door.

Raven let go of a tiny moan as we stepped out into the late afternoon light. I tried not to equate it to the same sounds she'd been emitting last night.

Hard as fuck, but somehow I kept it tamped and instead focused on the streams of sunlight that blazed through the spiked tops of the trees, painting the sky in blazing pinks and oranges. In the break of the woods, the lake was visible low in the distance.

There was a little round table set up in the perfect spot to take it all in, and we each took a seat.

Raven sighed as she looked out over the view. "I don't think I'll ever get over this place, Otto. It has to be the most gorgeous land in all of Moonlit Ridge."

"That's what you said then, too."

A soft smile edged that delicious mouth as she took a sip of her wine. "You remember?"

My brow pulled into a disbelieving frown. "How could I forget? You standing basically in that very spot with your arms hugging your chest as you gazed out on the lake. You looked at me and said, *This is it.*"

If it was *it* for her, then it was *it* for me.

Redness flushed her cheeks. "I didn't mean to sway your decision."

It was times like these when Raven would get modest. Like she didn't know the effect she had on me. The influence. Like she didn't get that she could ask anything of me, and it was done.

Still, I let playfulness ride into my expression. "You didn't mean to sway my decision? Don't act like you wouldn't have pouted and stamped those cute little feet if you didn't get your way."

Amusement danced across that stunning face, and it twisted my stomach in a knot of greed. "What can I say? I just have really good taste, and I wouldn't have wanted you to make any mistakes by purchasing different land. It would have been a tragedy."

A light chuckle rolled out of me. "Definitely a tragedy."

"Which is why you should always listen to me. My advice is impeccable."

"That so, huh?"

"Oh yeah," she said right before she took a bite of her chicken marsala. She groaned. The sound went straight to my dick.

My mouth watered and it didn't have a thing to do with the food.

I leaned over and took a bite like it might cover the reaction. Like it would actually suffice. Like it could stand the chance of sating the desire that thundered through my veins.

That damn vision still right there, bubbling right under the surface, ready to erupt and take over.

"As far as I'm concerned, you can do no wrong, Raven Tayte. So, you just keep giving me all the friendly advice, and I'll keep right on taking it."

She dipped her face like she didn't want me to see whatever ideas played through her eyes. A blush striking her cheeks. Fuck. Didn't think I'd seen Raven act shy in a long, long time, and I knew immediately where her thoughts had gone.

She was right back in that room with me watching down on her as she fucked herself with that toy.

I cleared my throat, doing my best to suppress it.

I took a sip of my wine since apparently she'd made me fancy like that, and I eyed her over the glass as I searched for a change of topic that would keep us in a safe zone. "Any progress on the apartment hunting?"

Frustration filled her sigh. "Not really. There was one place on the far end of Culberry Street, but the bathroom was so small I could barely stand in the shower, let alone find a way to shave my legs. It was not going to work."

And there I went, out of bounds, my mind racing right back to the obscene.

Apparently, no subject was safe when it came to her.

My jaw clenched as I fisted the stem of the glass a little too hard.

Discomfort pinched her face.

Shit. She thought I wanted her to leave. Thought I was itching in my chair due to entirely different factors than what really had me shifting in discomfort.

"I'm sorry it's taking so long. I really am trying to find a place," she said.

I reached over the table and set my hand on her forearm. Fire licked at the connection. "Told you, you're welcome here for as long as you want."

She narrowed that raven gaze, the darkened depths sparking like diamonds beneath the glittering rays of the sun. "I think you're just being nice, Otto Hudson. What man wouldn't want to sleep in his own bed at night?"

A groan got free.

Fuck me, she was trying to destroy me, words right there on the tip of my tongue, treacherous ones stating that I definitely wanted to sleep in my bed, but I wanted to keep her in it while I did.

"Meant it when I said you could stay for as long as you needed. My house is always yours, Raven."

Relief billowed through her expression, and then she shrugged a teasing shoulder. "I guess you don't have anyone else to dance with when you come home at night."

"And since you're the only one I want to be dancing with…"

Probably shouldn't have said it, but there it was.

Raven stilled, held in the energy that lapped. "I learned from the best."

"Nah, I was just teaching the best."

We got stuck there for too long, and I finally cleared my throat and started stuffing my mouth with food to keep myself from uttering any more reckless things.

We both fell into the silence, chewing and looking out over the view, making a few comments here and there, getting through the rest of dinner virtually unscathed.

A fuckin' miracle with the way she had me spun up so tight I was lucky I didn't split.

Standing, I gathered our plates. "I'm gonna do the dishes really quick. You go relax."

"But you made dinner," she argued.

Dipping down, I leaned in close to her ear. The scent of moon-flowers curled through my senses.

Intoxicating.

Mesmerizing.

My entire being off kilter.

"Yeah, and tonight I just wanna take care of you."

And this was going to have to suffice considering I wasn't doing it the way I really wanted to do.

By the time I finished cleaning the kitchen, Raven was stretched out on the couch. There was a show playing on the television, but the sound was set to low, and she was reading a book rather than watching it.

I wound around the island, hesitating for a beat, but then deciding if we were going to truly put what happened last night behind us, I was going to have to act normal. No tiptoeing my way around her.

So I did the same thing as I'd done most nights since she started staying here. I moved around the couch and lifted her legs by the ankles and set her feet on my lap as I sat down on the far end.

Raven had changed into the tiniest pair of cotton shorts I'd ever seen, this baby blue color, and a tight white tank top that barely contained her tits.

It seemed she had set out to cause me physical pain.

Did my best to control the tornado of lust that twisted through me.

"What are you reading?" I asked, no interest whatsoever in the show playing on the television when I could be watching her instead.

A flush of pink flared on her cheeks. God, was her mind back there, too? Was she thinking about it? Me watching her?

Her tongue stroked across her bottom lip. "Just this small-town romance."

Ah. Figured she'd be reading something sweet.

"Is it any good?"

"Really good. Definite five-star." A tinge of excitement filled her voice.

A slow smile crept to my mouth. "You love it? Escaping into your books?"

She'd always been a reader. When she'd been young, she'd constantly had her nose in these giant fantasy books, the thick paperbacks half her size. I knew she still read, but I hadn't had a clue how much until I found her on this couch or tucked up in my bed with a book night after night.

"I do. I love getting to have experiences through other people's eyes. Things that I might not ever experience for myself. It's different than when you're watching TV. It's like you're there."

"I can see that."

She was staring over at me, and it wasn't until then that I realized I was caressing my thumb up and down her calf, touching her like it was natural. Like I had the right.

I swore, her breaths had gone raspy, her body trembling as a new tension curled through the air.

Uncertainty.

Surety.

Our gazes tangled in this quiet intensity that keened between us on a tether.

Awareness spinning.

My throat grew thick, and I wondered if we both fucking knew.

Wondered if in that moment, we both knew if we'd met under different realities, if our circumstances were all different, we'd be doing this night after night.

Forever.

Two of us together in a real, permanent way.

But I think Raven knew it was impossible, too, because she suddenly hopped off the couch like she was about to catch fire. "I need to use the restroom."

She tucked a bookmark into the paperback and tossed it to the couch and padded on those bare feet to the powder room that was on the far side of the living area.

Black hair forever a messy pile on her head at this time of night, the girl a beacon and a light as she scampered across the floor.

She clicked the door shut behind her, and the second she was out of sight, I released the strained breath I'd been holding. Trying to rein this shit in because it was getting out of control.

Then I glanced at her book. The cover was illustrated, with what looked to be some kind of jacked-up lumberjack type of dude and a girl who looked like either a teacher or a sexy librarian on the front.

Looked like the whole opposites attract sort of deal.

Curious, I picked it up, needing the distraction, and turned to the page she'd marked, scanning the words just to see what kept her interest rapt.

My eyes nearly bugged out of my head.

"Spread those legs and let me see your pretty little cunt." Heath groaned and ran his fingers through my slit, and I thrashed, wanting to touch him but my wrists were tied to the bedpost, leaving me completely to his will.

"That's right, look how you're dripping for me. Good girl."

He brought his fingers to his mouth and sucked all my juices clean.

What. The. Fucking. Hell?

This was what she was reading? I'd expected tender kisses and damsels swooning. Not this. My thoughts immediately went back to last night, wondering what she'd been envisioning when she'd gone after her release.

Wondering if this was the type of shit she was imagining.

My fool mind went even deeper, wondering if this was what she liked when she was with a man.

I tried to suppress the riot of jealousy that pummeled me like a thousand fists, and I turned back to the page.

He reached over and ripped the ties free, and he leaned in close to my ear as he growled, "Now get on your hands and knees. We're going to see if I can fit in this tight ass."

"What are you doing?" Raven gasped. She might as well have caught me peeking at her through a gap in the bathroom door with the way the question whipped out of her mouth.

I dropped the book back to the couch like it was a hot potato, and I jumped to my feet and lifted my hands in surrender. "Just was curious about what you were reading."

Wasn't sure why it came out sounding like I was guilty. Like I'd pried my way into something that was her own secret.

But there was a tension that was suddenly there that hadn't been there before.

An awareness that I could feel thudding through her veins and pounding right back into me.

Or maybe I was just assuming it went both ways since my dick was instantly hard, thinking about Raven enjoying those things. In all the ways I'd spent far too much time imagining having her.

Overcome with the urge to pleasure her that way.

All while I wanted to rip out every hair on my head at the thought of some prick actually getting to touch her like that.

Raven's pale skin was flushed, but she huffed as she walked the rest of the way across the room, grabbed her book, and plopped back down onto the couch.

Though this time, she remained sitting up, crisscrossing her legs in front of her. "Newsflash, Otto Hudson, it's none of your business what I'm reading."

Did she think I was judging her? Not even close. I couldn't stand her thinking she should be ashamed.

So, I was murmuring, "Thought you said you were reading a small-town romance?"

"That's what it is." Her response was clipped. Not giving me more.

While I wanted to ask her a thousand things. Delve into her every fantasy.

Okay, so maybe we should have hashed out what happened last

night. It had to be the reason my brain was blipping. Too many fucking memories of Raven in a position I should never see her in.

Or maybe I should have helped her pack her things this morning and got her the hell out of here because I obviously couldn't act cool and controlled when my thoughts had skated in this direction.

The real problem was the possession that ripped through my nerves and fired into every molecule of my body when I thought of her experiencing it with some random guy.

I forced myself to sit, though my knee was bouncing a million miles a minute. Finally, I got myself together enough to look at her. Okay, *getting myself together* was a stretch. What I was really doing was letting a piece of myself go.

Traipsing a direction that I couldn't afford, but my mind had already spun there anyway, so what the fuck could it hurt?

"That's what you like?" My throat nearly closed off around the question.

She still had her attention fully trained on the book, though I got the sense she wasn't actually reading. She was just…staring at the page.

Creases dented the corners of her eyes, and her head barely shook as she muttered, "What do you mean, is this what I like? You know I like to read, and I like to read romance. I've never made that a secret."

"Not the books." I pointed at the words on the page. "Is that what you like men to do to you?"

Kept my voice as even as I could, but I still couldn't stop the wild rage of possession that burned me through.

Charring.

Incinerating.

The way I wanted to beat down any motherfucker who'd been anywhere near that sweet ass.

Her frown deepened, and her breaths turned choppy as some kind of hurt and incredulity seeped into her demeanor.

"Just want to know, Raven." Had no right to demand it. But there it was, out there like some kind of plea.

Raven suddenly whirled toward me, flailing her book around as she shouted, "Maybe I would, Otto. Maybe this is exactly what I would want a man to do to me if I ever got up the courage enough to let someone *actually freaking touch me.*"

She gripped at her chest when she said the last.

Okay, it could hurt a lot.

So much.

It felt like a hot blade had been driven right through my stomach at the pain that poured out of her.

At the torment.

At the grief I could feel flood the room. Clearly in need of something that had remained out of reach.

Fuck.

I hadn't known. I hadn't known.

I'd been too wrapped up in wanting to gut every little prick who I'd thought had had the fucking honor of touching her to see what was really going on with her. Jealousy eating me alive any time she stepped out the door with another man.

And still, my voice went raw, needing her to actually confirm it.

"What are you sayin', Raven?"

A tear slipped down her cheek. Fiery courage butted with the embarrassment that poured from her as she batted it away. "You know exactly what I'm saying, Otto. It's just like it was then. I can't let anyone touch me. I have a panic attack any time that I do."

Her brow pinched in misery. "Every single one of them except for you."

An arrow speared right through my middle because there was a goddamn plea weaved into her words.

That same desperation bleeding out as she stared at me.

Her lips parted and her chest heaved as both of us spiraled back to that one moment in time that I'd tried to eradicate from my memory. Bury it down so damned deep there would be no chance of ever uncovering it.

"So, you want to know about this, Otto?" She tossed the book toward me. "I read these stories because I want to be swept away. Because I want to imagine this happening to me. And every time, I wish it was you." She kept right on, that chin held high. "I touch myself, wishing it was you. It's you. It's always you."

I didn't know what the fuck I thought I was doing when I shifted onto one knee on the couch and angled her direction. I planted my hands on either side of her.

Shocked, Raven rocked back, her back pressed against the arm of the couch as I hovered over her.

Tension bound the air.

The energy so alive I could hear it sizzle and snap. Tiny lightning strikes that cracked in the room.

But in her eyes was also a distinct vulnerability. This brave, bold, beautiful girl who'd been done so fuckin' wrong. Scarred and wounded, and still she remained the brightest fucking light.

I didn't want to be another. Didn't want to be another who would only cause her pain.

My hand was shaking when I reached out and tucked a lock of her long, dark hair that had gotten loose behind her ear before I set my hand on her face, thumb stroking over that sharp cheek.

Our faces so close but an endless expanse raging between us as I gazed down at her.

"I'm not worthy of touching you, Raven. Not even close."

"To me, you're the only one who is."

God. How was I supposed to refute that? Deny her?

But I couldn't give in. Touching her would be a betrayal. I'd be nothing but a monster, taking advantage of this. This woman who didn't know me the way she thought she did.

"You deserve the whole fuckin' world, Raven Tayte. To be loved and adored. Touched in every way you want to be. But I'm not that guy."

I was vile. A demon who hunted the wraiths in the night. Hands so dirty that I tainted everything I touched.

Hurt blistered across her face, and I could taste the sting of rejection on her heavy exhalation. Dark, dark eyes flitted all over my face, searching for the truth. "You don't think I'm capable of making that choice for myself? You think I'm not wise enough to decide who that guy is?"

My head barely shook. "Not when it comes to me."

Pain splintered through her being, but it was anger that twisted her expression. She pushed at my chest.

Hard.

I fumbled back onto my side of the couch.

She heaved a sound of disbelief. "Right, I get it, I'm still that dumb, injured little girl who can't make decisions on her own."

She was on her feet before I had the chance to respond, her book gripped in her hand.

"Raven—" I attempted before she gave me a harsh shake of her head and shoved her palm out my direction to cut me off.

"Don't, Otto. Don't make excuses that don't mean anything. I don't want to hear them."

She turned on her heel and flew across the living room and up the steps, though she stopped when she got to the top of the landing. "Don't worry, I'll be sure I'm gone tomorrow."

Then she stepped into my room and slammed the door shut behind her.

Regret barreled through me. Chains so fucking heavy they nearly dragged me to my knees.

A beggar on the floor.

So fuckin' weak that I was a second away from going to her. Pushing into the places only a monster would go.

I'd promised I'd never hurt her, but fuck, that was exactly what this felt like.

Like I was hurting her.

Betraying her.

I dropped my face into my palms, trying to fight off the conflict that waged inside.

Heart and mind and soul.

Feeling like a piece of shit, I forced myself to turn off the lights, get undressed, and grab the throw blanket from the basket.

I just laid there on the couch, staring at the ghosts that writhed across the ceiling, unable to fucking sleep.

Wide awake and bleeding out.

Hours must have passed before I heard it.

Her cry from the depths of depravity.

There was no mistaking what was happening this time.

Her pain was so stark it was the only thing that I could feel.

There was nothing I could do. No wall or mountain or fucking cavern high or deep enough to keep me from going to her.

And I was there, crawling into the bed and pulling her into my arms, whispering her name over and over, "Raven, Raven, Raven."

She jolted when I first touched her, then her whole body gave when she realized it was me.

She whimpered as she clung to me with trembling arms. "Otto. Please. Don't leave me. Stay with me."

A fucking army couldn't have ripped me away.

"I've got you. I've got you. My moonflower." I murmured it at her head as I pressed a bunch of kisses to her crown.

A shaky sigh of relief pilfered from her, and when I laid down with her in my arms, her heart beating its trust against mine, I should have known things would never be the same.

I should have known this girl would be my complete undoing.

Should have known there would be absolutely no going back.

Because she whispered, "Otto, I need you to touch me. Please. Don't turn me away. I need to know what it's like."

Chapter
TWENTY-SIX

Raven

MY PETITION WAS CHOKED AND SMALL, BUT I MEANT IT WITH every fiber of my being.

I needed him to hear it.

I needed him to show me that I didn't have to be vulnerable. That I didn't have to feel small or insignificant. That I didn't have to be subject to the fetters that kept me bound.

I needed to know I could be free.

Free in him.

Even if it was only once.

Every hard, packed groove of his massive body flexed in a bid to suppress what urged and coiled between us. Bulky muscles twitched, and his beautiful heart battered at my chest.

I knew it now. I no longer questioned if this need was one-sided. No longer wondered if I was the only one who suffered this desire.

Being here with him for close to two weeks had proven what I'd hoped for all along. Those moments over all these years when I'd thought I was going crazy, imagining the energy that'd lashed between us before he'd turn around and call me his baby sister, assuring me I was only making things up.

But this could not be fabricated.

This need that blazed.

A fiery, incandescent bond that shined so bright it was blinding.

A connection that keened so loud I heard it as a reverberation at the back of my mind.

A sense so profound I felt it curling around me, body and soul, dragging me his way.

"Fuck, Raven." He muttered it in the lapping night. His room was nearly dark except for the vestiges of the moon that cast a murky haze through the windows behind his bed.

The outline of the soaring trees drawn in charcoal, and the endless sky smattered with a canvas of glinting stars beyond.

I could just see the shape of his fierce, glorious face within it. Could see the greed carved into every vicious line and the reticence scored into every harsh angle.

Tonight, there was no sign of the tease on his lips.

His jaw was clenched tight in sharp self-denial.

But it was his palm that slid down my side and over my hip that promised he recognized my need. What promised he saw me as something different than his sister.

What promised he saw me as a woman who needed this. To explore *this* with the one man she'd ever felt safe with.

Shivers raced in the wake of his hand, and I could barely breathe as he stared across at me with those blue, fathomless eyes.

Intensity thrashed, and his name whimpered from my tongue.

"Otto."

He groaned as his palm glided back up, lighting a path of flames as he went. "I don't want to hurt you, Raven."

"You won't. I trust you."

"I'm the last man you should trust."

I didn't believe that for a second, but I could somehow see that he had taken on that truth for himself.

But right then, none of that mattered. I didn't care about honesty or intentions or principles.

"I don't care. I need this. With you. You're the only person I've ever wanted this way. The only one who's ever touched me, and I wasn't afraid."

"But this is different." His voice was coated in gravel.

Was it? Because I swore that I'd felt it all along.

"Otto. I'm twenty-five. *Twenty-five*, and I have never let a man touch me. *Really* touch me." It was the most transparent I'd ever been. Opening myself up to him this way.

Charleigh knew. I could tell her anything. But this was different. This was cutting myself wide open for the man I'd kept like a secret for so many years.

Uncertainty knitted his brow as he kept smoothing his hand up and down, pulling me closer with each pass.

He was only in his underwear, the same way I'd found out he usually slept.

Heat blazed where our skin brushed, and my stomach flip-flopped in a rush of nerves and anticipation.

"I don't want to take advantage of that," he argued in that low, gruff voice.

My scoff was shaky. "How could it be taking advantage when I'm begging you? When it's the one thing I've wanted? Don't deny me that when you know you want to give it to me."

I put as much daring into it as I could muster. I wanted to find my inner strength. To flirt and tease and play like I did during the day.

Seduce him.

I wasn't quite sure how to do it in a situation like this. Not when he'd just found out this evening that I had zero experience. That I'd devolved into a panic attack any time I'd ever tried with someone else in the past.

But I also didn't want him to treat me like glass.

Fragile.

Something fractured and broken.

Because I was stretching my wings. Getting ready to fly. And I wanted Otto Hudson to make me soar.

I yelped when he suddenly shifted onto his back. He took me with him, bringing me up so I was straddling him.

I gasped when I realized I was seated on his thick, long shaft. My core pulsed with need, and my hands shot out to the hard, rippling planes of his chest for support.

"Oh God," I whimpered as I struggled to make sense of the change in position.

"Haven't even touched you yet, darlin', and you're already gasping."

I guessed he'd given in because there was little reservation that remained in his eyes as he peered up at me. Blue pools gleamed with desire as he coasted both hands up to grip me around the waist.

"It's not going to take much," I told him.

His brow arched in speculation.

"I've been dreaming about this for a long, long time," I admitted on a tremorous breath.

His tongue stroked out to wet his bottom lip. "Exactly what have you been dreamin' of?"

"You. Just you. You and…everything. You are the face of every hero in my books."

A growl rolled through him, the man pure beast where he lay on his back. Face carved in ferocity, two-day old stubble covering the harsh set of his jaw. Though his eyes and lips were soft, at odds with the rough edges of the rest of him.

My burly bear.

For a moment, I worried I might be hallucinating.

Because could this really be happening?

I'd better not wake up and find out I was dreaming. I had half a mind to grab my phone and snap a pic for proof. Maybe send it over to my bestie for confirmation.

"You been fantasizing about me, Moonflower?" he gruffed.

Lust billowed in the air, and his hands ran lower, gliding down over both my hips as he slowly rocked me against him.

His cock jerked where we were connected, and licks of pleasure lit up between my thighs.

The achy need inside me grew heavy, and my mouth went dry.

Completely parched.

This was real. It had to be real because there was no chance of a dream ever feeling this good.

"You were the first fantasy I ever had, and I never stopped," I admitted.

I sometimes wondered if it hadn't been old fear stopping me from allowing other men to touch me, but it'd simply been the fact that they weren't Otto Hudson.

"Fuck me, darlin'. Not sure what you think it is you're doing to me."

"I'll do anything to you that you want."

A groan infiltrated the air at the same time as a smirk hitched at the edge of his mouth. "You really shouldn't say things like that to a man like me."

"Maybe it's time I do, Otto. Maybe it's time I say exactly what I want. What I need. And for the record, what's in those books isn't what I want other men to do to me. It's what I want *you* to do to me."

His hips jutted upward.

I gasped at the sensation.

Tingles raced across the surface of my flesh, this feeling swelling from within unlike anything I'd ever experienced before.

Severity seared through his expression.

"You're sure that this is what you want? You want me to show you?" he rumbled.

"Yes. I want it. I want you."

"You know that's all it can ever be. I can't keep you, Raven. I'm a fucking bastard for even suggesting it. For even having you like this. Took an oath." Regret filled the last, and I could sense that he was having second thoughts and getting ready to withdraw.

My nails sank into his tattooed pecs, desperate to stop him. I dragged them down, over all that hard, carved flesh, all the way down to the scene depicted on his hip.

The moonflower blooming beneath the night.

"Don't tell me you don't want it, too." I wasn't quite sure where the obstinance came from, but it was there in the lift of my chin.

A challenge.

His cock that burned below me hardened further. No way for him to deny it.

That didn't mean I didn't understand where he was coming from. I knew his oath to Sovereign Sanctum. His oath to my brother. This man's loyalty was fierce and unending. Otto would never want to betray that.

But maybe it was time we were lifted above it.

"I told you it was time that I spread my wings. I want to spread them with you."

"Just this once, Raven, and no one can fuckin' know." Shame splintered across his face.

I hated that he would feel guilt over me. But I needed this so badly. To find myself in him. The courage. The strength. The belief. However short-lived it was going to be.

"I don't want them to. This is just for me. For us. If you want it."

"If I want it?" His hands slid lower until his fingers were splayed over my butt. I arched into it, needing to feel every touch.

"Don't think I've ever wanted anything so badly in my life." He ground out the confession. "The way you've been driving me out of my mind, here under my roof. In my house and under my skin."

Hope raced, his words so much bigger than temporary. But I needed to accept that's all this could be. I needed to put any foolish notions of this man actually loving me to rest.

Bury them right in this bed.

"I just need to know that you won't regret this, Raven." Otto reached up and brushed his fingers through my hair, eyes brimming with sincerity. "I need to know that things won't change between us. Need to know I'll always be your favorite person the way you'll always be mine. Can't stand the idea of anything coming between us."

Maybe we were both fools for thinking we could maintain who we'd always been, but as far as I was concerned, everything had changed anyway. When he'd walked in on me, and I'd bared myself to him the way I had. The way I didn't cower or hide but instead had continued, silently begging him to join me.

Tonight had been my breaking point when he'd asked about my book. The culmination of everything I'd tried to keep tapped.

My truth exploding from my mouth because I was so finished pretending. So sick of holding it in.

There was no going back on this.

"I would never regret a second spent with you, and I'm pretty sure I'm going to like you even better after you touch me. You're about to take favorite to new levels."

Somehow, I found the tease, my lips pulling up on the side, though that smile was completely obliterated when Otto suddenly flew up to sitting.

He wound a hand up in my mess of hair that I'd let down when I'd come to bed, and he jerked my face close to his, our lips almost touching.

His other arm banded around my waist, keeping me plastered to his chiseled front, and my legs were wrapped around his waist and tucked up close to his cock.

I gulped around the thickness in my throat. I'd imagined what he'd be like so many times, sure just from the brutal size of him that he'd be huge.

But this…this was so much more than I'd dared to imagine. The enormous press of him where he slowly rubbed himself against my center.

"Definitely, definitely my favorite person," I wheezed as I dug my nails into his shoulders.

He grinned. Grinned this salacious smile that tumbled through me like a dream.

Warmth and light.

Freedom.

That's what this was.

The letting of my chains.

"We're gonna see if we can discover a few more favorites for you, darlin'."

Then he softened. "But if you get scared or nervous or

uncomfortable, I need you to say it. Will never forgive myself if I take it too far, so I'm going to do my best to take it slow."

"I'm not sure I can handle slow." I wiggled on his lap.

He grunted a gluttonous sound. "Don't worry. I'm going to make my moonflower come. Right now. Going to watch her blossom in the night. Can't wait to watch you glow."

I let go of a shallow breath, and the fire spread as he began to grind against me.

Achingly slow as he watched me carefully, searching for any signs of distress.

A vibrancy raced beneath my skin, and I rocked myself against him. Sparks lit at the contact. Tiny flickers of bliss that flamed just beneath the surface.

Otto studied me, his chin just lifted as I rolled over him, his breaths shallow grunts as he gazed at me like he both wanted to protect me and set me free, one hand still twisted tight in my hair as if it was the only thing keeping him controlled.

"You good with that?" he asked in that rumbly voice.

I ground harder against him. "I need more."

A chuckle rolled through him as he yanked me closer against him. "Eager girl. Don't rush it. We've got all night. I'm going to take care of you."

The problem was, I wanted to rush toward this feeling that was taking me over all while finding a way for it to never end.

His mouth came to my ear, and his voice dipped into a gruff command. "Get up onto your knees."

Tingles spread through my body. Flames that licked as I complied.

He knew exactly what he was doing.

Playing into my fantasies.

Otto tipped his head back to gaze at me as I swayed on my knees, and my heart beat so erratically I wasn't sure my chest could contain it.

Breaths harsh and jagged.

His arm unhooked from my waist, and that hand smoothed across my lower back before his fingers slipped around to knead into my hip.

"Never have seen anything more gorgeous than this, Raven. Looking up at you. Lit up by the moon. Stealin' my breath. Fuckin' with my head."

I let my fingers play along the sharp edge of his cheek before I drifted them over his lips.

"It's my breath that's gone. Seeing you like this. Touching this face that has followed me into every dream. Being with the only person who could ever save me from the nightmares. The only one that ever made me feel safe. The one who made me sure I wanted to discover what it is like to be taken. Completely and fully."

His hand glided farther around to the front, and his knuckles brushed the top of my thigh before he pressed his fingers between my legs. He just barely rubbed me over my cotton shorts, never taking his eyes from mine as he did.

I jolted forward on a rasp.

"You good?" he asked.

"I'm not afraid."

I'd never been with him.

He shifted and dragged my shorts and panties aside.

Cool air rushed across my lips, then heat seared through me when he dragged the tips of his fingers through my folds. "Otto."

"Yeah?"

"Yes. Every yes."

He smirked, though it was almost pained as he nudged my legs wider, and his tongue stroked out across his lips as he dragged his fingers through me, back and forth, a fraction deeper with each pass.

His throat bobbed as he swallowed. "Fuckin' drenched."

I wheezed, holding on tighter as he started to push his fingers inside me. Desire whipped my insides into a frenzy.

A torrent of need that flooded the room.

Banged at the walls and bashed at my consciousness.

A tornado of greed spun with the faintest flickers of nerves at the disbelief that this was actually happening.

That I was being…touched.

And I wanted it.

Oh God, how much I wanted it.

He let go of my hair and looped that arm around my waist, holding onto me as he slowly...so slowly...pressed two big fingers into my pussy.

A tremor rocked through me. An earthquake of sensation that tumbled and rolled.

Leaning in, he ran his nose along my neck, and he inhaled as if he were trying to draw me all the way inside.

Take me in.

Consume me.

His words vibrated through me when he murmured, "So fuckin' tight. Wet and tight and needy. Do you shove that toy deep into this needy pussy when you fuck yourself thinkin' about me?"

I didn't think it was even a question. It sounded like a claim.

Lightheadedness swept through me as my head swished back and forth.

I felt half detached. Half grounded.

I could feel him everywhere, though it didn't feel like it could ever be enough.

He brushed the pad of his thumb over my clit.

The most embarrassing sound crawled up my throat as I clawed at his shoulders. "Oh God, Otto."

"Listen to you, my name on your tongue. Wait until I have you shouting it."

"I need..."

"Know what you need. I'm going to give it to you. That's what this is all about." He started sweeping the pad of his thumb over my clit.

Back and forth.

Back and forth.

"Showing you the way you deserve to be touched. The way you deserve to be adored. The treasure you are."

Pure electricity.

"I think it's working," I told him.

A dark chuckle rumbled in him as he dragged his fingers out.

I nearly cried until he pressed them back in, harder that time, and he swirled his thumb as he did. "The things I want to do to you, Raven Tayte."

"I want you to. I want you to have me in every way."

Affliction gripped his expression. "No, baby. We're not gonna go there. I'm going to show you that you can be touched. Show you that you don't have to be afraid. Then you can make that choice with a man who deserves you."

I wanted to argue, but all thoughts left me when he started driving his fingers in and out of me in deep, long strokes, his thumb rolling in time. With each thrust that feeling grew. The sensation crawling out from the secreted places where I'd kept my need for him hidden.

Shrouded and concealed.

I started grinding against his hand. Pleasure building to a breaking point, battering at my insides to get out.

Every cell inside me quickened, and I begged, "Harder."

I refused to be shy or subdue what I needed. Not with him. Not when I had this chance.

A squeal ripped out of me when I found I was suddenly on my back, laid out on his bed, my legs spread wide as the man hovered over me, eyes wild in the night.

"Fuck me, Raven, what are you trying to do to me?" he grunted.

Everything.

I wanted to do everything he'd done to me to him.

Chapter
TWENTY-SEVEN

OTTO

TUMULT RAVAGED ME, MY ENTIRE BEING SNARED IN THIS lawlessness.

In this sin that I knew was going to rack up the greatest penalty. But staring down at Raven right then? Laid out on my bed, thrashing as I fucked my fingers into her sweet, untouched pussy?

Any punishment I had coming to me would be worth it.

Her hypnotizing scent was all around, though tonight, it was coated in her arousal. The girl soaking my hand as I fucked my fingers into the heat of her cunt.

This beautiful, vibrant soul who I'd vowed to protect but instead was doing my best to corrupt.

Tainting her with each stroke of my hand.

Still couldn't fully process what she'd confessed. That she'd never been with a man. All the nights I'd spent stewing, tossing in this very bed thinking of some dirty motherfucker getting to lie with her, taking this body when some warped part of my psyche had always believed her mine.

There'd been no chance I could shun the petition she had made. No chance I could reject her when she'd confessed her fears and given me her desires.

Not when she wanted it to be me.

I wouldn't deny her that.

Problem was how fuckin' far I wanted to take it. The way I wanted to sink all the way in. Write myself on her in a way that could never be erased.

Possess and consume.

I couldn't go there. Couldn't.

So instead, I focused on pleasing her where she was laid out in the middle of my bed, long black locks splayed out over my pillow.

Her lips parted and those inky eyes raved with desire and need. Short gasps raked from her lungs as she kept whimpering my name.

A motherfuckin' goddess.

I pulled away for a beat, just staring down at her, the praise riding up my throat and dripping from my tongue. "So fuckin' beautiful, Raven. So fuckin' beautiful in every way."

Bucking up, she arched her back. "Please."

I planted one hand on the mattress up high near her head, and I slipped my other back through the crotch of her shorts.

Finding her slick, throbbing pussy still dripping for me.

I nearly came at the feel of it, my cock so heavy and hard I was afraid I was going to blow.

I drove my fingers back in, and Raven nearly levitated from the bed. "Yes, don't stop. I need...I need..."

I could feel every cell in the woman quicken as I began to pump her, driving her higher.

"Look at you. Coming alive. Glowing like I knew you would."

She was nothing but a light where the rays of the moonlight sheared in through the expanse of windows that rose behind her, illuminating her in a milky glow.

A beacon.

A sanctuary I couldn't seek.

Her mouth slack and those moonlit eyes fully focused on me.

I pulled out of her for a flash, and I swirled all my fingers around her engorged bud, making her whimper and plead before I shoved my fingers back in deep and pressed my thumb down on her clit.

She ripped at her tank that barely contained those tits, her gasps coming short as she got closer to the edge.

"You feel that, Raven? Embrace it, don't fight it."

She whimpered and those nails were clawing up my chest then sinking into my shoulders. "I want you."

"You have me. I'm right here."

It wasn't in the way she was begging for, but there was no chance I could go there. Not when I knew I'd want to stay there forever.

This was about showing her that she could trust herself to decide when she wanted to be touched. When it was right. When it felt good.

Made me irate, but I had to believe I couldn't be the only man on the planet who could make her feel this way.

An edge glowed around her, the woman barely holding on as she jutted and bucked. A sheen of sweat rose on her soft, delicate flesh.

I sped up my pace, shoving my fingers deep inside her, shifting them so I could rub at that sweet spot deep inside her. I kept sweeping my thumb over her engorged nub that I knew was going to send her soaring.

"Otto," she rasped.

Wanted to dip down and take that mouth and that tongue and every other delicious part of her that she would let me. Treacherous groanings inside of me. I tried to rein it, and I was only partially giving in when I angled in and kissed along the contour of her jaw, lapping up the taste of her flesh as I kissed up to her ear.

My voice was nothing but a scrape as I murmured, "Let it go, baby. Let me see you fly. Come for me, Moonflower."

At my words, she split apart.

Cracked wide open.

I could feel the maelstrom of her pleasure batter the walls of the room. Bursting from her middle. A volcano erupting from her body.

She was a hurricane in the middle of my bed. Sweeping me up in the cries that came from her mouth. "Otto...oh God...Otto. It feels so good. So good."

They were rasps. Barely intelligible. But I felt them all the way to my soul. "It's all I want, Raven. Only thing I want is for you to feel good. Want to make you feel that way forever."

There I went, tossing out more of those traitorous confessions that were going to destroy me. But I didn't know how to stop when it came to her.

This girl who was shaking and trembling below me, her arms curling up around my neck like she didn't ever want to let go.

"You okay?" I asked, terrified that I'd pushed her too far and too fast, and I edged back enough that I could look at that gorgeous, stunning face.

Sight of it ripped through me.

My insides a battlefield.

Fighting this feeling that welled inside.

This dangerous fucking feeling that I'd barely kept tapped for all these years, and there I'd gone and poured gasoline on the flames.

"I feel…" Raven blinked up at me with that enchanting gaze. Her delicate throat bobbed when she swallowed. "I feel liberated, Otto. Different in the best way. Or like maybe I just found a piece of myself that I had been missing."

My thumb swept across the apple of her cheek. "It's all I want, for you to be free."

"You make me feel that way."

Nearly came undone when that perfect fuckin' mouth suddenly latched onto my neck, her tongue stroking out to get a taste of the tats that swirled up my neck.

It happened too fast for me to prepare myself.

Lust colored my senses.

A swarm of red and black.

Disorienting.

So overwhelming I couldn't form a word.

She went south, kissing down my chest as her hands started to explore.

Riding up over my shoulders and then back down to my pecs. Wandering my sides and caressing my stomach until she was touching the spot that I'd had tattooed a few years back. Marking myself with an image that reflected all she was. Everything that I wanted her to be.

Then my entire body jerked when she ran her fingers over my dick.

My dick that strained against the thin material of my underwear, though it was just then that I became aware that my throbbing head had broken free of the confines.

"Fuck," I hissed. My hand flew to her wrist to stop her. "Raven."

She tore herself away from where her mouth was latched to my chest, and she rested her head on the pillow, distracting me with that stunning face as she pushed my underwear down a fraction to completely free my cock.

She wrapped that sweet little hand around my shaft. "I want to touch you."

I choked, barely able to speak. "Raven…fuck…this isn't supposed to be about me."

"Don't act like you don't want me to." She stroked me once.

Nearly cracked with that single touch, this woman coming at me with all her sass. A groan ripped up my throat at the same time as a grin pulled at the edge of my mouth.

Loving that she felt free with me.

Uninhibited.

Bold and abandoned.

"Will it make you happy, jacking me off with that sweet little hand?"

"Very happy."

And fuck, there was nothing I could do but sit up on my knees so she could get a better grip. I helped her, curling my hand around hers and guiding her, showing her she didn't have to be timid. "Like it hard, darlin'. Don't be shy."

Her tongue swept out on a needy exhalation. "Good because I think I like it hard, too."

A punch of surprise hit me.

Shit, she was definitely going to do me in.

She tightened her hold, adding a second hand, and the two of us started pumping me hard and fast. In a flash, I was grunting, pleasure stalking up and down my spine as she drove me straight toward ecstasy.

Because I'm pretty sure that's what she was.

Ecstasy.

A realm where I could never land.

I thrust into her hands. A fiend who would never get enough.

A twisted fuck who wanted to bury himself so deep inside her that I'd mark myself there forever.

"Raven...fuck...I'm gonna come."

Nearly cried when she pulled one of those hands away, only she was peeling her tank all the way up, exposing her belly and bare tits.

Sight of them nearly knocked me the fuck out.

Part of me wanted to fixate on the fact I was getting a real look at them for the first time. Her dusky pink nipples peaked and primed for me to suck into my mouth.

But I got sidetracked.

Fury ripping through me when I saw the scars that marred the flesh of her stomach and hips. Uncountable circular burn marks that made me feel like I was the one standing in the flames.

But it was the mangled one on her side that turned my guts to ash, the tattoo cutting through it where it was stamped on her side.

I will make it to the sunrise.

Raven's head shook on the pillow. No doubt, she knew exactly where my focus had gone. "Don't, Otto. Don't look at me that way. Look at *me*. At who I am. As a whole. As a person. As the woman who wants this with you."

"I've always seen you, Raven."

I'd just always wanted to protect that. Protect everything she was from me.

She pulled her shirt up even higher, and she lifted her ass from the bed. Begging me to mark her. The woman fisted me even tighter with her one hand that was still covered with mine. She had me captured by that gaze as she murmured, "Tell me you feel it, too, Otto. Let go, the way you asked me to."

And fuck, bliss gathered fast, her touch and her boldness, her aura taking me whole.

A sweet fuckin' moonflower.

It hit me like a landslide. A storm of pleasure.

I moaned as I jerked and spasmed, and Raven was writhing all over again, her eyes going wide with desire when I dumped myself on her flesh.

And maybe I'd known it all along, but I knew right then that I'd met my match.

This fucking gorgeous woman who was going to be the end of me. Because I wasn't sure I would ever be able to let her go.

Chapter
TWENTY-EIGHT

Raven

"**S**TAY RIGHT THERE." OTTO'S VOICE WAS A ROUGH SCRAPE AS he pushed back. He tucked himself back into his briefs, before he swung off me and slipped off the side of the bed.

While I struggled to breathe.

To push the air in and out of my jutting lungs and calm the violent race of my heart.

I watched him stride across his room and into the attached bathroom.

So beautiful in all his intimidation. Tall and wide and tatted. His butt and thick thighs flexed with each step that he took, and it nearly had me begging all over again.

My body twitched and jerked in tiny spasms while my mind whirled to wrap itself around what had just happened. My brain was having a hard time comprehending the shift. Accepting that it was real and not another one of the fantasies I'd given myself over to for so many years.

I listened to him shuffle around in the bathroom—the clatter of a cupboard and the run of water—while the truth of it sank down over me like an embrace.

Otto Hudson had touched me.

He'd touched me.

And I'd touched him.

And I hadn't been afraid.

I hadn't been afraid.

Truthfully, I didn't think I would be. Every part of myself had believed that I'd feel safe.

This was Otto we were talking about.

The one man who'd ever been able to keep my demons at bay.

The one who saw.

The one who understood.

But God, I'd be a liar if I said there hadn't been a small part of me that had been terrified that I'd freak out if one day he finally did.

Terrified that the anxiety would take over the rational.

If that had happened? There'd have been no chance that he would ever touch me again. The man was a protector to the extreme. He'd cut off his own hands before he'd dream of hurting me.

Or his dick.

And that would be nothing but an injustice considering how badly I wanted that dick in me.

Over and over.

Preferably without ceasing.

Dangerous thinking, I knew, wanting more when Otto claimed this was going to be a one-time thing.

Dangerous considering how horribly he'd hurt me just two hours ago when he'd rejected me. A spear that he'd driven through my soul.

Dangerous because now that he'd finally broken through the barriers he'd kept fortified around us, I never wanted it to stop.

No doubt, I was setting myself up to get demolished, this secret love I'd harbored for him for so long close to bursting out from within me.

No way to contain it.

But I didn't think there would be any talking me out of pursuing this with everything I had when he came rambling back out with that smirk licking across his striking face.

Swirls of color painting his flesh writhing beneath corded, hewn muscle as he walked.

A fortress in the middle of the night.

Every molecule in my body flared back to life when he slowly sat on the edge of the bed with a damp washcloth.

"Here." The single word was uttered so low I felt it reverberate rather than heard it. His attention was careful as he placed the warm, wet washcloth on my belly. He gently ran it over my stomach then up to my breasts, cleaning me.

I wondered if it made me some kind of freak that I would rather him have spread his cum all over me than have him wipe it away.

Mark every inch of me with himself.

Charleigh would tell me I'd been reading too many smutty scenes in my books, which I'd have to politely inform her there could never be too many. Especially if that meant I got to live them out.

With Otto. Freaking. Hudson.

I had to stop myself from squealing as a wash of glee sped through me.

He peeked up at my face with those eyes, sucking me down into that chaotic ocean of blue. His smirk inched higher. "What are you over there grinnin' about?"

"Grinning? I'm not grinning." My fingers flew to my lips to trace the shape.

Yep. Definitely grinning.

"Uh, yeah, darlin'. The grin is real. Want to tell me what's going on in that beautiful head of yours?" No question, he was trying to feel me out without coming right out and asking it, which was kind of ridiculous considering he'd just had his miraculous fingers shoved deep inside me.

"I'm just grinning because my favorite person is now my *extra* favorite person."

Amusement played across his delicious mouth. "Is that so? And here I was worried that little stunt might knock me down a peg or two." With the last, his expression dimmed, taking me in like he was terrified he had pushed me too far.

"Never," I told him. My voice went wispy, unable to find the lightness.

Not when this felt momentous.

He tossed the washcloth to the floor then reached out and fiddled with a stray piece of my hair as he gazed down at me. "You're sure you're okay?"

My nod was shaky. "More than okay. I would have stopped you if I wasn't."

A wistful silence stretched on between us. He finally broke it when he said, "It's my honor, you know…that you feel safe with me."

"I always have."

His gaze darkened, and a vat of sorrow suddenly poured out. I knew exactly where his mind had gone. To the moment he'd forever fault himself over when there was nothing different that he could have done.

No way to change it.

It had already been set into motion.

I'd tried to stop it myself.

My chest squeezed, and with a shaky hand, I reached up and set it on his cheek. I'd made that simple gesture many times through the years. But it'd always been…reserved. Held in an attempt for it to be appropriate for who we were supposed to be.

But this?

This *was* what we were supposed to be.

He kept brushing his fingers through my hair, appraising me as if he were waiting for one of my fractured pieces to break off. Worried he'd be the one responsible for it.

"Still having a hard time getting my head around the fact that you've never been touched before." He let a bunch of speculation hang unsaid in the air.

A twenty-five-year-old virgin wasn't exactly a common thing.

"Are you really that surprised? When I barely started dating a few years ago? After all the things you knew about me then?"

He flinched, my bringing voice to the point when a wedge had been driven between us. We'd still remained incredibly close, but an intrinsic piece had been cut off.

Shattered hopes left to decay.

"Think I'd chosen to believe that you'd moved on. That you'd found your way outside of me—the way it was supposed to be."

Air puffed from my nose. "How, when *this* is the way it's supposed to be? It's always been you, Otto. You have always been my safe place. My secret place."

Energy thrashed.

Our connection whipping a disorder that raged in between.

His eyes were full of truth but his words still reeked of reservation. "I wish I could be more, Raven. Wish I could be everything."

There was a warning behind it, and I couldn't stand the idea of him pulling away, so instead, I pulled him toward me. "For tonight, let's just be, Otto."

We'd face tomorrow when it came.

Hesitation billowed through him before he gave, plopping down so he was lying on his side next to me.

Laughter rolled out of me, joy uncontained. I scratched my nails through the scruff on his jaw. "You'd better be careful or you're going to toss me right out of this bed."

He curled one of those massive arms around me and pulled me close. Two of us face-to-face. His voice went soft. "Never."

I wanted to claim that forever.

I snuggled closer, clinging to the light, to the smile that couldn't be erased. "Good. I'd much rather you tie me to this bed than toss me from it."

A groan rumbled through his massive chest, and his lips tweaked into a grin. "You really do want to be the death of me, huh?"

"Death by orgasm?"

He chuckled low, and those big fingers threaded through my hair. "Death by your brother is what it's likely to be, but I'm fairly certain it would be worth it. Seeing your face when you came around my fingers. I'm never going to forget it."

He tucked me even closer.

I lit, a full body glow. The tease still rolled from my tongue, even though there was a small piece inside me that shivered, sure I was in over my head because I had no real clue what I was doing.

"Are you sure that was worth it? I could think of a few ways I could make it even better. You know, risk to pleasure ratio. Because I don't know about you, but I'd really like to see your face when you come a few more times."

A billion, but I probably shouldn't push my luck.

Otto took me by the chin, and he tilted my face in his direction. Moonlight streamed in behind him, and it cast him in a milky silhouette, though even in the shadows, I could make out the intensity in his eyes.

"You are worth it, Raven. You are worth everything. But I don't want to wreck what we are."

"What are we, Otto? Because this feels like *us* to me."

Chapter
TWENTY-NINE

Raven

Sixteen Years Old

"**Y**OU'RE HERE!"

Raven flew out the front door and down the sidewalk that cut through the yard. Haddie's smile was wide as she climbed out of her little red sedan, though she playfully rolled her eyes as she dug into the backseat to grab her bag.

"As if I wouldn't show?"

"Um, since you're miss popular now, it was a tossup."

"Pssh…like I would ditch my bestie for a couple acquaintances who only like me because I have a car now?"

Raven hurried to unlatch the gate and ran through it and out onto the sidewalk.

"Well, I only like you for your car, too, sooo…" She drew out the tease as she rounded the tail of the car parked at the curb.

Haddie playfully slugged her in the arm. "Shut up."

Giggling, Raven snuggled into Haddie's side as Haddie slung her arm over Raven's shoulders. "Okay, fine, maybe I still kinda like you because you're basically the most amazing person in the world and I can't live without you."

Haddie squeezed her tighter. "Now that is what I like to hear."

"Aww, did someone need their ego stroked?"

"I'll tell you about something I *stroked* when we get inside." Haddie whispered it salaciously at Raven's ear.

A gasp ripped out of Raven. "Oh my gosh, did you—?"

Raven's question clipped off when the front door of the house suddenly whipped open, and Otto came striding out. Big body bristling beneath the sun, a grin stretched over his entire face, his blue eyes dancing with mirth.

Raven's stomach tightened. To hide it, she dropped her gaze, worried it would be written all over her expression. Worried she'd be caught thinking thoughts she absolutely couldn't think.

But they'd been coming too much lately. This feeling that swelled inside her whenever he was near.

"Is that my baby sister?" he called.

Excitement buzzed from his spirit. Raven knew how much he adored Haddie. How close they were. Could see how he worried since their mom was a mess. Clean one minute and then relapsing the next.

Otto had wanted Haddie to come live with them, but Haddie had chosen to stay with their mom.

She'd been really good for the last three months, though, so Raven was hopeful.

Haddie unwound herself from Raven and did a little flourish and a bow. "In the flesh."

A rumbly sound echoed out of Otto's chest as he took the two steps down from the stoop and came striding her way. She dropped her bag and went running for him, and he picked her up and spun her around.

"Ahh…missed you."

"And I missed you. And Raven." Haddie slanted her attention to Raven.

Raven who was picking up her bag and slinging it over her shoulder and striding their way. "I'm impossible not to miss."

Haddie was still clinging to Otto as she teased, "Now who is looking to get their ego stroked?"

Another giggle fumbled out of Raven, and Otto stepped back, gesturing toward the door. "Come on, you two, let's get you inside."

Haddie didn't hesitate. She scampered up the steps and through the door and into the house where Raven lived with River and the guys.

Her family.

A traditional sort of family it was not, but to her, that's exactly what they were. They were the ones who'd protected her. Cared for her and raised her.

They'd kept her sheltered and secreted until River had made their mother sign off as her guardian, even though she'd continued to do classes online since she'd freaked out when she'd tried to attend school.

Too many people around her. Too many voices. Too many fears still lingering inside her that she still didn't know how to get away from.

She kept trying, though. She would never give up, and she knew one day, she would find her place.

Her comfort and her joy.

Her father might have destroyed a big part of her childhood, but she wouldn't allow him to destroy her entire life.

She was slowly finding her way, even though it was difficult sometimes.

Which was why she was really glad she had Haddie.

Haddie who'd been her best friend since Otto had introduced them when she was nine.

Haddie who was brave and bold and ran out into the world without a care, embracing everything that came her way.

They might have basically been opposites, but the two of them were inseparable, and they spent as much time together as they could.

Haddie went directly for Raven's room and tossed her bag to the bed right before she did the same with herself, flopping onto her back and bouncing on the mattress. Her light brown hair was spread all around her as she laughed toward the ceiling, so pretty that the guys lost their minds whenever they went out.

Ice cream shops.

Stores.

The few parties they'd gone to together.

The attention they garnered was something Raven was still trying to figure out how to deal with. How to handle it when her first instinct was to cower and hide.

Haddie sat up onto her elbows and cocked Raven a bawdy grin. "This is going to be the best weekend ever."

"What are you thinking? This is the worst idea you've ever had."

And Haddie had suffered more than a few of them. Raven rarely got into trouble, but when she did, it never failed that she was with Haddie.

They were supposed to be watching a movie and then going to sleep. At least that's what Haddie had told Otto before he'd left on *business*.

And there they were, slinking through the city under the cover of night.

"Your brother is going to be so pissed," Raven continued, trying to talk some sense into her best friend.

Okay, Raven's brother was going to be pissed, too.

Really pissed.

This endeavor was so off limits, so out of bounds, Raven would likely be grounded until she was twenty-seven, and she wouldn't put it past her brother to try to enforce it.

Raven clomped along a foot behind her, trying to balance on the outrageous heels Haddie had insisted she wear. What made it even worse was she'd pulled a sequined cream-colored miniskirt and a black lacy tank from her bag and had insisted that Raven actually put them on.

She'd never felt so exposed in her life.

Haddie was dressed pretty much the same, though her outfit was red.

"He'll get over it," Haddie said with a grin.

They rounded the corner to the sound of heavy music thrumming through the air and the hoots and shouts of inebriated voices.

Apprehension stirred Raven's conscience into unease. This was a bad idea. A really bad idea.

But Haddie just kept strutting along like it was the best one she'd ever had as they headed toward the bar and the buildings in the back where River's friends all hung out. Where they had their meetings and dealt their dirty deals. Some of them actually lived there.

Okay, she called them his friends, but she understood what they really were. She knew it from the long row of motorcycles parked at an angle out front and the leather vests they all wore. Knew it from the way the conversations often cut off whenever she came into a room, and the way River and the rest of his crew were always looking over their shoulders.

She hadn't gotten it at first, too young and naïve to understand, but she knew now.

They were members of a motorcycle club.

The Iron Owls.

And she was pretty sure they didn't partake in the legal, their illicit activities dangerous. But when she'd finally gotten the courage to confront River about it, he'd promised her he would be fine, and he would never let anything happen to him. Told her not to worry.

She knew it all the way down to her soul that River did it for her. That he'd gotten swept into this life because it was the only way he'd been able to care for a child. Knew the rest of the guys had gotten here because it was the easiest way when you started out on the streets.

Aligning yourself with those who would have your back.

That didn't mean Raven trusted any of the guys outside of her family, and her feet dragged in dread along the sidewalk while Haddie lifted her chin and sashayed right up to the door, sending the bouncer at the front a megawatt smile.

Raven's throat thickened. God, this was so dumb and reckless.

The jacked-up, heavily tattooed guy eyed Haddie up and down, gaze lascivious. "You lost?"

"Nope. I found my way just fine. I'm Otto's sister, and this is River's sister, and we just wanted to pop in to say hi."

Surprise filled the man's expression, and he cocked his head to the side. "Neither of 'em are here."

Haddie shrugged a casual, flirty shoulder. "That's fine. We'll just wait for them."

"You got ID?"

She leaned in close to his ear, and Raven could barely make out what she said. "Do I look like I need ID to you? Come now, we all know who you work for, and you wouldn't want to make any of them mad, would you?"

She pouted like she was concerned for him.

A puff of hot air left him, and he grunted as he said, "Go on in."

Haddie spun back toward Raven, barely able to contain the squeal she clearly wanted to release, but there was no hiding the gleeful triumph on her face, before she turned back around and started into the raucous vibe of the bar.

Raven gulped for confidence, and reluctantly, she followed Haddie into the fray.

Inside, the ceiling was low, and dingy yellow lights glowed from the pendants that hung above the booths that lined the walls. The music was loud and drowning the voices that lifted in an attempt to be heard over the blare.

A handful of pool tables and round tables took up the middle, and a long bar ran the back wall.

A ton of people were packed inside. Men clad in the same leather cuts that her brother and his crew wore. Most of the women were dressed in leather and lace, though they had more skin showing than not.

Raven didn't know if she wanted to gape or drop her stare when she saw a girl propped on the edge of a booth table with a man wound between her thighs.

Were they…?

Haddie grabbed her hand and tucked Raven against her as she

whispered in her ear, "Can you believe we got in here? This is amazing. I told you it was going to work."

Raven was too nervous to think it was amazing.

Too worried to even think about enjoying herself as Haddie towed her to two open stools at the bar. Warily, she sat, trying to adjust her skirt so she wouldn't give everyone there a peek at her panties.

"What will it be?" A bartender with a long white beard tossed two cocktail napkins to the bar in front of them.

"Two gin and tonics, please," Haddie answered before Raven had the chance to ask for a water.

Haddie gave her another winning smile when the guy turned and started making their drinks, and she leaned in and shouted so Raven could hear, "Relax. It's going to be totally fine. Stop being such a fun sucker and loosen up a bit, would you?"

Raven took a deep breath and decided she might as well try since she was there anyway, and she took a sip of the drink the bartender set in front of her, trying not to make a face at the bitter taste.

Haddie giggled as she slurped at her straw. "Delicious, am I right?"

"Wrong. Totally wrong." Raven drank a little more, anyway, deciding to fully let her worries drift.

Haddie stood from her stool, and she started shimmying her hips. "Come dance with me."

Raven slipped off her stool, and Haddie threaded her fingers through Raven's and lifted their hands high above them.

Raven had discovered she really did like to dance. Both with Otto who always goofed around with her, tossing her around like a ragdoll, and Haddie who never seemed to be able to sit still.

Raven let go, and the two of them danced like they normally did behind closed doors when they were messing around at one of their houses.

It only took a few minutes for Raven to be giggling.

"Admit it," Haddie said. "You're having a blast."

Raven stuck her tongue out at her. "Fine, I'm having a blast. You always have to be right, don't you?"

"Only if it means my bestie is wearing a smile like that…all while looking like a total fucking knockout."

Redness flushed Raven's cheeks. "I look ridiculous."

"Are you insane? You look hot. Have you seen the guys looking at you?"

Raven couldn't hold back her furtive peek around the bar.

That was just when a group of three guys came sauntering up. Wearing jeans and their cuts and lecherous grins on their faces.

Anxiety rolled through Raven's being.

A bottle of tequila dangled from the hand of the guy in the front.

"What do we have here?" He whistled low. "Looks like somethin' fresh and sweet."

Haddie kept swaying her hips, and the guy stretched out his hand, gripping it on her waist as he moved around her before he pressed himself to her back, that same hand gliding around to her stomach to hold her against him as he began to move.

Haddie kept moving, too, and she bit down on her bottom lip like she was enjoying it.

There was no shame in it, but Raven didn't come close to *enjoying it* when one of the other guys did the same to her.

She went rigid, the air heaving from her lungs as he curled an arm around her to bring her flush.

Nausea churned in her stomach, and she blinked, trying to see through the fear that flashed behind her eyes.

No, please, no.

The guy nipped at the lobe of her ear. "Bet you have a delicious pussy."

Fear ripped through her, and her gaze shot to Haddie, but Haddie was too busy gulping from the bottle the guy had tipped up to her mouth for her to notice. The two of them were writhing, the guy's free hand riding up the front of her thigh and under her skirt.

"Come on, baby." That vile voice crooned in Raven's ear, and panic surged through her body.

She started to shake, and she tried to pull away, only he grabbed her by the wrist. "Where do you think you're going?"

"Leave me alone." She wondered if there was even any sound to it, the way it wheezed out of her in a gush of desperation.

"Don't take too well to teases around here," he snarled as he yanked her back toward him.

She started to yelp, only everything froze when a thunderclap of rage suddenly broke over the mayhem.

"The fuck is goin' on in here?"

It was a roar, and the music clanked off as all the voices in the bar went silent.

Relief slammed her when she saw Otto stood in the middle of the bar.

She could almost feel what was dripping from him.

The violence that curled his fists into hate.

The man vibrating with an aggression so distinct there wasn't a soul in the bar immune to it.

The guy behind Raven stepped away, releasing her, and she gulped for the air she hadn't been able to get into her lungs, bending over like she could hide herself as she stumbled over to Otto.

Blue eyes toiled, torn, and he inhaled a vicious breath when he turned away from her and to Haddie who was still wound with the other guy.

"Otto," Haddie rasped when she caught sight of her brother glowering in wrath.

His enormous body convulsed with stormy indignation.

But the guy behind Haddie only grinned. "You got an issue, Hudson?"

Otto flew forward, and he ripped Haddie out of his hold and hauled her back. "Yeah, I got a fuckin' issue, Gideon, you fuckin' piece of shit. That's my seventeen-year-old sister."

A commotion broke out behind them, and Raven squeezed her eyes closed when a clatter of boots rushed in.

River was at the helm, and she saw the disappointment lash across his face when he saw her standing there.

Kane, Theo, and Cash came skidding to a stop on either side of him. "Fuck," Kane spat as he took in the scene.

Shame bit across her flesh, and she didn't resist when River grabbed her and pulled her against his chest, shielding her face like he couldn't stand for her to witness what went on inside these walls.

"What the hell are you doin' here, Raven?" he muttered to the top of her head. Anger buzzed across his flesh, though he was hugging her tight like he was making sure she was safe and whole.

Otto hauled Haddie behind him and jabbed a finger into the face of the guy Haddie had been dancing with. "Stay the fuck away from her."

He took one step back and whirled toward the guy who'd been groping at Raven. "Same goes for you, Dusty."

He pointed between them. Raven recognized the names. Two actual brothers who River had complained about being dangerous.

Trouble.

"Stay the fuck away from both of them if either of you motherfuckers want to remain standing. Do you understand what I'm tellin' you?"

"Fuck you, Hudson," the guy named Gideon cracked, lifting his chin in a show of dominance. "That pussy was willing and more than wet."

Otto had him by the throat and pinned against the bar top before anyone could make sense of the movement.

"Otto," Haddie cried, and Theo looped an arm around her waist to keep her from running to him.

"I'll end you if you even look at her again, and I'll do it gladly," Otto hissed as he angled over him. "You got me?"

Dusty and the other guy who'd been with Gideon edged forward, and Cash stepped in front of them, craning his head in a silent warning.

No one else moved. They all watched, agitation billowing through them as they waited to see what would happen next.

Otto finally shoved Gideon hard, and he turned on his heel and stormed back across to the rest of them. All the guys turned at the same time, making a circle around Raven and Haddie as they hurried them out of the bar, ignoring the jeers and laughter that suddenly went up once everyone realized there wasn't going to be a fight.

They all stumbled out onto the sidewalk, and Raven dragged heaving breaths into her lungs once they were out in the cool night air. Trying to calm the frantic flogging of her heart.

They kept ushering them down the sidewalk, looking over their shoulders as they steered them farther away from the bar and down the street. When the sound of the music was only a dull drone behind them, Otto whirled, fury on his face.

"What the fuck did you two think you were doing?"

Shame swept through Raven, and Haddie shifted on her feet, though she tried to shrug it off like it was no big deal. "We just wanted to have a little fun. See where you guys hang out at night."

Otto's laugh was hollow as he tilted his head toward the sky and scrubbed his hands over his face before he whipped his attention back to her. Venom coated his words as he threw them her direction. "You wanted to have a little fun? Those guys are fuckin' dangerous, Haddie. Fuckin' dangerous. They could have—"

He clipped off with a shout of fury, spinning around and ripping at his hair like he was envisioning exactly what could have happened.

Raven's guts twisted in horror, just then realizing how reckless their actions had actually been.

A tear slipped down Haddie's eye, and she swept it away. "I'm sorry. I just..."

"Don't *just* me. Just fuckin' listen to me for once. Please. You stay away from here. Stay away from all of them."

She scoffed as her brow pinched. "So, it's fine for you all to be here, having a great time, but not for the rest of us?"

Displeasure roiled in Otto, though Raven could feel the worry that underscored his demeanor. "You think this is fun to me? To us? We do it to survive, Haddie. We do it so we can put a halfway decent roof over our heads. So we can provide for you because no one else is going to fuckin' do it."

He leaned in closer. "We do it so you and Raven have good lives. And you're not gonna get that kind of life by comin' around here. Do you understand what I'm telling you?"

"I'm sorry," she whispered. It was clear she meant it that time.

Pain leached out of Otto's heavy sigh as he pulled her into a fierce hug. "Need you to listen when I tell you something, Haddie. Need you to hear me. I promise you I'm not makin' rules for the sake of it, but only to keep you safe."

Raven met Otto's intense gaze from where he looked at her from over Haddie's shoulder, his sister still plastered tight against him. She felt him trying to press the same desperation into her as he was to Haddie.

"Let's go," River said, voice low and filled with disappointment.

Haddie sent Raven a look. One of apology. Raven reached out and squeezed her hand. A promise that it was okay, all while she was praying Haddie would actually listen.

"No. No, no, no, no."

Raven thrashed, flailed and fought.

"No, please, no."

A wail tore up her throat. She shot upright, and her eyes pitched open to the darkness of her room.

Her hand went to her mouth like she would be able to reel back in the shout that she could still almost hear echoing against the walls.

Like she could hide it.

But she should have known better. Should have known the door handle was going to slowly turn and a massive figure cast in shadows was going to emerge in the doorway.

Only she wasn't afraid. She was never, ever afraid when it came to him, and right then, she felt both a wash of relief and shame.

Otto's bare feet creaked over the floorboards as he quietly crept across her room, and like he always did when she had a nightmare, he slid down the side of the wall and onto the floor next to her bed.

Only tonight, his spirit was all different. His own turmoil pulsed and undulated, ricocheting into hers.

"Bad dream?" he murmured into the quiet stillness.

Haddie had been relegated to Otto's room and he'd taken the

couch. It was the obvious punishment for the two of them breaking the rules.

A sticky sense of dread had followed Raven to her room, and she'd been sure in the moments before she'd finally fallen asleep that the fear was going to follow her there.

Torment her in her sleep the way the memory of her father so often did. Though tonight, that dream had been different.

It had started with her father, the same as always, only his face had changed to Dusty's.

"Yeah," she whispered where she'd shifted onto her side so she could look at Otto.

A strained sigh pushed from his lips, and he rocked his head back on the wall as he scrubbed his hands over his face. "Could have been bad, Raven. The things those fuckers wouldn't have thought twice about doing to both of you."

Rocks clogged her throat, and she struggled to form the words around it. "I know. I'm really sorry."

"Wouldn't make it if something happened to one of you. If you had any idea of how fuckin' scared I was when I came through that door and found you both there like that..."

He gripped his shirt right over his heart, his face contorting in agony as he swiveled his head to look at her. "If you had any idea, you would never have stepped foot through that door."

Part of her wanted to say she hadn't wanted to go in the first place, but she'd never throw Haddie under the bus like that. Haddie was just...going through a phase. Exploring and testing.

Things Raven would also want to do if she had half the courage and balls that Haddie had.

But sometimes when you were so eager to chase the good things in life, you made mistakes along the way. That's all this was. A mistake.

Raven reached over and picked up the mirror she always kept on her nightstand, and she peered at her distorted features. Silently chanting the things Otto had told her all those years ago. That she was brave and strong and smart. A fighter. The truth that one day, she would rise. Stand firm and without fear.

"Were you scared tonight?" Otto's voice was quieter than it'd been. Careful.

She could barely nod her admission. "I…I didn't like him touching me like that. It's the first time…the first time I've been that close to a guy, and it wasn't anything like I thought it might feel."

"Fuck," Otto seemed to say to himself, and sorrow curled through the shadows that played over his face.

Raven's stomach twisted. Twisted in regret and also that feeling she knew she wasn't supposed to feel. The feeling that made her want to reach out and trace her fingertips over the sharp angles of his face. The part of her that knew if it'd been Otto trying to dance with her like that guy had been, she wouldn't have minded.

She would have fallen into the bliss of it.

The traitorous thoughts fell away when Otto yanked at his hair again. "Told you I would never let anything happen to you. That you'd be safe here." He blinked in anguish. "And we were this close…"

He trailed off with a harsh shake of his head before he muttered into the lapping darkness of her room. "Never imagined it'd come to this. That we'd get so deep in this life there would be no getting out of it. So deep that eventually it was going to rise up high enough to consume those we care about most."

It was the first Raven had heard of any of them speak of the MC in a negative light, but it wasn't like she was privy to the inside. They tried to keep her protected from it the best that they could.

She'd seen a small piece of it tonight, though she imagined it went so much darker than she could ever imagine.

"What would you do differently?" she whispered like soft encouragement.

Air huffed out of his nose, and a sorrowful smile tugged at the edge of his mouth. He hefted his shoulder a bit. "Don't know. Do somethin' that makes a difference, I guess. Be a good guy. Somethin' that brings goodness instead of corruption."

Her heart clattered in her chest. It was the most candid she thought any of the guys had ever been, giving voice to the crimes and misdeeds she sometimes saw haunting their eyes.

"You do make a difference, Otto. For Haddie. For me."

His throat bobbed as he swallowed and roughed his fingers through his hair. "Would do anything for you, Raven. For both of you."

She got brave and she reached out over the side of her bed and found his hand. Heat blazed up her arm. "You are the one person who hears me when I need someone most, Otto. You're the one person who makes it better. The one person who makes me feel like I don't have to be afraid to go to sleep."

The tip of his smile was both agonized and adoring. "Would do anything to rid you of every single one of your monsters."

"I know you would."

He hooked his pinky with hers, his voice rough as he whispered, "That's why you've gotta be careful not to introduce any more monsters into your life, Raven. Know we've kept you shielded the best we can, but you're almost grown, and we can't do that forever. You need to know the real threat of these bastards. Take it seriously. Choose the type of people you hang with carefully." He hesitated before he rushed, "And fuck, Raven, don't let some depraved asshole use you up."

Before she could say anything, he hopped to his feet and moved to the door.

He paused when she quietly called behind him, "Thank you."

He hesitated before he looked over his shoulder. "For what?"

"For somehow always knowing what I need."

Chapter

THIRTY

OTTO

I BOLTED UPRIGHT TO THE SCREAMING OF THE ALARM. SO FUCKIN'
loud it was disorienting. My heart hammered at warp speed as my
eyes tried to adjust to the dim light.

Hands already in fists, ready to slaughter any motherfucker stupid enough to come around here.

Raven flew up to sitting, too.

Raven who was in my bed.

A surge of protectiveness pummeled me. Rage and possession.

I pushed an arm out in front of her to keep her shielded as I tuned
my senses to listen through the blaring of the alarm.

My room was still.

Empty of anyone else other than the two of us.

I was certain of it.

I could always scent out when some bastard was lurking. Could
feel it crawl across my skin in a roll of perversion. But I knew well
enough someone was nearby. On my property.

The alarm wouldn't call the authorities. It was only for me. A way
to alert me to anyone who dared tread into my territory.

"Wait right here until I figure out what is going on," I shouted
over the blare as I shifted and took Raven by the outside of the arms.

Those eyes were darker than ever, black pools that swarmed with fear. Fear I would do anything to decimate.

I cleared the rage from my throat and dipped down to be sure I got in her line of sight. "Don't move from this spot, Raven. Do you hear me? I'll be right back."

Her nod was frantic, and I pushed from the bed, going straight for my nightstand and to the gun case that I kept in the bottom drawer. I pressed my thumb to the sensor to open it, and I pulled it out, making sure it was loaded and ready as I crept across the room to the door.

Adrenaline thundered as I pressed my ear to the wood, trying to listen through the disorder that reverberated through my house. When I couldn't feel anything moving on the other side, I cracked the door open and peered out into the duskiness of the great room.

It was that dense hour right before sunrise. When the night felt deepest. The kitchen and living room were covered in a thick darkness only broken by the stars that shined through the wall of windows on the far side.

Anxiety ripping through me, I glanced back once at Raven. She was on her knees on the bed, those inky eyes wide with terror.

My chest squeezed, and I forced myself to move.

A fireball of aggression gripped me by the throat as I stepped out of my room, my gun lifted and my attention sharp as I scanned the area below.

Carefully, I edged down the three steps to the bottom landing.

Stillness echoed back. Zero movement. No sticky aura of some vile bastard waiting in the shadows, though I didn't let down my guard as I quickly moved to where I'd left my phone charging on the end table next to the couch.

Snatching it up, I turned off the alarm.

Silence cut through the house. As sharp as a knife.

So distinct it was palpable.

All wrong.

Blood pumping hard, I searched the alarm app for what had triggered the alarm.

Downstairs in the garage. The single window on the west side of the building. I was quick to thumb into the camera footage, watching as something busted through the window and toppled to the ground. The second camera caught a hazy figure outside the garage.

Fuck.

I didn't take the time to drag on my jeans.

I just shoved my feet into my boots where they'd been sitting by the couch, not bothering to tie them as I headed for the interior door that led downstairs into the garage.

Carefully, I unlocked it, cracking the door a fraction so I could peer out. Based on the footage, I was pretty sure no one was actually inside, but I couldn't be certain.

More stillness.

Sucking in a breath, I stepped through, quick to relock the door to make sure Raven was secure inside.

Gun swiveling from side to side, I edged down the steps, boots quietly thudding on the metal as I descended.

That sticky stillness echoed back. No one inside, and the last thing I was going to do was let the asshole get away.

I jumped into action, running for the regular door on the far side of the garage. I tossed it open to the night.

A chill crawled across my bare skin, a cold dread that sank like a stone to the pit of my stomach.

Someone was out there.

In the distance.

A fuckin' coward running to a safety I would never let them find.

I took off in that direction, boots pounding the ground as I hunted through the night.

It was my specialty. Sniffing out the demons that lie in the shadows. Dragging them out into the light.

The *light*, my ass.

It was judgement without grace. No room for sympathy. Karma at her fucking worst. When she was so sick of the depravity, her only goal was eradicating it.

Permanently.

No questions asked.

So this fucker had better run fast.

A foul energy emanated from the west, toward the dirt drive that led between the main road and my house. I used my phone as a flashlight as I ran over the loose gravel, my gun pointed out in front of it.

Not great for visibility, but it was going to have to do.

I pushed myself as hard as I could, wearin' nothing but my goddamn briefs and my boots, a beast that prowled beneath the darkness that loomed from above.

With each second that passed, I felt it increase—the vile presence that wept.

I was getting close.

I hit the bottom of the hill before it began to ascend, and in the distance, I could just make out the form that raced beneath the swath of branches that stretched over the drive.

The shape of what I assumed had to be a man, but it was too dark and he was too far away to make out any real details.

I increased my pace, my lungs screaming as I pounded across the ground. "You might as well stop, motherfucker. I'm gonna find you wherever you go."

With each furious step, I erased a fraction of space, bringing us closer and closer. Blood pounded in a violent beat through my veins, hatred so fierce for a faceless man. Didn't matter who he was.

He'd been here.

Near Raven.

He was going to pay for that.

Finally got close enough that I could see that he was tall and lean, though there was no chance I could make out his identity. I pushed harder, shouting, "Get down! On the ground. Might let you live if you do what I say."

Probably not, but I might need information. Might need to keep him alive so we could find out who had sent him and what his intentions were.

Our list of enemies was long, and we bore no pretenses that one day one of them might catch up to us.

Dread curdled my insides as my mind raced with who it might

be. Dread that he might have found me out, and rather than waiting around for me to come to him to show him his end, he'd shown at my door.

My footsteps echoed through the night, mixing with his as he pushed himself as hard as he could.

"One last chance, asshole. On the ground."

He didn't give, so I popped off a warning shot, aiming off to his left. Expected him to scream and drop to his knees.

Not the barrage of bullets that came from out of nowhere. Pings rang through the trees, dust flying all around and making it impossible to see.

And it was me who was suddenly on his knees.

Not even sure what had brought me to the ground.

A second later, I could hear the telltale sounds of a dirt bike being kicked over in the distance, the beelike screech piercing the air as the bastard raced away.

A roar burst out of me when a shock of pain bloomed on my thigh. Disoriented, I shined my light on the spot.

Blood poured out of a wound.

The motherfucker had shot me. I wobbled and swayed, before I fully dropped face down onto the ground.

Chapter
THIRTY-ONE

OTTO

I CHOKED, TRYING TO CATCH MY BREATH. TO SEE THROUGH THE disorder. To make sense of what had happened and to find the right course of action.

I realized I'd only been out for a blip since I could still hear the high-pitched engine far in the distance, fucker long on his way to getting away.

I slumped forward when I realized there was no immediate danger, and I rolled onto my back as I gulped through the rage that had taken me hostage.

Raven.

She was in the house.

Safe.

It was the only thing that mattered.

Finally, I got my shit together enough and forced myself onto unsteady feet. I lumbered back up the hill, ignoring the pain radiating down my leg.

Chaos whirled through my spirit as I caught sight of my house. The bedroom window glowed on the second floor. No doubt, Raven had flipped it on. Was in there. Pacing. Worried for me.

I didn't even know what to do with the feeling that swept over me. This possession and fury that took me over.

Couldn't stand the thought of putting her in danger. Of someone coming for me and Raven getting in the line of fire.

Old grief threatened to consume. I'd already endangered her enough, hadn't I? And here I'd touched her just hours ago, in a way I'd promised I'd never do.

My stomach toiled, torn between duty and the fact that I couldn't handle the thought of letting her out of my sight.

Everything was so twisted and convoluted I didn't know how to process it.

This…need.

This purpose.

Was supposed to cut her loose a long, long time ago, and the only thing I'd done was put a façade around my feelings. Treated her like a sister…a friend…when I'd never been able to staunch the desire for this woman. This thing that I'd kept like a dirty secret since she was eighteen years old.

I trudged up the drive as the faintest gray emerged at the horizon. Day getting ready to break.

The garage side door suddenly burst open, and my heart turned in my chest at the sight of her racing out.

Frantic as she searched.

Relief battered her expression when she turned and saw me coming up the drive.

"Goddamn it, Raven. What the hell are you doing out here? Told you to wait for me inside."

"I thought I heard a gunshot."

"Which should give you all the more reason to stay put."

She looked like she was going to argue the fact, only horror took her over when she realized I was limping rather than running to her the way I wanted to do.

"Oh my God, I did hear a gun. You were shot!"

It was the moment I glanced down to find blood seeping out of a wound and streaming all the way down to my boot.

I probably looked like a madman. Wearing underwear and my boots, gun in one hand and phone in the other. Caked in dirt and blood and the rage that I couldn't purge from my veins.

"I'm fine," I grumbled.

I wasn't fine. I was sick to my stomach. Couldn't fuckin' believe I'd let that bastard get away. That he was out there, free, which meant he continued to be a threat.

"You're fine?" Disbelief pinched that stunning face. "Don't you dare tell me you're fine when you just got shot, Otto Hudson." Her voice was frenzied, dredged in worry.

That dark, dark gaze dragged over me, searching for any other injuries.

It was a seriously inopportune time for my dick to take note, but now that she'd had those sweet hands wrapped around it, my cock was clearly all too eager at the prospect of going for another round.

Of pushing it farther. Taking her whole and complete, which was the most fucked-up thing I could do.

"Know when things look grim, Raven. Fucker barely nicked me."

I just needed to patch it up, and it *would* be fine.

"Don't ask me not to worry about you." Emotion came crashing through when she said it. Tears blurred the light in those eyes. "Don't ask me not to care about you the way you care for me."

A heavy sigh pilfered out, and I hobbled forward another step, coming up so close to her that I was assaulted by her aura.

Moonflowers and belief and a hope distinct.

"I'm just…" It trailed off when I was hit by a bout of dizziness, and Raven's hands darted out to steady me.

"It's okay. I've got you," she promised.

God, she did. She'd always had me. Didn't think she knew the extreme of what that meant.

She shifted around and looped her arm around my waist. "Lean on me."

I found a wobbly grin. "I'm bound to topple you right over."

"I'm stronger than I look." She glanced up at me as she began to lead me back toward the house.

I gazed down at her. At this fierce, fuckin' brave girl who I'd do anything for. The one who'd been through so much.

My voice went raspy as I clung to her as she guided me back through the door into the garage, my nose turning to dive into her hair as I whispered, "Nah, Moonflower. You are the epitome of strength. I just don't think the rest of us really know what that means."

Chapter

THIRTY-TWO

Raven

OTTO LEANED ON ME AS I CAREFULLY GUIDED HIM UP THE interior steps toward the main floor. I knew he was claiming to be fine, but he was bleeding pretty badly, and I could tell he was putting more weight on me than he probably wanted to.

Dread churned in my guts, and my spirit wept as my thoughts spun through a million scenarios. Terrified of who might have been out there and what they wanted.

I nearly scoffed out loud at myself. What they wanted? Whoever it was had freaking shot Otto, which meant they were after very, very bad things.

"Can feel you getting spun up over there, darlin'," Otto grumbled as I maneuvered to turn the knob to the interior door while continuing to balance him. "You don't have anything to worry about."

I rolled my eyes. "Newsflash, Otto. I have a whole ton to worry about considering I'm dragging you inside with a gunshot wound. You act like this is a normal occurrence."

I led him across the living area to the powder room on the far side of the living room just on the other side of the television.

I flicked on the light.

Otto lumbered forward, and he grunted in pain as he plopped down on the lidded toilet.

Though because it was him, he tossed one of those smirks my way like this wasn't a big deal. I wondered if he knew there was no chance that he could conceal the fact his face was contorted in hostility. I could almost see the fury blistering beneath his flesh.

No question, he was trying to keep the severity of the situation contained.

Like I wouldn't see.

Like I wouldn't know.

"And you're actin' like I've never been shot before." His grin grew, but I saw it for what it was.

A cover.

"And you say that like that should make all of this okay," I tossed back as I grabbed a washcloth from the cabinet and ran it under water. I didn't realize how badly my hands were shaking until I tried to squeeze it out.

I fumbled to get down onto my knees so I could press it to the wound. Nausea churned my stomach when I saw the butchered skin on the left side of his thigh. I gulped as I held the compress against it, barely able to get it together enough to look at him.

I wasn't quite sure what was in my features but understanding dawned on his as he gazed down at me. He reached out and ran his fingertips down my cheek. "Don't want to put you in a bad spot, Raven. Don't want you to get in the middle of my mess."

Confusion bound. He kept saying that. Implying that he was outside of what I knew. My family who I'd long accepted and had been *in the middle* of for basically my entire life.

"Anything you're involved in is my mess, too," I muttered.

He blanched, and my spirit shivered. God, what was going on in his head?

"Do you have any idea who was out there?" Why I was whispering, I didn't know.

His expression turned grim. "No. Couldn't get close enough and the video camera was fuzzy. Only thing I could tell was it was a man.

Gangly fucker who I'm gonna tear limb from limb once I get ahold of him."

Disquiet billowed, and my gaze dropped for a beat before I looked back up at him. "Is there…anyone you suspect? Has there been any issues in Sanctum that I don't know about?"

Again, something flashed through his expression. His jaw clenched tight before he forced it lax and he mumbled, "As far as I'm aware, Sanctum has been in the clear. But that doesn't mean someone didn't catch up to us."

Blowing out the strain, I stood and went to the sink and rinsed the cloth, then I returned, dabbing at it again, though this time I inspected the wound closer, trying to discern how bad it actually was.

"You're still bleeding. I'm going to need to call the doctor so he can stitch it."

Sovereign Sanctum had a doctor they worked with. Someone who was in the know. He often examined the women and children who came to Sanctum and administered any medical care they might need.

He'd also saved Charleigh's life at the beginning of the summer when her ex had caught up to her.

He was one of the best, both with his skill and the care he took with those in dire need.

Frustration heaved from Otto's lungs, and he roughed his fingers through the short crop of his brown hair. "Know it. And I'm going to need to let the crew in on what went down. See if we can catch a hint of who might have been sniffing around."

He seemed reticent to get them involved.

My insides quivered, and a tendril of awareness floated in my periphery. A wall I was butting against but somehow could see through.

Gaze downturned, I quietly asked, "Are you in trouble, Otto?"

Cagey hesitation radiated from him, and I tried to keep the fear out of my being as I looked up at him. At this man who had always meant everything to me. The one I'd had to pretend I didn't love the way I did. The one who likely had no clue the depths of how deep that love went.

The one who'd *touched* me just hours ago and had ensured that I would never be the same.

Because for the first time in my life—I believed.

I believed I could grow beyond the traumas I'd suffered. Believed I could find the strength within myself to seek my desires and wants and needs. Believed I could finally spread these wings and soar.

Believed that even though the fear might always remain, I could face it.

I just wondered if he would be brave enough to face them with me.

Wistfulness pulled through his harsh features, this gentleness that he'd always encompassed for me seeping out. "I'm going to be just fine, Raven. I promise you."

A wave of intensity rushed.

Tension binding the tiny room in bows of greed.

Shockwaves of energy banged against the walls and slammed into me on all sides.

His thumb traced the little freckle on the side of my lip, and those bottomless eyes dipped to the spot where he was touching me before they flicked back to meet my stare.

My heart jackhammered.

Kiss me.

Kiss me.

I wanted to beg it, but the words were lost somewhere in the landslide of rocks that rolled around in my throat. Were locked in the maze of obstacles that would always stand between us.

I could smell him. That patchouli and apple mixed with nothing but man. Dirt and the faintest vestiges of my arousal.

A shiver raced, and that anticipation sent butterflies scattering through my body.

But I guessed Otto must have run straight into one of those obstacles because he suddenly cleared his throat. "Gonna give everyone the word and get them over here."

A blunder of disappointment and confusion left me on a breath, and I forced myself to nod, to stand, to go back to the sink and rinse out the cloth like this man wasn't destroying me.

I stared at the blood-tinged water that circled the drain before it disappeared, and a stupid freaking tear got loose from my eye.

God, he was going to think I was needy and pathetic.

View me the same way as he always had.

A little girl he needed to protect.

He'd believe I couldn't handle what'd happened between us. That I couldn't move on from it like an adult.

But how was I supposed to actually do that?

Move on from it?

I didn't look up when Otto slowly stood, and I remained hunched over the counter as he edged up behind me.

A giant in the tiny room.

His presence overwhelmed.

A shudder ripped down my spine when he leaned in and murmured against the sensitive flesh at the nape of my neck. "Fuck, Raven. I wish you understood. Wish you understood I would give anything to be right for you."

Chapter
THIRTY-THREE

OTTO

"**T**HAT SHOULD DO IT." DR. REYNOLDS finished taping a bandage over the wound on my thigh, the elderly man's grin both knowing and worried, though he kept his voice light since I was definitely not the first of us to call him in the middle of the night needing his services.

Thank fuck he made house calls.

But he was paid pretty well to do the things we needed him to do and to do them in confidence.

Trusted the man, one hundred percent.

"He's in the clear?" River asked for what had to have been the tenth time since he'd come blazin' in ten minutes ago.

Rest of the crew had trickled in after that.

Each vibrating aggression where they gathered in some kind of semi-circle around the chair where I sat near the dining room table since the light was best there.

The sun was just breaking the horizon, the massive windows behind us striking with a gray glow and making them all appear like shadowy beasts. Beasts doing their best not to work themselves into a rage but pretty much failing.

I'd at least taken off my boots and pulled on shorts and a tee before anyone had gotten here, so maybe the madman look had ebbed a fraction, but there was no question every single one of us looked a bit psychotic.

"He should be completely fine. Bullet hit the side of his thigh and didn't lodge, though it took a nice chunk of skin with it. Seven stitches should do it. He might be sore for a couple of days, but other than that, he's good as new."

"See, what did I tell you? You can't keep a good man down, and this one is the best." I issued it with all the exaggeration I could enlist, hoping it belied the wrath that burned inside me.

My attention moved to Raven who stood on the other side of River. Distress radiated from her every pore.

I itched, wondering if her brother could look at her and see that something had shifted. That a change had been made. If he could see my filthy hands written all over her.

Really fucked-up thing was there was a part of me that thought I hadn't touched her nearly enough. Part of me that thought there was so much more to explore and discover.

I sucked it down and tried to act like this occurrence was no big deal. Everyone gathered around knew it was definitely an issue, though. Someone didn't just come around firing shots for no reason.

Dread clamped down on my spirit. Couldn't shake the worry that my actions had done this. That I'd been discovered before I'd had the chance to enact the revenge that had been coming for a long, long time.

But I wouldn't let it stop me.

Couldn't let it sway me.

The judgement had been cast, and it was on me to execute this wrath.

Dr. Reynolds stood, his knees creaking as he did. Felt bad that I had to drag him out in the middle of the night. Guy should be retired by now, and I was pretty sure half the reason he stayed in business was to be of aide to Sovereign Sanctum.

"If you're in pain, take up to 600 mg of ibuprofen every four hours. Stitches are absorbable, so you don't need to follow up unless you feel like you might be developing an infection, but in my experience, it isn't likely you'd come in even if I wanted you to, anyway."

The old guy had us pegged.

"Don't think you need to worry about me."

Dr. Reynolds chuckled. "Just as I thought. But try to lay low. Don't go running any marathons in the next week."

"Can't make any promises," I ribbed, keeping it light as I lifted my arms out to the sides.

He grunted a laugh then turned to everyone hovering close. "Let me know if you need anything else."

"Thank you," Kane told him.

"You know I'm at your beck and call," he said before he angled around them and crossed to the door to head downstairs.

The second it closed behind him, Theo whipped forward, venom dripping from his tongue. "Did you get a look at this fucker?"

Trepidation spiraled through my senses. Knew the second the doctor left, the inquisition would start. Wasn't sure I was prepared for it, though.

Guilt weighed so heavy I thought it might crush me.

A strained sigh rolled out of me as I scrubbed a palm over my face.

Hated it.

Keeping my crew in the dark.

My family.

The ones I trusted most.

"No. Best I could make out was it was a male. Tall and thin. Took off on a dirt bike. Camera footage was grainy as fuck and not a whole lot of use."

"Fuck," Kane spat toward the ground. He glanced around at our crew.

River was a dark cloud, that quiet, terrifying fury oozing from his being. Theo looked like he was a second from hopping on his bike and searching every square inch of Moonlit Ridge, murder pricking on his tattooed fingers.

And Cash…Cash lingered a couple steps behind, staring at me with his brown eyes narrowed into accusatory slits.

No doubt, he had an idea of who it was, though he was keeping quiet, waiting on me to make the right choice to come clean.

Agitation twisted my stomach into knots. Couldn't. Not yet. I had to see this through, and I had to do it without dragging my crew into this disaster.

It might be inevitable, though. Wasn't sure I could keep this secret if someone had found out what I was doing. Couldn't keep going along like nothing had happened if it put my family in danger.

Second I thought it, my gaze shifted to Raven.

Fuckin' gorgeous Raven.

Wearing those sleep shorts and that tank, shifting on her bare, pretty feet. Hair piled high. A total mess that I wanted to make messier.

Her face was contorted in a thousand things that I both adored and didn't want to recognize.

It was like standing there, she knew. Like she possessed some ability to see straight to the middle of me, dig around in my secrets, and discern exactly who I was and what I was up to.

"Has anyone heard anything? Had any sign that someone has discovered who we are?" River asked, attention volleying between each of us.

Kane and Theo shook their heads. "It's been quiet."

River shifted to Cash. Cash who looked like he wanted to call me out, his bearded jaw clenched as he looked from me to River. "My surveillance shows all current placements remain in their homes. I also haven't intercepted any indication of someone searching for us."

Frustration heaved from River's nose. "This can't be fuckin' random."

"Nah, there's no chance," Theo agreed, studying me like he was also searching around for some sort of clue hidden on my face.

"Did anyone look downstairs?" Raven asked. "See if any evidence was left behind? A window was broken, and whoever this was took off on a dirt bike, so there have to be tracks, right? There has to be some clue to find this creep." Her tone was harried. "He can't just get away. We can't let him get away."

Her words broke on the last, and she turned a forlorn gaze on me. A gaze I was worried said too much.

Was I the only one who could read it? Feel it? Her desperation? The way she looked like she was a second from running to me and crawling right onto my lap?

I guessed the rest of my crew was too disconcerted themselves to notice it.

"No, we're not letting this piece of shit get away," Kane growled. "Going to hunt the fucker down and let him know exactly what happens when you mess with one of us. And you're right, we need to go downstairs and see what we can find."

I'd attempted to before they'd all gotten here, but Raven had refused to let me, telling me I had to sit until the doctor showed or she was going to be the one to make me bleed.

Fiery little vixen had come at me full force.

They all started for the door, and I flinched with the bite of pain that zinged down my leg when I stood.

"Fuck," I grumbled.

"You stay," Theo ordered.

I scoffed as I limped behind them. "No chance I'm sitting on my ass while you all go off defending my honor."

"And what honor would that be?" Kane cracked, nudging my arm with his elbow.

I didn't miss the way that Raven flinched at the insinuation, though she covered it as she got behind me like she was going to follow us.

"Want you to wait here," I told her, nothing I could do against the wave of protectiveness that slammed me.

The way I wanted to lock her behind closed doors and keep her safe forever.

Even from behind, I could feel the roll of her eyes. "And what? You want me to sit on *my* ass? I don't think so. I am perfectly capable of looking for clues. I'm part bloodhound. Charleigh lost her keys a couple weeks ago. She was searching everywhere…and guess who found them, lickity-split? This girl right here."

"Don't like you getting involved in Sanctum business, Raven," River rumbled as he started downstairs, leading the pack.

Disbelief shot from her nose. "Do you think I haven't been all along, River? You all think just because you don't give me the details, it doesn't affect me? This is my life, too, and I care about Otto every bit as much as the rest of you, so don't ask me to stand aside and act like some helpless damsel who can't help find the asshole who hurt someone I love, because I promise you, that is not going to happen."

Her words struck me.

Arrows that impaled.

I tried to breathe around their impact while Kane let go of a low whistle. "Damn. Someone is telling it like it is."

"Well, I'm tired of not *telling* it."

A low laugh reverberated from Theo. "Girl said she was ready to stretch her wings. Just didn't know they were going to be coming up against all of us."

How everyone had gone light in the midst of this should have been impossible, but we'd seen enough shit in our lives that these types of situations weren't exactly rare. They came far less once we'd parted from the MC, but trouble still seemed to manage to make its way to us.

But this one?

I was pretty sure it was on me, and my guts twisted when we got to the lower level.

The lights were on full blast, bright and stark as they illuminated the area. Shining over my collection of restored trucks and bikes. But it was the broken window on the opposite side that held my attention.

I strode that way, forgetting the pain as I got close enough to see what had busted the glass.

It was a rock about the size of a fist, but wrapped around it was a piece of paper that was held by a bunch of rubber bands.

I knelt to pick it up.

"You find something?" River asked from behind.

"Looks like someone might be sending me a message."

I was likely outed. Right in front of my whole fuckin' crew.

Guilty.

I wouldn't deny it—what I'd been doing. What I *had* to do. The revenge I had to seek because those deranged bastards couldn't go on living after what they had done.

Thing was, I knew down to my soul they would have gladly jumped on their bikes and rode with me to enact the punishment.

But this wasn't about them, and this vengeance had to be committed by my own hands. Four of their deaths had already been stolen from me. I hadn't been willing to give up any more of them.

A lump the size of Georgia filled my throat, making it nearly impossible to breathe as I pulled off the rubber bands and unfurled the paper from the rock. Setting it aside, I lifted the paper to see what the message read.

Then that ball of dread in my throat dropped to the pit of my stomach.

A stone sinking to the bottom of the sea when I saw the words scrawled in red across the paper.

DID YOU THINK YOU WOULD GET AWAY WITH IT ? NO, BITCH, YOU WILL BLEED.

Any fury I'd thought I was feeling? It was nil compared to the rage that slammed me. A tsunami that threatened to knock me from my feet.

I turned to find her standing just behind me. Horror blanched her face, the color draining away to a pasty white.

A storm of madness whipped through the garage.

Every member of Sovereign Sanctum instantly riding a sharp, cutting edge.

Because it became immediately clear that the slur written on Moonflower's window wasn't random, and this motherfucker hadn't come for me.

He'd come for Raven.

Chapter
THIRTY-FOUR

Raven

TERROR RIPPED THROUGH MY CONSCIOUSNESS, TEARING AT MY insides and crawling into every crevice of my mind.

I took a faltering step back like it could remove me from the threat smeared across the paper.

Bile lifted in my throat as a whirl of sickness coiled in my stomach.

No.

This couldn't be happening. Not after everything I'd been through. Not after everything I'd overcome.

It wasn't fair.

And who?

Who would do this?

Otto slowly turned around, and it sucked the little oxygen I'd been breathing from my lungs.

The man was carved of viciousness.

Of a malice so acute I felt it shiver through the air.

Razors dragging across my flesh.

The happy-go-lucky guy who didn't take a whole lot seriously was completely missing.

And in his place was something…terrifying.

Menacing.

Predatory.

Sinister.

"Is this that Tanner cocksucker? Motherfucker is dead," Otto hissed.

River growled beside him, and grunts went up all around the rest of my family as if they were tossing out their votes and judgement had just been cast.

Thoughts churned through my mind. Everything Tanner had said. The things he'd done.

Intuition pushed against it, and I shook my head. "No. It doesn't track. He's kind of an arrogant asshole. But to come here...and...and shoot Otto?"

I attempted to swallow around the dread that thickened my throat. "There's no way. That would be insane. Besides, whoever was on the footage both here and at the stop doesn't match. Tanner is way bigger than that guy."

"Then who?" It was caution that filled my brother's voice. Warning me of what they would do to whoever they found was responsible.

But it was venom that dripped off Otto's tongue that sent a rash of chills streaking through me. "No one gets to fuck with you, Raven. Not on my watch."

"Yeah, any asshole who thinks he can come around here messing with you? Then takes a shot at Otto here? He should already know things aren't gonna end so well for him." Theo's voice was a blade.

Kane laughed a morbid sound. "Poor fucker picked the wrong people to get brave with."

"Pff," Theo grunted. "Brave? Spray painting threats on a woman's windows and taking shots while he's runnin'? Pussy bitch is gonna be screaming when we come for him."

"Who's got a grudge against you, Raven?" River's question was close to a demand, though it was soft. A prodding that warned we didn't have time to waste.

I tried to process through the disorder, and I shook my head to make sense of the chaos. "I have no idea."

River straightened to his full height, and the tattoos on his neck writhed. "Believe me when I tell you that we'll find out who it is."

I wanted to tap back into the casualness I'd used at the store when we'd found what had been painted on the window. Play it off. But this? I shifted my attention to Otto who looked like he was going to snap.

Barely holding himself together.

There was no playing this off.

But I wanted to. I wanted to pretend like this wasn't happening.

I wanted to be free.

For once in my life, I wanted to be free.

Wholly and completely.

Without the fear that had chased me down for my entire life. Without the chains that had kept me bound.

Pain splintered through the middle of me at the realization of how serious this could have been.

Otto could have been killed.

Gulping, I struggled to breathe.

"Until we find out who is responsible, I don't want you out of my sight. Get your things." River's voice was close to a snarl.

I was going to fight him. Argue it because I didn't want that.

I didn't want to go back.

I didn't want to regress.

But before I could get anything out, a single, gnarled word curled out of Otto.

"No."

River's attention whipped to him with a scowl of confusion on his face.

Otto seemed to wipe some of the animosity off his, inhaling deep and roughing agitated fingers through his hair when he said, "You have Charleigh and Nolan at your place. You don't want to take Raven back there. She should stay here with me. I'm not going to let this piece of shit get anywhere near her."

"But he knows she's here," River punted back.

"And I guarantee he'd know that she'd gone back to your place, too. Think it's safest if she stays put. Not gonna let her out of my sight."

River wavered.

Unsure.

And God, I hated that I was in this position. It sucked that the two of them were arguing about where I should stay like I didn't have a voice in it. But I didn't want to do something reckless and go off on my own, either, just for the sake of standing my own ground.

Obviously, it wasn't the best time.

And the truth was…I didn't want to leave.

"Agree with Otto," Theo said. "You get Raven back to your place, and you're going to be so spun up that you're not going to be able to sleep, and we know how things go down with you when you get inside your head."

"And I sleep light." It was a warning from Otto's tongue. An oath that he'd stand guard.

A shiver rolled through me, and I thought that maybe Otto scented it.

Could feel it.

Because those eyes dimmed to a deep, toiling blue.

River exhaled in discontent, though I could tell that he was giving in. "Know she's in no better hands than with you," he told Otto. "But are you sure you want to take this on?"

Otto looked at me.

Energy thrashed.

Alive in the space that separated us.

"Never have been so sure about anything. You know what she means to me. The lengths I'll go."

A tiny punch of air escaped my parted lips. A frisson of need curling out from my lungs.

I swore, I could still feel the marks of his big fingers pushing in between my thighs. Could still feel his thick, massive cock gliding through my hands.

A hard sound rolled out of Otto.

Was he envisioning it too? Did he want more? Would he give it to me?

My body burned with how badly I wanted it.

Thank God that my brother wasn't a mind reader and had probably chalked my reaction up to me finding out that some deranged lunatic was after me rather than actually seeing the salacious direction my brain had gone.

If he could, I was pretty sure Otto would be suffering a whole lot more than a superficial gunshot wound.

Pain coated River's expression when he looked in my direction. "Can I talk to you in private for a second?"

"Of course," I told him.

He guided me around to the far side of an old Ford truck, his voice quieted as he turned around to face me. "Did something happen that you don't want to tell everyone else about? Don't want to push you, Raven, but I need somethin' to go on if I'm going to be able to hunt this asshole down."

I rubbed my hands up and down my arms. "I truly don't."

Coming to Moonlit Ridge had been a new lease on life. A new beginning. Starting over from the traumas and the horrors of that lifestyle.

River and the rest of the guys had done their best to keep me out of it.

Hiding me away like they could shield me from the realities of who they were.

They should have known that was impossible.

That lifestyle would always trickle down and infiltrate.

Haddie's face flashed through my mind. Grief slashing and slaying.

I looked at Otto, my guts fisting in the sorrow. I thought I might be able to hear the ghosts from that time howl in the vacant space.

If only I could have done something sooner.

But I'd done the one thing I could. The one thing I would never regret even though I'd kept it secreted behind a veil of shock and shame.

He was here—alive and whole.

It was all that mattered now.

River must have taken the sorrow in my expression for fear because he reached out and tapped my chin with his thumb. He'd always done it whenever I was in distress. Whenever he wanted to reach me. Whenever he wanted to let me know I wasn't alone and he would never leave me.

I adored him for it.

"We're going to take care of this, Raven. I promise you, all of us are right here, and we won't let anything happen to you."

He looked over to the rest of the guys who had their heads together, clearly trying to come up with a plan from across the garage. His attention dipped back to me. "Is this where you want to stay? I support you, whatever you want."

"I think staying here is for the best." I probably said it a little too fast.

His nod was tight. "Okay. Just…be careful, and don't do anything reckless. Know you want to do your own thing, but it's not safe for you to be off by yourself right now. Just until we get this sorted, then you can find a place of your own. But for my sanity, let's put that on hold right now, yeah?"

"I can do that."

I could try to tell myself that it didn't have anything to do with the fact that this was where Otto was, but it would be a lie.

"Good. I'm going to head out, see if I can pick up anything along the drive. We're going to find this bastard." He reached out and squeezed my arm. "Promise you."

"I know."

"Text Charleigh. She's beside herself. She wanted to come to make sure you were okay, but we thought it best not to bring Nolan over here until we knew the area was safe."

"I will."

"Can't stand for you to be goin' through this." He pulled me into a tight hug. "Love you so damn much. Need you to be safe."

"I won't let anything happen to me because I know you need me here with you," I whispered back, a semblance of the promise he had always made to me.

His chuckle was deep and sorrowful. "Only thing I ever wanted in this life was to take care of you."

"And you have, and now it's time for you to let part of that go."

He nodded against my head, and I had to wipe away the tears that blurred my eyes when we both pulled back. "Now look what you did…you made me cry."

"You deserve it after the way I panicked on my way over here," he razzed, and I let go of a soggy laugh as we wandered back out to the rest of the group.

Otto, Theo, and Kane were speaking in hushed tones while Cash leaned against a workstation that sat along the wall, pretty much mute the way he usually was. Always outside the conversation. But I swore, there was something extra keen about him. The way he watched like he was decoding the situation.

A tiny drop of worry flooded my bloodstream when he lifted his chin as I approached. Immediately, his gaze flicked toward Otto and his expression hardened.

Was he on to us?

What we'd done?

Okay, it was ridiculous to even label it an *us*.

There was no *us*.

Otto had made it clear that it had been a one-time thing. I needed to stop getting my hopes up, but I wasn't sure I could keep it at bay.

This buzz that hummed just below the surface of my skin.

Theo and Kane each gave me a hug and murmured that they were going to take care of things, then proceeded to go to Otto to give him encouragement of the same.

Cash hung back until Theo, Kane, and River had slipped out the garage door.

He didn't hug me, not that I expected him to, he just angled in close as he passed by and muttered, "Both of you had better be fuckin' careful. Don't want your blood on my hands. Care too much for you both, just like the rest of them do, so don't be fuckin' stupid."

Shock pinned my feet to the spot, and I swiveled my body at the waist to watch him lumber across the garage and push out into the bright sunlight that had taken to the sky.

What the hell was that about?

It wasn't until I heard their motorcycles roar up the drive that I finally tore my attention from the door they all had disappeared through.

No doubt, shock marred my expression when I turned to look at Otto.

But something else entirely took me over when I saw what was written all over him.

Fury and desire.

Fear and desperation.

Hunger and rage.

And he was coming straight for me.

Chapter
THIRTY-FIVE

OTTO

THE SECOND THE DISCORDANT BRAWL OF ENGINES ROARED INTO the distance, there was no stopping what came over me.

The overpowering rush of protectiveness and possession.

A need so fierce there was no way to deny it.

I let go of the foul words scrawled across the paper as I stalked Raven's way and took her stunning face in my hands.

The paper littered with the threat fluttered to the ground, and I gripped her by the sides of the head, my fingers delving into the soft locks of her hair as I urged her to look up at me.

Ink-stained eyes blinked at me in surprise, her breaths coming in short, jagged puffs.

That intoxicating moonflower scent invaded.

"Who's after you?" I basically croaked the words, unable to keep the desperation from bleeding into them.

She struggled to inhale, to breathe through the heat that flamed around us.

A circle of fire that kept us trapped.

"I truly don't know."

"What about someone else you've dated the last couple years?" The question was shards.

I was barely able to tolerate thinking about someone else having their hands on her. Except I didn't have to contend with that any longer. The truth that she'd never let anyone get close enough to actually touch her the way I'd been dreaming of doing. The way she'd let me do last night.

This fuckin' fierce, innocent, beautiful girl who was nothing but a light in the middle of the darkness.

And some motherfucker was trying to drag her back into it.

I could see her process through each one, calculating their risk.

The faintest line dented between her brows when she whispered, "None of them were really anything. A couple dates here and there. A kiss on the cheek. Most of them got bored and stopped texting when they realized I moved way too slow for their tastes."

That made me fuckin' ragey, too. Seemed there wasn't one thing about her that didn't send me into a tailspin.

"Anyone at the shop set you on edge? A customer or a supplier? Someone who might have gotten obsessed?"

She gulped, and she was barely able to shake her head with how tight I was holding onto her. "I don't think so. No one has given me the gut sense that something was off."

"Anyone in your past?" I grasped for anything.

Straws.

A needle in a giant fucking haystack.

I mean, how many goddamned people had she come into contact with over the years?

I felt the slightest flinch beneath my palms, the tiniest indication that maybe her brain had gone to a moment in time that might have meant something, before she blinked it away. "No. There's no one."

"Are you sure?"

"Yes."

I pushed closer, and my nose brushed hers as the urgent words fell from my mouth. "If you think of anything…absolutely anything…I need you to tell me, Raven. Trust me with it. Because I can't stand the thought of something happening to you. Of letting some asshole get to you. I need to stop this."

"And I hate that something in my life has brought this on you," she rasped. "I hate that you were hurt because of me."

She stared at me through the dense air that swirled around us in a disorienting cloud.

A haze that distorted everything I should cling to.

The reality that I couldn't have this girl.

But I couldn't find that footing right then.

"You think I wouldn't stand in front of every bullet for you? Take every blow for you? Suffer any consequence?"

"It's not your place." Even coming from her mouth, it sounded like a lie.

Both my thumbs brushed under the dark hollows beneath her eyes. "Isn't it? Isn't standing for you what I'm supposed to do? Isn't it what I've always been meant to do?"

It'd been me she'd come to when she was afraid. Me who'd held her. Me who'd chased away the nightmares.

But when everything had gone to shit, I'd known I had to put a barrier between us. Erect and fortify it.

See to it that neither of us could break through.

No question, what had gone down between us last night had put more than a dent in the surface.

It'd created a crack right through the foundation.

And I was afraid I'd already done it—crossed a line of no return. Because I couldn't step back. Couldn't peel myself away from this woman who held me like a magnet.

Gravity.

Luring me forward as I gazed down into the fathomless depths of those dark, entrancing eyes.

"Maybe you are meant for me. In every way." She answered my demand in that throaty lilt. Pushing even farther into the perilous territory I'd been toeing.

Pure fuckin' temptation.

My gaze dipped to her lips, and a pained groan rolled out of me when they parted at the attention.

A silent plea.

Coaxing me into disaster.

"Raven." Her name was a warning.

Praise and a riot of lust.

Her hand fisted in my shirt, and my thumb brushed across her plump bottom lip. My gaze jumped between the action and her eyes.

Hoping to God that she might be the one to stop this madness because it'd become clear that was not going to be me.

Apparently, I lost all power when it came to her.

"Tell me to stop. Tell me not to touch you. Tell me you don't want *this*," I demanded.

She laughed a brittle, disbelieving sound. "The only thing I've ever wanted is for you to touch me. Haven't you heard my body begging for it?"

Had tried to ignore it. Pretend as if I hadn't felt the desire radiating from her flesh. The way that gaze had always tracked me, and her heart raced an extra beat whenever I got into her vicinity.

All of it was the exact same thing mine had done.

Her body a match to mine.

"Touch me again," she rushed, her voice so low, her breath skating my face and infiltrating my senses. "I don't want it once. I want to feel it again and again."

I could scent her arousal. Way her entire being trembled with desire. With this desperation that had built for so long, and now that it'd been released, it'd become a life of its own. Grown into a volatile, charged entity.

"You want me to touch you again, Moonflower?"

"Yes. So bad. I need it. I need to feel you. Whole and safe. I was so scared—"

Before she could get the confession I was terrified of her saying free, I crushed my mouth against hers.

A promise that she was going to make it through this. A promise that I'd take the brunt of whatever was meant for her. Stand in the way of any motherfucker who would dare to do her harm.

A promise that I was going to take care of her…in every fuckin' way.

Only the second our lips touched, a roll of pleasure hit me so hard that I couldn't see.

Motherfucking bliss.

Dizziness spun, and my pulse careened through my veins.

Should have known better than kissing her. Tasting her. It was bad enough with what I'd done last night.

Now, I was instantly consumed. Delirious with the greed that spiraled through me.

A despairing hand fisted in her hair as my lips moved against hers, devouring her delicious mouth like I was tasting my favorite treat for the first time. Sucking at her top lip then the bottom before I got extra greedy and swept my tongue inside the hot, wet well of her mouth.

Raven gasped the second our tongues met. And that match lit.

Sparks and fire and need.

Rising up on her toes, she pressed those tits against my chest and her fingers came up to yank at the short pieces of my hair.

The woman kissed me back like that was exactly what she was made to do. Meeting me lick for lick, her tongue stroking and tangling with mine.

My cock hardened to steel, and my free arm looped around her waist so I could tug her delicious body against mine.

All that soft against my hard.

"Otto," she rasped against my mouth, every bit as delirious as me, and I was hoisting her up into my arms, no care to anything but this.

On instinct, her legs wrapped around my waist and her arms wound around my neck, though she jerked back far enough to see me. Concern was carved on every line of her expression.

"Not that I haven't fantasized about you tossing me over your shoulder and carrying me off to have your way with me, but you're hurt."

I grunted in return, diving back in for that mouth, though I was rumbling against her lips, "Doc said I will be just fine."

"And he also told you not to overexert yourself."

"You think carrying you three feet is gonna hurt me?" My voice dipped between a tease and coarse, raw need. "You think these arms weren't made to hold you? You think I'm not made to carry every-fucking-thing that you are?"

I was spilling things that should never be said, making claims I couldn't keep, but they were leaking out, anyway.

I kissed her wildly as I carried her over to a workbench on the far wall. I used my arms to scatter the tools from the top, the clang of metal crashing to the concrete floor.

A tiny bump of surprise rolled out of her when I propped her on top of it.

I forced myself back a foot so I could get a good look at her.

Attention roving, dragging over her, head to toe.

So fuckin' pretty where she sat on the table.

Black hair a matted mess and those eyes the most potent things I'd ever seen. Black diamonds that sparkled in the rising of the sun.

Pale skin flushed, still wearing that tank and those shorts.

My moonflower aglow.

She held onto the edge of the worktable as she wiggled in discomfort, needing the only thing I could give her.

"You need to come, sweet girl, and I'm not about to leave you wanting."

It sounded like another promise that I shouldn't make, but it was out, anyway.

I pulled my shirt over my head and tossed it aside, before I reached out and grabbed the hem of her tank, hesitating for a second as I grunted, "You mind if I get you naked? Been dying to see every inch of this body."

She choked a surprised sound before seduction went barreling through her demeanor. "All yours, Otto Hudson."

Yeah, she shouldn't be talking like that, either, but I'd never claimed that I wasn't a selfish prick, so I peeled the tank up her torso, and she lifted her arms so I could drag it over her head.

I tossed it to the floor, and my stomach fisted as I gobbled up the sight.

Fuck me.

"Look at those fuckin' perfect tits. Number of times I felt them pressed to my back while you clung to me on my bike. Wondering what it would be like if I ever got to see them like this. Last night it was a dream. And this…seeing you like this in the light of day?"

Raven let go of a wispy sigh at my confession.

I ran my knuckle over a hard-peaked nipple. She whimpered and arched in my direction.

"You like that, Little Moonflower?"

"Yes, I like everything you could possibly do to me."

My cock jumped, far too interested in all the ways he could have her. By the things I could do to her.

But I needed to rein it. Remember this wasn't about taking what I wanted. This was about giving Raven what she needed.

"You've always glowed beneath the darkness, and you're about to glow for me."

Angling in, I hooked my thumbs in the waistband of her shorts, and I pressed my lips to her jaw, kissing down the column of her neck at the same time as I started to wind her sleep shorts and underwear down her legs.

I kept kissing south, licking a path over her chest to the swell of her breast before I was taking one of those pert nipples between my teeth.

I gave it a nip before I sucked it into my mouth and swirled my tongue around the hardened bud.

Raven's fingers flew back into my hair. "Yes. That. I like that."

A rough chuckle skated up my throat. Loved that she wasn't shy to say exactly what she wanted. That she wasn't shy with me.

I licked and sucked for a second, rolling the other between my thumb and index finger, before I shifted back so I could twist her shorts the rest of the way off her ankles.

And there she was.

Fully bare.

Sitting propped on that worktable, swaying with desire.

She looked like the perfect pinup.

Dark hair and big eyes and swollen lips.

Perky breasts and thin waist and wide hips.

The sight of her dropped me straight to my knees.

Completely floored.

"Otto?" There was a question behind it, like she wasn't sure if she should argue the situation, thinking I was too banged up to get on my knees for her.

But I was already there.

A worthless beggar at her feet.

"You good?" I asked her instead. Knew I had to be careful with her. That I couldn't just gorge and devour.

Funny considering I was being the most reckless I'd ever been.

Hurtling in a direction that was only going to bring desolation.

Ruin everything.

But there wasn't an iota of rationale inside me that could stop me right then. Nothing that could stop me from giving her the pleasure she was begging for.

"Yes." It was a breath.

"Good. Then hook your heels on the table and spread your knees wide."

I rumbled it low.

Raven didn't hesitate to comply, and I nearly fuckin' died at the sight.

Her pussy was pink and drenched and swollen, so needy I could almost see it throb.

"Knew your pussy was going to be just as gorgeous as the rest of you." I took a single digit and pressed it all the way in to the knuckle, pumped it twice, before I pulled it out and circled the tip of my finger around her engorged clit.

She jerked and whimpered, "Yes, yes, I like that even better. Keep that up, and you're definitely going to be my very favorite person."

She attempted the tease, though the words were strangled.

Would have laughed if it weren't for the roil of possession that held me hostage.

"You're already mine, Raven. You're already mine."

Then I wound my arms under her thighs and dove in.

Tongue diving into her cunt, pushing in as deep as I could go all while trying not to come undone from the taste of her.

Nails sank into my shoulders, digging deep and holding on as I dragged my tongue through her slit and lapped up to that sweet, swollen nub.

"This…this. Don't stop." She was rasping it as she struggled to get closer, her hips bucking off the table in little jerks.

I ate her up, rumbling, "Don't intend to stop until I hear you screaming my name, Little Moonflower."

I used my shoulders to keep her legs propped open, and I let my hands glide around her hips so I could spread her pussy with my fingers. Exposing all her glistening, perfect heat.

I sucked at her clit, licking her into a frenzy, before I went back to dragging my tongue through her folds.

"Otto, please…I want…"

"Know what you need. Promise you I'm not going to leave you hurting. Going to make you feel good. So fuckin' good."

"Yes…so good…I…"

I knew she was winding up, the way her body started to tighten, pleasure gathering up from the edges as I drove her toward ecstasy.

It was the only place I wanted to take her. Where she had every fucking thing that she'd ever desired. Everything she'd ever needed.

I couldn't give her all of that, but I could give her this.

For now.

For this moment.

Those fingers were tugging at my hair, pointed nails raking at my scalp and drawing me closer as she lifted her butt from the table.

I swept my tongue back through her slit and up to her clit, then I shoved two fingers deep into her pussy.

Fingers ripped at my hair, and she widened her legs, a plea falling from her mouth, "More."

Fuck me.

Only Raven.

Begging for what only I could give her.

I added a third finger, pumping her hard and deep as I flattened my tongue against that throbbing nerve, swirling and licking in time.

She writhed and jerked and clawed at my neck as I drove her toward the pleasure that was waiting.

Felt it when she snapped.

When she rended apart, her walls spasming and clenching as the orgasm tore through her body.

An explosion that had her shouting.

And the one thing she was shouting was my name.

Chapter
THIRTY-SIX

Raven

BLISS. BLISS. BLISS.

It sped through me on a shockwave. Wave after wave of this unfound pleasure that careened through my body. Sparks and fire and flames. So good and perfect I thought I would black out.

Float off into space and disappear forever.

Except my fingers were locked in Otto's hair and his fingers were still burrowed deep inside me, though he'd slowed, and he barely pumped them in and out as he lessened the intensity of his tongue.

The man was wrenching every last drop of pleasure out of me.

Every molecule in my body shook with the disbelief that this had happened. That he'd touched me again.

Like *this*.

It was something I'd really wanted to experience. The number of times I'd imagined what it would be like with Otto's head between my thighs as he ate me into oblivion.

And oblivion it was.

I was gasping when he withdrew, my heart a mangle of love and relief and desperation when he edged back a couple inches so he could peer up at me.

My arousal was smeared all over his face, worry in his eyes and half a smirk on his mouth.

In that moment, he had to be the hottest thing I'd ever seen.

Every bulging muscle in his arms and chest flexed in need and restraint, skin slicked in a sheen of sweat, tats dancing and pulsing over his taut, golden flesh.

"Good?" he asked.

I scoffed a disbelieving sound. "I think you know exactly how good it was."

That smirk widened. "Maybe I just want to hear you say it."

"You want me to tell you that was the best thing I've ever felt? You want to hear me say that every time you walk into Moonflower, I imagine you propping me on the counter and doing the same thing? You want to hear that I wear dresses in the hopes that one day you'll walk in and push it up over my hips and drop to your knees so you can peel me out of my underwear?"

Lust blazed across his face, though he tried to keep it light. "And I thought you only wore them to torture me."

"Oh, believe me when I tell you that you're the one who's been torturing me." I slowly slipped off the table. He was still on his knees, and for the first time, I was the one who towered over him.

Naked.

There was a tiny part of me that thought I should go for modesty and slip back into my clothes. Maybe cover the scars on my abdomen and hips that were completely exposed.

But no.

Not this time.

I swayed in front of him as I scratched my fingers through the stubble on his cheek.

Otto groaned.

The sound crawled over me like he was gliding his fingers over my flesh. My stomach twisted in a knot of need.

I wasn't sure how it was possible after what he'd just done to me, but apparently, I would never get enough of him.

"Look at you," he murmured. "A fucking goddess standing over me. You have any idea, Raven, what seein' you like this does to me?"

"I hope it's half of what you do to me."

His chuckle was raw as he reached out and squeezed my bare hip. "Don't think you have the first clue. The first clue of what I want to do to you."

I lifted my chin. "Do it."

He winced. "You know we aren't going there."

I slowly eased down onto my knees in front of him. I didn't care that I was kneeling on hard concrete.

Those blue eyes flared. A battering of waves on an endless sea.

"What do you think you're doing?" His words were rough, scraping over me and sending another rush of desire coursing through my center.

Over his shorts, I curled my hand around his cock the best that I could.

He was hard.

So hard and big that a tremor rolled my throat.

It'd been dark earlier, and I hadn't gotten to take him in the way I'd really wanted to. I wanted to see him the way he'd just seen me.

"Raven," he warned.

My tongue swept across my bottom lip. "I want to taste you."

A guttural sound of restraint rolled in his chest. "Think it's best to leave well enough alone, don't you?"

"Is it?"

"Think you're playing with fire."

"I want to stand in it." I tugged at the waistband of his shorts. "Let me taste you."

That fire blazed.

"Not sure you know what you're asking for."

"Show me." I let a little of the vulnerability seep into my voice. The truth that I didn't know what I was doing. That I'd never experienced this, and I wanted to experience it with him.

Something shifted in his gaze.

A darkness that flashed through his features. His voice went gruff as he reached out and ran the pad of his thumb over my lips. "You want me to fuck this hot little mouth?"

A hurricane roared in my middle, and I had to shift and press my thighs together to try to staunch some of the ache that lit in my core.

I leaned in close to his ear and whispered, "Yes. I want you to fuck my mouth. I want you to show me what it means when you say you like it rough."

An earthquake rocked the ground, and his expression ignited in sheer possession.

He slowly climbed to his feet.

A fortress that stood.

A tower that reigned.

Magnificent and terrifying.

So glorious and fierce and rough that another tremble rocked my being. I stared up at him, at the muscles that flexed and bowed, at his cock that pushed at the fabric of his shorts.

He reached out and dragged the pad of his thumb down by my lips before he pushed it inside. Hard and deep.

My belly twisted as I sucked.

It was a precursor.

A warning.

I wasn't sure.

The only thing I knew was I wanted more. I wanted to see him. Experience him.

Have him.

I edged up enough so I could hook my fingers into the waistband of his shorts. I started to wiggle them down, careful of his wound as I tugged them free and he stepped out of them, though I was basically knocked senseless the second I freed his dick.

Lightheadedness nearly sent me sideways.

Holy fuck.

I had only felt the shape of him last night. Of course, I'd known he was big. I'd known he would be before he'd ever let me touch him. Every part of him was.

But this I was unprepared for.

He was massive, his giant cock bobbing as it strained for the sky.

Thick and obscenely long, the purpled head bulging and dripping at the tip.

My stomach toppled over, and my tongue stroked over my lips as a flash of heat pitched through my bloodstream.

"Careful with the way you're looking at me."

Otto's voice had gone completely different. Different than it'd ever been with me before.

It was cut in steely possession. In a command that rumbled from his throat and sliced from his tongue.

"I can't look away."

"You want it?" I knew he meant it as a warning as he fisted himself, stroking all the way down his length and back to the top.

"Yes. I want it. I want it everywhere."

A groan rolled out of him. "Tryin' to wreck me. Tryin' to ruin me in every way."

I wrapped a shaky hand around the base of his cock and leaned enough that I could lick across the tip.

Otto jolted forward. "Raven, fuck."

"Like that?" I asked, unsure, but also letting instinct take over. I'd read about this at least a thousand times. I'd have thought I would at least be part pro. I'd even deigned to believe I'd be pretty amazing at it.

But this was different. Experiencing it in this element.

Real and whole and in the flesh. Otto standing over me with barely contained need vibrating through his intimidating body. "You couldn't do it wrong, Moonflower."

A twinge of softness filled his gaze, though every other part of him was stone.

This man who I knew would do anything for me. A man who I knew was breaking all his oaths to allow us this.

But it was time.

Time to break free of the chains that had held us trapped.

I just hoped I could get him to see that he could fly with me.

"Show me," I told him.

Desire licked out of him as he gazed down, eyes hot and his body hotter.

"Show me how you like it," I begged.

I could feel the flashfire of heat rush through him. "You sure?"

"Yes."

For a moment, he hesitated, wanting to protect me the way he always had, so I tipped my head up at him and said, "I'm not breakable, Otto. And if I was, I'd want you to be the one to break me."

"Sweet fuckin' moonflower." He pressed the tip of his dick to my lips. "Open."

His tone filled with a command, and I obliged, parting my lips. He pushed the tip inside.

"Suck it," he grunted.

I did, sucking his head before I swirled my tongue around it and started licking him the way he'd been licking me.

"Fuck yes, Raven. Now take me deeper."

My chest buzzed at the feel of him, and a rush of excitement and adrenaline rolled through me as I edged up higher on my knees. I wrapped both hands around his base and drew him deeper into my mouth, flattening my tongue on the underside of him as I went.

My mouth was stretched so wide I finally got a little sense of what pleasured pain might mean.

He fisted a hand in my hair, and the words gritted from between his clenched teeth. "Just like that. Take it deep."

I drew him in as far as I could, gagging a little because on all things holy, the man was huge, and I literally had no idea what I was doing except for the fact that I wanted to please him the same way as he'd pleased me.

I barely got half of him into my mouth before he hit the back of my throat, and I rumbled a garbled semblance of his name around it.

"Good girl," he choked. "Such a fucking good girl with my cock stuffed down your throat. Like you were meant to do it."

I hummed around him, and his fist tightened in my hair. He

tipped my face up toward him, those sea-ravaged eyes burning into mine.

"You have any idea what it's like to have you like this? On your knees with that sweet, dirty mouth wrapped around my cock?"

I couldn't respond, couldn't do anything but stare up at him as he slowly began to withdraw before he pushed back in with a slow, measured thrust.

Energy crackled. The connection that had always shimmered between us coming alive. A frisson in the dense, dense air.

He grunted when he hit the back of my throat. "So fuckin' good. Just like that. Take it like you mean it."

He did it again, a little harder that time. "My sweet moonflower. You want me to dirty you? Wreck you? Ruin you?"

His tone volleyed between regret and possession.

I nodded in frantic, short jerks, need blistering through me, my skin seared with the flames that consumed.

I wanted it.

I wanted him to wreck me. To wreck me in the very best way.

I squeezed him tighter with my hands, and I was the one to pull back that time, staring up at him as I swirled my tongue around the tip before I plunged back down.

A vicious sound rippled from his chest, and I almost grinned, the way I felt powerful and beautiful right then, driving him toward the chaos I could see whirling through his eyes.

"This mouth. This dangerous fuckin' mouth and this sweet fuckin' soul. What am I supposed to do with you?"

I guessed he knew, though, because he started to rock, picking up the rhythm he wanted. A rhythm I matched, using my hands to stroke him as I sucked him deeper with each thrust.

"So good, baby." He grunted each word as he started to fuck my mouth in long, desperate strokes.

His hips snapped as he jutted forward, and the hard, packed muscles of his stomach flexed as he worked us into a disorder.

It felt like a claiming.

That's exactly what I wanted it to be.

A claiming.

I wanted him to take me. Own me.

My gaze locked on the moonflower tattoo that bloomed on his left hip. Was it me? Did he feel the same? Or was it a symbol that only promised he would forever look out for me? Protect me like a little sister?

I thought I had my answer the instant I looked up at him. When I saw the searing intensity that blazed from his gaze and erupted from his soul.

I knew it. I knew it.

I just didn't know if he would ever admit it.

I curled one hand tighter around him as I let the other wander up to the tattoo, and I brushed my fingers over the statement, hoping he could feel the statement of my own.

I love you. I love you.

I always had.

Probably long before I'd really understood what it meant.

An agonized sound rolled through his body, and a second hand dove into my hair, the man lifting me higher by both hands as he surged into my mouth. Guiding me exactly where he wanted me as he muttered, "Moonflower…baby…what have you done to me?"

He pushed himself deeper than he'd gone before, a hand at the back of my head drawing me forward.

I swallowed around him, taking everything I could.

That was all it took, and he shattered.

A roar of pleasure ricocheted through his garage as his cock throbbed and pulsed in my mouth. He poured and poured, grunting and groaning as I sucked him clean, making sure that I eked every last drop of pleasure out of him, too.

He slowed then stilled, and I carefully eased back to stare up at the man who'd always been everything to me.

The one who'd made me feel safe.

The one who'd seen me in a different light than anyone had before.

The one I'd always been willing to sacrifice for. The one I'd do anything for.

My spirit thrashed.

He could never know.

He could never know what I'd done or the lengths I'd gone.

His thumb came to trail along the edge of my mouth. "You're fuckin' perfect, Raven Tayte. So goddamn perfect. You got me wrecked."

But he was the one who'd wrecked me long ago.

Chapter
THIRTY-SEVEN

OTTO

Twenty-Seven Years Old

"**W**HAT THE FUCK WAS THAT ABOUT?" OTTO SPAT IT AS HE tore through the double doors of the club, heading right for that piece of shit Gideon Marsdon who was already at the bar, swilling down a bottle of tequila.

This bar was private, tucked behind the public bar out front, and was overflowing with Iron Owls at two on a Friday afternoon.

A ton of speculative eyes flew Otto's way as he stormed in, a path of fury lit behind him.

Gideon cracked a condescending grin. "Don't know what you're talkin' about, Hudson."

Otto hated this motherfucker. Had despised him since the moment he'd met him. But that scorn had taken on whole new levels after he'd been messing with Haddie a couple years earlier.

Otto knew the fucker had done it on purpose. Knew he'd known exactly who she was when he'd gone dragging his slimy ass around Otto's little sister.

Around Raven.

He still wanted to come unglued every time he thought about it, and this prick was only driving the nail that much deeper.

Otto scoffed. "You don't know what I'm talkin' about? Well let me remind you that it was your fuckin' job to sit lookout while I did my drop."

It'd been Gideon's duty to have his back, only when Otto had come out of the warehouse down by the docks, he and the rest of his crew had been missing.

Alarm had tremored through him the second he was out in the light of day. A feeling that somethin' had gone bad.

Loathing rolled through Otto as he thought of what his own *job* had been. It was the part of being an Owl that still made him sick, the drugs they ran through the city, contributing to the poverty and desolation that ran rampant. It was his duty, though, nothing he could say that could get him out of the pact that he'd made.

Not that he would have stopped, anyway. Not when it was on him to keep a roof over Haddie's head. On him to pay her tuition now that she was attending USC. He'd promised her if she got in that he would take care of the rest.

Trent Lawson rose from the shadows where he lounged on a high-backed stool, his head cocked to the side as he approached.

He was their vice prez, and his *duty* was making sure the club ran smooth.

Dude was as intimidating as they came. Stealthy and quiet and filled with demons so dark the last thing you wanted was his animosity pointed at you.

"The fuck is this?" he asked, purely a threat as he came up to the two of them.

Gideon grinned, and his brother Dusty chuckled low beside him, as if they were sharing some kind of inside joke.

"Got a call from Cutter that we were needed elsewhere." Gideon shrugged. "President always takes precedence."

"Yet you didn't contact me to let me know so I could send Otto backup?" Trent demanded.

Gideon feigned a flinch. "Must have slipped my mind."

Otto wanted to rip the asshole's throat out.

Trent scrubbed a hand over the top of his head, sighing, before he returned a glare at Gideon. "Make sure you don't forget next time, yeah?"

"Wouldn't dream of it."

Otto's hands clenched in a bid to subdue the violence skating through his veins.

Trent turned his attention to him, head inclining. "You good, brother?"

He took a step back, gritting his teeth when he muttered, "Yeah, I'm good."

Otto wasn't good.

He wasn't fuckin' good at all.

He was fuckin' face down on the ground, cuffs being slapped around his wrists. "You're under arrest for the distribution of narcotics. You have the right to remain silent…"

The officer's words were muddled, like the rushing of water in his ears, rage and regret a crashing waterfall that gushed through his senses.

His gaze caught on the front door of the house he'd shared with his crew for the last nine years, only none of the guys were there to witness this.

It was Raven who stood on the stoop, a hand covering her mouth as tears poured down her face.

His chest squeezed tight, his brow furrowing as they hauled him to his feet. "It's gonna be okay, Raven. Don't worry. It's gonna be okay. Tell the guys what's going down, and tell my sister—"

He didn't get the chance to say anything else before he was shoved into the backseat of a cruiser.

He stared out the window at the girl who'd become a woman in the blink of an eye. Torment shearing through her being as she mouthed, *I will.*

The cruiser pulled away, leaving her behind while he wondered if he just had bad fuckin' luck or if he'd been set up.

Chapter
THIRTY-EIGHT

OTTO

WRECKED.

Completely fuckin' wrecked.

And I didn't know what the hell I was supposed to do about it. How to move on from here. How to stop the spiral that Raven and I had fallen into. Madness took over any time I looked at her precious face.

This fiery temptress with all that soft vulnerability underneath.

And I kept marring it. Tainting it at every turn. Should have known when I brought her here that I was going to take that treacherous path. That everything was going to change, and there'd be no keeping myself from that trajectory.

But they say trauma either brings people together or forces them apart. It'd been true back then, in those days when I'd been skating that line and we'd smacked heart first into a grief so severe that we'd been fractured by it.

It'd been a glaring awakening. A reminder of who I was. A monster who didn't deserve someone like Raven Tayte. So I'd put up every barrier that could be fabricated all while still being the glutton who'd kept her near.

Close but out of reach because there was no way I could fully cut her off.

And there I was, all these years later, scooping her off the floor and into my arms.

God, she felt good. All that bare flesh tucked up against mine. Her warmth saturating my skin and sinking way down deep into my soul.

I was flooded in a wash of satisfaction.

In a feeling of contentment while tumult loomed around us.

Of course, she went all sass when I started carrying her toward the steps.

"Otto Hudson, what do you think you're doing?"

I arched a brow at her. "What does it look like? Carrying you."

She knitted that pretty face into a scowl. "Um, yes, I realize you are carrying me, but the question is why on earth you think it's a good idea to do it after you've just been shot!"

The last part she shrieked.

"You didn't seem to mind so much when I was carrying you to the worktable to give you an orgasm."

She gasped a choked sound before she tossed out, "Temporary insanity. I couldn't be held responsible for my actions."

God knew, I was going to be held responsible for mine. Letting myself go astray, touching her the way I had, though I was having a damned hard time worrying about the consequences right then.

"Now put me down, you burly bear, before you bust a stitch, and when you do, my brother is going to ask if you were following the doctor's orders, and I'm going to have to tell him the circumstances. We wouldn't want that now, would we?"

If she were standing, she would have been tapping a stilettoed toe.

A chuckle rolled out of me.

"You're going to tell your brother, huh?" I asked as I started up the stairs, taunting her a little.

Honestly, I barely noticed the wound. My body was still riding that Raven Tayte high. No pain in sight. This woman was the ultimate balm.

"Okay, fine, no, I'm absolutely not going to tell him that because the whole point here is to keep you healthy and safe and not dead." She bugged her eyes out at me.

"Would deserve it," I told her, my voice going gruff and some of the lightness wilting on my tongue.

Raven stopped struggling in my hold as I climbed the stairs. Two of us naked and exposed. Delving into a place we weren't supposed to go. Somehow going there felt inevitable, anyway.

"How can you say that, Otto? How can you say that after everything you've done for me? After all the times you've been there for me? After you were just *shot* because of me?"

Her words slanted in emphasis.

"Told you I'd stand in front of every bullet if it meant keeping you safe."

Problem was, I would likely have a million others coming at me. The things I was doing risky. Hazardous and grave.

Both with the beasts I had sworn to destroy and the wedge I was driving between me and my club.

I'd pretty much spat in the face of every oath I'd ever made, and the greatest one of them was currently in my arms.

"And how could that ever make you wrong for me?" she asked.

"You already know the answer to that, Raven. You know why we can't do this."

She wiggled in my arms, her bare ass brushing my dick that still stood at half-mast.

"Based on what just happened between us, I'm pretty sure we can."

A groan got free.

When I got to the top of the landing, I shifted so I could turn the knob and edged open the door, then I carried her across the great room and up into my bedroom. I strode straight for the shower in the en suite bathroom, and I balanced her in one arm as I reached in and turned the faucet to high.

While it heated, I turned and sat her on the counter. I stepped back from her, though I still was standing between her thighs.

Her pussy was right there, still emitting heat.

My cock jolted, hungry to just give in and fully take her over.

I brushed back the matted hair from her face before I set my palm on her cheek, staring down at the beauty that was this girl.

The goodness.

The kindness.

The belief.

My moonflower that had forever shined in the night.

I was terrified that I might be the one to stamp it out.

"I need to know how you're feeling. If I pushed you too far?"

Understanding dawned on her features, and her hand came up to cover mine as she leaned deeper into my touch. "No, Otto. I wasn't afraid. I know you would never hurt me. Know that you never *could* hurt me. I wanted it. I *want* it. I want to feel you in every way."

"Afraid I can't give you what you're looking for, Raven. Can't give you what I see playing in your eyes."

I couldn't give her forever, and that's the one thing she deserved. And if I took any more of her? I was never going to want to let her go.

She'd get so far under my skin there would be no way to get her out, not that she hadn't been there all along. Winding and weaving into me.

Body, spirit, and soul.

Disbelief shot from her mouth, and her eyes pinched at the corners as she lifted her chin. "Because you don't want to, Otto? Because you really don't see me the way I see you? Or because you're the one who's afraid?"

Fuck.

She just laid it out.

I took her chin between my thumb and index finger and angled in close. "Because I'm no good, Raven. Because you don't know who I really am. Because you'd be disgusted if you knew."

Because I'd failed my sister, and I'd be damned if I failed her, too.

"Because yes, Raven, I'm *terrified* of hurting you."

Surprised dread rippled through her features, and that sexpot mouth dropped open a fraction as her attention flicked all over my face. I knew she was searching around for something to say, for an answer, for a rebuttal, so I cut her off before we could let this spiral any farther than it already had.

"Now let's get you in the shower and clean you up, then I'm going to take you to Moonflower and I'm gonna stand outside and watch over you the way I was meant to do, and we're going to forget what happened between us last night and this morning."

What fuckin' bullshit.

There was no forgetting Raven Tayte because no matter how painful it was, this woman was carved on my heart and written in my soul.

Chapter
THIRTY-NINE

Raven

So let it be said that Otto Hudson was delusional.

Completely, freaking delusional.

Forget?

Seriously?

Yeah, I think not.

My mind was a foggy haze of lust as I struggled to focus on arranging a birthday bouquet that a man had ordered for his mother who'd turned eighty today.

Everything ran on a slow-moving reel as my mind replayed every time he'd touched me in the last twenty-four hours.

In the darkness of his room after I'd had the nightmare.

In the garage.

The feel of him as he'd stood behind me in the shower, my head tipped back as he'd massaged shampoo into my hair. His eyes tracing the trails of where the sudsy rivulets had streaked down my body.

His drenched, gorgeous flesh written in the horrors of his past writhing with restraint as he'd touched me gently.

Adoring me even though he didn't want to admit what it really meant.

Not to mention the protection that had roiled from him when

he'd brought me to work on the back of his bike. I loved that he'd already known that I would insist on coming in today. That he'd already known there was no chance I was going to allow some asshole to chase me from the one place I'd created for myself.

Besides, I needed a moment away from him. A breath. Some clarity.

Fat chance since Otto loitered across the street, leaning against the brick wall to the right of Sunrise to Sunset Café.

Tattooed hands stuffed in his jeans' pockets, so big and intimidating that I felt his presence covering me like a shield.

Refusing to let me out of his sight, just like he'd promised my brother.

Brutally intimidating and still tossing out easy grins at people who passed. It seemed most were uncertain whether to grin back or run because the man was rabid and likely to bite.

From over my shoulder, I peeked that way, through the panes of glass at the man who toiled intensity, his focus unending as his attention continually swept the street.

I turned back to the pile of fresh-clipped flowers and started tucking the pink roses and white irises into the bright green sprigs. I didn't even realize I'd gotten lost in my thoughts until I startled when the door banged open from behind.

I whirled around, silently chastising myself for getting caught up and lost, not that Otto was going to let some deviant get to me, anyway.

Unnecessary since a giant smile took to my face when I saw who was coming through the door.

Nolan started bouncing and clapping his hands overhead like he was doing jumping jacks when he caught sight of me on the other side of the counter. "Auntie Raven! Auntie Raven! Hi, we came to see you because you've been staying at my uncle Otto's all the time and I miss you so much."

His blond curls bounced around his cherub, chubby face, his blue eyes alight.

My heart panged with the adorableness that was my nephew. Panged with how much I'd missed him, too.

"What, you came all the way over here to see me?" I enthused, playing it off like I was shocked.

He giggled like it was absurd. "What are you even talkin' about, Auntie? We got here in only thirty-five seconds. I counted."

Charleigh's grin was wry as she stepped through the door and let it drift shut behind her. Her warm blonde hair glinted in the rays of sunlight that sheared in through the window.

"He might have lost count a couple times and had to start over," she said.

"Okay, maybe it was a hundred seconds, but I'd count all the way to a million if I needed that many to come see you."

Adoration clutched my spirit, and I stuffed the last rose into the vase and came around the counter, and I bent down so Nolan could bounce the rest of the way into arms. My eyes squeezed closed as I hugged him tight, breathing in his sweet innocence as I did.

His little arms were locked around my neck, squeezing me, too, though he was gritting his teeth with the effort.

A grunting laugh rolled out of me. "Goodness, when did you get so strong? You're squeezing me so tight I can hardly breathe."

He let go of me like he'd been holding hot potatoes. "Oops, sorry, but you know I gotta be liftin' my weights so I can get as strong as my daddy and my uncle Otto."

Affection rolled as I reached out and ran my fingers down his plump cheek. "I think you're almost there."

I glanced up at my best friend whose brow was pinched in worry, though she didn't say anything since it was clear we needed to keep the incident that had occurred at Otto's this morning from little ears.

I sent her an encouraging smile.

I'm fine.

It's fine.

Okay, I'm really not fine because I'm freaking out and I really need to talk to you and it has nothing to do with the reason you're actually here.

"It's about time you came to see me," I told her, hoping she could read the rest through the tease.

She grunted a soft sound, and she chose her words carefully. "I'm lucky I was able to make it out at all. But River figured it wouldn't hurt for him to stop by to check up with Otto."

She gestured out the window, and I saw there were now two brutes loitering off to the side of the restaurant. It was a wonder they hadn't had the sheriff called on them.

"Of course, he did."

Her frown deepened, and she mouthed, *Are you okay?*

I gave her a look that said we needed some privacy, and I scrambled around in my brain for an excuse to earn us some. I turned my attention back to Nolan. "How about doing a special project for me?"

Excitement blazed through his expression, his smile so wide that it actually tipped down on the sides and showed off his teeth. The spot where the baby tooth he'd knocked out a few months ago was partially filled with an adult tooth. "What kinda special project? You know I got all the skills, Auntie."

I loved the confidence this kid had.

"I need ribbons tied around a bunch of flowers. Since you just learned to tie your shoes, I think it will be the perfect job for you."

"Like a real job? Do I get paid? I don't have to get paid because I already got five dollars, but if you got a job, I think you get extra money."

Laughter rolled out of me as I set my hand on his back and guided him through the door to the back where there was a regular-sized desk. "I'm definitely going to have to add you to the payroll."

He popped onto the chair on his knees. "I'll do the best job ever."

"I know you will."

I set him up with a handful of violets and ribbon that had already been cut, then I slipped back out into the main area to where Charleigh was waiting at the end of the counter.

The second I did, she rushed, "What the hell is going on?"

Cringing, I crept forward as I shook my head. "I don't even know, Charleigh. Some idiot who has no idea what he's up against has decided to mess with me, I guess."

Her brows shot for the ceiling. "Mess with you? Someone shot Otto. I would hardly call that *messing* with. This is serious."

Dread clamped down on my chest. "I'm not trying to downplay

it. I totally know this is crazy serious, and I know the guys are freaking out right now."

"Completely. Then I got your text saying you really needed to talk to me, but you didn't want to do it over the phone. You should know that *I'm* the one who's really been freaking out."

"I'm sorry, I didn't mean to worry you more than you already were, I just…" I trailed off.

"What?"

I glanced over her shoulder to make sure my brother and Otto were still across the street, then I leaned in so our heads were close to touching and lowered my voice like I was sharing the most scandalous thing.

Which when it came to this, it was.

"Otto." I said his name like a dirty, beautiful secret.

"Otto?" She frowned, completely not tracking.

"Otto." I drew it out even lower, letting the insinuation bleed into my whispered words. "Otto, you know, the one who is my favorite subject? Otto, the one who I really want to put his dick in me?"

I tipped my head to the side, trying to lead her back to the one thing that I'd sworn her to secrecy about. She was the only one who knew the way I felt about him.

Of course, she also knew that that desire and hope came from zero experience. Knew the issues I had with trust. With allowing someone to touch me when the only touch I'd known in my life was pain.

"Oh my God." She grabbed me by the elbow and whipped her attention around like my confession had immediately garnered an audience. When she turned back to me, her brown eyes were wide with surprise, her voice hushed and excited. "You had sex with Otto?"

I released a frustrated moan and covered my face. "No…" I hesitated, then gushed, "But we did get naked."

"What?" she screeched, then she winced when she realized that the whole block had likely heard it, and she was quick to drop her voice right back to a secret. "You actually got naked? With Otto? The man you've been salivating over your entire life?"

I peeked out at her through my fingers. "Freaking finally, yes. Can you believe it? And God, he is the most gorgeous thing I've ever seen, Charleigh. And the orgasms…"

I groaned some more.

She pried my hands from my face. "How did you finally make that man come to his senses?"

"I think living with him proved the attraction was more than either of us could handle."

Not that I'd ever tried to resist him. Hell, I'd given him so many signs it'd gotten embarrassing.

"I finally told him last night that I've never been with a man—that I freak out when one even tries to touch me. I think we both hit a wall. Me telling him that he was the one I'd always wanted, and him giving him some crap about him not being good enough for me. I told him I was leaving this morning, getting out of his way because there was no way I could stay there with him after that." My throat tightened. "But then I had a nightmare, and he came to me."

Charleigh's face twisted in empathy. She and I were a lot alike. Our experiences different but similar. Both of us traumatized. Hurt by the people who were supposed to love us most.

I think it was likely what had bonded us first.

She didn't specifically know about the dreams, but she knew I remained haunted and chained.

"And when he did come to you, you weren't afraid?"

"Not even for a second. There was zero hesitation. Like, I didn't think I'd ever felt anything more perfect. I wanted it, and I didn't want him to stop." A little irritation wound into my tone. "Which I basically begged him not to, but of course, he went right back to telling me that *we* couldn't happen."

"How in the world did he resist my bestie? The man has to have a will of steel."

"And a cock of steel. You should see it." I fanned myself.

Charleigh curled up her nose. "Um, I'll pass, thank you very much."

Amusement rolled out of me, and I shook my head. "No. You're right. You definitely shouldn't. That man is mine, and I don't need anyone else ogling him."

"I'm perfectly fine ogling your brother."

I pushed her shoulder. "Eww. I do not need the reminder. You both are lucky I didn't go blind. That bleach was painful."

Charleigh giggled before her demeanor softened, and she knocked her arm into mine, my best friend eyeing me in care and curiosity. "Don't think I missed that you said that man is yours…"

I sighed. "I want him to be. That is if he could ever get over this whole idea that he isn't good enough for me. He keeps saying these things, implying that he's a bad man and I don't really know him."

Worry infiltrated. It was the part I didn't get. I *did* know him. I knew the casualness he wore like armor and the pain he held beneath it. I knew his grief and his loss. I knew his joy and his belief.

Charleigh's brow knitted in uncertainty, though she kind of shrugged as she speculated. "I think they all have a sense that there is something wrong about what they do. I don't see how they couldn't…the things they've seen, the things they've partaken in. It doesn't matter that it's for good, it's still bound to scar them in some way. Plus…you know it was really bad when they were a part of the MC."

Her words deepened in sympathy and dread. "In the end, they're still criminals. They still have blood on their hands. River was terrified of letting me in. Of loving me. Afraid of what his involvement in Sovereign Sanctum could mean for me."

"Yeah, and look what it did *mean* for you. It meant you found everything you'd lost. You found your family. How could that ever be bad?"

Charleigh's head barely shook, and her gaze filled with compassion. "They all have their demons."

I chewed at my bottom lip as I glanced back across the street. Even in the distance, I could tell that River and Otto were speaking in hushed, secreted tones.

I turned back to my bestie. "I'm worried that there's more. That he's hiding something. But you can't tell River that I told you that."

I would never betray Otto that way.

Concern twisted through her expression before she seemed to land on a resolution. "I think everyone has secrets, Raven. We each have things we hide because we're ashamed of them or afraid of them or worried they're going to hurt the people we love."

My spirit shivered. I understood it intimately. The truth that some things couldn't be shared.

Guilt bottled in my throat, but I swallowed around it and gave her a shaky smile. "Yeah. I know. It's human nature. I just want him to see past it. See me and who we could be and not let anything stand in our way."

I inhaled a deep breath. "He says he wants to fight for me, Charleigh, and I want him to fight for me. For all of it. That is, if he wants me that way."

A bit of insecurity rippled in, my stomach sick with the idea that maybe he didn't feel the same.

That maybe what had happened between us was purely superficial. Brought on by stress. Or worse, pity.

Charleigh blinked. "Are you crazy? Have you seen the way that man looks at you? He goes completely rabid. I think he has to restrain himself from tossing you over his shoulder and carrying you to his bed every time he sees you. I honestly don't know how River doesn't know or hasn't noticed. Otto's entire being shifts whenever you come into the room. You're his gravity, Raven."

In emphasis, she squeezed my wrist. "I promise you, this is not one-sided."

Nervously, I chewed at my bottom lip. "And what about River?"

A tiny flicker of annoyance washed through her features. "I love that man with every fiber of my being, but it's time that he views you as who you really are. A resilient, brave, capable woman who gets to make her own choices."

Her gaze deepened as she angled around to make sure I was in her line of sight. "You are the only one who can decide how you live, Raven."

"I know. The only problem is getting the rest of these overprotective bobbleheads to accept it." I tossed it out like a tease.

"The only question here is exactly how my amazing bestie is going to get Otto to accept it?"

"By my sexual prowess, of course." I let a dose of lightness wind into my voice. "Operation seduce Otto Hudson is officially in full force."

Charleigh giggled. "Oh, the poor man isn't going to know what hit him."

"I plan on bringing him to his knees. I mean, not that he wasn't already on them for me."

I wagged my brows at her.

She choked over a laugh. "Oh, I can only imagine. You're going to have that man crawling for you."

"That is the plan."

She let go of a breath, and her tone turned serious. "Just be honest with him, Raven. Let him know what you want and what you need, demand it in return, and if he can't give it to you, then let him go. You deserve every joy this world has to offer, and you can't wait around your entire life for someone who isn't willing to return it."

"I will," I promised her. "It's time. It's been time for a while, and I'm not willing to pretend any longer."

"Good." Then she frowned, taken back to what had brought her here in the first place. "Be careful, okay? It's so scary that someone is threatening you like this. Are you sure you can't think of anyone it might have been?"

A face rose up from the depths. From the darkest place where I'd kept my own secrets hidden.

But it was impossible.

There was no chance.

I shook my head. "No. There's no one. I keep thinking it has to be random. Some weirdo who saw me walking down the street or saw my picture or something. I don't know…it feels unreal. Like another one of the nightmares I suffer."

"You know they'll figure out who it is and take care of it."

A quiver rolled through my insides when I thought of the way it would be handled.

"I know," I told her.

"Auntie, I finished the whole thing, and I think I did a really good job, so I think you should probably pay me about a million dollars."

Nolan's little voice broke through the tension that strained the atmosphere, and I pulled away and pinned a smile on my face as he came bounding out into the main area of the shop.

"You finished them already?"

"Yup, because I'm a really good worker."

He held the bundle up for inspection. Most of the flowers had been smashed, the stems bent and petals falling off, half with crooked bows and the other ribbons were in knots.

I suppressed a laugh. "Wow, you did amazing."

"Do I get a million dollars?"

I ruffled my fingers through his hair. "Not quite, but how about twenty?"

He lifted the flowers overhead. "What? Twenty whole dollars? It's a deal."

He shoved the flowers into my hands then jumped toward Charleigh. "Mommy, you gotta take me to the store to get a new toy because I worked really hard, and when you work hard, you gotta play hard. That's what my uncle Otto told me."

Stark affection rolled out of her as she brushed back his messy hair. "Sure, we can do that. Why don't you go use the restroom really quick before we leave?"

"On it!" he said as he fist-pumped the air then went scampering into the back, the door of the restroom slamming behind him.

When he was out of earshot, Charleigh slanted her attention my way, mischief on her face. "And Otto is working extra hard today, so I bet my BFF is hoping he wants to play extra hard tonight."

I tried to stop it, but a cackle got out. "How did you know exactly what I was thinking?"

"It's written all over you."

My gaze moved to Otto. It didn't matter that cars were traveling back and forth on the street between us. I could still feel the intensity of his stare cutting across the distance and burning into me.

Anticipation slithered down my spine. It was precisely what I wanted.

I wanted Otto Hudson written all over me.

Chapter
FORTY

OTTO

"Y OU ABOUT FINISHED?" I STOOD JUST INSIDE THE MAIN DOOR of Moonflower, a sentry standing guard, watching Raven as she flitted around her shop, finishing her daily tasks. All her orders had been picked up or delivered, and she was tidying and wiping down her workstation.

Wearing another one of those dresses that drove me out of my damned mind, though this one was short as fuck, pure black and frilly, a pair of five-inch heels to match.

Of course, now that I knew the real reason she wore them, it only made it five-thousand-times worse. The greed that rolled in my stomach as I watched her move through her space.

Fluid and lush.

The girl in her element. So fucking free and beautiful as she managed this shop that I knew brought her a ton of pride and joy.

"Ten minutes max." She peeked back at me, playing innocent, like maybe she was attempting to do what I'd asked of her earlier and forget every delicious thing that had gone down between us.

Acting typical.

The way we always interacted.

Would have bought it, too, if it weren't for the way those inky eyes dragged over my body in a slow slide of appreciation, flaring as she succumbed to what clearly played out in her mind.

With that single look, I was hooked, my dick kicking in my jeans and the greed I'd barely kept tamped all day threatening to bust out of its confines.

Doing my best to ignore it, I busied myself by glancing at the giant farmhouse clock on the wall.

Five o'clock.

Thank fuck.

Closing time.

I reached over and flicked the lock on the door, then I turned back to her, rumbling, "What can I do to help?"

Needed a distraction. Something to get the temptation that was this woman out of my head. Quite the quandary considering it was my duty to keep her within fifty feet of me.

"Um…you could finish wiping down these counters while I close out the totals for the day?"

"Sure." I pushed off the doorjamb and ambled through rows of flowers that took up the center of the store and around the long counter. Each step I took, it brought her closer to me. Her aura becoming more potent.

The sweet honeysuckle moonflower scent hitting me like a landslide.

Her kindness.

Her belief.

The vixen underneath.

Was never going to get over the way she'd shouted my name when she came. Would never get over the way she'd gazed up at me with those eyes as she had my cock shoved down her throat.

I scrubbed a palm over my face to try to break up the onslaught of visions, and I edged her aside and took the rag from her. I started wiping down the counters while she turned to the computer she had set up facing out toward the main part of the shop.

She started humming as she worked, her throaty voice floating through the air, winding around me and twisting me in greed.

"How'd it go today?" I asked, trying to divert the out-of-control train of my thoughts.

"It was good, busy until late this afternoon. Not that you couldn't tell from across the street." There was a bit of a taunt to it, a pressing that told me she'd known I was watching too close.

I grunted as I swept the little pieces of leaves and petals into my palm so I could toss them into the trash.

"Couldn't hear what you were saying, though. Couldn't tell how you were feelin," I admitted.

I felt her still a fraction, her movements slowing as she murmured, "I felt safe, if that's what you're wondering."

But what about your heart?

What about your body?

Were those safe, too? Was she regretting everything that had happened between us? Would she take it back if she could?

I'd fretted like a fucking hen about it all day, barely able to keep still as I'd watched over her from across the street, lying through my damned teeth to her brother about how it was my privilege to take care of *our* baby sister.

So damned fucked up that I wasn't even sure what the truth was anymore.

"Only thing I want is for you to feel safe. To be safe," I murmured.

She slowed even more, though her voice twisted into this seductive, disorienting thing. "Is it, Otto? Is it the only thing you want?"

My guts tangled in possession.

I slowly turned around, compelled, the woman a magnet I'd seemed to have lost all power over.

She stood facing the computer screen, her stomach up against the counter.

Her tempting, lush body vibrated beneath that dress, her legs so fuckin' long in those heels.

The soft sway of her hips was mesmerizing.

The heavy thud of her pulse hypnotizing.

Could feel it, the erratic thuds that beat through the air.

My lungs squeezed as I slowly inched her way, coming up behind this woman who'd wrecked me so completely that I didn't recognize myself any longer.

Couldn't seem to stop myself from treading farther and farther into this depravity.

Her hair was piled on her head, twisted up in some kind of braid with a bunch of tiny white flowers poking out of it.

Her delicate neck exposed.

A magical sprite who'd taken possession of my mind.

I eased up until there was only an inch of space separating us, and I leaned in so my mouth was close to her ear.

"You wear this dress on purpose, Little Moonflower?"

She arched back. "Yes."

"You like teasing me? Tempting me?"

She rocked back, her ass hitting my cock that was stone, and she barely peeked at me from over her shoulder. "Is it working?"

"Clearly."

"That's what I thought," she murmured.

I buried my face at the back of her neck, then rumbled, "Fuck," as she ground herself against me. My hand moved of its own accord, riding up below that dress where I splayed my hand over her bare bottom.

She whimpered, and I groaned, my mouth at her ear. "We need to get home, Raven."

We needed to get out of here before I lost my mind.

Chapter
FORTY-ONE

Raven

OTTO'S HAND RESTED ON THE SMALL OF MY BACK AS HE LED ME out the front door. His gaze swept both directions.

"It's clear."

His voice was gruff. Harsh and shallow.

"Maybe it really was just random."

"Wound on my thigh begs to differ."

Right.

We couldn't forget that, even though I wanted to. Even though I wanted to erase all of this business and focus on what mattered.

Us.

Well, finding out if there actually could be an us.

I locked the door, and Otto's hand was right back on my lower back, stealing my breath as he guided me toward his bike that sat like a black beast at the curb.

Butterflies scattered in my belly.

How it was possible that just looking at his bike still riddled me with excitement, I didn't know, but it happened every time.

"Raven!"

My attention snapped up when I heard the voice shouting from across the street.

Sienna waved her hand frantically overhead.

I grinned and waved back, and she looked both ways, waiting for a truck to whizz by before she jogged across the street, a big canvas bag bouncing on her back as she ran toward me with a giant smile.

She hopped onto the sidewalk next to me. "Hey, Raven."

"Hi, Sienna." I stepped up and hugged her. "How are you?"

"Good, good. It was super busy today, so tips were great."

"That's awesome."

"I was worried for a minute because I wasn't sure if someone here was going to chase all our customers away…" There was a teasing question to it as she cast a sidelong look in Otto's direction. "Or maybe he just suckered them in. Our brand-new mascot."

She winked at me.

Yeah, the man was something to look at.

A brutal monument.

I didn't know how every woman in Moonlit Ridge hadn't flocked to Sunrise to Sunset Café to see him.

He grunted.

I laughed. "Sorry about that. Otto here thought he needed to keep an extra eye out for me today."

I lowered my voice on the last.

Worry pinched her face, and she glanced around. "Did something happen to your shop again?"

I blew out a sigh. "No, but some jerk came sniffing around Otto's place and broke a window."

I left out the shooting part. No question, that was information Otto did not want anyone else to know.

Shock ripped out of her. "What the hell?"

"I know. It's super annoying. But, of course, this guy thinks he needs to go all papa bear on me." I hooked a thumb in his direction.

"Well, it's good you have someone looking out for you." She widened her eyes, her message clear.

Especially him.

"It is good, isn't it?" I looked at Otto when I said it, and he grunted again, roughing one of those massive, tatted hands through his hair as he shifted in impatience. I turned back to Sienna. "We'd better go. This guy gets hangry if he doesn't eat by six, and you don't want to see him reach that point."

She giggled. "I can only imagine."

She rushed forward for another hug, mumbling, "Be safe."

"I will. I'll still see you on Saturday at Kane's, right?"

"If it's still happening, then absolutely yes."

"Um, yes, it is absolutely still happening." I cut Otto a warning look to stop him before he spouted something ridiculous like we were canceling.

The one he sent me back was pure disbelief.

This wouldn't be the last I heard about it.

"Okay, I'll see you then."

"Bye," I called as she ambled away, watching her go as I felt the heat of Otto's stare searing into the side of my cheek. I made sure to maintain all the sass I could muster when I turned back to him.

"You don't actually think we're going to celebrate my birthday on Saturday when all this bullshit is goin' down, do you?" he gritted.

Taking a step toward him, I touched his chest as I murmured, "Yes, Otto, I very much plan on celebrating you."

I let my fingertips brush down his abdomen as I pulled away, dipping low enough that I nearly touched the bulge still evident in his pants.

He growled as he took a lumbering step forward, his head angling down so close to mine, my senses swelling with his scent.

Patchouli and warm apple pie.

"Watch it, darlin'. You don't want to push me to the edge."

Oh, but driving him to the edge was precisely what I intended to do.

Chapter
FORTY-TWO

OTTO

Fuck, this woman was set on doing me in. Driving me out of my ever-lovin'-mind. Her hot as sin body tucked up close to my back, those bare thighs that were exposed by that godforsaken dress wrapped around the outside of mine. Tits I'd finally gotten a good taste of plastered against my back.

Could feel her dress flapping in the wind, could scent her breaths that she exhaled at my neck, could sense her arousal as she curled herself around me as my bike carried us up the mountain.

I kept my speed contained, though we were still going fast enough that the trees whisked by in green flashes as we hugged the curves.

The powerful engine a roar in our ears.

The road a blur beneath us and the sky a blaze of oranges and pinks strewn across the fading blue.

Here…here was where I found peace.

Freedom.

A feeling of completion.

The open road and this woman tacked to me on the back of my bike.

Which shouldn't give me so much satisfaction considering she didn't belong to me, but I was having a harder and harder time thinking of her as anything but that.

Mine.

Her arms tightened around my waist as I took an especially sharp curve, though I could feel the exhilaration roll through her body.

Raven loved it.

Being on the back of my motorcycle like she was cut from the cloth. Hewn from the metals.

I was sure it was here that she felt all of those freedoms, too. In sync with me on the open road.

I slowed when I finally approached the turn-off to my place, and I made the right onto the dirt drive. My attention remained keen, searching through the forest that grew up tight along the path, searching for any sign that the motherfucker had returned.

It was quiet. Exuding that peace, and I relaxed a bit, sure that Raven and I were alone.

We wound down the hill and back up the other side to where my cabin was tucked in the woods. The metal and glass glinted with the rays of sunlight that pierced through the tops of the trees.

Coming to a stop, I stretched my boots out to balance us as I grabbed my phone from my pocket and tapped into the app to turn off the alarm and lift the garage door. The metal rolled up, and I pulled my bike into its spot and killed the engine.

In that one passing second, silence wrapped us whole.

Dense and deep.

An awareness so thick that I could taste it on my tongue.

"Off you go, darlin.'" I went for normal. Same way as I would have talked to her a month ago, except that was fool's thinkin' since there wasn't one goddamned thing that remained the same.

Raven swung off. There was no reason for me to warn her to be careful since she knew the drill. She had already removed her helmet, and she took a couple steps back, facing me, wearing those heels and that dress.

God, she was a vision.

An innocent temptress.

A dark angel.

I didn't know.

Just knew that I couldn't breathe when I looked at her like that. Those ink-stained eyes doing dangerous things, watching me like they knew me. Like they had me pegged.

I swung off my bike, and the second I did, Raven turned and started up the stairs.

I followed, keeping three steps back like that would offer enough distance that I wouldn't want to reach out and touch.

Only thing it accomplished was every time she stepped up, the skirt of her dress would shift and give me the barest glimpse of the perfect round globes of her ass.

Lust clutched me in a vise. Took everything I had not to stretch out a traitorous hand and glide my palm up the outside of her thigh so I could take a good fistful of that ripe, juicy bottom like I'd done at her shop.

Maybe sink my teeth straight into the flesh.

A quiver rocked through her like she had a tap to my brain, and she inhaled an unsteady breath as she pushed open the door into the house. I stalled out at the doorway, watching her stride into my place like she belonged there.

Like she'd become a permanent fixture.

A painting inscribed on the walls.

So stunning it was hard to look at her without dropping to my knees.

The problem was it went so much deeper than the physical. So much deeper than the need that barreled through me on a rampage of greed so severe I didn't know how I remained standing.

This woman who deserved every fucking thing the world had to offer.

A normal life.

A three-bedroom house with a white-picket fence.

Some dude who would check in to work at eight in the morning and be home by five-thirty in the evening.

Loyal.

Kind.

One who didn't kill and maim.

She needed out of this life. To stretch those wings and let them carry her someplace safe.

Raven waltzed into the kitchen, light on those heels, hips swishing from side to side in a spellbinding sway.

The woman nothing but a snare.

A hook directly in my soul.

She pulled open the refrigerator and pulled out the half empty bottle of pinot she'd drank last night. She reached into the cabinet beside it and grabbed two glasses, and she waved one in my direction. "You want?"

Fuck, yes, I wanted.

"Why not?"

She poured us each a glass, and I carefully edged her way, feeling like I was making my way through a field of landmines. Unsure of which step was going to cause the blast that would completely annihilate.

Do us in.

Implode the very shaky ground we were walking on.

"Here you go." Raven passed me a glass, and she tipped those gorgeous eyes up to me.

"Thank you," I told her, voice rougher than it should be. Standing too close to her as I lifted my glass so I could clink it against hers.

"What are we toasting?" she asked.

"That you're here. That you're safe."

"I think what we should really be celebrating is that you're still standing."

"Of course, I'm still standing, darlin'. It's going to take a whole lot more to take me down than some candy-ass fucker who goes runnin' scared. Tossing out threats like the night is going to keep him concealed. Going to end him. Make sure he is no longer a threat to you."

I just laid it out. It wasn't like she wasn't fully aware of what was coming for the bastard.

"I never believed for a second that you would let anyone get to me."

"I won't. I promise you I won't let anyone get to you. Promise I'll stand in the fire."

She took a sip of her wine, never breaking our stare. "That's what I want, Otto. I want you to stand in the fire with me."

A charge struck the air.

A crackle of greed.

Electricity.

Hunger curled through my guts.

I took a sip of the wine, the tart but fruity flavor on my tongue, my gaze glued to hers before I set the glass aside. I reached out and ran my fingertips down the sharp angle of her cheek, overcome with the urge to touch her.

"Thought we discussed that we were going to forget about what happened last night and this morning?"

Raven leaned into the bare connection, her voice going raspy. "You know that I can't, even if I wanted to. And you'd be a liar if you said you didn't want it, too."

Keen eyes flashed with the challenge.

"What fuckin' man wouldn't want you, Raven? What man wouldn't want to get lost in this fuckin' perfect body? Wouldn't want to get lost in these eyes?"

My fingers brushed the corner of her right eye before I moved to settle my hand over the raging in her chest. "Who wouldn't want to get lost in this kind, magnificent, brave heart?"

She tipped up her chin. "I don't want any of those men."

"Fuck, Raven." It was a last-ditch effort that only served as a call.

"Tell me you don't want me," she demanded.

I had her hoisted in my arms and propped on the island before I could even make sense of the movement.

A knee-jerk reaction.

My hips wound between her lush legs, my jean-covered cock pressed up close to her mind-numbing heat.

Raven gasped, and her glass clinked against the granite as she set it aside. One second later, her arms were around my neck, holding on but leaning back far enough that she could read every desire scored on my face.

"I'm not what you need, Raven." It fucking hurt saying it. Thinking of some squirrely motherfucker's hands on her. Sharing meals with her. Curling up with her at night. Putting a baby in her belly. Lucky bastard getting to live in this tight, hot body.

"I know exactly what I need," she refuted.

My hands glided down her sides until they were cinching around her waist. Half in possession and half in restraint.

Leaning in, I ran my nose along the delicate flesh of her neck, inhaling that intoxicating moonflower scent. Voice a rumble of reticence. "Don't you see? I'm no good. No fuckin' good. I can't be the one to hurt you. I can't."

The words cracked on my desperation. With the plea for her to see.

I rocked back in surprise when her hands suddenly shoved against my shoulders.

Girl a flame.

A fire.

She slid off the edge of the counter and onto her feet. Appearing so damned tall, a force of nature, spite and determination in her stance.

She shoved me again.

"Don't you dare tell me what I need, Otto Hudson. Don't you dare. And don't you dare try to convince me that you're not a good man because that's a lie, too."

Clenching my jaw, I forced myself to move across the kitchen from her. Searching for a way to put an eternity between us all while wanting to erase every inch that could ever separate.

"I'm not. The things I've done…" A warning lined the words.

Disbelief shook her head. "Do you think I don't know the things you've done? Do you think I don't understand this life? Do you think I don't understand the cost? Do you think I don't see that you're scarred and carry the burden of setting people free? Do you think I don't know that always comes with a price?"

She took another step toward me as she said it, the woman a riot of emotion. Anger and hope and belief.

Every single one of those things were directed at me.

But she didn't know. She didn't know everything.

I had to wonder right then if it would even matter, though. If it would change a thing. If it would dim the light in those magic eyes.

"I'm finished pretending, Otto. I'm finished pretending about the way I feel about you. This either begins tonight or it ends tonight."

She jammed a pointed finger toward the floor.

Alarm churned through my being. "What are you saying, Raven?"

"I'm saying I'm finished tiptoeing. I'm finished shuttering. I'm finished keeping this inside."

She took another step toward me.

Intensity thrashed.

The woman an earthquake.

"Raven." Her name murmured out of me while urgency battered my chest. Ribs stretching so tight around the fullness I thought I would blow.

Come apart.

"I might be inexperienced, Otto. I might have been wounded so deep that I've been terrified of letting anyone get close to me, but you are the only one who's ever been able to do it. The only one I've wanted right next to me."

Her entire body angled toward me as she whispered, "I love you, Otto."

She touched her chest right over that beautiful heart as she took another step forward.

"I love you so much, and I have my entire life. And it's not infatuation or hero worship or bred of this trauma. It is what my heart knows. It's my truth. And if it's not yours, then I'll accept it. I'll walk away and I'll never look back. But the one thing I'm asking right now is for you not to lie to me. Don't be a coward and give me some camouflaged truth. Tell me what you feel when you look at me."

She gazed up at me with that boldness that was underscored in all her vulnerability.

Bared.

Chin lifted and those eyes weeping with her petition.

This?

This I couldn't resist.

I couldn't form a lie that great. So I let the truth ride free.

"You want to know how I feel, Raven? You want to know if my heart fuckin' bleeds every time I look at you? You want to know if I toss at night thinking about holding you in my arms?"

My brow pinched in emphasis. "You are the first thought I have when I open my eyes in the morning and the last one before I go to sleep. You are the thunder in my veins and the chaos in my spirit. You are everything I want and the one thing I'm not supposed to have."

I took a single step toward her, voice going gruff. "What I feel for you is endless, Raven Tayte. So, you want me to tell you exactly what that means?"

My hand fisted against the center of my chest. "It means I'm so fuckin' in love with you, so fuckin' gone for you, that there's no chance my world could spin right without you in it. So fuckin' in love with you that I feel like I'm ripping apart every time I look at you. You are my heart, and that's the truth."

Moisture blurred her eyes, and her delicate throat bobbed as she swallowed, and there was absolutely nothing I could do.

No restraint left.

No barrier high or wide enough that could hold me back.

I stormed across the space separating us, and one second later, I had my girl in my arms.

Chapter
FORTY-THREE

Raven

THE GROUND TREMBLED AS OTTO SWEPT ME OFF MY FEET. A grunt ripped up his throat as I wrapped my legs around his waist and curled myself around his big, beautiful body.

"Otto," I whimpered, and in a flash, he had one arm locked around my waist and the fingers of his other hand tangled up in the twist I had in my hair.

His mouth crushed against mine in a landslide of desperation.

His lips demanding and his tongue beseeching.

In a passion and need so intense it crashed through my veins. The same way as his.

A life-beat that pounded through our beings.

I thought I'd known it all along. Sure that I'd felt the yearning locked tight within him, but I'd never been able to sense the magnitude of it until right then.

"Love you, Raven," he mumbled against my mouth, his hand twining tighter in my hair as he carried me across the kitchen and toward his bedroom. "Love you so much. I can't keep it back any longer."

"Don't. Don't keep it back. Don't keep it from me."

"Won't. Won't ever again."

Joy saturated my spirit, and I arched into him, rubbing myself against his hard, packed body as he started up the three steps.

Rather than walk through the door, he pinned me to the wall next to it.

His big body covered mine like a shroud.

He pressed his hard cock to my center as he kissed me into disorder.

Madness took us over as we clawed and yanked at each other, anything to get the other closer.

"You're mine, Raven. Always have been." It was a growl of possession as his lips roamed from my mouth to my jaw and down my neck.

My head rocked back against the wall to give him better access, and my fingers dove into the short pieces of his hair.

"Just like you've always been mine."

It whipped out of me.

An unmitigated claim.

He edged back for the flash of a second. A wicked storm glinted in the depths of his blue, blue eyes. "Yeah, darlin'. You've always had me enchanted."

He hiked me up again, his kiss potent.

Exquisite.

Though I felt the tiniest bit of hesitation as he stopped right in the doorway.

He edged back to look at me.

His voice was low as he warned, "This is gonna change everything."

"The second you touched me last night, it already did."

"And now that you have me, there's no going back."

A desirous sound got out of me as he edged into the hazy light of his bedroom. Twilight had taken to the heavens, scattering fading pink wisps and sparkling diamonds that floated through the air.

Otto's boots thudded heavily across the floor, and one hand glided down and up under my skirt before one of those big hands was palming my bottom.

I whimpered and rocked myself against his abdomen. "Please."

"There will be no begging tonight, Raven. Gonna give you everything you need."

Without putting me down, he leaned over and grabbed the comforter and dragged it all the way off before he carefully laid me in the middle of the soft gray sheets.

He remained at the end of the bed. The man a pillar that stared down at me.

A dark defender. Brute strength and bulky intimidation.

But I'd never felt safer. Never felt safer than in the sanctuary of this man.

My burly bear.

I writhed in antsy anticipation. I still had on my heels, and they were planted on the mattress, my hips arching from the bed and sending my skirt to bunch up high on my thighs.

My body afire.

Aglow.

Singed at the searing intensity that blazed from his gaze.

"You have any idea, Raven? What it feels like to have you like this? A needy ball in the middle of my bed, waiting for me to take you? Consume you?"

He reached out and dragged the fingertips of his right hand from my knee down to my ankle.

Sparks flew at the contact.

Enraptured, he watched the movement before his attention flicked to my face.

"Going to possess you the way you've been possessin' me."

A scoff of a tease gusted out of my lungs. "You think I'm the one who's been possessing you? I already told you that you are my every fantasy. The face of every desire I've ever had."

My hand slipped from my sternum and down to my stomach. As if it could quell a portion of the necessity that pounded through my bloodstream. Urging me toward one thing.

Him.

Otto groaned as my hand smoothed over my dress, and my knees rocked from side to side in a show of supplication.

His tongue stroked out over his bottom lip. "You sure this is what you want? You sure you want to be mine?" It sounded almost of a threat.

"I already am."

His expression deepened.

Wicked and ravenous as he took me in.

Slow and sure as if it were marking what was his.

Reaching back, he grabbed the collar of his tee from behind and drew it over his head.

It left him bare from the waist up.

Wings flapped frantically through my belly.

God, no man should be that violently beautiful. A mountain of quavering stone, a mammoth that vibrated in the middle of his room.

So tall he blocked everything out except for the vision of him.

His chest carved and packed and rippling with muscle, every divot and edge of his abdomen flexing with the need that powered through his body.

He reached out and took me by the ankle, and he pressed his mouth to the sensitive flesh as he pulled the Louboutin from my foot. "Gonna fuck you in these heels, and I'm going to do it soon, but tonight, I need you completely bare."

A tremor rocked through me. "Yes, please."

A rough chuckle raked his throat. He clearly knew that I didn't even know what I was pleading for.

Everything, I guessed.

I wanted him in every way.

He did the same with the other foot, peppering kisses around my ankle as he removed my shoe and let it drop to the floor.

He set my feet back onto the mattress, and he didn't look away from me as he leaned down and unlaced his boots.

My heart jackhammered as I waited for him.

The anticipation growing with each second that passed.

Otto was going to take me.

My insides burned, and need throbbed at my center, an assault that battered through my entire being when he slowly pushed to standing.

Rising to that full, intimidating height.

The man a brutal bear.

But I wasn't afraid.

The air transformed around us, and a whirring hummed in my ears.

The oxygen coming alive, the intensity shifting as he slowly climbed onto the bed.

My legs spread to make him room, and he crawled up to hover over me. On his knees, he planted his hands on either side of my head.

His gaze traced my face. My expression. Searching for my fears. For my belief. For my trust.

I reached up and scratched my fingers through the stubble on his jaw. "I love you."

It was the one thing he needed to know. The one thing that had the power to erase every doubt and reservation.

He traced the pad of his thumb down the curve of my cheek. "My moonflower. Can't wait to watch you glow. To see you fully bloom in the middle of the darkness."

My chest squeezed, swamped by the attention, engulfed by the affection. I wanted to tell him the only thing I saw when I looked at him was a light. A beacon that glowed.

A safe haven.

But there was no chance for that because he dipped down and took my mouth in a kiss.

A deep, desirous, mind-bending kiss.

This kiss was slow and thorough.

Unhurried.

Like we had all the time in the world. Like we had no end.

Our tongues danced and played, and our breaths mingled as our hearts beat in sync.

I let my hands explore, palms riding over the glorious muscles of his shoulders, fingers dragging over his massive pecs and scratching at his rippling back.

Otto moaned and dropped down a fraction, letting his heat burn through my body as he kissed me into a puddle.

A needy, helpless puddle.

"Otto."

"I know, baby, I know."

He pushed up high on one hand and let the other glide up my outer thigh until he was gripping my hip. I felt his fingers tremble. Felt his nerves. The concern he forever held for me as he pulled back, breaths heaving from his lungs as he studied me.

"You say, Raven. If you get scared or anxious or just fuckin' change your mind, you say."

"I promise."

He sat back on his heels, and I sat up. He reached around me and drew down the zipper of my dress.

Cool air brushed my back, and chills lifted across my flesh. He bunched up the material and began to slowly drag it over my head. He tossed it aside, and my chest rattled as he gazed down at me.

I didn't have a bra on under the dress, and it left me completely bare except for black, lacy underwear.

"You have no idea, do you? What it's like seeing you this way?"

He leaned in and started to pluck the pins out of my hair, letting it fall around my shoulders.

The fresh baby's breath that I'd tucked into the twist earlier this morning rained around me.

"Goddess. How's it I'm touching a goddess like this?"

My nails raked his chest, coasting all the way down until I was tugging at the button of his jeans.

"And how is it that I'm finally getting to experience this fantasy with you?"

A ridge of cockiness rode the edge of his mouth. "Going to make sure you get to experience it again and again. In every way that you've imagined."

He eased off the end of the bed and hooked his fingers in my underwear as he went, and I arched as he peeled them down my legs.

Otto hissed. "Fuck me. Never have I seen something so beautiful.

This fuckin' gorgeous body laid out on my sheets. You said I was every fantasy you've ever had, Raven. But you are my only dream. The one wish I'd never dared to make. And now I have it in the palm of my hand."

He let that palm slip up around my hip before he squeezed at the same time as he leaned in to inhale the flesh on my inner thigh.

Need flash-fired, a riot in the middle of the room.

Otto edged back, never looking away as he shoved his jeans off his waist. He took his underwear with them as he shucked himself free of the denim.

Then he straightened.

Naked.

So dangerously gorgeous that a wave of dizziness pummeled me.

A sharp inhale wheezed down my lungs as I took him in. His big body covered in swirling colors and designs that vibrated over that rugged, hazardous power.

My throat thickened as I took in his hard, thick cock. It sent a slick of arousal rushing to my core. Desire banged against the walls and ricocheted between us, awareness spinning and spinning.

Wrapping us whole and complete.

A bond that we'd tried to forsake but could never be broken.

Energy lashed, and my throat grew thick as he climbed back between my legs.

No barriers left to separate us.

"Can I have you like this, Raven? Bare?" he rumbled, like he had direct access to my thoughts. "Promise you, I've never been with anyone else like this."

"I know," I murmured because I did. I knew this was different. I knew neither of us had experienced anything like this before.

Maybe he'd been touched a million times, had a million other women, but he'd never had *me*.

And still, caution filled his gaze as he swept his fingers through my center before he slowly pressed two inside. Gauging me as he drew them in and out. Making sure I was ready.

No question since I was soaked.

Then he gathered me up, took one of my hands and threaded our fingers together, and curled me fully into the safety of his arms.

Nose to nose and breath to breath.

I could feel the blunt head of his cock perched at my center, and the air locked in my lungs.

"Are you sure, Moonflower? Last chance before I make this body mine."

My nod was frantic, and my heart beat wild. Something that wasn't quite fear fluttered beneath the surface of my skin.

The thrill of the moment when you were stepping right up to the edge. The shaky exhilaration when you were looking out over a vast horizon and saw the beauty laid out beneath. Knowing you could never truly experience the completion of it without fully stepping into it.

That one last second before you jumped.

"Take it."

Every part of him darkened as he slowly started to nudge himself inside me. Lines were carved deep into the harsh angles of his face, muscles flexing taut, his nostrils flaring with the care he took.

All while my breaths turned short and choppy as he slowly, slowly spread me.

Fire licked a path up my spine and flamed through my being.

I struggled to adjust to the size of him. The stretch blissfully painful.

The toys I'd played with had done absolutely nothing to prepare me for the feel of him, not that I'd expected they would.

No comparison to this man.

My nails sank into his shoulder, and I gasped and clawed at him as he broke me apart and filled me full.

Otto kept watching me. Carefully. Tenderly beneath all the brawn that rippled and pulsed.

"Fuck," he grunted, the single word a rasp as he seated himself completely inside me.

I couldn't breathe. All the air had fled.

"You okay?" he asked, voice strained, expression tight.

My nails were burrowed deep in his shoulder as I whispered, "I've never felt anything as right as you."

He edged back an inch so he could gaze down at me, searching my expression as he remained painfully still. Every part of him was held in sharp restraint yet fully given.

His heart and his spirit and his mind.

"Was terrified of believing it…that you were meant for me," he murmured as he lifted my hand that was still twined with his and brushed his lips over my knuckles. "But you were, Raven."

He eased back a fraction before he edged back in, a little deeper that time, stealing the oxygen all over again. "You were meant for me. Do you feel it?" he grunted.

I could barely nod, trying for a tease but unable to find it. "The only thing I feel is you."

"That's right, Moonflower. That's the way it's supposed to be. My cock buried so deep inside you that you can't process anything else except for me. When you can't think about anything else but the pleasure I'm going to bring you."

He brushed the thumb of his hand still entwined with mine along my jaw, voice gruff and raw. "Nothing as perfect as this. Your pussy hugging me tight. You in my arms. This heart beating against mine."

"Nothing," I told him. "Nothing could be better than this."

A smirk hitched on his delicious mouth. "Oh, I think it's going to get better, darlin'. I haven't even begun with you yet."

I lifted my hips, urging him on, needy and desperate for him to show me. "Then you'd better start."

It was close to a chuckle that rolled through his chest. "Needy girl."

Though that lightness shifted to something close to predatory when he pushed up onto his hands.

His eyes raked down my trembling body, my body that was already covered in a sheen of sweat. A slow slide of ravenous appreciation in his hungry gaze. He paused when it landed on where we were joined.

"Look at that, my cock possessing you." His tone hardened in potency.

He pulled back then drove back in. The thrust was powerful and hard, and my back arched from the bed at the sublime intrusion.

"Otto."

"That's right, Raven. That's exactly what I want to hear. My name on that sweet little tongue. Going to have you chanting it forever."

A gasp ripped out of me as he drew back out then drove back in deep. He began to move in firm, measured strokes. Each one of them sent flames licking up my spine and lapping at my insides.

A beautiful burn that gathered strength with each rock of his hips.

I met each one, urging him to take me harder, to find the reckless rhythm we'd been racing toward all these years.

It took all of a few seconds before we were a writhing, gasping mess in the middle of his bed.

Grunts and drags of nails and grumblings of need.

"Fuck, Raven. So good. The way your cunt feels wrapped around my cock. So tight. So fuckin' tight and perfect. Never have felt anything as good as this. Nothing can compare. Gonna do me in."

He didn't take me gently. Like I was fragile or breakable. He took me the way my being begged him to do.

Unshackled and unchained.

I relished in it. Felt my wings that had been clipped flapping in the wind, freedom laid out right out in front of me.

He worked us into a frenzy. Energy frenetic as it buzzed through the room. Sparks of lightning flickered at the edges of my sight.

Pleasure billowed and swelled.

The threat of bliss blooming on the horizon.

His hips snapped as he drove into me, the man an onslaught of greed.

He curled a big arm around the top of my head, covering me whole as he surged down to capture my mouth in a kiss that nearly sent me sailing.

At the same time, he wound his other hand between us and circled his fingertips around my clit.

Fire flashed.

A wave of heat that blistered beneath the surface of my skin.

"Oh God...please...yes...harder."

Otto groaned. "You don't know what you're askin' for, Moonflower."

It was close to a warning. Maybe a promise.

I smoldered beneath it, sure it was the man who was going to be the one to do me in.

Ravage and devastate.

"I want everything you could ever give me."

He looped an arm under my thigh so he could spread me wider and shifted the angle.

The fat head of his cock hit that sensitive spot inside me as he took me again and again.

I started gasping, jutting up in desperation as the pleasure grew and bound. Gathering strength with each slam of his body.

It was hard and messy and desperate, and he was suddenly on his knees, keeping me open with one hand as he played me into disorder with the other, thumb circling and circling my throbbing bud as he pounded into me.

He looked like a beast right then.

The light had dimmed in his room as the sun melted away, and the man had shifted to shadow.

Skin glistening with sweat, every muscle in his body taut and flexing.

Eyes a scourge of dominance.

I loved it. Loved the claiming. The way he marked himself so deep inside me there would be no way for me to unwrite him.

My fantasy.

My secret.

My heart.

"I can feel you gettin' ready to split. Let me see you glow, Moonflower. Let me see you come alive beneath me."

He lifted my hips from the bed and rocked into me as he swirled his thumb around my clit.

It cracked me wide open, and a rush of ecstasy tore through my body.

A shockwave of bliss.

A torrent of pleasure.

And I swore that the ground no longer held me.

Swore that I soared and flew.

A darkened sky all around where I floated in the paradise that was Otto Hudson.

He thrust two more times before a shout burst from him, and he clutched me so tight there was nothing to separate us as he jerked and spasmed and groaned my name. "Raven."

He grunted as he poured into me. I could feel every twitch and pulse of his cock, and my pleasure fluttered around it, capturing him the same way as he'd captured me.

He held us there for the longest time.

In this rapture that could only belong to us.

We both knew it then. Knew it in the way our gazes were locked as we let go.

As we gave ourselves over.

As every wall and brick that had been built around us was top-pled to the ground.

Completely demolished.

It was *us*.

Forever.

And there was no turning back.

Aftershocks twitched through our muscles, and harsh pants heaved from his lungs as I struggled to drag oxygen back into mine.

As I struggled to catch up to this.

Otto had had me.

Had taken me.

Fully and completely.

I nearly wept when he pulled out, though he had me in his arms and was rolling us onto our sides and curling me tight against the heated flesh of his body before I could get out any sound of displeasure.

And through the lapping shadows that filled the room, those eyes were on me.

Searching my face as if they could get all the way down into my soul.

He let his fingertips trace the edge of my jaw. My lips. Before they were brushing along my brow. "You good?"

I snuggled into him, resting my cheek on his biceps as I let my own fingertips play along the intricate designs he'd tattooed there. "I knew there would be nothing like you, but I wasn't prepared for how good it was going to be."

Cockiness laced his words. "Good to hear, darlin', because you're about to have a whole lot more of me." Then his lips were at my temple, his words seeping deep into my spirit. "You're mine now, and I have every intention of making good on it."

Chapter
FORTY-FOUR

Raven

OTTO DROPPED THE PECK OF A KISS TO MY LIPS BEFORE HE ordered, "Don't move," in that rumbly, powerful voice.

"I don't think I could move from this bed if the house was on fire."

I was nothing but a puddle of mush.

Languid bones and sated muscles.

And a little sore on top of it.

Otto squeezed my hip with one of those massive mitts. "Don't worry, gorgeous, house catches fire, and you'll be over my shoulder so fast you won't know what hit you."

"I already know what hit me," I said, words laden with a tease and wonder.

His chuckle scraped across my overheated skin, and he squeezed a little tighter. "That was me goin' easy on you, Raven. You don't have the first clue what I have in store for you."

I snuggled down deeper into the rumpled sheets of the bed, still completely nude, skin sticky with sweat, limbs so heavy I couldn't move. Still, I was unable to stop the ridiculous grin that spread across my face. "You say that like I might object. Bring it, Burly Bear."

Otto laughed a little harder, though his tone went predatory as he leaned in closer to my face. "You think you can handle me, do you?"

"I was made to handle you, Otto Hudson."

"Ah, my little moonflower really is ready to bloom."

"I've been waiting for half my life."

His features softened, tenderness and something that resembled regret. He stroked his thumb over the freckle at the side of my upper lip. "Didn't mean to make you wait, Raven. Didn't mean to keep you from what you needed. Just didn't think I could ever be worthy of holding something as beautiful as you."

I set my palm on the stubble of his cheek. "Everyone deserves to be loved, Otto. No matter what you've done. But you? You deserve it more than anyone else I know."

He flinched. "Nah, baby, I'm just the lucky bastard who somehow is fortunate enough to get someone like you to look at me the way you do."

"It's not just looking. It's seeing, Otto. I see you. I see you for who you are."

Blue eyes dimmed, and he leaned in, so close to my face that our mouths were nearly touching. "One day, I'll let you see all of it, Raven, then you might change your mind."

It hit me like a threat.

Like shame.

Like fear.

He pushed off the bed before I could say anything else, and he strode for the bathroom.

Completely bare.

I rolled that direction and propped my head up on my hand so I wouldn't miss a second.

His back rippled with strength and his perfect ass flexed with each step that he took.

He flipped on the light since the sun was steadily sinking behind the trees, and I listened as water ran and a cabinet banged before he returned to the doorway with a washcloth, so close to the way he'd done last night, though everything had changed.

He wavered at the threshold. Greed gripped him as he froze there to take me in.

Ravenous eyes glinted beneath the fading rays that speared through the floor-to-ceiling windows, the man lit up in a glittering spotlight.

A treasure that had been unearthed.

A crude, rugged, priceless stone.

His hard, packed body vibrated with lust.

His giant cock twitching where it bobbed, still partially hard.

The designs on his flesh writhed, like each depiction had come to life.

And I swore that somehow I saw the petals of the moonflower on his hip unfurl further beneath the shower of the moon.

His head cocked to the side as he let his attention devour me. "If I could only paint you like that, Raven Tayte. Capture the absolute splendor that you are. Woman lying there in my bed like a portrait. Fuckin' stunning. Stealing my breath and my mind. Stealing my heart."

"It seems only fair since you've always had mine."

"Want to keep you right there, just like that, for the rest of my days."

"I wouldn't mind. All except for the fact that I'd need you over here in this bed with me."

Arrogance rolled through his demeanor, and he started across the floor. Though he took it slow, like he was relishing every second that he got to keep me like this.

"I intend on taking you right back to my bed, but I think I need to feed you first. You're going to need your energy."

Excitement pranced in my stomach, and I pressed my thighs together as he made it to the side of the bed.

He dragged a fingertip from my chin and down to my chest. A shiver rolled, but he didn't stop, he kept moving lower across my belly until his fingers fluttered just at my pubic bone.

"On your back and spread your knees."

Surprise jutted out of me, though I was quick to comply, my

thighs shaky as I bared myself to him. He pressed the warm wash-cloth to my center.

A little moan climbed my throat as he gently swept it over my tender flesh. "You sore?" he asked, voice low.

My nod was tentative. "A little. But I like it."

"You like feeling how I marked you? How I claimed you?"

That time, my nod was erratic. "Yes."

He wiped the cloth between my legs before he stood and moved to take me by the chin. "Gonna write myself on every inch of you."

My teeth clamped down on my bottom lip. "That's where I want you. Everywhere. In every way. Forever."

Chapter
FORTY-FIVE

OTTO

I T FELT ODD AFTER YOU'D SPENT SO MUCH TIME IN YOUR LIFE fighting against something you thought you couldn't have, doing your best to deny yourself the very thing that felt like it sustained you, then turning around and letting it slam directly into you.

The way it rocked through you. An earthquake that knocked you from your axis. Crumbled your foundation.

But the epicenter remained the same.

The one single focus that guided everything.

I watched her through the increasing darkness of the room as I moved to the end of the bed and snatched my underwear from the floor. I pulled them on, before I turned and started for the dresser against the wall.

I did my best to ignore the picture that screamed at me from the top, the voice that demanded vengeance.

Haddie. Haddie.

I felt torn between two destinies.

Unsure which of them would be the end of me.

I pulled open the top drawer and grabbed one of my tees, then I turned and moved back for Raven who anxiously awaited me.

An enchantress in the middle of my bed.

Just a glance, and a spell was cast.

She sat up as I approached, as if she was compelled, drawn to me the same way as I was drawn to her.

All that black hair rained around her, brushing her delicate shoulders and rolling down to caress her breasts. The pebbled tips of her pert nipples peeked out between the lush locks.

My mouth fuckin' watered.

My attention wandered, gliding down over the scars that marred her abdomen. The cruel intentions meant to be evidence of a sadist's schemes. To whittle her down to surrender.

My gaze skated to the deeper scar on her lower left side, the one that was covered by the words that rolled up her ribs.

I will make it to the sunrise.

Fury glinted at the edges of my mind. In the darkest recesses where the demons howled and played, my own scars carved inside of me ragged and weeping and still begging for retribution.

But Raven's scars?

They only shouted of her resilience.

Of her bravery.

Of the goodness that radiated from her spirit.

"Arms up," I told her, and there was the tiniest grin playing at the edge of that sexpot mouth when she obeyed. I slid the shirt over her head. It was enormous on her, swallowing her tight, enticing frame, coming all the way down to her knees.

I scooped her up without warning. She squealed in surprise, and she threw those arms around my neck at the same time as she wrapped those long legs around my waist.

"What are you doing, Otto Hudson?"

"Told you I needed to feed you."

She edged back, arching a brow, her face so goddamn striking in the wisping light. "I think you forgot something important."

"What's that?" I asked as I started to carry her from the bedroom.

Her brow arched higher. "My panties."

"You aren't gonna need those."

Swore, it was glee that sprinted through her being, lighting as sparks in those dark, dark eyes. Excitement and greed and her own wicked, wicked things.

Fuck me. She really was meant for me.

"Is that so?" she challenged, playing along.

"That's right," I told her as I ambled down into the main part of the house. I strode right into the kitchen and perched her on the edge of the island.

"Want that sweetness ripe and ready for me."

A shiver rocked her, and she gripped the counter, wiggling in the spot. She looked like a temptress there, a siren sitting beneath the hazy rays of light that danced in through the windows that overlooked the lake beyond.

View might have been magnificent, but it didn't hold a candle to her.

I strode to the refrigerator, whipping open the door and riffling around inside to find something to sustain us. There wasn't much that wasn't going to require effort, but there was half a cake that Raven had picked up at the restaurant across from Moonflower a few days ago.

My favorite fuckin' cake from my favorite fuckin' girl.

It was exactly what we needed.

Chocolate and carbs.

I pulled out the platter and set it beside her on the island.

"We're having chocolate cake for dinner? And here I always thought you were a steak kind of guy."

I wedged myself between her legs that dangled from the counter, and I tipped my face up to hers. "Turns out, I'm a Raven Tayte kind of guy."

Her fingers sifted through the longer pieces of my hair. "I think you were always a Raven Tayte kind of guy."

I took her hand and kissed her palm, sucking down her intoxicating moonflower scent. It was like pressing my nose into a spray of honeysuckle. Imbibing all the sweetness that she was. "Yeah, think you're right."

Raven eyes stared down at me. "Did you then? Did you want me?"

Wasn't prepared for her to give voice to the past.

I pressed my face a little deeper into her palm. "Think I knew it the moment I got released from prison. When I walked in and you were standing in the middle of the room. The way you looked at me right then…"

I trailed off, unable to fully give it voice, knowing the way it'd all gone to shit. The way it'd spiraled. The tragedy that'd come.

Still, I took her palm that'd been against my lips and splayed it over the boom that clanged in the middle of my chest. "It's always been yours."

Didn't matter how long I'd ignored it. Didn't matter the way I'd gone after every distraction, every pleasure, like the quick encounters and easy lust that came from that kind of life would ever sustain. Like it could ever fulfill what had been lacking.

Shaking myself out of the heaviness, I pulled the foil from the cake. Didn't bother with utensils. I dug into the spongy concoction with my fingers, ripping free a big chunk, all too eager to feed my girl.

"Open," I told her.

Delight raced across that stunning face, and she indulged me, opening that sweet mouth before she closed it around the giant piece, moaning as she did.

A decadent sound that went straight to my dick.

I pulled back and watched as she chewed, then I reached out and wiped away a glob of chocolate that had gotten stuck to her lip with the pad of my thumb.

I moved real slow when I drew my thumb into my mouth, sucking it, watching Raven's stare flare with her own lust.

"No fair, Otto Hudson."

"What's not fair?"

She rolled those pretty eyes. "Don't act like you don't know what you're doing to me."

"And what am I doin' to you, darlin'?" I played it innocent, a tease, loving the lightness that flitted between us.

"You know exactly what…making me all squirmy and needy." She whispered the last like it was a secret.

"Looks like you caught me. That was the whole plan." I leaned in close, and that time, I licked the bit of chocolate remaining from her lip, voice lowering to a rasp. "Only thing I want is you squirming and needy."

Raven was the one who reached over and dug into the cake that time, basically coating her fingers in it rather than picking up a piece. She pressed all four fingers into my mouth, and I sucked around them, licking them clean, making her shake.

I kept feeding her little pieces, watching her the whole time, loving that she was mine. I dragged messy fingers down her neck, licked that up, too, didn't mind one bit that I was smearing chocolate all over my white tee that she wore, my hands making imprints all over her.

She whimpered, and it was clear she was no longer interested in eating as she pressed her chest toward my face. Over the shirt, I pulled one of those diamond tipped nipples into my mouth, giving the bud a tiny nip of my teeth.

Raven yelped then giggled as she curled her arms around my head, and I was pulling her from the counter and into my arms and swinging her around.

Letting this joy overflow us. A rising tide powerful enough to sweep us away. Our feet unsteady with the amount of happiness that rushed.

I reached over and grabbed her phone from her purse where she'd left it on the counter earlier, and with her still in my arms, I thumbed into her music app. Put it on a slow song so I could dance with her the way I'd always wanted to.

Completely wrapped up and wholly given.

Strains of the soft melody filled the room, and I carefully set Raven on her feet and tucked her against me, and she breathed out a tremulous sigh and gazed up at me.

Understanding in those eyes. The truth that it really had always been her.

"You don't have to be afraid of loving me," she murmured.

Wistfulness filled the shake of my head. "Since there is a very real chance that your brother is going to kill me when he finds out, there's probably going to be a little pain."

I tried to keep it light.

A tease.

But the severity of it rang around us.

She was forbidden, and I'd taken the one thing I was never supposed to have.

"He won't."

We swayed, and my thumb traced the freckle on the edge of her lip. "He might, but I promise you, any second I get to spend with you is worth it."

"He doesn't need to know. What is between us is between us."

Both of us knew that was impossible. There was no way we could keep this under wraps for long. No way to conceal the fire that burned between us.

Air puffed out of my nose. "I'll figure out a way to tell him. Just gonna need some time, and I need to be the one to do it."

Time to figure out what the hell I was doing. Time to decide if I was going to continue on this suicide mission. Chasing down death as I chased down vengeance.

I was beginning to wonder if *that* was worth it. If it was going to change anything inside me once it was done.

Most of all, I needed the time to figure out who was after Raven.

Then I'd face what I'd done, and I'd take any penalty that was coming my way.

She was worth it.

She was worth it.

"I will never be ashamed or regret loving you." She said it simply. Like nothing could touch us.

Nah, I had no regrets, but there was plenty of shame.

"No, Moonflower, there never could be any regretting you," I murmured, swaying her soft.

Nose pressed into her hair and my arms curled tight around her body.

It didn't take long for the air to change.

To come alive.

A charge that sparked in the room.

The connection that pulled taut between us a live wire.

Greed twisted my guts, the need to get lost in her greater than any need I'd ever felt.

She sensed it, too, and a sensual exhalation escaped her lips.

I leaned down and fitted my mouth against hers, drinking that provocative sound down, sucking it into the well of my lungs.

Filling myself with the taste of her.

Chocolate and temptation. Goodness and light.

My hands began roaming, gliding along her gorgeous curves, taking handfuls as I went. The second my fingers hit the hem of my shirt she wore, I peeled it over her head and tossed it to the floor.

The break in our connection gave me a second to take her in.

Standing naked in the middle of my kitchen.

A goddess who reigned.

Raven tipped that chin my direction, going coy as she took a step backward, swaying those hips to the enthralling beat of the song. Her tits bounced a bit as she did, woman nothing but delectable curves and sleek lines.

The shape of her my perfection.

In an instant, she had my cock stone.

"You really are a little temptress, aren't you?" I said, barely able to get the words out around the knot of lust that thickened my throat. "A tease. Driving me wild."

"You deserve it. Every time I ever looked at you it felt like a tease."

"You can rest assured the feeling was mutual."

I took a step toward her, peeling myself out of my underwear as I went. I pushed them down my legs and shucked them off my feet.

A throaty moan rolled out of her. A thrashing as every molecule in the atmosphere intensified. A dense, sumptuous heat billowing through the space.

And that moan was turning to a gasp when I slowly knelt on my knees in front of her, peering up at her as I took her by the outside of the thighs and spread her legs enough to make myself room.

She jolted forward and her hands dove into my hair when I dipped in and licked through her seam.

"Otto."

Pulling back, I rumbled, "Love this sweet cunt."

My fingers took the place of my tongue, and I shoved them deep into her pussy. She arched and rasped and clawed at me. Already two seconds from coming apart.

I pulled my fingers free and played with her clit, before I pushed up to standing. Towering over her, covering her in my shadow. "Turn around, Moonflower."

Her rotation was slow, the woman peeking at me from over her shoulder as she went.

I hissed.

I hadn't gotten a real good look at her ass until then.

Pert and firm and full.

I reached out and let my fingers travel the delicate slope of her spine, riding down to the small of her back before I edged forward and took her by both cheeks, spreading her and pressing my dick to the crease.

Chills raced her flesh, and she shivered as she whimpered, "Yes."

My mind spiraled back to what I'd read in her book just last night. Seemed impossible that only that short time had passed. The way my mind had been blown at what she was into. The things she'd confessed.

"You like it dirty, don't you?" The question was pure greed.

Raven trembled. "Yes."

I took her by the arms and turned her to the side, and I bent her over the island counter.

That gorgeous ass jutted out. I let my palms smooth down her sides until they were cinching around her waist, and I was groaning as I leaned down and peppered kisses along the small of her back.

She was scarred there, too, and I nearly succumbed to the rage. To the fury that pumped through me in a riot of hate at thinking of what she'd been through.

I tucked it down, though, kept it as a promise that I would never again allow anyone to get to her. Never allow anyone to touch her when she didn't want to be touched.

My lips traveled south, and I was kneeling again, taking her ass in both palms and spreading her. I circled my tongue around her puckered hole.

Surprise rocked out of her, sending her forward before she pushed back with a strangled plea flying from her lips.

"You like that?" It left me on a growl, and she frantically nodded her head, hair swishing around her where she was bent over the counter.

I dipped in, lapping at her ass as I fucked my fingers into her pussy. Her walls clutched around them.

Throbbing.

The girl an instant toil of need.

I pulled them out and rubbed my hand between her thighs from behind, hitting her clit each time as I slowly rose to standing.

Rising high behind her where she writhed and whimpered with her chest pressed against the countertop.

"Gonna fuck you so good, Raven. So hard and deep you will always remember me."

No matter what happened.

"As if I could ever forget you. As if I'd ever want to."

I lined the head of my cock up at her swollen lips. "Hold on. This one is gonna be rough."

I surged forward, taking her in one hard thrust.

She cried out, and I grunted, my hands going to her hips as I seated myself deep.

I nearly passed out at the impact of her gripping me in a fist.

So goddamn good I couldn't see.

"That's right, Moonflower. You're never going to forget me."

I pulled out to the tip, my dick coated in her arousal, then drove back in.

She rocked forward on a jolt.

My fingers sank into her hips. "Nothing in the world is as good as this. Your cunt hugging my cock. Squeezin' me in a fist."

"So good," she whimpered. "Better than I ever imagined."

I started fucking her, as hard and as desperate as the mewls that were slipping out of her mouth. Her nails clawed at the granite countertop as I took her again and again. She pushed back, meeting me stroke for stroke.

Bliss sparked and flickered, glowing like a fire in my balls and at the base of my spine.

"Heaven. Your pussy is heaven. Every fucking thing I could never deserve. An angel I'm going to dirty."

I edged back enough that I could swirl my thumb around her asshole. I barely pressed it inside on the next plunge of my cock into her slick, hot body.

She tremored and shook.

"Do you like that, Little Moonflower? Does it make you want to glow?" I muttered through the fever that had taken me hostage.

Raven went wild, gasping and begging. "Yes."

"Wait until it's my cock filling this tight hole."

A discordant sound climbed out of her, heat sprawling far and wide, radiating from her being and into mine.

I pushed my thumb deeper on the next thrust, picking up a heedless rhythm as I filled her again and again.

"Otto, oh my God, please..." Her words were garbled, incoherent, her flesh slicked with a sheen so bright I swore that she glistened.

A glittering diamond.

A moonflower blooming in the night.

I wound my other hand around her front so I could get to that bud, and I rubbed at that sweet little nub.

In one single second, she was wound into a thrashing, urgent bow.

Energy thickened. The air so dense I could barely drag oxygen into my aching lungs, our grunts and pleas thick vapors that curled around us like smoke.

A hazy perfection that made me lose sight.

The only thing I could see was her. This fucking stunning girl.

She exploded around me, an orgasm ripping through her so fiercely that she screamed.

Shattering.

Erupting.

Fracturing.

She throbbed and spasmed around me, and that bliss gathered strength, prowling up and down my spine like a predator hunting its prey.

I hauled her up, turning her in my arms at the same second as I was spinning around and pressing her to the door of the refrigerator.

Surprise left her on a gush, then she moaned when I shoved my dick back into the warm, wet well of her perfect body. She arched, nails scratching at my back as I took her whole.

"Need to see your face when I come in this sweet pussy. Need to see that you're mine."

I rocked into her in hard, possessive thrusts, taking her and taking her, driving myself to that plane that I'd never dared to believe could exist.

A plane that was meant only for Raven and me. A place only our own.

Paradise.

Raven started moaning again, pleasure rebounding.

"Come for me again, Little Moonflower."

I snapped my hips in erratic, powerful juts, plunging into her and driving her up the side of the refrigerator before she would drop down and I slammed back into her again.

Her fingers yanked at my hair as she arched forward.

"Do you feel it? What you do to me?" I demanded. "Show me what I do to you."

She split at that, shooting high as she cried my name.

She took me with her. An explosion of ecstasy breaking free of its chains and lighting through the middle of me.

A supernova so bright that I was blinded.

Nothing else to be found but this woman who was coming apart in my hands.

The pleasure that ripped and tore and screamed.

I pulsed as I poured into her, my cum so deep in her cunt she was never going to be rid of me.

While she whimpered and wiggled and writhed as a thousand spasms rolled through her body.

Took the longest time for either of us to come down, and I just held her there, pinned to the metal as she panted.

Once she caught her breath, she grinned. There was no containing the euphoria that split on her face. "So that's what it's like to be fucked."

My chuckle was gruff, and I let my hands wander her thighs that still shook where they were wrapped around my waist. "Is that what you wanted? To be fucked?"

Her fingers were gentle when they reached out and danced along the edge of my jaw. "I told you I wanted every experience with you."

My cock jumped where I was still seated inside her. "Going to show you every pleasure you ever imagined."

She wiggled, bouncing on my half flaccid dick. "I can't wait."

I growled at her, the sound mixed with a low laugh as I pulled her from the fridge, never releasing her as I started to carry her back toward my room. "You are askin' for trouble, aren't you?"

Her arms curled tighter around my neck, and her lips moved to my ear. "I want all the trouble with you, Otto Hudson. In every way you'll give it to me."

"In every way, huh?"

"That's right, and I don't ever want you to stop."

We didn't make it to the stairs before I had her on the floor and was fucking into her tight heat all over again, just as I was murmuring, "You have everything, Raven. You own every part of me."

Chapter

FORTY-SIX

OTTO

THIS TIME WHEN I CARRIED HER INTO THE EN SUITE BATHROOM in my bedroom, I didn't do it telling myself lies. There was no trying to front some bullshit line that we were going to forget what happened between us.

There was no turning back.

Boundaries broken.

Toppled into nonexistence.

I kept her against me as I turned the faucet of the bathtub to high and leaned in to plug it. Steam filled the room, and the dim light that burned from the ceiling wound through it to create an effect that appeared like a dream.

A misty sanctuary that could only belong to us.

Wasn't sure how long it was going to last before everything imploded, so I intended on cherishing it for as long as possible.

When the tub filled halfway, I stepped into the claw-foot tub.

A tub Raven had picked out because she'd teased me and said it reminded her of me.

Her burly bear.

Thought it was ridiculous then, but I got it now.

"You're going to be sore. You need to soak," I told her.

The water was just shy of too hot as I settled us into the water. I rested my back against the tub, and Raven sighed as she edged off just to the side, turning toward me and tucking in the safety of my arm. She rested her cheek on my chest, and those fingers started playing along my pecs, tracing the lines of the horrors and hope that I had tattooed on my skin.

She was still breathing hard, her heart still thrumming, though I could feel her begin to relax in my hold.

I pressed my lips to the top of her head. "Was I too rough on you?"

Her cheek smooshed into my chest as she shook her head, her breaths almost cool with the heat of the water. Her scent was all around, though it was distorted, painted with me.

Kind of wanted to keep it that way forever.

"Tell me it wasn't obvious how much I liked it?"

A chuckle skated my throat, low in the quiet that encapsulated us in a hedge of protection. "Guess the way you were shouting my name made it pretty clear."

Then I sobered, nudging her chin up so I could study her face. "But I'd never forgive myself if I hurt you."

"You would never hurt me, Otto."

"Have though, haven't I? Ignoring this? Pretending like I didn't feel it begging between us?"

"You did what you thought was right," she whispered.

A contrite smile pulled at my lips. "Or maybe I'm just being selfish now. Taking you for myself."

"If giving into the need you have for someone is selfish, then call me a glutton."

I ran a palm down the back of her head as amusement rolled at the base of my throat. "Haven't had your fill yet, darlin'?"

"I think that is going to happen at precisely..." Raven played it up looking at a nonexistent watch on her wrist. "Never."

"That seems pretty exact."

"I'm willing to bet on it." Her voice was quiet and light.

I fiddled with a lock of her hair, breathing in the peace. Silence wrapped around us, a comfort that we both sank into.

I didn't know how much time had passed before the question finally broached my mouth. "What do you want from this life, Raven?"

I'd asked her before, but that was under the context of us being friends.

A *sister*.

Should have known anything baked under that guise was nothing but a falsity.

"Other than you?"

My laugh was low. "Yeah, other than me."

"Well, other than my number one which now belongs to me…" That part was playful before her voice slipped into contemplation. "I want to continue to grow Moonflower. I feel like it's important, what I do. I believe a bouquet isn't just some simple decoration, but an expression of love. A sympathy or a well wish. An apology or a promise."

I hummed, and the silence thickened, and I could almost feel the tension glide through her being. "And someday soon, I think I'd like to have a family."

She whispered that.

I blew out the strain. "That's what I'd hoped for you. Might have killed me to think about it, but I'd hoped that you would find some lucky motherfucker to love you. Someone to treasure you. Treat you like a queen. Thought the two of you would move into some cute little house with a slew of flowers growing in pots on the porch. Imagined you'd have two or three kids playing out in the yard, too."

I hesitated before I forced myself to speak. "Thought you might get away from the life. Away from the danger that comes from being affiliated with Sovereign Sanctum."

Kept wondering if that's what this was. This threat that loomed. If some monster had figured out who we were and was using the sister of one of our members as intimidation. A warning for what was coming.

Raven's brow pinched, and she shifted so she could peer up at me. It sent the water sloshing around us. "How could you think I would ever want to distance myself from you? From my brother? From the rest?"

She made it sound like it'd be a betrayal.

My thumb stroked her cheek. "Because then you'd be safe."

"I don't want to be safe if it means being separated from the ones I love. From my family."

Pain splintered through me. That old grief that had always made me terrified of getting too close. Terrified of loving. Terrified of the idea of losing someone I cared about more than life all over again.

Certain if it happened again, I would never survive it.

"You've always said you'd be willing to fight for me. Die for me. For all of us." Raven's words filled with urgency.

"Of course." That went without question.

"Do you know so little about me that you would think I wouldn't sacrifice the same?"

A swell of protectiveness tumbled through my guts, and my hand twitched where I set it on her face. "I'm not worth that kind of sacrifice."

Whatever my fate was going to be, I had it coming to me.

I didn't want her anywhere near it. Fucked up considering I didn't think there was a chance I could let her go.

Something passed through her features. Something haunted. Ghosts that swept through that ink-stained gaze. "I've always been willing to fight for you."

"But that's supposed to be my job."

"No, that is supposed to go both ways. Caring and loving and protecting. It can't be one-sided, or it will never work," she argued.

The quiet settled around us for a moment, her words weaving and winding, searching for a way to penetrate. To find a way to seep through the cracks whittled in the broken places inside me.

"Do you want that, Otto? A family?" she finally asked through the thick air.

Trepidation hammered through me, spirit clutching in a vise of regret. Part of me wanted to keep it locked inside, but I found myself admitting, "Tried to be that for Haddie and it didn't turn out so great."

Sorrow rolled. It'd become a taboo subject between us. Words left unspoken. But I wasn't sure we could maintain that any longer when we were this close.

Raven barely shook her head on my chest, her words so quiet I could hardly hear them. "She was amazing, Otto. The kindest, most genuine best friend I could have asked for. And so much of that was because of you."

Grief cut through me. A dull, bitter blade. "She's gone because of me."

"She got caught up. Made mistakes like we all do. That doesn't make someone a bad person. The only bad people are the ones who stole her from us." A tremor rolled through her, dark and ugly, palpable in our connection.

I wondered if there was a chance that she hated them as badly as I did.

If she'd understand what I had to do.

If she'd accept the resentment I still bore at the fact that I hadn't been the one to be able to end them all.

"Did it so wrong." It scraped out of me.

Her fingers drifted over my pecs. "They're the ones who incited it all. They're the monsters."

But she didn't know it all. My retaliation that had cost everything.

A stupid fucking choice. A bomb dropped, and I hadn't been able to stop the fallout.

"You were fighting for us all along," she added.

My eyes squeezed closed on the trust she kept trying to impart on me that I couldn't receive, and I swallowed some of it back, the agony that kept wanting to rise to the surface, and changed the subject.

"Is that what you did tonight? Fought for me? Drawing that line in the sand?"

She settled her head back on my chest, the words wisps. "I was fighting for *us*. Fighting for what I deserved. For what you deserved."

"Can't say I'm mad that you did."

"Oh, you'd better not be mad. If you were, you're not going to get any more of this." She squirmed against me, her skin slick with water.

I choked over a groan that became a laugh, and I hugged her against me. "That so? Now which of us would be paying the price?"

Could feel the heat race across her flesh. "Okay, fine, you're going to get all of this. All the time. Whenever you want it. I'll just have to find a different way to punish you."

"Oh yeah?"

"Definitely." A tease scampered all over her stunning face.

"Does it make me a masochist that I really want to find out what that means?" I needled, wanting to know how far she might take it. "Time out? A spankin'?"

I wagged my brows at her.

She giggled, and God, I loved the sound of it. Fingertips swept along my jaw as those dark eyes danced. "I think you might like that too much, Otto Hudson."

"You can rest assured I like it any time that you're touchin' me."

"Like this?" she asked. She slid her hand down my stomach until she was gripping my cock.

A thunderbolt of pleasure struck me.

"Fuck, Raven," I groaned, caught off guard, taken by surprise, the girl so fuckin' bold, I had no idea how we hadn't ended up here years ago.

But I guessed when she'd claimed she was ready to stretch her wings, she meant it.

"That's a really good start," I told her, words going jagged as she began to stroke me.

One touch, and she had me so hard it was painful. Dick thickening in a fit of desire.

Seemed now that I'd had her, I was never going to get enough.

Raven shifted, and she tossed a leg over me to straddle me at the waist.

The woman a vision beneath the hazy rays of light that filled the bathroom. Rivulets of water glided down her flesh, that shock of black hair a tangle, the ends dripping wet as she drove me to madness with that wicked little hand.

My hands flew to her waist. "What do you think you're doing, darlin'?"

There was no timidity in her when she raked her teeth over her bottom lip. "Taking this fantasy. Seducing you."

My chuckle was a scrape of greed, and I sat up and took a fistful of her hair, words shifting to a deep, guttural awe. "You can go ahead and tick that box, Little Moonflower. Call me seduced. Never gonna break the spell you have me under."

Then I stood with her in my arms, stepping out of the bathtub, both of us dripping wet, and I carried her to my bed.

Chapter
FORTY-SEVEN

Raven

Eighteen Years Old

HADDIE HAD RAVEN BY THE HAND AS SHE HAULED HER DOWN the sidewalk toward the house that was lit up like a stage.

Lights glowing from the windows and music thrumming from the walls.

People were scattered all over the front lawn and porch, and it was almost impossible to maneuver their way through the crush as they stepped through the front door.

Raven could feel Haddie's excitement. The exhilaration that buzzed through her as they stepped into the bedlam of the party.

Haddie squeezed her hand as she tossed her a grin. "I'm about to get sloppy drunk tonight."

Raven rolled her eyes though she couldn't help but smile. Her best friend was a wild one. Eager to race into every experience.

Raven wished she could be more like her.

Bold and daring.

But it'd taken Haddie three hours to even convince Raven to

come tonight and then another two to coerce her into putting on the slinky, short dress.

She felt out of sorts and out of place. Exposed and unprotected.

But she yearned to step out. Find herself. Embrace who she was hungry to become.

That felt almost impossible since her fears had been more intense lately. The nightmares coming more often and leaving her terrified where she'd wake thrashing in the night.

It was painful without Otto there to come to her. To comfort her and remind her that she was strong and brave.

A fighter.

Her spirit flailed as she thought of him. Behind bars. She missed him. God, she missed him so much that she ached.

Haddie dragged her directly to the kitchen. Booze covered the countertop, and Haddie grabbed them both red cups and poured them each a drink. She handed Raven one and tapped the plastic cup against hers. "To all the fun the night will bring."

"That sounds dangerous," Raven said as she tapped her cup back, though she smiled as she brought the rim to her lips and took a sip of the vodka Haddie had mixed with cranberry juice.

Haddie giggled over her cup. "You're always so worried. Time to let go, Raven. Tonight is going to be a blast. I mean, how couldn't it be when you're with me?"

A rush of excitement rolled through Raven, and she tipped her cup back, making the choice to let herself get carried away on the vibe.

And she was having a blast. Dancing with Haddie in the living room with some of the girls that Haddie knew from her neighborhood. They were actually really cool and welcoming to her, so Raven let go of some of her insecurities and instead chased down the thrill.

Hours passed like that. Laughing and dancing and having the best time.

Until Raven's stomach bottomed out when she saw who came striding through the front door.

Gideon and Dusty and the rest of their crew.

Dread crawled down Raven's spine. She didn't have all the details, but she was pretty sure from the rumblings she'd heard between River and the rest of the guys that these assholes were responsible for Otto being sent away.

She knew it way down deep the second Gideon's gaze landed on Haddie and something wicked passed through his features.

She knew it. She knew it.

But Haddie didn't seem to have a clue. That or she didn't care.

Because she only pressed her back against him when he slinked up behind her and wound his arm around her stomach, and she begged Raven to keep it a secret when she left with him that night.

Five Months Later

Nerves rattled through her when she heard the clatter at the front door and a commotion of voices in the living room.

"You're back."

"Thank fuck, brother."

"You made it out."

Raven edged through the kitchen to the entryway so she could peer out.

All the guys were giving Otto hugs and clapping him on the back, welcoming him home.

Once they all finally pulled away, it left Otto standing in the middle of the room. In an instant, that blue gaze was on her. A sea where she could drown.

So viciously tall and wide where he stood like a fortress.

A pillar of strength and volatility.

Her being trembled. Shivered and shook at the impact of seeing him after all this time. That feeling swept through her like a firestorm, an awareness that flamed to life, scorching her in the truth of what she'd felt for so long.

He slowly came her way, his big boots thudding on the floor as he came.

Then he wrapped the strength of his arms around her and tugged her close.

She breathed out in release as she hugged him back, his scent all around her.

Patchouli and warm apple pie.

Home.

"I missed you so fuckin' much," he murmured.

"I missed you, too. So much. So much," she whispered back.

Raven flailed before jerking upright to the darkness of her room. She might have been jolted awake, but the nightmare still tormented her mind.

A ravaging that thundered through her veins and pounded through her spirit.

The fear that held her hostage.

Shackles and chains.

The door creaked open, and a small gasp ripped from her, then it was relief that slammed her when she realized he was there.

Otto was there.

An imposing shadow that moved through her room.

In it, she'd never felt so safe.

He came to the side of her bed. "Another bad dream?"

She nodded against the pillow, and he started to slide down the wall to the floor the way he always had.

Only Raven got brave. She reached out and grabbed his hand, and she scooted into the middle of her mattress to make him room.

Otto hesitated, the energy he was emitting so thick she could taste it.

"What are you doin', Raven?"

"Lay with me." She didn't care that it sounded like she was begging.

He warred with his reservations before he roughed a hand over the top of his head and carefully settled himself on her bed, though he was rigid, trying to keep a foot of space between them.

His hand was still in hers, and he was the one to shift and face her, moving so he was hooking his pinky with hers as he searched her face in the night.

"They're still coming at you bad?" he asked, voice low and coarse.

"They were worse while you were gone," she admitted around the thickness in her throat. Her heart was pounding so hard in her chest she wondered if he could hear it. If he could feel what whooshed and slicked through her veins.

Regret curled through his expression. "I'm so sorry I wasn't here for you."

"It's not your fault."

Blue flicked all over her face.

Studying.

Memorizing.

Maybe rewriting.

"It is, though, isn't it?"

She got brave—brave in a way she'd never done before—and she unhooked her pinky from his and reached out to scratch her nails through his beard. "You do what you have to do."

"And I'm beginning to wish I had a different choice."

The bed creaked as he rolled, and he fumbled around on her nightstand and grabbed the mirror. He started to hold it out for her to see, and she wiggled closer to him, carving out a space at his side and resting her head on his shoulder.

His spine went rigid, and she could feel the shallowness of his breaths, before he gave and curled that arm around her and dragged her closer. With the other, he lifted the mirror. "Hope you were looking at this while I was gone. Hope you saw what I see. This brave, strong, beautiful woman."

The last of his words were brand new.

Beautiful.

Woman.

A buzz rolled through her, and she snuggled closer.

He came night after night. When she dreamed and when she didn't. She'd begun to wait. Anticipating his arrival. The quiet thud of his boots across her floor and the creaking of her bed as he climbed in beside her.

When her stomach would churn, and her heart would race.

He held her close, and he whispered his belief into her ear. Filled her up with his praise. But he never touched her the way she craved for him to do.

She wanted him to push her onto her back and peel her out of her clothes.

Take her in a way she'd never been taken.

But Otto always maintained the distance. Kept an invisible barrier between them.

She wanted to push through it. Climb over it or under it. Whatever it took to get to him.

But there was an obstacle she had to face first. This guilt that soured in her conscience. The secret she'd been keeping that she wasn't sure she could keep any longer.

She was worried about Haddie. About how reckless she was being.

But the betrayal locked on her tongue. Unable to form the words that she knew would drive a blade between her and her best friend.

She couldn't do it. She couldn't.

Haddie trusted her, and she couldn't break the bond that they had formed.

Chapter
FORTY-EIGHT

Raven

I GLANCED AROUND, ALL COVERT-LIKE BEFORE I TAPPED A MESSAGE on my phone.

> Me: This is a 9-1-1. I'm in dire need of my bestie.

I mean, I needed to tell *someone*, and she was the only one I could really trust, and really, she was the only one I wanted to tell. The one who just got me in every way.

And I really, really needed to squeal about this.

Her response was almost instant.

> Charleigh: Are you in trouble?

My fingers flew across the screen.

> Me: If you mean am I in trouble because of a six-foot-five hunk of a man, then absolutely yes.

> Charleigh: Oh crap. You're definitely in big, big trouble.

> Me: Oh, it's big, all right.

I could almost hear her splutter from across the miles.

Charleigh: I did not need the vision.

Me: Karma, baby 😉

Charleigh: You're cruel...and also lucky River isn't standing over my shoulder.

Me: Like I don't trust you to keep all our conversations in confidence.

Charleigh: True. But this one is...delicate.

I took in a deep breath.

Me: Which is why I need to talk to you. Meet for lunch?

Charleigh: Absolutely. Where?

Me: Sunrise to Sunset Café across from Moonflower. It's delish. Noon o' five.

Her lunch was always during the noon hour, and I'd just close up shop for a little bit so I could meet with her.

Charleigh: It's a date.

Me: See you soon!

I felt the presence wash over me from behind. So powerful. An inundating wave.

I shifted to look over my shoulder from where I stood in the kitchen to find Otto slowly coming down the stairs from his room.

Fresh from a shower. Shorn hair damp and a clean tee stretched across his massive chest. Jeans snug and barely able to contain everything that he was underneath.

The man was a riot to my senses.

Cataclysmic.

He drove his big fingers through his hair, pushing it back, the tweak of a grin scampering over his mouth as he lumbered closer. His boots were heavy on the floor as he edged my way.

I was struck with a fresh dose of his aura.

Encircling.

Invading.

He didn't hesitate to pull me into his arms and press his nose into my hair. He breathed out what sounded like relief.

My knees went weak.

Is this what it felt like to swoon?

Yes, yes it had to be, because I felt lightheaded and my heart careened and my stomach was nothing but a toil of tumbling butterfly wings.

"Way the sight of you knocks me sideways. Way I can't think about anything else when you're standing there like that. Wearing one of these sexy as fuck dresses that you know damned well drive me out of my mind. Can't fuckin' get enough." Otto dragged his lips down the side of my neck, peppering kisses along the sensitive flesh as he went.

It knocked a whimper loose, and my head tipped to the side to grant him better access. Somehow, I managed to force myself to say, "You need to stop right there before you get carried away or else you're going to make me late."

"Thought you said I could have this delicious body any time I wanted it?" His words were nothing but bait.

Those butterflies spun. "Well, it's also said good things come to those who wait."

He grunted, and I could feel the force of his grin against the side of my neck. "So, you're saying you want me to spend the day conjuring up all the dirty things I'm going to do to you once I get you home?"

A shiver ripped down my spine. A big, big hand followed it, riding all the way down until he was gripping me by a butt cheek and tugging me against the hard, packed planes of his merciless body.

And that's what I wanted.

No mercy.

I wanted him to take me until I couldn't handle it any longer.

It was honestly a wonder that I was even walking today, the mark of him scored so deep inside me that I felt like I'd been cut in two and sewn back together.

Body achy and legs weak.

"Yes, that's exactly what I am saying to you." I shifted so it was me who was whispering in his ear. "I want you to dream about me all day while you watch me work. I want you to be thinking the whole time about the way I'm going to be wet for you, needy for you to get back inside me."

I saw no reason to act shy any longer.

A wave of lust rolled through him. Palpable and distinct. An overwhelming energy that crashed into me.

His chuckle rumbled with a delicious threat. "You are in so much trouble, Little Moonflower."

"That's what I like to hear, Burly Bear."

Otto let go of a low, ardent laugh, and he edged back, thumb tracing the contour of my cheek. "What am I going to do with you?"

"The question should be, 'What aren't you going to do to me?'"

He shook his head as he stepped back. The most arrogant smirk had taken to his expression. "Come on, let's get you downtown before I tie you to my bed so we can start answering that question."

"Well, now you're really not helping things." I shooed him farther away because I needed the man out of my vicinity before I begged him to make good on the idea.

"But I can't be late...Jimmy is going to be at the store in fifteen minutes. He's delivering a bunch of irises for a wedding that's at the lake tomorrow. I have a ton to do to get ready for it. It's going to be gorgeous."

I always made sure to get all the arrangements for big events that happened over the weekend done on Friday so it would be all set for when Millie came in on Saturday morning.

I had slung the strap of my purse over my shoulder and had started for the door when a hot hand landed on my wrist and spun me around.

Otto stood there, all the teasing gone, an intensity so profound in his features it rocked the ground beneath my feet.

A clash of conflict and hope and despair.

"That what you want, Raven? You want one of those weddings?"

I looked up at him. Unafraid. "I won't lie and say that hasn't been one of my fantasies."

Then I unwound myself from his hold and sauntered across the room toward the door that led downstairs, and I glanced at him from over my shoulder as I pulled it open.

"Besides, can you imagine what I'd look like in that dress?"

I strode through without looking back.

Deciding it was his turn to fantasize.

"Charleigh!" I shouted as I jogged across the street.

My best friend turned from where she'd been getting ready to pull open the café door with a massive smile on her face.

She was wearing pink scrubs, and her hair was in a ponytail. It was her normal work attire for where she worked at the medical office a few blocks down this same street.

She was shaking her head as she watched me beeline across the road, balancing like an expert on my five-inch heels.

These were killer skills I possessed, and I looked good while doing it, too.

There was no questioning it since I could feel the heat of Otto's gaze from where he watched me through the plate glass windows of my flower shop. He'd convinced me that he could keep it open while I went to lunch. It wasn't like he had anything better to do considering he was on guard duty.

No chance of letting me out of his sight.

But it was the way of Sanctum. If they protected strangers the way they did? You could bet that would extend to the ones they loved by a hundredfold.

"You could go for a ten-mile hike in those things, and I bet you wouldn't even twist an ankle," Charleigh called as I hopped onto the sidewalk in front of her.

I scoffed with a grin. "Hiking? Do you think I'm some kind of masochist?"

My bestie lifted a wry brow as she swung open the door. "As evidenced by the fact you make Otto carry you on his back every time we take the trail out to the lake."

"Two birds with one stone and all of that. No hiking *and* I get my legs wrapped around the man's waist."

Unfortunately, it had been from the wrong direction, but I didn't have that nasty little problem anymore.

"And it sounds like that's where they've been." She lowered her voice conspiratorially as we stepped into the cool air of the restaurant.

My heart pattered, and I angled my head in her direction. "Things might have changed a little bit since we talked yesterday."

She started to ask more, but she clipped off when Sienna rounded from behind the coffee counter and came striding our way, welcome on her face. "Hey, Raven. What are you up to?"

I hooked my arm through Charleigh's. "Having lunch with my bestie. I've been wanting to introduce you two. Charleigh, this is Sienna, my new friend I was telling you about. Sienna, meet Charleigh, my brother's fiancée, even though she was mine first."

I tacked the biggest pout I could onto the last.

Charleigh laughed, giving my arm a tug. "The two of them love to fight over who met me first."

"Obviously me." I widened my eyes in a way that claimed it. "My surly, grumpy brother would have chased her off if it hadn't been for me."

Sienna's laughter was soft as she glanced between us. "Well, Raven definitely has a way of making us feel welcome, doesn't she?"

Charleigh's gaze was soft. "She definitely does. And she's told me a lot about you. It's nice to finally meet you."

"It's nice to meet you, too."

"Sienna is going to join us for Otto's big birthday bash this weekend. She gets to finally see all the hotness that is my brother's friends."

"Well, I already got a peek at one, so I'm ahead of the game," Sienna teased.

Speculation filled Charleigh's expression.

"Theo came in for lunch one day," I explained out of the corner of my mouth as if it were a sordid secret.

Understanding dawned on Charleigh's face. "Oh…so you like them dark and terrifying."

Sienna's brow arched. "From what I've seen, I'd say you do, too. I've seen your man hanging around here."

Charleigh laughed a self-conscious sound. "He can be a little intimidating, but I promise, there is nothing but goo underneath."

Okay, that was a bald-faced lie, but we couldn't admit the real truth in front of Sienna. This world classified and contained. It made it hard to get close to anyone outside of it, but I still intended on trying.

"Well, hopefully Theo isn't too soft because I don't mind my men a little rough around the edges." Sienna let the innuendo wind into her voice.

"I already warned you that man will eat you alive."

"I'm counting on it."

She turned to the nook where the menus were stored. "So, two for lunch, or are you grabbing something to go?"

"We definitely want a table. We have some conspiring to do."

Sienna grinned. "Well, then we'd better not delay. I'm actually serving today, so I'll put you in my section."

"That would be great."

She led us to a cute table on the far side of the restaurant, the place a cross of posh and cozy. Charleigh took a seat on the long couch that ran along the back wall, and I pulled out a wooden chair across from her.

Pride filled me when I saw the dainty bouquet of flowers that sat in a vase in the middle. I loved that my floral shop made a splash here.

"Today's special is a Mediterranean salad with grilled chicken, or if you want something with a little more substance, we have a grilled ham and cheese with gouda and cheddar. It is delish. I just scarfed one down half an hour ago."

"Sign me up," I said, slapping the menu down onto the table. "I am definitely in need of some sustenance. I am starving."

From over the table, I sent Charleigh a scandalous look.

She pursed her lips, clearly dying to get the scoop.

"I'll take one, too, and an iced tea," she agreed.

"Same here," I added.

"On it," Sienna said before she walked away and disappeared through a swinging door to the back.

The second she did, Charleigh leaned forward, the eager words hushed. "Tell me everything."

A thrill left me on a shimmy of my shoulders and an ecstatic stamp of my feet under the table.

"Okay, wiggle worm," she teased. "You're more wound up than Nolan was that one time he snuck that energy drink out of Kane's cooler."

"I can't even sit still."

"I can see that. You are flying."

"Oh, believe me when I tell you I've been soaring."

"So how did all of this go down?"

"I did what you suggested yesterday. I just laid it out and told him exactly how I felt."

I took in a breath as the scene from last night played through my mind. "I told him that I was in love with him, and I'd been for a long, long time, and I demanded that he not be a coward and tell me exactly how *he* felt."

"I bet you put it to him," she mused. "My bestie is all fire when she sets her mind to something."

I hummed. "I basically told him that was it. There was no more pretending. We were either together or I was walking away."

Her brows shot for the sky. "You were pulling no punches."

"Nope. I was over it. No more tiptoeing. No more pretending."

"And I take it he manned up and confessed what's been so blatantly clear to me since the first time I saw you two together?"

Emotion crested, waves that battered against my swelling heart. "He told me he's been in love with me for just as long, but that he'd never believed himself good enough for me, so he tried to ignore it, but he couldn't do it any longer, either."

We paused when Sienna showed at our table and set two iced teas in front of us. "Here we go. It shouldn't be long for the sandwiches."

"Thank you," we both said, stalling out the conversation as she walked away before Charleigh returned her attention to me.

"I'm so incredibly happy for you. I knew he would see through his fears to what really mattered, and that's you."

Tears burned my eyes, and I swallowed it back and shot her a grin. "I am proud to announce that your girl here no longer has her V-card."

I lifted my tea for a toast.

She giggled as she clinked her glass against mine. Her expression turned cunning. "Now that much was obvious. That man's hands are written all over you."

"Oh, you should really see what's written on me."

She choked a laugh, though she let her grin wind into something shameless. "He clearly did my bestie right. You looked so loved up crossing that street that you basically floated across it."

"Pssh. Those are just my mad skills in these shoes."

She chuckled a soft sound before she sobered, reached out, and squeezed my hand where it rested on the table. "This is truly amazing. I know what you've gone through to get here. I know the pain you suffered and the fear you've carried, and I'm so thankful that you found the one you can trust with it."

A tear got free. "When he looks at me, Charleigh?" My head barely shook as I fought the crash of emotion. "When he looks at me, I simultaneously feel safe and brave. Vulnerable and powerful. I feel like I can really be me."

"And who are you being yourself with?" Sienna's voice was soft as she stood at the side of the table with two plates in hand.

Surprise lurched me back. I hadn't even noticed she was there. I swept the tear away and smiled up at her. "Can you keep a secret?"

"Hello, what are friends for?"

"Otto loves me."

It felt so good to say it.

Confusion spiraled around her as she set the plates in front of us. "Wait, this is supposed to be a secret? I thought you two were already a thing? The man looks like he wants to ravage you every time he looks at you."

Charleigh's laugh was knowing as she turned her gaze on me. "Told you."

Charleigh and I laughed and giggled and whispered our way through lunch, a lightness taking us over as we enjoyed a meal together. It felt simple and right, the way we'd always been together.

Gratitude overflowed my chest.

We talked a little about River and the rest of Sanctum. About what they would think. Charleigh agreed that Otto needed to be the one who broke the news to River.

We skated over the topic of what had happened at Otto's place the other morning, neither of us wanting to bring voice to something so heinous, though we could feel the weight of it hovering around us in the distance.

Charleigh grimaced when she looked at her phone to check the time. "Crap, I need to get back to the office before I'm late."

"As if Dr. Reynolds could ever be angry with you."

Charleigh had been working as a medical assistant at Dr. Reynolds' office before she'd known his connection to Sovereign Sanctum. Before she knew his part in helping women and children make their way to safety. Before he'd saved her life.

Now, she was taking night courses to become an RN with hopes of moving forward with becoming a nurse practitioner, her goal to slide into Dr. Reynolds' position once he retired. She wanted an active role in changing the lives of those who came to Sanctum for help.

She chuckled. "Well, I don't want to push my luck."

"I'm pretty sure he couldn't function without you," I said as I pushed out my chair and stood.

Charleigh stood, too, mischief in her voice when she leaned in and said, "I guess I am pretty great."

I gasped and touched my heart. "Oh, my goodness, I can't believe it. I'm finally rubbing off on my bestie. Look at you, not hesitating to claim how great you are."

It was something Haddie had taught me. Something I'd taken with me from the tragedy.

Never be afraid of claiming who you are.

"I guess you are, aren't you?"

We walked to the front counter and paid, and I hugged Sienna like mad and told her I couldn't wait to hang out with her on Saturday.

Then Charleigh and I stepped out onto the sidewalk. The sun stood proud at the center of the sky.

Warm rays rained from above, though there was the hint of cool at the edges of the air.

Fall approaching.

I leaned forward and hugged Charleigh with all my might. "Thank you so much for everything you've done for me, Charleigh. The way you've changed so much inside of me and made me look at myself differently."

Her scoff was soggy. "I'm pretty sure it's the other way around."

"That just means we both needed each other."

She took one step back, her smile soft as she squeezed my hands between us before she turned and started up the sidewalk in the direction of the medical plaza. I watched her go, and she tipped her attention down as she typed something on her phone.

One second later, my phone buzzed in my hand. I grinned when I opened it to see the message.

Charleigh: Have fun, you sexy bitch.
Make sure that man loves you up right.

Glee skated through me. I really was rubbing off on her.

I tapped out a response, my head downturned as my fingers flew across the screen.

Me: I intend to.

I started to straighten when I felt the shift in the air.

The cool breeze that had brushed my skin in comfort turned to a chill.

An ice slick that streaked down my spine and pooled as dread in the pit of my stomach. I started to whirl toward it, toward the foreboding that covered me like a dark shroud.

To pinpoint it.

To stop it.

Only there was no time.

No time to process anything except for the blur at the corner of my eye. A thunder of footsteps and a clamor of evil. The flash of a man raising an arm with a brick in his hand.

A brick that he smashed against the side of my head.

Chapter
FORTY-NINE

OTTO

IT WAS A COUPLE OF MINUTES BEFORE ONE WHEN RAVEN AND
Charleigh stepped out of the café.

My insides stirred, a whipping of need to get back to my girl.

I was so fucked.

So fucked considering I hadn't seen her in all of fifty minutes,
and I was already sick to my stomach at missing her.

She and Charleigh were huggin' it out in front of the restaurant.

The two friends who'd become sisters clinging to each other in
the middle of the sidewalk as they whispered something under their
breaths.

Could feel the emotion radiate from all the way over there. It
clutched my chest in a grip of thankfulness that Raven had someone
like Charleigh.

Someone to confide in.

Someone to trust.

Knew their relationship had changed both of them, their belief and encouragement in each other pushing the other toward their
goals and dreams.

Didn't mind that I had likely been the main topic of conversation
during their lunch, either. Without question, Charleigh had Raven's

back, no matter what, even when her heart belonged to the man who was going to hate me when he found out.

He would.

The oath I'd made him all those years ago swirled through my head.

Raven might have liked to believe that he would see through it to support us, but she didn't know the full extent of the promise I'd made to her brother.

But I wouldn't be so much a coward that I would keep it from him for long. No chance I would keep the woman like a dirty secret.

Charleigh pulled away, then turned and started up the sidewalk. Raven watched her go, her expression filling with a grin when she lifted her phone to look at it.

I started to round the counter so I could meet her at the door, just needing to get her back into my arms, when I felt it.

A change.

An omen that blustered through the atmosphere.

The sense that I always got when something bad was about to go down.

Nothing but a slick of wickedness.

A thick stench that coated the oxygen and turned it evil.

I went clamoring for the door, shouting her name from within the confines of Moonflower.

"Raven!"

But it was too fucking late.

Too fuckin' late because some vile motherfucker came from out of nowhere. Manifesting from thin air, emerging from the crowd in a flurry of depravity.

Panic surged through me when I saw he had a brick in his hand.

My hand was on the knob at the same second as Raven whirled his direction.

Sensing it, too.

No, Raven, no.

My heart leaped to my throat, and I ripped open the door and tore out onto the sidewalk at the same time as he brought the brick down hard and struck her on the side of her head.

She didn't scream or fight.

She didn't do anything but crumble to the ground.

"Raven. No!"

Fury and fear bashed at my senses, hate careening through my veins and sickness churning in my guts.

No. Raven. No.

Head spinning, I darted out into the road. Horns blared and people shouted their disdain. I just dodged the cars that screeched to a stop to avoid hitting me, zigzagging through the chaos as I raced for her.

Confusion bound, and I could hear the shouts of concerned bystanders, though it was a dull drone that could barely penetrate the tumult that cluttered my mind.

Second my feet hit the sidewalk, I was shoving people aside so I could get to her.

Anguish cut through the middle of me when I saw her. Cleaving and flaying as I looked down at this beautiful girl with blood pouring out of a wound on the side of her head.

I dropped to my knees, my hands shaking out of control as I brushed back her hair so I could get a better look at where she'd been hit. "Oh God, Raven."

Feet came clattering up from behind, and Charleigh was on her knees beside me, horror in her expression as she began to inspect her.

"Is she okay?" I grated through the clawing pain.

Charleigh's hands were much surer than mine, going to her wrist to check her pulse and then brushing her hair back so she could inspect the wound.

"She was knocked out. The cut is probably less of an issue than the concussion she likely has."

Raven moaned, and I nearly wept with the surge of relief that slammed me.

She blinked those inky eyes at me in confusion.

"Baby." It gushed out of me, then I turned to Charleigh, my voice urgent. "Stay with her. Need to find this asshole."

I jumped to my feet and started pushing back through the crowd. The bastard had fled in the direction that he'd come from, disappearing around the corner of the building.

Motherfucker was dead.

Bloodlust reeled through my being, violence twitching in my hands.

I ran that way, my boots thundering against the sidewalk as I followed the same path he'd taken. My heart beat a manic rate, so fuckin' heavy that I could hear the thud of it in my ears. A tempo that screamed that I had to find this piece of shit. End the threat that had been made.

I made it to a T where the alley met the backside of the buildings, a long chain-link fence boxing the area in.

My attention darted from one direction to the other, trying to discern which way this pussy might have gone.

A forest rose high beyond the fence.

Monster had left no trace, no indication of which way he'd went.

The alleys were basically empty except for a few cars parked at odd angles behind the back entrances to the buildings.

There was no movement.

No sign that he'd escaped down either direction.

Frustration blustered. I couldn't give up. I ran for the fence that was about seven-feet high, and I jumped up and hauled myself over the top.

I dropped to my feet on the other side. My attention raced, delving through the thick foliage and leaves, looking for any suggestion that someone had come this way.

I could see that the wild grasses had been freshly trampled, and I took off, following the same path. My breaths grew heavy and harsh as I raced through the woods, ducking and diving beneath the branches, smacking the ones that whipped into my face out of the way.

A frantic desperation lit inside me.

The outright need to find who would dare harm Raven.

The trail curved right, and I increased my pace as I wound around a giant tree. Then I skidded to a stop when I found the tracks had shifted.

Dirt bike tracks.

My hands fell to my knees as I bent in two.

Heaving for air.

"Fuck," I spat, whirling around like I was going to catch the motherfucker, all while knowing he was already long gone.

"Goddamn it."

Gulping for oxygen, I turned around and ran back through the woods, no chance of catching up to him.

The aggression riding my being didn't abate as I made it back to the fence and threw myself over it.

The frenzy still buzzed through me in electric shocks as I flew around the building to where a crush of people were huddled around Raven.

It looked like every person on the block had piled out of the restaurants and stores and circled her.

I shoved back through, and I nearly crumpled in a ball when those big raven eyes blinked up at me. Arrows that impaled. They dropped me straight to my knees, and I took her face in my hands. "Fuck, Raven, are you okay?"

She nodded against my palms. "I think so."

"I'm so sorry. So fuckin' sorry I let him get to you." Guilt ate up my insides.

"It isn't your fault."

"Should've been nearby. Right next to you."

Only my fiery little vixen would scoff in a situation like this. "I'm the one who told you I wanted some privacy with Charleigh."

"Yeah, well I shouldn't have given it to you when I knew someone was after you," I murmured quiet enough that the spectators wouldn't be able to hear.

She looked at me, the question clear. My head barely shook, a silent confession that I'd failed her in that, too.

Bastard had gotten away, and I wasn't any closer to having an idea of who it was.

"It seems like maybe it wasn't as bad as it looked," Charleigh cut in, no doubt trying to assuage the regret that flayed me wide. "But we do need to get her in to see the doctor to get her checked out to make sure."

It was right then that the blare of sirens whirred in the distance. Dread sank to the pit of my stomach. Someone had called 9-1-1.

But why wouldn't they?

They were only doing what was right.

Helping.

They didn't have the first clue that this all had to remain under wraps, which really pissed me off, too, the fact that Raven was trapped in this life that put a target on her head.

With the bleep of a siren, an ambulance came to a stop in the middle of the road with its lights flashing. Carefully, I picked Raven up and nestled her in my arms, one under her back and the other under her legs.

I carried her toward the tail of the ambulance, shouting at the paramedic who hopped out.

"We need to get her to Dr. Reynolds' office."

He started to open his mouth to tell me why it was against protocol, but I cut him off, grinding out, "You can check her inside the truck." My tone told him there was no room for argument. "But right now, you're going to get her to Dr. Reynolds' office and you're going to do it fast."

I wound around him and climbed into the ambulance with Raven still in my arms. I sat down on the bench, holding her tight against my chest while the paramedics piled back in.

Charleigh hopped in, too.

Casting me a glance of worry as the siren blipped again before we took off down the street.

"CT scan is clear."

My head rocked back against the white brick wall as Dr. Reynolds delivered the news that we'd been waiting on for the last half hour.

He'd had her taken to the small local emergency room in the building next to his to get the scan.

"Thank God," I muttered as I scrubbed both palms over my face like it might be enough to eradicate the worry that had held me hostage.

Guilt constricting.

Nerves going haywire that I might have allowed Raven to have been severely injured.

A gush of air heaved from River's lungs. "Fuck. You sure she's okay?"

"The CT scan showed no brain swelling or trauma. It was likely it was the pain of the impact that brought her down and not a true unconscious event. There is no evidence of a concussion, but there is still a chance she sustained a mild one, so I expect a full recovery without any issues. Two stitches in her head are all it took to close the wound. She should be ready to go home soon."

Without saying anything else, Dr. Reynolds dipped back out of the private office where River and I were waiting.

River nodded, relief and rage in his stance as he stared at the linoleum floor. "Can't believe this monster, coming up on an innocent like that. In the middle of the fuckin' day on a busy street."

I pushed to standing, knees wobbling beneath me with the amount of shame that bore down on my shoulders. "So damned sorry."

A vicious frown carved into his face as he turned his attention to me. "Not your fault, man."

"Should've been there." I could say it a billion times, but it wouldn't rewind time. It wouldn't take me back so I could stop it from happening.

"You *were* there," he said, giving me his belief and encouragement.

It only made me feel insurmountably worse. Guilt eating me alive at the secret I was keeping. At the betrayal I was committing.

"Should have gotten to her before it happened." My throat was so thick I could barely get the words out.

River took the two steps required to bring him to standing in front of me, and he reached out and squeezed my shoulder as he stared at me in emphasis. Eyes that were the same color as his sister's boiled like black, menacing flames. "We're going to get this fucker. We're going to hunt him down and make sure he doesn't have the capacity to ever hurt her again."

My hands curled into fists.

Yeah, this bastard was going down.

Before I could say anything else, the door nudged open, and Charleigh poked her head through. "Raven is ready for you both to come back in."

River tipped his head at me and immediately strode for the door. He pushed his face into Charleigh's cheek when he got to her, breathing her in like it was the only thing that tethered him to sanity.

Raven was the only thing that did it for me.

Seeing her sitting up on the examination table when we pushed into the room, still wearing a medical gown, her hair tied back and better exposing the spot where she'd gotten two stitches at the very farthest edge of her left forehead.

"Raven," River wheezed, going straight to her side.

"I'm fine," she said.

"Can't believe this is happening. Have done everything…everything in my power to make sure you aren't touched by the choices we've made." His apology rasped in the tense air.

"We don't know that it has anything to do with Sanctum." She kept her voice low, her brow knitting in emphasis. "And even if it does, I'm just as much a part of Sanctum as the rest of you."

Those eyes met mine from over her brother's shoulder.

It was the last place I wanted her. In the middle of our mess. And I was only dragging her deeper into the depths of my own depravity.

A strained sigh rippled out of River. "Shouldn't be that way. Only thing I've ever wanted is for you to be safe."

His sentiments echoed mine. Of course, that's what we both wanted. Except he didn't have the first clue how deep that ambition really went. How I felt like my insides were being shredded, thinking of her in the line of fire, all while knowing it would devastate me— leave me in complete ruins—if I were to have to let her go.

Raven glanced at Charleigh, then her brother, before her attention hooked on me.

"We all have to make choices for ourselves about where we belong. About what is most important to us and what risks we're willing to take. And I choose to be here. With you all. As a part of you. It has always been worth the risk to me, and it always will be."

It was delivered with quiet, determined strength.

A hushed ferocity.

Beautiful, brave girl.

My throat trembled as I took the silent message she was delivering.

River let go of a disbelieving laugh. "Guess it's in your blood, huh?"

"Pumping strong right through the middle of me."

His amusement was short-lived, no one quite sure how to traverse this disaster. "What do you want to do from here, Raven?"

And that bottomless gaze was on me when she murmured, "I want to go home...with Otto."

I didn't know if it was the way she said it. What he heard or felt or sensed.

But there was no missing the suspicion carved deep in River's brow when he swiveled to look at me.

We were both held in it for an eternal beat.

Then he blinked it away like he refused to believe something so foul in me.

Chapter

FIFTY

Raven

"**I**CAN WALK, OTTO."

He grunted at me as he dipped into the passenger side of my car and slipped his arms underneath me. "Not gonna happen, darlin."

"And why is that?"

"Because I need you as close to me as I can get you, and I can't think of any better way than having you in my arms."

"Oh, I can think of ways for us to get closer," I told him, letting the innuendo wind into my voice, going for light.

We were in dire need of it since this afternoon had been too much.

Too dark and strained and terrifying.

I might have tried to play it off, but I didn't think there would be any way for either of us to shuck the horror that had taken us prisoner.

Those old chains that had tried to keep me down cinching tight around my wrists.

The worry and dread and reservations that Otto had carried slithering back from their confines, weaving their way back through his consciousness.

I saw it, so clear in the seething blue of his eyes. The way he watched me when he straightened with me in the stability of his powerful hold.

He thought he was to blame, but he also wasn't cowering behind it.

To me, it felt as if a new fire had lit.

"And that is not going to happen, either. You are going to rest. Doctor's orders."

"What does the doctor know?" I let my arms dangle loosely around his neck as I sent a pout his way. "I think you are the only medicine I need."

He sent me a look that told me he was on to my game. "You already know you have the seduction down pat, Raven. How about you do me a favor and don't tempt me, yeah? Need to make sure you're whole and healing before I ravish you."

My pout deepened, though I settled my cheek against the surety of his chest, letting him hold me as he carried me up the interior steps of the garage to the door. He maneuvered me around easily, like I didn't weigh anything, getting it open with hardly jostling me at all. He carried me directly to the couch and laid me across it.

"Don't move," he ordered.

"So bossy. The doctor said I needed to rest tonight, not that I'm bedridden."

Otto climbed to his knees beside me, leaning in close. "Don't care if you barely have a headache. I'm gonna take care of you. You haven't met the meaning of *bossy* yet."

A shiver rolled through me. "Why do I like the sound of that?"

Otto sighed, half in frustration and half in affection. "Always askin' for trouble, aren't you, Little Moonflower?" He gathered my hand and kissed across my knuckles as his expression turned somber. "Scared the fuck outta me, baby. Seeing you go down like that."

I reached out with my free hand and trembled my fingertips over the sharp edges of his face. "I was scared, too. But I'm fine. I'm right here. Whole and healing. It was nothing."

"It's not *nothing* when someone was able to get that close to you.

Close enough that they made you bleed. If I said I wasn't going to let you out of my sight before, I'm going to be stuck to you like glue now."

"I like the sound of that, too." There was no teasing to that. It was pure softness. My gratitude to him.

A strained second passed before he croaked, "Who is this bastard?"

He asked it against the back of my hand, pressing it to his forehead and squeezing his eyes closed as if he were praying for the answer to drop out of the sky.

"I don't know…but we will find him."

Otto slowly opened his eyes. Determination roiled in their depths. "We will. I'm going to toss every speck of dirt until I uncover who this asshole is."

"I know you will."

"Good." Then he stood, a buttress of intimidation and fortitude.

"Where are you going?" I asked.

"To make you some soup."

I didn't know whether to giggle or roll my eyes. "I don't have the flu, silly boy."

Leaning down, he pressed a growl to the uninjured side of my head, though it rumbled with affection. "I'm going to take care of you and you're going to like it."

A patter fluttered in my pulse, and I grinned as he pulled away. "Fine, Burly Bear."

He rounded the couch, and I could feel his heavy footsteps thudding across the floor as he headed for the kitchen, the man an earthquake to my senses.

"But if you really want to take care of me, then you'll bring me a glass of wine," I shouted, trying to keep from smiling when I did.

Already anticipating what was coming.

"You little vixen. What am I supposed to do with you?"

It wasn't a question because I had a hunch that we both already knew.

Chapter
FIFTY-ONE

OTTO

Twenty-Seven Years Old

OTTO STARED AT HER THROUGH THE DUSKINESS OF THE NIGHT. Face so fuckin' pretty he couldn't breathe. Couldn't move. Couldn't do anything but lay with her on that bed with her tucked tight against him.

What the hell am I doing?

This was Raven Tayte he had in his arms. So goddamn off limits it felt like he was committing a mortal sin just inhaling her air.

Those jagged puffs that kept jutting from her lungs as she gazed across at him. Looking at him in a way she shouldn't.

And for the last two weeks, he'd been looking at her in a way he shouldn't, too.

He didn't know what'd happened between him getting sent away and then. But it'd struck him like a bullet when he'd looked up and found her standing in the doorway to the kitchen when he'd come back to the house after he'd been released.

A thunderclap.

A lightning bolt.

The feeling that had jolted through him so intense he was sure he'd sustained burn marks across his heart.

He couldn't do this.

But still, he came to her night after night, holding her this way, ensuring that the dreams never came.

Raven smoothed a timid hand up his chest, and he struggled to drag the oxygen into his too-tight lungs. Because when he did inhale? He was only inhaling her.

Her innocence.

Her goodness.

Her sweet moonflower scent.

"I'm so glad you're back," she finally whispered.

"Hate that I was away from you," he muttered into the shadows that crawled the walls and pelted at the windows.

"I hated that you were, too. The whole time...I felt like...like a piece of myself was missing." She whispered the confession through the hush that infiltrated the room.

He pulled her closer, in a way he knew better than to do. Her heart beat violently at his chest, the air dense and rippling with dark, decadent things. Things he couldn't contemplate. Things he knew would make him the biggest monster of all.

But he couldn't stop the way his spirit pitched toward hers, as if she had a hook impaled directly on his being. Connected to her in a way he couldn't be.

But it was there, a bright light that radiated around her and drew him close.

A connection.

One that was deep and profound.

Shifting, Raven propped herself up onto her elbow, and Otto rolled to his back. His guts stretched tight, and his fingers moved on their own accord, brushing over the gorgeous swell of her cheek before they were threading up into her hair.

Her lips parted, and those inky eyes dipped to his mouth. His mouth that watered with the urge to draw her against him.

To taste and devour.

"I shouldn't be here like this," he forced out.

Rejection of the notion billowed across her face, all mixed with a muddling of hope. "I think this is exactly where you're supposed to be. Here, like this. With me. I..."

Hesitation brimmed through her, though he could read everything she was trying to say in that gaze that covered him in an embrace.

In trust and truth.

"Do you feel it?" she asked, voice timid and brave.

His chest stretched tight. No doubt, he should keep the words locked tight, but he was unable to hold them back. "Yeah, I feel it, Raven. But that doesn't mean we should—"

Raven's phone suddenly started vibrating from where it sat on her nightstand, and Otto glanced to the side to see the screen light with Haddie's name.

Worry instantly gripped him, especially when he saw the same damned thing ripped through Raven's expression.

She bit down on her bottom lip.

Reservations and fear spiked through the air.

Otto grunted, "Answer it."

With a trembling hand, Raven reached over him and grabbed it, and she pushed back to sitting, her voice quiet when she muttered Haddie's name.

Haddie started rambling, obviously crying, her words just loud enough for Otto to be able to make out since Raven had the phone pressed to her ear. "He just dumped me. On the freaking street. He's such a jerk, Raven."

Otto's baby sister gasped and choked, while a vat of rage plunged into his stomach. It took everything he had not to rip the phone out of Raven's hold.

"Where are you?" she whispered as those eyes came up to meet with his.

Guilt and dread roiled in them.

There was a break, then Haddie mumbled the crossroads.

What the fuck? She was halfway across town from where she was supposed to be. Near Iron Owls' club.

Agitation barreled through his senses.

"I'll be there in a minute to get you," Raven said.

"I'm so sorry. I'm really sorry," Haddie rambled.

"It's okay," Raven promised. "I'll be right there."

The line went dead, and Raven slowly let the phone drop to her lap.

Otto eased up to sitting, careful since he felt like he might split apart. "The fuck was that?"

Raven gulped, and she looked away like she was trying to hide whatever secret she was supposed to keep.

"Raven…please. This is my sister we're talking about."

She looked back at him, that guilt in full force. "I don't want to betray her confidence."

His eyes squeezed closed for a beat, then he was urging, "Is Haddie in trouble? If she is, I need to know."

A single tear slipped down her cheek, and warily, she nodded. "She's been seeing Gideon."

Horror belted through him.

Alarm and a hatred so fierce that he couldn't contain it.

He flew out of the bed and started for the door. "Don't worry about pickin' her up. That's on me."

The words were coated in disgust.

"Otto, please, don't…" Raven scrambled off the bed behind him.

He whipped the door open, then he came to a crashing halt when he slammed into a body on the other side.

River.

Fuck.

With his hand trembling like a bitch, he reached behind and closed Raven's door.

Darkness reigned in the narrow hall, though he could make out the speculation and something that looked too close to animosity glow in River's dark eyes.

"What the fuck is goin' on?" his best friend growled.

A landslide of shame slammed into Otto, and his throat constricted so tight he could hardly speak. "I heard Raven having a nightmare."

What bullshit.

She hadn't had one in two weeks.

Not since he'd been going to her.

Not since he'd been holding her.

River took a step toward him. He might have tried to keep it in check, but Otto could feel the combativeness roll through his body as he backed Otto up to the wall. "You sure that's all it was?"

An accusation lined the words.

"River…" Otto didn't even know what to say, but River had plenty to fill the tension that curdled the air.

"You think I haven't noticed the way you've been lookin' at her? You think I don't know you've been slinking into her room night after night?"

Otto's head shook. "No, man. Would never fuckin' cross you like that."

River came closer, getting right up in Otto's face. "She's innocent, man. Want to keep her that way. Outside of this life."

"You know I'd never touch her like that. She's a sister to me, and that's all she's ever going to be. That's it. Swear it. Swear it on our friendship. On our brotherhood. You never have to worry about me goin' against that."

Otto wanted to vomit saying the words.

The lies he had to force between clenched teeth.

But he had to cling to those lies. Believe them. Take them on for himself.

Because he couldn't…he couldn't stoop to being so vile.

Raven deserved so much more than he could ever offer. More than he could ever give. He wanted the world for her, not the Hell their crew had made their home.

A bit of the suspicion drained from River's expression, and he stepped back and gave Otto a tight nod. "I know it, man. I just…she's grown now, and I don't fuckin' know how to handle that. How to keep protecting her from the evil in this world. Can't fuckin' handle the thought of someone doing her wrong. Not again. She's too good. She's far too good."

Otto reached out and squeezed his shoulder. "Know it. We can't stand aside and watch it happen. Not to either of our sisters." Otto hesitated then leaned in and murmured around the rage that was still seething inside him. "Which is why I'm gonna need your help."

"You're all sure you want to get involved in this?" Disquiet whirred through Otto's senses as he peered out into the night where he and his crew lurked in the darkness of the alley, waiting on the right moment to strike.

"You think we're gonna let you go this alone?" Kane scoffed. "Asshole messes with you, he messes with the rest of us."

"That's right," Theo and River agreed, and Cash barely gave a nod from where he leaned against the wall.

Still, nerves rattled through Otto, his mind a slog of second thoughts that he was having about dragging his brothers into the war he was about to start.

But truth be told, Gideon and Dusty had started that war that night almost three years ago when they'd sought Haddie and Raven out at the club's bar, and he'd sealed it when he'd set Otto up to go down for possession.

Otto was sure that Gideon had been responsible.

Sure that it hadn't been random.

Gideon had never liked him. A sentiment Otto had wholeheartedly returned.

He was supposed to be his brother.

Iron Owls swearing an oath of loyalty to each other.

But there'd always been something about Gideon and his group that had set Otto off kilter. No trust to be found. And the bastard had proven Otto had a right to be leery time and again.

Now, it'd grown to this rampant hate that tore at Otto's insides.

He still couldn't believe that Haddie had been with this fucker the whole time he'd been locked away. Killed him to think of his sister being used up by this scumbag.

Otto had confronted her when he'd picked her up in the middle of the night two days ago. And he'd nearly gone on a murder spree when Haddie had admitted that Gideon had hit her earlier that night when they'd gotten into an argument.

Otto had demanded that she never talk to him again. Warned her all over again how dangerous he was. Told her he was pretty sure he'd been responsible for setting him up.

Haddie had promised she'd cut things off, but that didn't mean this betrayal wasn't going to go without retribution.

This motherfucker was going to get the message that Otto wasn't one to be trifled with. He'd fuckin' destroy anyone who messed with his sister.

Strains of country music infiltrated the air from the dive bar that sat on the outskirts of the city. Trent had given Otto the inside that Gideon and his crew were going on a run on that side of town, and Otto knew from experience that the assholes would likely end up here.

It was another clue that things had gone amiss in the ranks of Iron Owls, fact that Trent was giving them up. Trent wasn't going to stand for someone fucking with River and Otto's sisters. Gideon should have fuckin' known what was coming for him.

"You ready to let these motherfuckers know they messed with the wrong Owls?" Theo spat as he flicked his cigarette to the ground and stubbed it out with the toe of his boot.

"Yup, let's do it," Kane said, tossing his neck to the side to crack it.

Each of the men shared a look. Their own loyalty. They might have been part of the Owls, but there was no oath greater than the one the five of them had made to each other.

Then Otto scooped up the can of gasoline, and the five of them strode around the corner, steps long and full of purpose as they moved for the row of seven bikes parked out front. The ones they knew well.

The ones they made quick work of toppling into a pile and dousing with gasoline.

And Otto?

His grin was far too satisfied when he struck the match and watched the bikes go up in flames.

Chapter
FIFTY-TWO

Raven

I awoke held in the strength of Otto's arms. His breaths were long and deep, and his lids barely fluttered as he searched through his dreams.

Joy gushed from my spirit.

A deluge that surged and flooded, spilling through my body and overriding every question and reservation I'd ever held in my heart.

My gaze raced to take him in like this—so at peace—all the volatility that he radiated washed away, like he was captive to the same joy that bound me to him.

Affection pulsed as I traced the harsh, gorgeous edges of his face. Over his sharp brow and distinct nose, down to his jaw that was covered in stubble and the designs that covered his neck.

Carefully, I moved, slipping out from under the sheets and swinging a leg over his middle. As if he sensed the movement in his sleep, he followed the action, his hands gliding over my bottom and up to my waist as he rolled onto his back.

He groaned when I pressed myself against his cock. He was hard, so big beneath me that I had to wonder if what he'd been chasing behind his closed lids was me.

I thought maybe so because when they fluttered open there was no surprise on his face. There was only a cocky contentedness in the tweak of the smile that stretched across his full, plump lips.

I rolled slowly over him, making that smile grow.

"What do you think you're doin'?"

My own grin took to my mouth, and I tried to play coy. "What does it look like I'm doing? Wishing you happy birthday, obviously."

His hands smoothed back down my bottom as I slowly rocked over him. "Best fuckin' birthday I've ever had. Waking up with you like this. A goddess hovering over me with the sun shining all over her stunning face."

I edged forward, planting a hand on the mattress beside his head so I could whisper close to his lips. "And it's only six in the morning."

I had on a tank, and he reached over and pushed the fabric up a fraction to reveal the words tattooed on my side. Gentle fingertips trailed up the ink as if he were making the statement for me.

I will make it to the sunrise.

Here, with him, I wanted to stand in the sun.

Still, his voice was a grumble as he said, "And you're supposed to be resting."

My head barely shook. "I'm fine. I don't even have a headache."

"Raven," he started to argue, and I closed the distance between our mouths, breathing the words through the brush of my lips. "I intend on celebrating you all day, Otto Hudson. Again and again. In every way that brings you pleasure."

"Raven." That time my name was a needy moan, and a ripple of satisfaction went blazing when I realized he was giving in.

He nudged me back so he could stare up at me, and a big hand cupped my cheek. "Are you sure you're not hurting?"

"Oh, I'm hurting, Otto. Aching because I'm empty, and only you can fill me up." I went for flirty. A tease. Hoping he would take the bait because I truly was hurting.

Hurting because of the way I needed him. The way I always had, and now that he was mine, I wanted to sate that need time and again.

Forever.

Endlessly.

"Yeah, you have that seduction part down pat, don't you, Little Moonflower? You know I can't deny you."

"Why would you want to?"

He sat upright, bringing our chests flush. Flames sparked at the connection. A greedy sound worked its way up my throat, and my nails sank into his bare shoulders.

The muscles flexed and danced below them, his strength undulating through me on a wave.

"I can't, Raven. Can't resist you any longer." His voice was hoarse.

Our noses were an inch apart, and my eyes flicked all over his face. "That's because this is exactly where you're supposed to be. Here, like this. With me. No longer denying what we were meant to be."

"Is this what you were meant to be, Little Moonflower? Mine?"

"Yes. Just like you were meant to be mine."

"Then it sounds like this is definitely going to be the best birthday I've ever had."

"I think I know how to make it even better," I murmured as I edged back so I could pull him from his briefs.

Otto groaned as I fisted him, stroking him slow and hard as I watched the pleasure rattle through his features. "Oh, yeah. This birthday is definitely gettin' better and better. Only one thing might make it extraordinary," he rumbled.

"What's that?"

"Unwrapping you."

A gasp rocked free when he suddenly tossed me off him and onto my back. I bounced on the mattress, and I was giggling as he climbed onto his knees.

Fully predatory. Sporting the most scandalous smirk I'd ever seen.

Excitement buzzed through my belly. A torch of anticipation glowed bright.

He reached out and took the hem of my tank, lifting it before he carefully pulled it over my head.

Cool air breezed over my flesh, and goosebumps erupted as arousal rushed to my core.

"You sure are wasting no time. And here I was worried you might be one of those guys who carefully unwraps a present so the paper can be reused."

Okay, I totally knew he wasn't. I'd watched this man tear into every gift I'd ever given him, far too eager to find what was hidden inside.

"Nah, darlin'. The real treasure is what's underneath."

He had the tiny scrap of undies I was wearing tattered with a quick jerk of his hand.

I yelped at the tiny sting against my skin, shivers rolling through me because I liked it so much.

"And look at that. Best gift I've ever been given. One I'm going to cherish for the rest of my life," he said, gaze devouring me as he hovered high on his knees

I spread mine in invitation. "All yours, birthday boy."

Otto chuckled a dark sound. "That's right, baby. All mine."

He was out of his underwear and picking me up and spinning me around in the flash of a second. He pressed my front to the headboard at the same second as he thrust into me from behind.

Bliss raked up my throat on a surprised shout, then I whimpered his name when he withdrew and then drove right back in.

"Otto."

"Fuck, you feel so good," he growled as he wound a fist up in my hair.

He pulled my head to the side and laved kisses along the sensitive flesh of my neck. "So goddamn good. Nothing in my life, Raven Tayte. Nothing in my life has ever felt as good as this. Nothin' in this world as good as you. Not one thing."

I held onto the headboard as he filled me to the brim. He kept himself plastered against my back, his arms wrapped so tight around me I knew there was no chance he'd ever let me go.

His movements were deep and hard as he began to move.

Intensity filled the morning air. A dense awareness that consumed. His grunts low and his whispers soft.

Passion bound, a rippling of energy that crackled through the room.

Warm rays of sunlight cut through the lush trees that surrounded his house, but it was still dim enough outside that I could see our reflection through the panes of glass over the top of the headboard. Could see the ecstasy carved through his expression as he possessed me in a way I'd never been possessed.

No question or reservation left.

Just us.

Just this.

He took my hands and pressed them to the window, his fingers threaded through mine as he kissed along my jaw as he rolled into me.

"Nothing, Raven. Nothing as good as this. You are the piece I've been missing."

I turned my head toward him, taking his mouth in a fervid kiss as I arched my hips back, basically sitting on his lap as I ground against him, desperate to chase the feeling that swept through me like a windstorm.

A howling of pleasure that whipped through my body and wept in my ears.

"Otto...please. Yes...I'm..."

"I can feel it, Raven. Your sweet cunt gripping me tight. Can sense it. The way every inch of you glows. My moonflower. Most gorgeous fuckin' bloom...shining in the darkness and leading me to the light."

I came apart at that. The bliss breaking me in two.

A torrential downpour that gushed through me in a flashflood of rapture.

A desirous moan erupted with it, and Otto swallowed it down as he kissed and kissed me, his fucks hard as he gripped me against the fiery planes of his drenched flesh.

Pleasure throbbed and rolled, and Otto fully curled himself around me as he gave. I could feel its sparks. His own glow that burst wide open. Blinding bliss that ruptured the air and streaked through our bodies.

We both were panting and covered in sweat when the shocks finally stopped shooting through us. Otto pried me from the headboard, and I sagged against him when he picked me up.

He shifted and laid us down on the bed, facing each other.

Silence stretched between us.

An awareness.

A promise.

Just this knowing that we had no end.

"Happy birthday," I finally whispered, no tease to my voice.

Otto reached out and ran his knuckle down the side of my face. "Best birthday ever."

"I want to spend every one of them with you," I admitted through the calm stillness that had taken over his room.

A soft puff of air escaped his nose, and he kept tracing his fingers over the contours of my face. "Have spent the last seven years wanting that, Raven. Wanting to belong to you. Wanting to be the lucky bastard who got to sleep next to you and wake up with you in his arms. The lucky bastard who got to love you and cherish you and give you everything in this world that you've ever wanted."

"And the one thing I wanted was you."

"Guess we spent a whole lot of time wishing for the same thing. And now, I'm gonna watch my moonflower glow beneath every moon and shine beneath every sun. Can't wait to spend my life getting to watch you stretch those wings and soar."

Euphoria singed through my being, scorching my heart and blistering my soul.

A dent furrowed between Otto's eyes. "Just don't ever want to be the one to hold you back."

I raked my nails through the shadow that covered his jaw. "And what ever made you think you would do that?"

Those eyes had become a toiling, raging sea. Wrought with so much turmoil it was terrifying to contemplate their depths.

"Because of Sovereign Sanctum?" I asked, needing to understand every intricacy about him.

A heavy sigh suffused the air between us, and he kept caressing my face, though I was unsure which of us he was trying to give comfort to.

"Yeah. Because I always envisioned a better life for you. One above what we do." He hesitated, then muttered, "Because of your brother, of course. But none of those things really had true bearing on my fear of giving into my love for you."

"And what kept it from me?" I kept scratching my fingers over his jaw, letting them glide over his lips, my heart pinned to his as I waited for him to completely open up.

Shame wrenched through his expression. "This hatred inside me, Raven."

I didn't have to search around to grasp his meaning. Didn't have to hunt for what he was referring to.

It hovered over us. A grim, bloodthirsty specter that clung to our psyches.

Did he think I didn't understand it? That I didn't feel it myself?

"You've always blamed yourself," I murmured.

Otto flinched. "Of course, I've always blamed myself. It was my fault."

My head barely shook. "I don't think so, Otto. I don't think there was anything that either of us could have said or done that would have stopped her from pursuing him."

Haddie had thought she was in love with Gideon, and he'd convinced her that he was in love with her. But it'd all been a ruse. Gideon using her as a puppet to stoke the contempt between him and Otto.

I still didn't know why Gideon had despised Otto the way he had, the way he'd wanted to ruin him.

But they'd felt the scourge of it after Otto had retaliated.

Grief seized my heart as I thought of it, the loss that permeated the hole that had been left after she'd been stolen from us.

Agony tore through Otto. Palpable and alive as he stared at me, never looking away.

"That right there, Raven. What I just saw play out in those beautiful eyes. The demons and scars that remain. That's why I've been terrified of giving into my love for you. Because I bear the same wounds, but they are so vile and ugly and gnarled that I know the only thing I'm going to do is taint you with it."

"I hate them, too," I admitted on a devastated whisper.

Sorrow pulsed through his features, and he ran his callused palm over my cheek before he set it on my jaw. "I don't just hate them, Raven. I want to destroy them. End them. And I won't stop until I do."

Knots curled in my stomach, and his thick throat bobbed as he swallowed hard. As he opened up to me the way I'd wanted him to do.

Begged for him to do.

But I didn't know how to handle this.

"I'm sick with the need for revenge," he continued, his voice coarse and jagged with the admission. "So sick that I hate that someone else got to end four of them that day. Hate that they took the vengeance that was mine. Have hated them for so long for taking that from me. But no one is going to steal the vindication of ending the rest."

What did he mean? Was he…actively seeking them out?

Oh God.

I couldn't breathe as I flew upright. My back was to him as I struggled to get oxygen into my lungs. Trying to suppress an anxiety attack from bubbling up and taking over.

I could feel his shame roll over me in surging waves.

His reticence.

His acceptance of the conviction he was sure was coming.

"That's why, Raven. That's why you should stay away from me. That's why I'm terrified I might be the reason someone is after you. That's why I'll never be good enough for you. I'm fuckin' sorry I'm not better. I want to be. Fuck, I want to be better. But I'm not, and there's no stopping this part of who I am."

Tell him, tell him, tell him.

My insides screamed, but I couldn't get the words to form on my tongue.

Otto released an agonized sigh from behind, and I felt the bed shift as he sat up on the opposite side. "I'll take you back to River's."

Is that what he thought? That I'd reject him because of this?

I flew around and had myself plastered around his back in a flash, my arms banded around his body. I pressed my face into the side of his neck, gasping as I breathed him in, and I told him the one thing that I could manage. "Do you think I could ever blame you? They're monsters, and none of them deserve to live. Not after what they did."

Chapter

FIFTY-THREE

OTTO

"**N**OT SURE THIS IS A GOOD IDEA."

I wasn't sure if I was talking about actually going forward with my birthday party tonight or the skirt that Raven was currently wearing.

God knew I was going to lose control in front of everyone there with her dressed like that.

Woman looking like the only place she belonged was on the back of my bike.

Wearing this black leather miniskirt that came up high on her waist and a lacy black tank with her bra showing underneath. She had on those same five-inch heels she'd had on the first night I'd had her. When we'd crossed that line there'd been no coming back from. The ones I'd promised that I was going to fuck her in one day.

The long black locks of her hair were done in cascading waves, and they draped down her bare shoulders, caressing all that soft flesh.

She peered back at me through the mirror where she was applying mascara, the makeup she'd already applied covering the bit of her bruising on her left forehead.

But it was her ass perched in the air where she was bent over the counter that sent a cyclone of greed spiraling through me.

The woman was pure mind-bending temptation.

Body a lure and that heart a magnet.

But it was those inky eyes that nailed me to the spot.

So dark and mesmerizing they held me like a trap.

A thunderbolt of lust gripped me by the guts, same way as it always had, though now, everything was different.

"I already told you that I'm going to spend the entire day celebrating you, and I'm not about to stop. Besides, all the Lawsons came from Redemption Hills. We wouldn't want to disappoint them, would we?"

She pouted a little as she painted her lips with red stain.

"You could have called it off."

"Not a chance." She turned and sauntered my way, and she tipped her face up my direction. "It's your first birthday I've gotten to spend with you this way, and we are going to make it memorable."

"You think it hasn't already been memorable? You think it's not already carved on me forever? Spending the whole damned day wrapped around you, taking this tight body again and again?"

Heat flushed her flesh. "I think it started out pretty good, and now we're going to end it with a bang." Then she softened. "Everyone wants to celebrate you. Not just me. This family loves you."

Looping an arm around her waist, I tugged her close, gazing down at my girl who swayed in my arms. "You stick to my side the whole fuckin' night. Don't want you out of my sight."

"You act like I'm going to have a problem with that." She fiddled with the collar of my shirt, pointed black nails scraping at the bottom of my throat.

A groan rolled in my chest. "Don't know how I'm supposed to keep my hands to myself tonight...not when I want them all over you."

I needed to tell River, and I needed to tell him soon. All of it. Both about Raven and the way I'd been hunting the monsters in the night. The lies I'd been telling. The betrayals I'd cast.

He might hate me, but I couldn't go on keeping it from him. I loved and respected him too much for that.

Guilt tried to wind up into my conscience, but Raven just pressed her chest against mine and sent me a sly grin. "By knowing that the second you get me home, you're going to be having me in any way you want me. By knowing I'm yours, even when the rest of them have no clue. By knowing that's the way it's always going to be, no matter what anyone else has to say about it."

My smile went gentle, and I brushed back a lock of her hair as I gazed down at her. "Endless."

Her gaze softened and she whispered, "Yeah, Otto. Endless."

Night covered us in a blanket as we took the winding curves down the mountain. The roar of my motorcycle filled the air, the metal vibrating beneath us and the wind whipping through our hair. Raven's arms were locked around me, and her heart beat a steady, beautiful rhythm against my back.

Her aura all around.

Her spirit consuming.

Her love abounding.

Didn't think I'd ever felt better than right then. This moment in time when it was just me and her, no boundaries around us, just the freedom that we'd found in each other.

I slowed when we made it into town, and I took the couple turns required to get onto Culberry Street as I headed toward Kane's.

The gravel lot was already packed when I made the left into the club, and I wound my bike through the mess of cars and trucks to the front where a slew of bikes were parked in a row. I came to a stop then planted my boots on the ground so I could walk the bike backward to park it next to River's.

I killed the engine.

There was no missing the frenetic energy that filled the atmosphere, the music that thumped from within the club seeping out through the thick walls, something wild and untamed driving the mood.

Or maybe it was just the excitement I could feel roll through Raven that spurred it, the woman eager as she unwound herself from me and swung off my bike.

Pure fuckin' vixen where she stood at the side of it smiling my direction as she unbuckled her helmet.

A knockout who'd gone and sucker punched me.

No reserves left, I was at her mercy, nothing but a beggar at her feet.

"Are you ready for the best night of your life, Otto Hudson? I mean, there's little chance it won't be considering you're spending it with me. I am kind of a blast."

A grin cracked the edge of my mouth, chest feeling light as I climbed off my bike. It brought me to tower over her, this gorgeous woman with a sly smirk playing over the delicious curve of her lips.

"Oh, you're a blast, all right, Raven Tayte."

"I aim to please."

The woman was intoxicating.

Entrancing.

I was probably a little too close to her when I leaned in and rumbled in her ear, "And please you do."

Chills lifted in a wave across her skin, and she edged back with a grin. "Then it seems we have something in common."

"Oh, Little Moonflower, think we have plenty in common."

She raked her teeth over her plump bottom lip, her expression shifting to this gentle thing as she fiddled with a button on my shirt.

Took everything I had not to kiss the hell out of her right then, but somehow, I managed to straighten. "Come on, let's get inside before I change my mind and take you home."

I ushered her around my bike, my hand just barely resting on the small of her back as we treaded over the loose gravel to the entrance of Kane's.

Ty and Jonah were manning the door, and they let us directly through.

Inside, the club was cramped, people packed shoulder to shoulder. A country band played onstage, and the dance floor was crowded with couples two-stepping beneath the strobing lights, the reflection from the stained-glass windows high above glinting over their faces.

I sent a smile down at Raven as we angled through the crush, heading toward the booth at the very back.

Our crew was already there behind the rope that sectioned off the area that contained three high-top tables and the big horseshoe booth.

Kane saw me first, and he lifted his tatted arms out to the sides as he called, "Ah, the birthday boy has arrived. It's time to get this party started."

The rest of our crew looked our way.

River and Charleigh. Theo and Cash. Plus the whole family from Redemption Hills.

Sienna, Raven's friend from the café across the street from her shop, was there, too, standing at a high-top table chatting with Charleigh.

A round of hoots went up. "Ah, the man of the hour."

I lifted my arms high, letting the lightness take me over. It wasn't like I was one to reject the finer things in life. Always ready for a good time. Only that definition had shifted a bit, the *finer things* in life standing right next to me.

"That's right. The fun may now begin," I shouted as I lifted the rope so Raven could duck under it.

Everyone gathered around us.

River first, with his hand outstretched, shaking my hand hard before he pulled me in for a clap to the back. "Happy birthday, brother."

"Thanks, man."

Theo edged forward next. "Happy birthday, old man."

A rough chuckle got out of me. "Fuck off, asshole. You're only a year younger than me."

"Might as well claim it, Otto. It's called wisdom," Trent Lawson said as he strolled up with his wife Eden tucked under his arm.

Owed Trent a ton of gratitude. The way he'd stood beside me when all the shit had gone down with the rest of the Owls. Wasn't long after that when the MC had fallen apart after his father, the Owls' president, had tried to take him out.

Trent and his brothers had ended up in Northern California in Redemption Hills, not that far from here.

When we'd left Los Angeles so River could find a place to raise Nolan, Trent had convinced us to come here. Had been sure it'd be a good place for Sovereign Sanctum to fly under the radar.

"That's right. Pure wisdom right here," I said.

"Pssh," Raven said from beside me. "I guess since it's his birthday, we should go ahead and let him believe that."

"Watch yourself, now," I warned, cutting her an eye that promised wicked things.

Could see the thrill roll through her limbs. She hid it behind a coy grin. "Okay, *old man.*"

She emphasized what Theo had said.

"Can you believe this nonsense? Look at her, busting my balls," I razzed, hooking a thumb in Raven's direction.

"She always was the smartest one of the bunch," Eden said as she came forward and gave me a hug.

I squeezed her back. "Ouch. It appears this is a roast rather than a party."

"I've always said our family's love language is giving each other shit." Raven's smile was wide.

Love.

It pulsed inside of me. A heavy current that swept me off my feet.

The rest of the crew from Redemption Hills came up to wish me happy birthday.

Jud and his wife Salem.

Logan and Aster.

Milo and Tessa.

"Glad you all made the trip out here to celebrate with me."

"Wouldn't miss it, brother," Jud said. Dude was a giant, a mountain of strength. Cool as could be, too. All of them with sordid pasts but hearts of fuckin' gold.

"Means a lot."

"Like we're gonna miss a party like this," Trent said as he snagged a bottle of dark whiskey from the table and passed it over to me.

I took a big swig from it and let the warmth glide down my throat and pool in my stomach.

From the side, I felt the searing burn of Raven staring up at me.

Yeah.

Best birthday ever.

Chapter
FIFTY-FOUR

Raven

"**S**OMEONE LOOKS LIKE HE'S HAVING A GOOD TIME," CHARLEIGH said where me and my friends were gathered around one of the high-top tables.

Otto and the rest of the guys were in a huddle across the roped-off area, laughing and joking and giving each other shit as they told stories of the old days.

I loved it for him. Loved that he was surrounded and supported. I wished he knew how far that support extended. I wished he could see through the fog of his tragedies to recognize that every single one of those guys would get it—would see him—would accept him fully if he'd just open up about it.

No question, it'd taken a whole lot for him to do it with me this morning. The man leaving himself flayed open wide, his afflictions on full display, even though I could feel that he was keeping some piece of it secreted.

Unable to fully state what had been going on in his mind.

"Looks like it," I said as casually as I could, like it really didn't affect me all that much.

"Looks like it? Are you over there acting like you haven't been staring at that delicious man like you want to eat him for dessert the entire night?" Tessa never was one for subtlety.

Salem choked on her margarita, laughing as she pulled the salt-rimmed glass away. "Way to just go for the jugular, Tessa."

"I am not one to beat around the bush. I mean, it's not like every single one of us isn't thinking it. Am I right?" Tessa looked around at the rest.

A titter of agreement went up around Charleigh, Eden, Aster, and Sienna.

Charleigh and Sienna shared a secret glance that I was pretty sure the rest of them caught.

"I don't even know what you're talking about." I took a guilty slurp of my chocolate martini.

"Oh, come on, Raven. You think all of us couldn't feel what was coming off you two when you came strolling in acting like you hadn't just been rolling around naked with that bad boy?" Salem lifted a perfectly arched brow.

I cringed as worry slithered through me. "Is it that obvious?"

Cracking up, Tessa reached out to steady herself on Aster's shoulder. "Is it that obvious? That man is written all over you." She waved a hand over me like she was offering proof. "You might as well tattoo big handprints all over that body because he has clearly claimed you."

My attention traveled back to Otto who was laughing at something my brother said.

Crap.

"I take it River doesn't know?" Eden asked, her voice cautious.

"Nope."

"Well, don't worry. Those brutes are all completely oblivious," Salem said. "It's the rest of us who are in tune."

She sent me a sly smile.

I'd never in a million years thought I'd have friends like this. Never thought I'd be surrounded by those who cared about me. I'd never thought I'd have it again after I'd lost Haddie.

No, she could never be replaced, but I could feel some of those fractured pieces inside me beginning to heal.

"I actually had thought they were together this whole time, and I just found out it was a secret yesterday." Sienna cocked her head.

"We're just…keeping it on the down low until Otto can find the right time to tell River," I explained.

"I have faith that River will accept it," Charleigh promised. "He just worries about you. Especially right now with everything that's going on."

Concern rippled over the group, everyone going quiet as they carefully watched me, unsure of what to say or how to handle it.

"How are you feeling?" Sienna asked. She let her gaze drift to the two tiny stitches at my hairline that I'd almost forgotten were there.

"Fine. It was just a small cut. Not a big deal."

"Well, it freaked me out when I heard the commotion out there," Sienna said, the words laden with questions.

A frown carved Aster's expression. "I heard what happened."

Uncertainty and frustration shook my head. "Yeah, some jerk came from out of nowhere and assaulted me."

"And you have no idea who it was?" Salem asked.

"No." I rocked back on my heels. "Some sicko is after me for no reason. But they'll find him."

I lifted my chin as I shifted my attention back to the guys, my belief distinct.

Only Otto was already looking at me.

Energy crackled across the space that separated us.

An intensity so hot that I shifted on my feet, my throat growing thick and my stomach roiling with need.

"Oh no, not obvious at all," Salem mumbled into her margarita.

"Shut it," I told her.

She giggled, then she softened when she fully looked at me. "I think it's wonderful, Raven. I saw what was in your eyes the first time I met you both, and I'm really glad the two of you have clearly *made your way* to each other."

She let the innuendo wind into the last.

Everyone laughed.

"All of you, shut it." I pointed around the group as a feeling of lightness swept through me.

So good.

So right.

And that only amplified tenfold when the DJ switched the song. The band had long since finished playing, and now the dark beat filled the murky club.

Charleigh knew it was my favorite, and she grabbed my hand. "All right, everyone on the dance floor. Time to shake all those hot booties."

Sending her a big grin, I touched my chest. "I really am rubbing off on you."

She winked, and all of us wound onto the dance floor. It took all of five seconds to completely let go.

Each of us getting swept up in the hypnotic beat. To the energy that curled and twisted through the throbbing crowd.

We were all laughing and having the best time together for a few songs before, one by one, the guys joined their partners.

I didn't want to keep dancing right next to them by myself like some kind of weirdo when they were all caught up in each other, so I edged away from them, dipping into the fray, and I let my eyes drop closed as my hips moved in time with the beat.

Lights strobed and darkness reigned.

Then a tidal wave of energy crashed against me.

Something so fierce that it nearly brought me to my knees.

My eyes flashed open to find Otto weaving through the crowd with a bottle of whiskey dangling from his fingers.

One destination in mind.

So ferociously gorgeous the ground trembled beneath my feet. All power and stealth and cocky arrogance. So sexy my entire body tremored as he approached, shivers raking across my flesh.

I tried to play off my reaction and threw my arms in the air the way I always would have done, voice shouting over the deafening decibel of the music. "You want to dance with me, Burly Bear?"

His aura swamped me as he slowly angled around me, demeanor predatory, feral as he edged up to my back.

Heat seared through me when his arm wrapped around my front and he hauled me against his hard, rigid frame. His words were gluttonous as he leaned in and murmured in my ear, "I can't fuckin' stay away."

Chapter

FIFTY-FIVE

OTTO

THE ENTRANCING BEAT OF THE DANCE MUSIC THRUMMED through the space.

Alluring.

Spellbinding.

Though it was this woman who lured me like a trap, only I was a willing prisoner.

Captivated.

Enthralled.

Hers.

"Thought I told you I didn't want you to leave my side," I grumbled at her ear. Panic had seized me when I'd looked up to find the table she and the rest of the girls had been huddled around empty, though it hadn't taken but a blip to find the lot of them out on the dance floor, having the best time.

I didn't want to rob her of that, but I couldn't evade the dread after what had happened yesterday and the weeks leading up.

Some faceless psychopath out for blood.

I'd spent most of the night trying to keep distance between us because I wasn't sure I trusted myself to be close to her, but I hadn't been able to stand it for a second longer when the rest of the guys had paired up with their women and Raven had gotten swallowed by the throng.

I had to seek her out.

"I knew you'd come to me," Raven murmured over the din, glancing back at me as she leaned her weight against me.

"I'll always come to you, Moonflower."

Couldn't stand spending one more day without every-fucking-person in this place knowing she was mine, and I made the decision right then that I'd go to River tomorrow and confess it all, consequences be damned because loving Raven Tayte was worth any repercussion.

She writhed to the rhythm.

Seductive.

Provocative.

Lust barreled through my being, and a needy groan rolled up my throat that I buried at the side of her neck.

It wasn't like we weren't known to dance together, but this was wholly different.

The way I couldn't get her close enough. The way our bodies moved together. Way my hand was splayed across her belly as I ground my hard cock against her ass.

I guided her deeper into the fringes, tucking us away at the far edge of the dance floor, beyond the reach of the strobes that flashed over the toiling crush. We were hidden in it, buried in the frenzied swell of bodies that raved in the ecstasy that boiled in the club.

Heat curled and climbed, and I edged closer to the flames, getting lost in the feel of her against me.

I lifted the bottle of whiskey to my lips, taking a long swill, before I did the same for her. She rocked her head back against my chest as she swallowed it down before she went back to rolling her body against mine.

She bunched up the lush fall of her hair and lifted it high.

Her skin was slicked with a sheen of sweat.

I leaned in and kissed a path along the slope of her neck, tongue roving over the soft, delicious flesh.

A haze clouded my mind, the only sense I had left was her.

The feel of her. The smell of her. The taste of her.

"Otto," she whimpered as I somehow pulled her even closer, my dick rocking against her ass, seeking friction.

"Need you," I mumbled, half delirious.

Okay, I had to be completely delirious since I was basically mauling her in front of everyone.

"Then take me. It is your birthday, after all."

Fuck.

I only had a flash of reservation before I snagged Raven's hand and began to wind her through the crowd. Needy expectation radiated from her as she fumbled along behind me.

I scanned the faces on the dance floor, making sure no one was paying us any mind before I slinked through the opening to the hall that led to the restrooms.

There was another door at the very end of it that read *Reserved.*

It was a rambling room that was normally used for private parties, but I had far better intentions for it right then.

I turned the knob and poked my head inside to make sure it was vacant, then I glanced over Raven's head and down the hall once more before I pulled her inside.

She giggled as she stumbled a little on those heels as she strode into the dimness of the room. The only illumination came from a row of dull lights that ran the backside of the wall, giving it a dusky, twilight glow.

I clicked the door shut behind us and locked it, before I slowly swiveled on my heel to the woman who was vibrating in the middle of the room.

A vision.

A dream.

This treasure that I was going to cherish forever.

"You tryin' to wreck me, Little Moonflower? Make me lose my mind?"

"Think I lost mine a long, long time ago."

Lust rolled out of me on a low grunt as she kept backing away, using that body as bait.

I stalked for her, taking a deep pull from the bottle of whiskey as I approached. I swiped my mouth with the back of my hand as I kept erasing the space between us.

Those eyes raked over me.

Needy and hungry.

Energy lashed.

Whips of greed that scourged across my overheated body.

With the bottle still in one hand, I looped an arm around her waist and hoisted her up, and she wrapped those toned legs around my waist.

I carried her two steps to the long table that sat in the middle of the room and propped her on the edge, never stepping out of the sanctuary of those thighs as I tipped the bottle back to her mouth.

She took a long swig, gasping at the burn.

But I didn't think it was the alcohol that had us intoxicated.

It was this.

Us.

This chaos that bound.

"Raven." Her name was praise as I set the bottle aside and fisted the fall of her hair up in my hand. I angled her head so I could kiss along her neck. "Sweet fuckin' Raven."

Though the woman didn't look so sweet right then.

So goddamn fierce and powerful in that skirt.

"So fuckin' beautiful, I can't see. Blinded by you."

A charge flashed through the room.

Sharp nails dragged down my chest. "You've always been the one I've seen, Otto. The one I needed. The one I loved."

"I'm right here, honey, and I'm not goin' anywhere."

I shifted so I could capture her mouth.

In an instant, a fire lit. Our kisses frantic and crazed as we struggled to possess the other.

Tongues and lips and teeth.

Hands gripping and seeking.

Flames erupted, a fire that'd been smoldering all night.

An inferno that consumed.

I jerked her closer to the edge of the table as she yanked at the button of my jeans. She had me free as I was pulling the slip of lace covering her pussy aside.

I drove inside her.

So damned deep.

Pleasure ricocheted through every cell of my body, no better feeling in the world than my dick buried in the throbbing clutch of her cunt.

So fuckin' tight a rush of dizziness spun through my head.

She cried out as her fingers clawed up the back of my neck. "Otto. God…how…every time?"

"You love it, Raven? You love being stuffed full of my cock?"

"Yes. I love it. I want it. I need it," she rambled, close to incoherent, nothing but pleas rolling from that sweet tongue.

I splayed my hand over the base of her spine and brought her to the very edge of the table, her ass hanging off the side. I pulled out then drove back in.

A delirious moan jutted out of her, and I swallowed it. Drinking it down as I began to move inside her.

She kissed me back, frantic and wild as she rose up from the table to meet me thrust for thrust.

A fever raced across our flesh.

Our desperation pouring into the other.

Impassioned kisses and groping hands.

Our bodies thrashed and bucked as I fucked her deep, clinging to her to get her closer with each drive of my hips.

My ears filled with the sounds of it. The slapping of skin and the whimpered cries and the shout of our souls.

"You feel so good." The words scraped through our kiss, her breaths jutting from her lungs as I filled her full again and again. "So good."

"You are my heaven, Raven. Fuckin' paradise. Everything I never thought I'd have."

"You had me all along."

"I'm never letting you go."

Heat crackled across our flesh. Pinpricks of rapture that whispered over us like a prayer.

Like a promise was being made.

"You are the light inside of me, Raven. Only thing that could ever lead me out of the dark. Gonna love you through it all. Under every endless moon. And when dawn finally breaks, I will watch you rise."

The words raked out of me as I drove into her, my hands up under that skirt, palming her ass as I urged her against me.

A swell of intensity bellowed.

Winding and whipping.

Dragging us closer.

Chains I no longer wanted to resist.

Bound with this girl for eternity.

Body and heart and mind.

Pleasure glowed like a halo around her. Girl a beacon that would forever guide me home.

"Otto."

"You feel it?" I demanded.

"Yes," she gasped.

I shifted her so I could reach my hand in between us to get to her throbbing, swollen clit. I rubbed my fingers against it as I pounded into her in torrid, frenzied thrusts.

Hot little sounds kept mewling from her mouth, and I swallowed them whole as I drove her toward the bliss that swarmed around us.

The air alive.

Snapping and buzzing as it encircled us in a hazy cloud of greed.

Pleasure grew and gathered with each rock of my hips, both of us wound so tight as we climbed for that height.

To that place where the two of us reigned.

Where it was just me and Raven and there were no obstacles to be found. The chasms filled and the fractures healed.

"Want to hear my name coming from that sweet mouth when you come, Little Moonflower. Want to hear you shoutin' it."

"I'm going to—"

I swept in and took her mouth, stealing the words as I shifted her back, driving into her so fuckin' hard as I swirled my fingers over her engorged nub.

"Let me have it, Raven. Give me your pleasure."

"It's yours. It's always been yours."

On the next thrust, I felt her splinter apart. An orgasm rending through her on an obliterating wave. Racing through her as she shouted my name.

Nails raked down my back, almost painfully as she flew.

The girl soaring through the night.

She took me with her.

Carrying me on her wings.

That heaven set out above me that I could only reach with her.

A rapture so complete that I was shouting, too, her name forever on my lips.

"Raven. Fuck, Raven."

I poured into her hot needy cunt, pulsing and pulsing in spastic quakes. My fingers sank into her thighs as I dragged her even closer, so close there was no room for anything else.

Just us.

Just us.

She kept clutching me as she searched for the oxygen that'd gone missing.

Sweat slicked our skin, the flames still licking through us, though they'd been subdued.

Quiet, crackling embers.

Inhaling a shaky breath, I curled an arm up her back and wrapped my hand around the nape of her neck, hanging on as I brushed back the hair matted at her temple with the other.

My throat felt sticky and thick.

Too full.

Overwhelmed.

"I love you, Raven Tayte. For every single one of my days."

"I love you so much, Otto. You're my favorite person." There was no tease to it that time. Only stark adoration as she brushed her fingertips over my lips.

I grabbed them and kissed across the tips. "No one can compare."

We stayed like that for a moment, just gazing at each other through the lapping darkness of the room before I pulled out of her, more than reluctantly, and started to tuck myself back into my jeans as I helped her readjust her underwear.

But it wasn't soon enough before the door crashed open behind us.

Not soon enough to conceal what we'd been doing.

Not soon enough to stop the fury that lanced through the room.

Because River was there, raging in the doorway, Kane's key hanging from the lock, his mouth twisted in venom. "You fuckin' lying piece of shit. I fuckin' knew it."

Then he was storming across the room toward me.

Chapter

FIFTY-SIX

Raven

I T WAS DISORIENTING, FLOATING ON THE HIGHEST HIGH ONE second, then being sucked down into the mayhem that suddenly spiraled in the room.

A vortex swilling all air and light from the space.

An animosity and disbelief and hurt so thick that I didn't think my brother could see anything in front of him other than a man who'd violated his sister.

Someone who'd lied and betrayed.

Someone he no longer recognized or loved.

Someone who'd *hurt* me.

Not when he flew across the room at the same second Otto had fully turned and taken two steps toward him with his arms stretched out at his sides like some kind of offering.

River gave no warning before his fist flew. A violent crack ricocheted off the walls when it landed on Otto's cheek.

Shock ripped out of my lungs, for one moment stunned that my brother would attack Otto this way.

Probably more stunned that Otto just let him.

Like he was inviting the punishment.

Otto grunted a low sound at the connection. Pain that he tried to keep contained.

He just stood there while River delivered another punch, that one to the other side.

No doubt, he believed he deserved it.

Blood splattered with the crunch, and Otto rocked to the side, inhaling a sharp breath before he forced himself to upright stand again, shaking himself off as he readied himself for another blow.

"You fuckin' vile piece of shit. You think you can touch my sister? Behind my fuckin' back? You fuckin' swore to me, you bastard. Come on, you twisted fuck," River taunted.

Otto didn't take the bait, though, he stood stock-still, welcoming the malice that oozed from my brother.

"River," I begged, trying to break through the madness. "You don't understand."

"Oh, I understand perfectly, Raven. Can't believe you'd let this disgusting prick touch you. After everything you've been through? Thought you knew better."

River spat it like an accusation, one I wasn't sure if he was issuing to me or Otto. But it was the one thing that got a rise out of Otto, his own fury brimming to the surface. "Don't fuckin' talk to her like that."

Cold laughter rolled out of River, and his face pinched in disbelief. "You think you have something to say to me about being her *brother?*"

He emphasized the last, spite dipping into the word, driving the blade in deep.

I started to slip off the side of the table, and Otto held out a hand without looking at me, his voice gruff as he muttered, "Stay back, Raven."

A hollow sound echoed from River, and he lifted his chin at Otto. "Is that it? You tell her what to do? Manipulate her? Take advantage of her vulnerabilities? Of her trauma? Use her up the way you use the rest of the women you burn through?"

It was the one thing that cut into Otto's reserve. Rage bubbled out of him, the man vibrating hostility before he suddenly lunged at

River and tackled him to the ground. They hit the wood floors with a thud, and in an instant, they were a grappling mess in the middle of it.

Punches and grunts and kicks as they fought to outdo the other.

I jumped off the table, rushing up to them as a shout tore up my throat. "Are you kidding me? Just stop it. Stop it! Both of you!"

It didn't come close to penetrating the tumult that raged between them.

A commotion suddenly burst through the door, and Kane, Theo, Cash, and Trent came barreling through.

Charleigh, Eden, and Sienna hovered at the door behind them, their eyes wide as they took in the scene.

The guys rushed forward to the tussling pile that was River and Otto.

"Enough. Break it up."

Theo and Kane grabbed ahold of Otto who was currently on top, and Trent and Cash hauled River away.

River tried to break free, sneering at Otto from where he was being dragged across the room. "You're dead. Fuckin' dead to me. The one thing I ever asked of you?" Hurt curled through his features before he spat, "Can't fuckin' believe you."

Shame burned through Otto's expression, his face smeared with blood and guilt flaming in the depths of his blue eyes.

I stumbled out in between them. Sickness churned in my stomach. "What? You think I have no say? That I'm so small and insignificant and *vulnerable* that I can't make my own decisions for myself?" Hot tears streamed down my face as I looked at my brother.

"He fuckin' promised me, Raven. Promised me he'd never touch you."

"And what about what I want?"

Pain fractured through his expression. "Then you want the wrong thing."

My focus swiveled to Otto. Otto who wouldn't even freaking look at me, let alone stand up and tell my brother he was wrong.

Tell him he loved me.

That he'd stand for me.

That he'd do anything for me.

That he'd been the one who'd comforted me for all those years. When I was tortured by the nightmares. The only one who'd ever made me feel safe.

Hurt cut me in two, and I barely nodded as I fumbled back before I turned and ran for the door because I didn't want to be around either of them.

Charleigh met me, taking me into her arms the second I was out in the solitude of the hall, hugging me tight as she muttered, "It'll be fine. They'll cool down and it'll be fine."

But that wasn't the point.

My brother should support me.

My decisions.

The same as Otto should stand for them.

Angrily, I swiped at the tears on my face as I glanced around at my three friends. Sorrow pinched Eden's brow and concern twisted through Sienna's expression.

"I just want to leave," I said.

Charleigh curled her arm around my waist. "I'll take you wherever you want to go."

"Okay, I didn't mean here. Are you sure about this?" Doubt filled Charleigh as she glanced between me and my shop.

"Yeah. I really just want to be alone."

I didn't want to be around either River or Otto right then. Didn't want to go to either of their houses.

Sienna wavered, too, rubbing her hands up and down her arms as we stood in the cool breeze that wisped through the night.

"But you're going to sleep in your shop?" she asked, full of speculation.

I looked back at the darkened panes of glass, and I shrugged when I turned back to them. "Flowers make me happy. This is my happy place."

Concern churned between them, both clearly reluctant to agree.

"Don't worry—I'll keep the doors locked and I'll set the alarm. I'll be fine."

Charleigh's nod was slight. "Okay."

She surged forward and hugged me tight, muttering at my ear, "Call me if you need me."

"I will."

When she stepped back, Sienna reached out and squeezed my hand.

"I'm really sorry this messed up your night with Theo," I told her.

A grin hinted at the edge of her mouth. "Who knows...I might head back to Kane's and see what he's up to."

I giggled. "That sounds like a solid plan."

Then she frowned. "I'm sorry your night got messed up, too."

A heavy sigh whispered free. "It's okay. It was coming, and I'm pretty sure all those old feelings needed to be dragged out into the open. I just wish Otto and River would have done it with a little respect."

"They're fighters, Raven. It's what they know," Charleigh said.

"Yeah, but they're also brothers. Family. That should come first."

Chapter
FIFTY-SEVEN

Raven

Eighteen Years Old

RAVEN AWOKE THRASHING IN THE MIDDLE OF THE NIGHT. C OLD and alone. The way she'd been the last week.

She felt abandoned. A new fear rising up to take her over. One that felt almost like a broken heart, though she'd never been close enough to anyone to understand what that was like.

Throwing off the covers, she heaved for breath as she tried to calm the dark storm that bellowed inside her. A tacky awareness that slithered through her veins, more toxic than the bad dream.

She squeezed her eyes closed, praying for sleep, but none would come.

She stilled when she heard the soft thud of footsteps outside her door.

Come to me, she silently begged. She still couldn't understand what had happened over the last week.

All except for the call Raven had gotten from Haddie.

Otto had been distant since.

Barely looking at her in the day and completely ignoring her at night.

Those footsteps changed course, backing away, before she heard the soft click of a door latch before it quietly snapped shut across the hall.

Sorrow threatened to tie her to the bed, to keep her shackled. But she couldn't do that anymore. She didn't want to be small and ashamed. She didn't want to hide or conceal.

For once—for the first time in her life—she wanted to be seen.

She rose from the bed and crept across the floor. Her heart fluttered madly in her chest when she set her hand on the knob. Inhaling a steadying breath, she searched inside herself for fortitude.

For courage.

For the bravery and strength that he'd always affirmed that she had.

For everything he'd been instilling in her for all these years.

She opened the door, and her attention swept from one side of the hall to the other to make sure it was clear, then she tiptoed to the door directly across from hers.

She didn't hesitate or knock.

She pushed it open the same way as Otto had always done hers.

He was lounged on his bed, and he lurched upright. Only wearing jeans and his boots.

Thickness filled her throat and butterflies scattered in her belly as she took in the sight of him.

So viciously beautiful it made her feel weak.

Designs inscribed across his flesh, flexing and contracting over the shock of muscles that bulged beneath.

Magnificent.

It was all she could think.

This man who she trusted more than anyone else.

"Raven." It gusted out of him on a low roll of surprise.

Her brow pinched as she squeezed the door handle, though she lifted her chin, refusing to back down. "Where have you been?"

He scraped a hand over the top of his head, diverting his gaze to the floor. "Busy."

Stepping forward, she let the door swing shut behind her. "Too busy for me?"

"Guess so." He kept his head down when he said it.

A shockwave of pain reverberated the air. She wasn't sure which of them it originated from because it felt like they both were washed in it. Dragged down to the dark abyss of an endless sea.

"You should go back to bed, Raven," he said, still not fully looking at her.

"Why?"

"Because you shouldn't be in here."

She choked out a sound of disbelief. "But it's fine for you to come to my room whenever it's convenient for you?"

He flew to his feet, so tall and imposing she sucked in a shattered breath.

Anguish contorted his face. "No," he hissed quietly, the sound a mere reverberation. "It's not okay for me to come to your room, Raven. Think you know that."

"How can you say that?"

"Because it's not my place."

Hollow laughter curled up her throat, and she blinked as she stared at him. Trying to understand why he was doing this. What would have changed. "It is your place, Otto. It is your place because you're the only one who's ever made me feel safe. The only one who gives me peace. The only one I want coming into my room."

His head barely shook. "No."

She barreled right through the resistance. "Otto, I want you—"

"No." It whipped off his tongue, a sharp, bitter blade.

It pierced her.

An arrow driven right through.

Then he sighed and stepped forward, and he pulled her into his arms. He was hot. Burning up. He ran his fingers through her hair as he pressed her cheek to his chest. "Please don't say it, Raven. Please don't say it. Because I love you. I do. So fuckin' much."

The air held, time slipping away between them, his breath shaky before he cast the final blow. "But not like that. Not the way that you're thinking. I think you got confused along the way. Turned this into something it's not."

Confused?

She choked around the statement. She wasn't confused. She knew. She knew exactly what glowed inside her.

"Otto…" She blinked against the moisture that gathered in her eyes, and he hauled her closer, his lips murmuring at the crown of her head. "You're amazing, Raven. Beautiful and strong and courageous. Hold onto that. Keep it close. And I know you're going to find everything in this world you want. Everything you deserve."

It's you. It's you.

But she couldn't say it.

The rejection he'd cast splintered through her like a thousand fiery darts.

Then he completely finished off. A fatal blow that speared through her heart. "And I'll be right here, at your side, cheering my baby sister on every step of the way."

Baby sister.

Baby sister.

Numbly, she backed away, doing her best to staunch the tears that brimmed in her eyes as she turned and fled.

She didn't let them fall until she fell face down on top of her bed.

"Haddie, please don't give into him." Raven nearly begged it where she sat in the front passenger-seat of Haddie's car.

Haddie cut her a glance as they traveled beneath the streetlamps that glinted above them as they headed toward the house party where Gideon was waiting for her.

"He said he was sorry. Really sorry."

Worry churned in Raven's guts, and she blinked out the windshield at the glittering clubs and bars they passed.

"And it's Hollywood. Like, seriously, this is going to be so much fun." Haddie reached out and squeezed Raven's knee.

Raven couldn't find any excitement. There was only dread. Something deep and dark that lurked in the recesses of her mind.

An omen that crawled over the dense fog that hung from the heavens and blotted out the stars.

City lights shined against it, creating a silvered canopy that covered them whole.

Something about it felt like a prison. A trap.

"He hurt you, Haddie," Raven whispered.

A shiver rolled through her best friend before she straightened in her seat. "He won't do it again. He promised." There was almost an apology on Haddie's face when she peeked at her. "You don't have to come if you don't want to."

Disquiet pulsed through Raven. There was no way she *wasn't* going. Going to a party in Hollywood was probably the last thing she wanted to do.

The faint vestiges of courage she'd been wearing had been demolished by the rejection Otto had inflicted the previous night. Her heart tattered. Her edges frayed.

But this was her best friend.

Her best friend who wouldn't listen to her no matter how much she begged her.

Haddie made a right onto a neighborhood street. It was darker here, the small houses a bit dilapidated and run-down. It wasn't like any of the parties she attended with Haddie were in upscale neighborhoods, but something about this felt all wrong.

Off.

Haddie pulled to a stop in front of a single-story house that matched the address. The white paint was peeling, the yard was overgrown, and boards covered the windows.

Only a single pickup truck was parked in front of them.

Anxiety billowed, a queasy feeling that clawed up her throat. "I don't think this is a good idea. Where is everyone?"

"Probably parking on another street so the cops don't get called."

Haddie hesitated before she rushed, "I know you're all up in arms about this, Raven, and I get it, but I chose to forgive him, so I'm going in with or without you."

Haddie snatched her small purse from the middle console and stepped from the car.

Warily, Raven followed, her throat thick as she trailed her best friend up the crumbling sidewalk that had weeds growing through the cracks.

The front door swung open before they even got to it, and Gideon grinned as he leaned an arm up high on the jamb. "Ah, our guests of honor."

A flirty giggle rolled out of Haddie. "Were you missing me?"

"Oh, yeah," Gideon drew out.

"I missed you, too," she said, pecking a kiss to his lips.

He stood aside to give her room to slip by, then he widened the door for Raven who hesitated ten steps back.

"No need to be shy," he drawled.

Raven looked around, swallowing around the lump in her throat, before she forced herself to move inside.

Gideon closed the door behind her.

But there was no music.

No revelers.

No party.

Just the malicious stares of the group of men who stood waiting for them.

Ice slicked down Raven's spine when she heard the lock clicking into place.

And in the flash of a second, she was back in that small room. Her father lurking above, that maniacal grin on his face. His sadistic hunger to inflict pain written all over his smile.

Except her vision was filled with seven faces then.

All Owls who watched them with sadistic, salacious hate.

Panic drove through Raven, and she whirled around to run back to the door. Her hand curled around the doorknob at the same second as Dusty snatched her wrist. She cried out when he wrung it back.

"Little bitch…nothing but a cock tease. Been waitin' for this for a long, long time. Now it's come due."

Haddie stumbled back a step, her gaze flitting over the faces of the men before it landed on Gideon. "What's going on?" She tried to demand it, but it trembled.

Gideon cracked a grin. The same kind of grin Raven's father used to wear. He stepped forward, angling his head. "Otto and his whole crew have it comin'. And I'm gonna enjoy getting that payback through you."

Fear weighed down on her body where she hid under her covers. So heavy. Shaking and shaking as she listened to the door creak open. "No, Daddy, no." But she had no strength, and there was nothing she could do but succumb to her own screams.

Raven fought against it, the terror that wanted to consume, and she lifted her foot and rammed the sharp point of her heel into the top of Dusty's boot. He howled and she jerked free of his hold.

Raven bolted forward, grabbed Haddie's hand, and shouted, "Run!"

She hauled Haddie the only direction they weren't surrounded by the Owls, running through the cutout that led into the kitchen. Raven prayed the back door was unlocked. It was their only chance.

Only they didn't make it halfway there before a hand fisted in her hair and ripped her back. She screamed at the pain that tore across her scalp, then a sob ripped from her lungs when she was thrown to the ground, her hip taking the brunt force of the impact.

Dusty loomed over her, a malignant smirk on his face as he came to straddle her.

She cried out, kicking and flailing her arms.

The back of his hand cracked across the side of her face. Blood filled her mouth, acrid and foul, and she spit it in his face.

"You fuckin' bitch. You're gonna regret that."

He started to rip at her clothes, and she struggled against him when he yanked at the button of her jeans.

She fought and fought. Kicking her legs and bucking up.

He grabbed her by both wrists and pinned them to the floor.

He leaned in close and licked her cheek, and Raven closed her eyes like it could keep her from the horror of it all. Remove her.

But it didn't block anything. Not the stench of Dusty's presence or the bite of his nails or the weight of his body.

Not the agony that was coming from Haddie a few feet away.

Wail after wail.

Raven managed to get one of her hands free and she scratched her nails down Dusty's cheek. Tiny lines of flesh opened. They bloomed red with the blood she'd drawn.

He struck her again.

And then…

Hope blossomed through the terror.

Because she heard it above Haddie's sobs and the shout of the men.

Motorcycle engines roared in the distance, growing louder with each second.

Otto. River. Oh God, they were coming. They would save them.

"Fuck. They're comin'. Everyone get the fuck out and get clear," one of the men shouted from the living room.

"Finish it," Gideon growled. "They're finally gonna feel our pain."

Dusty spat a curse, and she almost breathed out in relief when he edged back, until she saw the flash of metal when he pulled something from the back of his jeans.

A knife.

Horror raced through her when he came forward, going for her throat, and she flipped around just in time to deflect it, trying to push up from the floor to get away.

"You bitch."

She clawed at the slick tile.

Desperate.

Praying for one more second.

For River and Otto to bust through the door.

Only a scream tore from her when that relief didn't come, but instead, a hot blade was thrust into her side.

Chapter
FIFTY-EIGHT

Raven

Okay, fine, so maybe sleeping on the hard floor in the back of my shop wasn't the best call I'd ever made.

My body was stiff as all heck as I blinked my eyes open to the gauzy morning light that filtered in through the small window on the door that led to the alley at the back of the building.

I lifted my head, scowling at the drool that soaked a small spot on the scratchy embroidered pillow that I'd snagged from the gift display out front.

Awesome.

But at least I'd had it and the matching throw blanket. They'd been my only saving grace—that and the tee and shorts I'd had stored in a drawer for emergencies.

The accommodations might not have been comfortable, but at least I hadn't had to sleep in leather and lace.

Not that there'd been a whole lot of sleeping.

The entire night had been fraught with anxiety. Tossing and turning on the unforgiving ground as my mind had played through the way things had unfolded last night.

The accusations River had thrown out.

Ones that Otto had received as if he were deserving of them.

He'd warned that River was going to kill him when he found out, but I'd chosen to believe that on some level River would understand. That he'd accept us.

But what had hurt the most was that Otto had just stood there mute.

Head slumped with shame between his shoulders.

As if loving me was a sin? A mistake he'd made? As if I were some crime that he'd committed?

A brand-new scar marked on his heart when I was supposed to be helping heal the ones he'd already had inflicted.

Standing, I rubbed my palms over my face to break up the conflicting emotions as I shuffled barefoot into the tiny bathroom. It didn't help much at all, so I splashed cold water on it, instead, praying for the clarity I couldn't find.

Blowing out a sigh, I grabbed a hand towel and blotted my face, then I looked up to my reflection in the mirror.

"Look at you, Raven. Look at who you are. If you could only see the way I see you. You are brave and strong. So goddamn beautiful. A bloom in the middle of the darkest night."

But I didn't want to only be his in the night. I wanted to be his in the light of day.

For him to stand for me. Beside me. Love me in front of everyone.

So much of my life had been secret. Hidden behind my fears and traumas.

I wanted to soar, and I wanted to soar with him.

I tossed the hand towel to the sink and padded back out through the door and into the main area of the shop.

Dawn was barely breaking, and I moved to the bank of windows and peered out at 9th Street. There was very little activity this early on a Sunday morning, though the little coffee shop next door and Sunrise to Sunset Café across the street would be open.

My chest squeezed when I noticed who stood on the other side of the road.

Kane was there, casually leaned against the wall with his hands tucked in the pockets of his jeans. Barely moving as he watched my shop.

Of course they would have sent someone to watch over me.

It was just their way, and I had a feeling he'd been sent by Otto.

Otto who was likely at his house, stewing in regret and guilt.

Dropping my eyes closed, I attempted to clear it all. To break myself from the hazy pain that threatened to suck me under.

Blowing out a sigh, I forced myself to move. Millie would be here soon, and I didn't want her to find me an emo mess. I might as well get busy and get everything ready for her.

I dipped back into the backroom of the shop, going for the ribbon I'd need for a couple orders that had come in, then I slowed to a standstill when someone rapped at the back door.

Apprehension rippled through me.

It was too early for a delivery, wasn't it?

Carefully, I edged up to the small window, keeping myself to the side of it so I wouldn't be seen when I peeked out. A grin took over the unease when I saw Sienna on the other side.

I moved so she could see me, and she waved wildly from the other side.

What a goof.

A soft laugh rolled out of me, and I mumbled, "What in the world are you doing?" as I tapped the code to turn off the alarm on the panel next to the door. I worked through the locks, a smile full on my face as I opened it.

"Hey, Sienna. What are you doing back here?"

"Hi, Raven." Her smile was soft as she reached for my hand. Only when she grabbed it, she cinched down tight, and her nails dug into my skin as she jerked me out into the alley.

What in the world?

Surprise lurched through my consciousness, my head spinning as I tried to process what was happening. The harsh grip of her hand and the unexpected sneer on her face.

But it was the barrel of the gun that was suddenly pressed to my side that sent a slick of dread through my being. A thick, oily sensation that oozed through my spirit and dripped into my soul. "Sienna? What are you doing?"

"What I came here to do."

She grabbed me by the arm and jostled me around so she was behind me, and she locked an elbow around my neck.

Slowly, she turned to face me out into the right side of the alley.

To the man who stepped out from behind a large dumpster.

Sickness pooled in my stomach when I saw who it was.

Gideon.

Sienna pressed her mouth to my ear, whispering, "Your friend was totally right about me. I do like them dark, but I already have myself a man. And he's been waiting on this day for a long, long time."

Chapter
FIFTY-NINE

OTTO

Twenty-Seven Years Old

OTTO AND HIS CREW TORE UP THE ROAD THROUGH THE SEEDY area in Hollywood. His hand was cocked back on the throttle, their engines roaring as they blazed beneath the cover of night.

His teeth were gritted in spite and fear.

His guts gnarled with dread.

He'd had a feeling that things had gone bad when he couldn't get in touch with Haddie this evening and Raven's room had been empty when he'd gotten himself together enough to go ask her if she'd heard from his sister.

He'd still been reeling from the disgusting lie he'd had to tell her last night.

How he felt like he was splitting in two as he severed the trust Raven had given him. As he cut the bond that had tied them with the snip of his words.

Words that were nothing but blasphemy.

But he'd had to do it. He had no other choice. He couldn't betray River that way. But more than that? He couldn't saddle Raven with a life like theirs.

When he'd found Raven's room empty, he'd called her, but her phone had gone directly to voicemail. Intuition had kicked, an angsty sense that promised things weren't right, and he'd gone to River who had her location on his phone.

There was no other reason for them to be headed this way other than chasing down trouble, and he was sure Gideon and his friends had something to do with this.

Thankfully, the girls weren't that far ahead of them.

Otto and his crew had all jumped on their bikes, and now they raced, bullets that rocketed through the city. They barely slowed when they made the right into the grungy neighborhood.

It wasn't that far off from the depravity Haddie had grown up in, so it wasn't like showing up here was going to cause her a whole lot of concern.

But Otto?

He was *concerned*.

Spirit bashing with a turbid awareness that wouldn't let him go.

Especially after they hadn't heard a word from Gideon and his crew. He'd expected immediate retaliation. Sure it was gonna come to a head.

But God, he would never survive it if it came to *this*.

He nearly breathed out in relief when he saw his sister's car sitting at the curb, all while a fresh shot of adrenaline spiked through his senses.

They all came to grinding halts behind it, parking at odd angles as they jumped off their bikes and ran for the door.

Otto was out front, and his hand darted for the knob. He rattled it. It was locked.

He didn't bother with knocking.

He grabbed both sides of the doorframe and lifted his leg, and he rammed the sole of his boot against the door near the doorknob.

Wood splintered, though it didn't give.

He did it again.

Twice more before it finally busted open and slammed against the interior wall.

All five of them piled in, ready for a fight, eyes scanning the area.

Confusion wound through him when they found the living room empty. No motion at all. Until he heard the tiny moan echo from somewhere deeper in the house.

He shared a look with River before they went running, boots thundering across the floor before they dove through a nook and into a kitchen.

A howl of pain ripped out of Otto when he made it inside, and he slipped through the streams of blood weaving across the floor as he fumbled to his sister's side. He dropped to his knees with a wail.

She was surrounded by a pool of blood, her brown hair saturated, her throat slit and gaping wide.

Gasping, he pulled her into his arms, begging, "Haddie. Oh God, Haddie. I'm so sorry. I'm so sorry."

Grief bound. So tight he couldn't breathe. Couldn't see.

"Haddie. Oh God, Haddie. Please, no. No."

River was shouting, "Raven, Raven!"

Otto could hardly look that way. His stomach revolted when he saw Raven in her own pool of blood, face down before River turned her over. He brushed back the black locks from her hair as he felt for her pulse.

She moaned again, and River screamed, "Call an ambulance!"

Raven. Oh God, Raven. And Haddie. His spirit moaned. A guttural cry that begged for the both of them.

The rest of their crew gaped in horror from the opening before Kane snapped out of it and pulled his cell from his pocket and called 9-1-1.

"Hurry," Otto mumbled, brushing back Haddie's hair, rocking her and rocking her.

Hurry.

Except he knew it was too late. Haddie was too light. Too still. All wrong.

The loud rumble of a truck engine turning over thundered from outside. It revved high, tires squealing as it sped away.

Motherfuckers running.

He didn't make to chase them. He held his sister knowing it was going to be the last chance that he got to do it.

Let them fuckin' run.

Let them know what was coming for them.

Because if there was only one thing that remained in his life, it would be hunting them.

And when he found them, they would come to their end.

"We ride tomorrow." River gripped his shoulder, dipping down to try to get in his line of sight.

Otto sat on his bed propped against the headboard.

Numb.

Dead inside.

All except for the rage that simmered in a place inside him that he hadn't known existed. The famished need for vengeance that fermented in the hollowed-out hole that had been carved in the deepest, darkest recess of his soul.

It was the only feeling that remained.

He gave River a limp nod, and River squeezed his shoulder again before he left Otto's room and closed the door behind him.

A week had passed since Haddie had been killed.

A week of this detached torment.

It felt like he was floating outside his body. Outside of reality because he couldn't process what was true.

The fact Haddie was gone, and he was the one who was wholly responsible for it.

He sat up from the bed, shoved his feet into his boots, and laced them up. His breaths were shallow when he went to his closet and opened the large gun safe hidden at the back. He took his rifle and three loaded magazines, fitted himself with his back holster and shoved the gun into it before pulling on a long jacket to conceal it.

Then he slipped out his window and carefully lowered himself to the grass below.

His attention darted all directions, checking that it was clear, before he slinked across the yard, ducking low as he hurried to his bike.

He wouldn't wait for tomorrow.

Because this retribution was on him.

For Haddie.

For Raven.

For the two people he loved most and hadn't been strong enough to protect.

He kicked the stand on his bike and pushed it down the street beneath a sheath of darkness, and when he was sure he was far enough away, he slung his leg over it and turned over the engine.

One destination in mind.

One he was sure was going to be his last.

He left his bike five hundred yards up the alley. He crept slow, keeping his footsteps quieted and his back against the dingy buildings as he made his way to the warehouse hidden in the sleaziest, most depraved part of the city.

Gideon and his crew were there every Thursday night. Unpacking the blocks of cocaine that were hidden in straw in the back of a truck, getting them ready for distribution.

Otto had gotten word that the Owls' prez had given Gideon and his mob the clear. Found them not responsible, claiming they'd been on a run that night so there was no chance they were involved in Haddie's death and Raven's injury.

Otto knew it was bullshit.

A cover.

Same as he knew he'd never be loyal to that motherfucker again.

Cutter might deem them clean, but tonight, Otto was going to be the judge.

He made it to the chain-link fence that surrounded the whole perimeter. Dull lights droned from the sides of the building, and he could hear the distant voices rambling from within the building.

He gripped hold of the fence and hoisted himself over. He landed with a dull thud, and he crouched down, ensuring that no one had heard him before he stole forward. He hid himself behind a metal container.

Kneeling low, he peered out.

There was no movement, only the intermittent discordant bark of laughter.

That rage boiled. Climbing his throat and speeding through his veins.

They were laughing.

Fuckin' laughing while his sister was dead in a grave. While Raven was lucky to be alive.

She'd been in intensive care for two days, though she was now home safe where she was slowly recovering, though he was sure the wounds these demons had inflicted were going to devastate the progress she'd made. She'd carry them like scars that would drag her back into the darkness.

For a moment, he pinched his eyes closed against the grief of it. His sister stolen from them.

And Raven...

He gulped as he struggled to breathe.

Warring with the love that he was forbidden to feel.

A love that made him no less than a monster. No better than these bastards who hooted and howled, no fuckin' sweat off their backs.

Otto shucked off his jacket and dropped it to the ground, and he reached over his shoulder and pulled his rifle from its holster.

He checked to make sure it was loaded and ready before he stood and began to wind around the trailer.

Right before a clatter of footsteps rushed up behind him, so fast he barely had time to whirl around right as the butt of a gun was bashed against his temple.

Dropping him straight to the ground.

They dragged him out into the dirt lot and shoved him onto his knees. Blood poured from the wound on the side of his head as fury pulsed through his veins.

Anger that this was it. Anger that he wasn't going to get justice for Haddie. That he wasn't going to get justice for Raven.

These motherfuckers were going to get away with what they'd done.

Gideon and his pathetic posse made a semi-circle around Otto where they loomed about ten feet back.

"Been expectin' you," Gideon said, amusement in his voice.

Hatred burned through Otto's conscience.

"You killed my sister, you fuckin' bastard. Murdered her in cold blood." His teeth nearly cracked from the pressure he was exerting as he ground out the words.

Gideon tsked. "I wouldn't call it cold blood. It was coming, after all. You disrespected me in front of everyone at that bar that day. Not that I didn't hate you to begin with. So fucking high and mighty with your crew. Turning Trent against the rest of us."

"You thought I was just gonna stand aside and let it happen with my sister? I don't think so."

"Yet I had her, didn't I? Time and again. Slut had a sweet little cunt. It was a shame I had to end her."

Otto roared, trying to get to his feet, only he sank back down when Gideon lifted the handgun that had been dangling at his side and pointed it in Otto's direction. "But there was no chance I wasn't going to make her bleed. After what you and your crew did? Fuckin' with our bikes?"

It was the ultimate disrespect. Otto knew it. It was why he'd done it.

"You should've known that pain would come. It's been coming all along. Years spent with you getting in the way. I lost the trust of Trent because of you. Lost my chance at every promotion within the club because he had some kinda hard-on for you. You made me lose the respect of the rest of the Owls, knowing you spat in my face that way. That ends today."

Rage and grief and sorrow pounded through Otto.

And for one fleeting second, he wished he could go back. He wished he could go back and tell Raven how he really felt. Hold her. Protect her.

Go all the way back and keep Haddie from ever stepping foot into his world.

Maybe never enter it himself.

"Don't be sad, the rest of your crew will be close behind."

Gideon cocked the gun, and Otto closed his eyes.

And it was a vision of Raven that manifested behind his lids.

Lying in that bed curled in his arms. Tucked to his chest.

And he prayed that she'd run. Get fully free of this life.

Fly.

He prepared himself for the gunshot.

Only there was suddenly a ton of them. Ringing out, pings and flying dirt.

Shouts and cries and chaos erupted.

Confusion bound, and Otto threw himself to the ground as a flurry of gunshots ricocheted. Coming from somewhere outside the fenced-in area.

A slew of shots were fired back.

And he could hear the stampeding of footsteps and the roar of motorcycles and the quiet of death.

Because when Otto finally hauled himself up onto his feet in the aftermath, when the dust had settled and the sound of sirens shouted in the distance, he was standing in the middle of four dead bodies.

Dusty, Zeke, Lane, and Decker.

Gideon, Brek, and Lye had escaped.

Otto searched the darkness beyond the fence for who was responsible.

Unsure of what he felt.

The opposing emotions that clashed and conflicted.

The hate. The thirst that remained unquenched. The resentment that he didn't get to end the four who lay bleeding around him.

All mixed with a tiny spark of something bigger. A tiny glow beneath the moon that rained a murky, silvered haze from above.

The fact that he was alive.

Chapter

SIXTY

OTTO

I PULLED MY TRUCK UP TO THE CURB IN FRONT OF Sunrise to Sunset Café. A heavy sigh puffed from my nose as I shifted it into park and looked out the driver's side window at Moonflower across the street.

The panes of glass glinted beneath the rays of the rising sun.

A beacon.

Blinding like the woman.

I killed the engine and grabbed the two to-go cups from Morning Dew Brewhouse.

Raven's favorite.

And considering I had some groveling to do, I needed everything available in my arsenal.

River had taken off right after Raven had, not saying another word to me, though the spite in his expression had said everything he needed to.

I'd thrashed, wanting to go after Raven. Pick her up and hold her and wipe the hurt I'd inflicted from her gorgeous face.

I'd seen it, what my silence had done. But I'd been gripped by shame, my throat constricted and unable to give any defense as I'd stood guilty in front of my best friend.

But that guilt wasn't greater than the remorse I'd felt for not standing up and claiming exactly what Raven was to me.

Kane and Theo had held me back, telling me to cool off, that everyone needed to process what had just gone down. Kane had promised to find out where Raven was staying and keep an eye on her.

He'd texted me forty minutes later and told me she'd gone to Moonflower.

Fuckin' Moonflower.

Without a bed.

She was stubborn, all right.

But I didn't blame her. Wanting to shut herself away from the rest of us when we'd acted like imbeciles.

Kane had told me he'd be here and that I needed to keep my ass at my own house and lay low.

Give it the night.

I hadn't slept a fuckin' wink, so I'd been out the door with the sun.

Now, I clicked the truck door open and stepped into the cool air of the morning. I tossed the door shut with an elbow, and I jutted my chin at Kane from over the top of the hood.

"How's it goin'?"

He scoffed with a smirk. "My ass is tired thanks to you dippin' your dick where it isn't supposed to be, so one of those coffees had better be for me."

Except the asshole grinned when he said it, and I shook my head as I rounded the truck and stepped onto the sidewalk.

"It's not like that," I told him as I came to stand by his side, hating that any of them would think I was toying with Raven.

That she was just a fuck.

Not when she was everything.

Kane blew out a huff as he raked his fingers through his hair. "I'm just giving you shit, man. You think we all haven't known it?"

I inhaled a shaky breath. "And what's that?"

"That you're fucking mad over Raven? I've spent the last seven years watchin' you watch her. It's plain as day. Not sure how River never saw it."

A flicker of that guilt bubbled up again. "He did, but I swore to him that he had it all wrong. That I'd never look at her like that. Would never touch her."

Kane gave me a shrug. "It was bound to happen. You can't keep something that profound contained for long. Honestly can't believe it hadn't happened sooner."

"Should've done it all different, though."

"What, like not fuck her on a table at my bar?" An amused accusation lifted his brow.

A contrite chuckle skated out of me. "Yeah, that probably would have been a prudent start. She makes me crazy, though. Can't think straight when I'm around her."

"Love drunk fool."

A heavy shot of air blew from my nose. "Apparently."

He clapped me on the shoulder and pulled me close to him. "You'll make this right. Fix your shit with your girl, then fix your shit with River. He loves you, man. He's going to see through the anger to what's been clear to the rest of us for years."

"Thanks, brother."

"You owe me big." His grin was all teeth.

I handed him one of the cups which was, in fact, for him, and he lifted it in the air and pointed at me with his index finger of that hand. "Now *this* is a prudent start. If only it had a shot of whiskey in it."

He winked and brought it to his lips. "Now go get on your knees and beg her to forgive you so I can drag my ass to bed."

I let go of a short laugh before I was jogging across the street, feeling both heavy and light as I went straight to the door. It was still two hours before opening, so I knew it'd be locked.

I knocked at the glass, waiting a few seconds.

Nothing. No movement or sound.

Disquiet pulled through my chest, and I pressed my nose to the pane, peering inside as I knocked again.

Harder that time.

Nothing again.

Dread seeped slow, licking across my flesh and sinking into my stomach.

Throat growing thick, I dug into my pocket for the set of keys I kept. I found the right one and slid it into the lock, hand shaking as I turned it and opened the door.

Silence.

No alarm.

I could feel the concern emanating from Kane from across the street, and I rushed inside, gaze frantically jumping in every direction.

I searched up and down the two aisles, under the white wooden displays slotted with buckets of flowers, like there was some kind of chance that she was going to be hiding underneath.

I rounded the counter, eyes sweeping her workspace.

Empty.

My pulse started chugging hard in my veins, and I rounded back out just as Kane was bursting through the door.

"What's going on?"

"Can't find her." I croaked it as I ran into the backroom, heart crashing in my chest. It was a small space, not a ton of places to hide, though I went for the cupboards anyway, ripping them open to find nothing inside. I ran to the small bathroom. The vacancy echoed back, and I shot back out, gasping, "She's not here."

It was a lament.

Horror.

Agony.

My brow pinched when I noticed the back door was slightly ajar, just resting on the frame. I bolted for it, whipping it open and stumbling out into the alley. Spinning around as I searched the emptiness.

"Raven!" I shouted, pain leaching into the single world. "Raven!"

Kane suddenly stumbled out behind me, his face ashen as he

held up a sheet of paper. Same kind that had been wrapped around that rock.

> *You think you're coming for me? I've been coming for you both all along. Now the bitch will bleed for what she's done. For what you've done. Don't be sad, you're all next.*
>
> *G*

Kane and I blew into River's driveway with the tires spinning, barely coming to a stop before we both jumped out. The front door whipped open at the same time, and River stormed out onto the porch. Wrath surrounded him in a halo, same as I could feel surrounding me.

"It's fuckin' Gideon," I choked as I strode toward him, fully prepared for another attack because God knew I deserved it, though I didn't slow my approach. "He has her."

"What?" Horror pulsed with River's question.

"Gideon." His name stuck on my tongue, terror gripping me in a fist.

"How the fuck is that even possible?" he wheezed, hands going to his head as he attempted to deal with the blow. "That asshole has been missing for seven years."

Gideon, Brek, and Lye had all been missing that whole time. I'd hunted them, and it'd taken me forever to sniff them out. The few clues I'd found not enough to fully unearth them.

I'd gone to Cash when I'd gotten desperate.

Played it a game, though he'd known all along.

He'd given me what I'd needed to take care of Brek and Lye, but Gideon had remained elusive.

Disappearing without a trace.

And now he was here.

"Need to tell you something," I grated, pushing the words out around the razors that lined my throat.

River glared at me, cagey as all fuck, though he was uttering low, "Tell me what the hell is going on, Otto. No more fuckin' lies."

I scraped my fingers through the short pieces of my hair, barely able to speak, just knowing I had to get Raven back. Bile gathered in my throat. "I've been hunting them," I admitted, words gravel.

Shocked confusion knitted his brow. Alarm rushed in behind it. "What do you mean, you've been huntin' them?"

"Couldn't let them get away with what they did to Haddie. With what they did to Raven. Ferreted out two of them. Brek and Lye. Put them in the ground."

"You did what?" His disbelief was abraded, the full scope of what I'd been doing becoming clear.

I pressed on. "Couldn't find a trace of Gideon."

But he'd obviously found me.

River blinked while Kane buried a curse in the fist he pressed to his mouth like it was the only thing that would keep the torrent of his anger from rushing out.

"Without us?" River pressed. "Without letting us in on it? You're supposed to be our family, Otto."

My head shook before the confession started spilling out, seven years of grief and torment woven in the words.

"He killed my sister, River. He stole the one person I was supposed to protect. I couldn't drag you all into it. Not when I was doing it out of revenge and not for Sanctum. Not when it was done out of hate and not for the sole reason of protecting someone. It was on me to seek justice for her. For them."

My voice snagged on the last, sure he'd know exactly what I meant.

His sister was included, and my hatred had extended to what they'd done to her.

He winced, and I continued, voice low as I angled his way, "Going behind the club was wrong. I know it. I should have just told you, but I couldn't risk getting you involved. Know you'd be on your bikes in a second flat. You'd all moved beyond it, beyond that life, beyond the immorality and wickedness, and I've been fucking stuck there."

I sucked in a distraught breath.

"Stuck seven years ago. In that moment when I failed my sister. In that moment when I'd tried to retaliate but instead it was me who was about to be buried. In that moment when I was saved for God knows what reason except to be able to take these monsters down."

My chest tightened with the onslaught of emotions. With the truth that had come to fruition over the last month. One that I'd been avoiding for so long but wouldn't ignore anymore.

"In that time when I broke your sister's heart because I thought it was the right thing to do. Because I thought I couldn't give her the life she deserved. Because I thought I wasn't good enough for her. And fuck, I'm not…don't think there's a man alive who's good enough for how amazing she is, but I'm going to spend every one of my days trying to be. Trying to be good enough for her. Trying to give her *that* life she deserves. Whatever *she* wants it to be."

River dropped his gaze to the porch. Tension wound through every muscle in his body.

Could barely swallow as I forced the words up my throat. "I love her, River. I love her so fuckin' much. I've fought that love for seven years, and the only thing it did was hurt her, and you can hate me for it, but I refuse to fight this love for a second longer. We're going to get her back, then I'm never going to let her go."

I felt the weight of Charleigh's presence when she stepped into the doorway. Tears blanketed her cheeks, and she hugged herself across her middle.

"We have to," I reiterated, looking at her, a silent promise that I wasn't going to let this bastard hurt her.

I had to get to them. Find her. Stop it the way I hadn't been able to do before.

Desperation streaked through my veins when my cell rang, and I yanked it from my pocket. My lungs closed off when I saw it was Cash.

I fumbled to answer it, praying to God he had news as I pressed it to my ear. "Please tell me something good."

"Think I got a lead."

"What is it?"

"Been hunting for anything on Gideon since you asked me for information." The repercussions of that request hung heavy in the dense air. Echoes of his warnings of what my thirst for revenge might do.

"I finally got a possible hit. The spelling of his last name was different, but the birth date and social security number matched. It was a marriage license to one Sienna Perdue. I was able to locate a picture of her. It's from about five years ago, but I'm ninety-nine percent sure it's the same Sienna who met Raven at the club last night. I thought she looked familiar, but I didn't make the connection until this morning when I got the call that Raven is missing."

"Oh fuck," I wheezed.

River angled down, listening the best as he could, and Kane came up on my other side, also inclining his ear.

"She rented a house over on Pine. Way on the outskirts of town," Cash continued. "Saddle up. I have the address incoming. Theo and I are already on our way. And this time, this motherfucker is going to feel the wrath of us all. Of this entire family. The way it's supposed to be."

He ended the call.

A crash of hope and despair ripped through me.

A drive of ferocity and hate and the love that shined so fuckin' bright.

River looked at me for a beat before he stretched out his hand with the stacked Ss tattooed on the back and muttered, "That's fuckin' right. That's what this club does. It's what this family does. Now let's go get your girl back."

Chapter
SIXTY-ONE

Raven

ROPE BIT DOWN ON MY SKIN WHERE THEY HAD MY WRISTS AND ankles bound to a hard wooden chair that had been pulled out from a small dining table.

It'd been placed in the middle of the kitchen.

Plastic covered the floor underneath, and duct tape sealed off the whimpers that groaned in my mouth.

Gideon loomed ten feet away, a demented smile on his face as he studied me with a hunting knife dangling languidly from his right hand.

Sienna was on the couch in the living room, appearing to be bored as she flipped through a magazine. Completely indifferent. Her friendship fabrication and deceit.

It wasn't hurt from her betrayal that drummed through me.

It was fear.

Harsh pulses that thrummed like poison through my veins.

Sickness pooled in my stomach as bile lifted to my mouth. I tried to swallow around it, but it was impossible. No way to subdue the way it felt like I was being strangled by the horror that ensnared every cell in my body.

Sweat slicked my flesh as I sat there waiting for this fiend to have his way with me.

He slowly stalked forward, a gleam in his eye when he reached out and ripped the tape from my mouth, leaving a burst of pain in its wake.

Gasping, I struggled to bring large gulps of air into my aching lungs.

To stay calm. To believe.

But I'd seen firsthand what this monster would do. I'd seen the evil that occupied every recess of his mind.

"I've been waitin' for you." He said it softly like we were old lovers, and I tried to edge back from the foulness he exuded when he leaned in and dragged his nose along my cheek.

Recoiling against the filth that oozed from his spirit.

"Always so shy," he murmured, and he reached out and dragged the blunt edge of his fingernail down my cheek where his nose had been.

I wanted to spit in his face. Fight him. Tell him I was so much stronger than any of them had ever given me credit for. Shout the lengths I would go.

But I was bound, trapped the way I'd been when I'd been nothing but a helpless little girl.

His eyes glinted in some sort of victory, as if he'd seen my internal reaction. "But you're not so innocent, are you?"

His voice transformed in a flash, and he moved before I could make sense of the action.

A scream punctured the air when he drove the blade deep into my thigh.

Agony sundering. Rending through me on a hot, searing burn as he knelt in front of me, twisting the handle as he did.

I nearly blacked out from the pain, and I sniveled and choked through it, trying to keep my composure that was quickly slipping.

"I know it was you," he seethed, getting close to my face. "They blamed it on the Demons, but I know it was you. You, little bitch. You killed my brother and the others, didn't you?"

He cranked the knife as he gritted, "Did you think I was gonna let you get away with it?"

Another scream.

Anguish clutched me in a fist, and a sob catapulted out with it. Saliva poured from the side of my mouth as I wheezed around the misery.

"I saw you running through the shadows. Saw you thinking you could slink through them unnoticed."

Lightheadedness rushed through my mind, and the hazy blur of my thoughts tumbled to Otto. Back to the time when everything had changed. I'd known the torment he'd suffered. I had watched him wilt away in the week after Haddie had been killed. I had witnessed his despondency.

I'd known exactly what was happening when I'd heard him moving around in his bedroom after River had walked out. I knew he was going for them himself. Without the help from the rest of the family.

I couldn't let him do it. Couldn't let him become some kind of martyr lost to his grief.

Because of Haddie, I'd known where Gideon and his friends went on Thursday nights. The many times she'd sneaked off to meet him there during the time that Otto had been in prison.

I couldn't let him do it.

Alone.

The guys had made sure that I knew how to protect myself. That I knew self-defense, even though it hadn't done me any good when I'd been pinned under Dusty in that kitchen where I'd lost so much of myself. But the one thing they'd taught me that I could use was how to use a gun, River drilling it into my head that it was only for my safety when he'd take me out into the desert for target practice. Drilling it into my head that I should only go that route if I had no other choice.

And I was sure that night when I'd heard Otto leave that there was only one choice to be made.

So, I'd stole into River's room and had taken one of his rifles, and I'd gone, riddled with pain from my wounds. Riddled with the sorrow of losing my best friend. Riddled with the anguish of the man I'd loved turning his back on me.

Then I'd been riddled with desperation when I'd found him on his knees, Gideon pointing a gun and getting ready to shoot.

I hadn't thought twice about it.

I'd opened fire.

As if I wouldn't protect Otto the way he'd always protected me.

As if I would hold an ounce of remorse over it.

I lifted my face to the monster who snarled three inches from my face. "You killed Haddie."

"Just punishment for what Otto did. She was a good fuck. Would have kept her around until he set our bikes on fire. A straight disrespect. No one fucks with us like that. There was only one thing left I could do. Thing was, it wasn't just Otto involved, now, was it? It was the whole crew, and you were supposed to bleed out that night, too."

His voice twisted to that low, disgusting thing again. A crooning as he turned the hilt of the knife. Pain splintered, and I struggled to remain conscious.

"But since you survived, our plans changed for you. Oh, the ways we were all going to have you. Figured we'd get rid of Otto's crew first and then we'd get to keep you all to ourselves."

I gasped and choked as he continued, "Otto showed just like we knew he would. Only you were there, weren't you? You were there and you killed my brother. You killed the others."

Hot air puffed from his mouth, hate and his own twisted grief. His nostrils flared as he leaned in close.

"I've been waiting to find you for so long. All of you. But you disappeared just as deep as I did. Had to since the cops had linked me and my boys to everything inside that warehouse. I had to leave all four of them there, lying in pools of their own blood, our fingerprints all over those drugs, set right out for the cops that showed after all that gunfire. Wasn't about to lose my brother and get locked up because of you and Otto."

He sighed an exasperated sound. "Been on the watch for years, no clue where you were hiding. I can only thank Otto for coming for us, thinking he was gonna finish us off. I got a hit that someone was searching for us, and I was able to track it back to this little town in the middle of nowhere. And surprise, surprise, here all of you were. Living lives like you deserved to have them. Probably couldn't have done it without my Sienna here, keeping tabs on you. Getting me on the inside. Makes all of this so much easier."

He jerked the knife free. Agony fractured through my body, and I knew he was only getting started.

"Now, I'm gonna kill you slow…drag it out so when I dump your body in Otto's house, he feels the pain. So he knows exactly what you've gone through. Then I'm going to do the same to every one of them. One by one."

He pressed the tip of the blade to my other thigh, and I held my breath, waiting for the fresh round of torment…when I heard it.

A swarm of power in the distance.

A gathering of strength.

Motorcycles.

Relief thundered as loud as the bikes.

My family was coming for me.

Chapter
SIXTY-TWO

OTTO

River and I were already poised at the window and Kane was at the back door when the hum of motorcycles penetrated our ears.

It was our cue to move.

Knowing the second Gideon heard them coming he'd be set off balance.

Caught off guard and unprepared. Thinking he had only a minute to get ready before we came busting through the door.

And that was the *minute* we were using to our advantage.

But that was only going to last for a beat.

Acting while we had the chance.

River smashed the lock on the window with a rock. It gave easily, and he tossed it wide open. The second it was, I dove through the narrow opening, and I tumbled into the house, rolling twice before I pitched onto my feet.

I remained low, two guns drawn and pointed at the motherfucker who flew around Raven with shock and rage littered across his horrid, disgusting face.

River toppled in behind me, guns drawn, too.

Didn't know if it was relief or rage that I felt when my gaze fell on Raven.

Raven who'd already been battered.

A stream of blood trickled from a cut on the side of her mouth, but what lurched my heart was the thick pool of it that had gathered on the floor beneath her from a gash on the top of her thigh.

But she was alive, and she looked at me with those inky eyes. Dragging me down into the depths. To her love and her belief. To her strength and her vulnerability.

To every complex, beautiful, perfect thing that she was.

I hoped mine conveyed everything that I felt inside.

That I'd live for her. Die for her. Shout for her. That I loved her with every fiber of my being. That she was the light that called me from the darkness, and I was ready to bask in it.

But I couldn't relish in it since that bitch Sienna screamed as she jumped off the couch, and Gideon yanked Raven up from a chair. The ropes that had bound her had already been cut and fell to the ground, fucker likely doing it when he heard us coming and thought he was actually gonna drag her away.

Now, he hauled her back against his chest and pressed a knife to her throat.

Sienna hovered just off to the side, antsy as fuck as she looked between me and Gideon.

Trepidation had my insides quaking, but I refused to let it show as I ground out, "Drop the knife."

A crazed smile pulled across Gideon's face. "Yeah, that's not goin' to happen."

"She doesn't have anything to do with this. This is between us, so drop the knife and you and I will hash this shit out."

Derision rocked from him, and he yanked Raven harder against his chest. "This bitch killed my brother, and she's not going anywhere until she gets what's coming to her."

It was my turn to be unprepared. The stake of questions that arrowed through me and pinned me to the spot.

What the fuck was he talking about?

I didn't have time to contemplate it before the roar of a motorcycle revving from outside rang in the atmosphere.

It was the second cue. The one that had the front door busting open with Cash and Theo banging through, at the exact same time as Kane burst through the back door.

My whole crew piled in, guns drawn, hostility vibrating from their beings. Theo went for Sienna, pushing her down onto her knees before he turned his attention to Gideon and River.

"Now!" I shouted, praying to God Raven would get that single word was meant for her.

Since the woman knew me better than anyone else, she did.

She angled an elbow into his gut and took all the weight from her feet at the same time, using one of the techniques we'd taught her when she was a teen, tearing herself free of his vicious hold and dropping to the ground onto her knees.

It left him exposed.

He shouted, "You fuckin' bitch."

Last word barely got out of him before I squeezed the trigger, letting the single bullet fly.

My whole family would have been firing if it wasn't for the fact that Raven was in a ball with her hands over her head in front of him.

I was aiming for his heart, but was too far to the left, and I hit him up closer to his shoulder. Roaring, he stumbled back a step, and the knife slipped from his hand.

That was all it took to send me running, raging across the room, throwing myself on top of him to keep him from coming back for Raven. I hit him with a thud, and the two of us toppled to the ground. We scrambled around, trying to get on top of the other.

A grunt heaved out of me when he got a punch in low at my ribs, bastard thinking he was gonna get the upper hand when he tossed me just to the side. Only I threw a fist at the same time, clocking him in the jaw. In a flash, I was right back on top of him, pinning him down while I pressed the barrel of a gun to his temple.

Teeth gritted, I pulled the trigger.

And somehow, I recognized it didn't have a thing to do with the hate. No bearing on the thirst for retribution that had consumed me for so long.

It was for Raven. For the simple fact that I'd give anything to keep her safe.

He went limp below me, and I was washed in a vat of relief.

Only it didn't last because a feral scream cut through the air. A pain so great as Sienna jumped to her feet and came running across the room with a knife held in one hand above her head.

And she was coming for me.

I could feel the reservation pummel the air. The way not one of my crew wanted to take her down since they'd committed their lives to helping women in need.

"Get down on your knees!" Theo shouted at her, but she kept coming.

A single gunshot popped off. I saw her stumble when it struck her low in the back of the leg, no doubt, Theo trying to injure her rather than end her.

Only she was already right there, refusing to let it stop her as she went to drive that knife straight into my back where I was still straddling Gideon.

Only Raven had pushed to her knees, and I saw a flash of metal. A blade.

She had Gideon's knife, and she drove it straight into Sienna's stomach right before she got to me.

Shock dropped Sienna's mouth open and froze her to the spot, her knife toppling to the ground as her hands went to the hilt of the blade that was buried in her abdomen.

Two seconds later, she dropped to her knees as a gush of blood poured from her mouth. Her eyes were wide as she gurgled and wheezed, before she faceplanted against the floor. Sprawled out dead in front of Raven.

Discordant breaths raked from Raven, horror tearing through her as she scrambled away. Only she was scrambling for me, throwing those arms around me as a sob erupted from her throat.

"Are you okay?" I begged. "Baby, tell me you're okay."

She could barely nod, sniffling as she rambled, "You came for me. You came for me."

Relief sped through my veins, and I curled my arms around her as I pulled her onto my lap. She kept wheezing through the disorder, through the trauma and shock, and I was pressing a thousand kisses to the top of her head, murmuring, "I will always come for you, Little Moonflower. Always."

Chapter
SIXTY-THREE

Raven

I couldn't stop crying. Couldn't stop the emotion that flooded out of me on a torrent.

The relief.

The horror.

The vestiges of terror and the lingering pain.

But most of all, it was the feel of Otto. The surety of his arms that were held fiercely around me. His heart that thundered a savage beat against my ear. His promises that he mumbled at the top of my head.

"Always. I will always come for you. It's over. It's over."

Hot tears kept bleeding from my eyes and into the fabric of his shirt as I choked and whimpered.

"I'm so sorry," he mumbled, trying to get me closer. "I should have—"

I shook my head and fisted my hand in his tee. "No more *I should haves*. All that matters is the now. That you're here. That we move on from here. Together," I rasped.

I was finished living in the past.

Finished being chained.

The time had come that we were freed.

He clung to me the same way as I clung to him, his warmth

saturating me, his strength surrounding me with an overwhelming force.

While our family stood in a semi-circle around us. Their harsh pants ricocheted from the walls as everyone processed the scene.

It'd all happened so fast.

In a flash.

A blink of events that closed the book on years of history.

Otto carefully shifted me, sweeping an arm under my legs and banding the other high up on my back.

Slowly, he stood.

Carefully.

Cradling me against his chest.

"Need to get her to the doctor," Otto grumbled low, his lips still pressed to my forehead, unable to tear them away.

I wound my arms tighter around his neck, and I stared up at the man who I'd loved for all of my life.

My safety.

My security.

The one who'd whispered belief into my spirit for all those years.

And I didn't need the mirror to see myself right then. To know who I wanted to be. To feel the fulfillment of who I'd become.

"I don't want to go to Dr. Reynolds' office, Otto. I just want to go home. With you. He can come to the house."

He edged back enough that he could peer down at me with those blue, fathomless eyes.

"That where you want to be?" he murmured. "With me?"

"It's where I've always wanted to be."

His attention slid to River.

The two of them shared a silent conversation.

One that transpired as quickly as the events that had just taken place.

A flash and flicker.

But in it, a thousand things had been said.

A claim.

An oath.

A new understanding.

River's voice was gruff when he said, "We'll clean up this mess. Looks like a domestic dispute to me."

He looked to Kane, Theo, and Cash, getting a round of agreement from them on how they were going to handle the situation. How they were going to cover it.

Then he lifted his chin when he looked back at Otto, a clear message woven in the words. "Get her home. Where she belongs."

Otto's nod was clipped, and he carried me across the room and out of the house.

It had to be midmorning, the sun steadily climbing the sky, the warmth of its rays expanding out over the earth and wrapping us in its embrace.

Otto kept me in those arms as he ambled down the steps and through the yard. Below the ramble of trees that were beginning to turn, the leaves a glorious patchwork of oranges, yellows, and reds.

He kept moving past the bikes that had been left at haphazard angles out front, and he headed down the pitted dirt drive.

"Where are we going?" I asked, my throat sore from the screams.

"Left my truck about a quarter of a mile up the road so they wouldn't hear us coming."

No question, they'd planned it all, utilizing their skills of getting vulnerable women out of bad situations to their full extreme.

As if he read the questions that played out in my mind, he explained, "Knew I had to get to you as quickly and as stealthily as I could. River, Kane, and I plotted it on our way out here, praying that we'd make it soon enough."

"And you came."

"Promised you I wouldn't let this bastard get to you. Had almost been too late."

"But you weren't, and I'm fine and whole."

A furor of fury rolled through him, and he pulled me tighter. "Can't stand that he still managed to get to you. That we missed it."

"None of us knew Sienna was involved."

I wanted to hate her, but in the scheme of it, it didn't matter. I didn't have any space left inside myself for the animosity to infiltrate. No room for the fear, humiliation, and shame.

I was letting it go.

All of it.

And I was doing it today.

Otto peered down at me, and his brow arched in speculation. "You want to tell me what he was talking about when he claimed you killed his brother?"

I curled deeper into his hold. "I don't know why I was always so afraid of telling you."

Unease rolled through his being. "Tell me what?"

"That I followed you that night. That I knew what you were doing. That you were somehow going to go and make the ultimate sacrifice. Thinking that it would make up for what happened to Haddie and me. But I couldn't let that happen."

He slowed a fraction, and he pulled me even closer as old pain wisped from his mouth. "It was you."

My throat clogged off, and he hugged me tighter.

"You were the one who saved me. Gave me a new lease on life."

I peeked up at him. "Because I always knew you were destined to spend this life with me."

"Fuck, Raven, you…" He trailed off.

I looked up at him without shame. "I never regretted it, Otto. To me, what I did was the exact same thing as what you all do for Sovereign Sanctum. Stopping an atrocity from happening. And no, I don't love the way I had to go about it, but would I take it back? Change it?"

I stared up at him as the rays of sunlight speared through the breaks in the trees, the glittering rays flaring around him like beacons.

"Never." It was an urgent whisper. "Because you were always worth it to me. Because I would always fight for you, the way you promised to fight for me."

The wings on his throat thrashed as he swallowed. "You found me at my lowest."

"Just the way you always found me in mine. And now it's time we both rose above it."

He inhaled, those arms strong, and his boots crunched over the uneven terrain.

When we made it to his truck, he angled around to the passenger side. He opened the door and carefully settled me inside. He shut it and ran back around the front, sliding into the driver's seat.

He turned it over and let the engine roar to life, then he turned to look at me, hand gentle as he brushed the pad of his thumb over the tiny freckle near my lip. "Thought I was going to die when I got to Moonflower and found you missing."

"Were you coming to tell me how much you love me, my burly bear?"

I wound as much lightness into it as I could manage, though it was thick and soggy.

"Yeah, baby, I was coming to shout it from the rooftops and pray you'd shout it back."

Love filled my chest to overflowing, years of it that had been shrouded and contained.

Love that was no longer trapped.

I blinked and another tear fell. "You're my favorite person in the world, Otto Hudson."

Otto reached down and hooked his pinky with mine. "And you, Raven Tayte, are mine."

Then he dragged me across the bench seat to tuck me to his side. He put the truck in drive, then curled his arm around my shoulders as he whipped a U-turn in the road. "And now, Little Moonflower, I think it's time you learned exactly what that means."

EPILOGUES

Raven

Nine Months Later

I REARRANGED THE FLOWERS IN THE BOUQUET THAT I'D PLACED in the middle of the small table under the wall of windows in the great room at Otto's house.

Correction: Our house.

It turned out I hadn't been looking for my own place. I'd been looking for where I belonged. Where my heart and my feet and my body would be set free.

Sunlight shined in through the windows where they sheared in through the dense woods of the forest that surrounded the house, their glittering rays glinting over the lake that sat low in the distance.

It was breathtaking.

Stunning.

I pulled an iris from the bouquet and resituated it, making sure the arrangement was perfect.

A giant, full array of my favorite flowers.

Irises and lilies.

Tulips and hydrangeas.

Moonflowers, of course.

All surrounded by lush leaves and green foliage.

Pride swelled inside me when I thought of my little shop and what it'd become. What it stood for.

For the moments in our lives that marked us.

Weddings and anniversaries and birthdays.

Get wells and funerals and apologies.

Achievements and milestones.

And sometimes, they just represented the day to day.

But to me, each of those days were a milestone. Something to be remembered and cherished.

Each a reminder that my wings were no longer clipped.

This girl had decided to soar, and I no longer held back.

Excitement blazed in my belly when I heard the low grumble of a motorcycle coming up the drive in the distance, that anticipation growing to a furor as the sound of the garage door rolling up echoed through the walls before it wound back down.

I was in a full body buzz by the time the steady thud of heavy footsteps climbing the stairs reverberated the floors.

Then my heart pressed full when the door opened behind me.

His presence rolled over me from behind.

His aura profound.

Patchouli and warm apple pie.

I could feel his slow slide of appreciation as he stilled in the doorway. The heat of his ravenous gaze dragging over my back.

"You tryin' to wreck me, darlin'?"

"I must be since you ask me the same thing every day," I told him with a coy glance over my shoulder.

Okay, so I was totally trying to wreck him. Bring him to his knees the way he always had me on mine.

Because the man stole my breath where he stood just inside the door.

Otto Hudson was so hot it was unfair.

So hot it was physically painful.

I'd once thought that staring at him was like standing in the sun and knowing you were going to get burned, but you did it anyway because it felt so good while you baked in the blistering rays.

But I knew now that I did it because it was where I belonged.

Held beneath that fierce gaze of blue, loved by a man hewn of rugged stone.

Skin covered in tats and muscles rippling beneath the tight white tee stretched over his massive chest.

What else was I supposed to do but throw on one of those dresses and heels that I knew drove him wild?

"Dream I'm livin' every day…coming home and finding you standing there like that," he rumbled in that deep, lust-inducing voice.

He ambled into the kitchen, carrying a bag of ice and a twelve-pack of beer that I'd sent him to pick up at the store. He put the ice in the freezer and the beer into the fridge.

One of those smirks that hadn't left his mouth for the last nine months rimmed his full, plush lips, desire glinting in his eyes as he let the refrigerator door drop closed before he slowly edged up behind me.

Each step an earthquake that resonated across the floor.

I had my hair pinned up in a loose twist, and he pressed his mouth to the nape of my neck as he gripped me by the waist.

Need licked through my veins.

He let his palms ride around to my belly.

Splaying wide as he kissed a path across my shoulder.

A whimper rolled out of me, and I leaned back against him, welcoming the teasing kisses that moved back up the side of my neck and to my ear. "And dressed like this. You know exactly what you do to me."

Chills flashed as he slowly smoothed his hands back down my body to my hips to gather the material of the dress's full skirt.

He leisurely dragged it up.

"Everyone is going to be here in thirty minutes." It was supposed to come out a rebuff of the direction he was traveling, but instead it came out a question.

Or maybe a challenge.

He emitted a low chuckle, lips nipping at my ear. "While I prefer to take my time with you, I'm willing to make it fast. Last thing we want is me hard and thinking about getting in this pussy during the entire family barbecue."

He cupped me over my pelvic bone, and his fingers pressed between my thighs over my underwear.

Energy crackled. Though it was light. A tease. Zinging around us in the joy that we'd found.

"Like you aren't going to be, anyway." I tried to play it a taunt, but it came out breathy when he pushed the fabric aside and dragged his fingers through my slit.

Arousal rushed, a throbbing ache that instantly lit.

This man had me in a puddle of need in a second flat.

"Now that is no lie, but I think I'm going to need to have my moonflower, anyway. Seeing as how you're already dripping for me."

"I think that would be a very good idea," I whispered, words barely audible as he played with my clit. Fingertips just brushing over my nub.

Tiny flickers of pleasure sparked across my flesh, and surprise jolted from me when he suddenly pushed my chest down onto the table and tossed the skirt of my dress up high.

Cool air brushed my backside, then heat followed it as he leaned down to drag my underwear down my legs, the man kissing along the cleft of my ass as he went. He wound them free of my heels, then he straightened.

The man a tower behind me.

Strength and volatility.

Softness and greed.

He was everything. Every element that I needed.

I heard the jangle of his belt and the zipper of his jeans, then I moaned when he lined the fat head of his cock up with my center.

"You ready for me, Little Moonflower?"

"I'm always ready, my burly bear."

He drove into me, taking me whole.

My nails raked at the tabletop as a desirous cry jutted from my mouth.

The man filling me so full I couldn't breathe. So full I couldn't feel anything but the abject pleasure that he brought.

"Fuck, Raven. Doesn't matter how many times I have you, I can't get enough. Pure fuckin' heaven."

That pleasure glowed as he withdrew and rocked back in.

"My paradise," he rumbled as he seated himself to the hilt.

He picked up a reckless rhythm, fucking into me with long, hard strokes. Big hands gripped onto my hips as he pounded relentlessly.

Perfectly.

Because I'd not found one thing in this world that felt better than him.

He grunted as he took me again and again, mumbling his praise as he consumed me.

"This body. This heart. Nothing better than you. Such a good girl."

An arm slipped between me and the table, and he yanked my back against his chest.

I gasped at the sudden change in position, then I was moaning loud when he grabbed me by the back of the right knee and lifted my leg to hook my heel on the edge of the table.

Spreading me wide.

And God, it felt so good…miraculous as he drove into me from behind. His fingers found my clit again and his other hand wrapped around the front of my neck.

I felt consumed. Taken whole. The man everywhere all at once.

Only he wanted more, and he turned my jaw to the side so he could capture my mouth with his.

Those tiny sparks of pleasure caught fire.

Increasing with each possessive thrust as he kissed me like he didn't ever want to stop.

One second later, I was shooting off, soaring amid the fireworks that burst behind my eyes.

And he was shouting my name as he throbbed and pulsed

inside me. We stayed that way, both of us gasping for the breath that we'd lost.

Then he carefully took me by the knee and settled me back on my unsteady, trembling feet. No doubt, he knew he'd set me off balance, my knees and body weak. He looped an arm around my waist to keep me supported and brushed aside a lock of hair that'd gotten free of the twist.

Then he murmured at my jaw, "That should do it."

A giggle got free.

Apparently, he got cocky when he was trying to put a baby in me.

"You think so?" I asked, peeking back up at him from over my shoulder. Anticipation and this dream we were living weaving into the words.

He gathered me closer and breathed me in. "I hope so, Raven, because I want to give you every single thing in this life that you desire."

OTTO

I leaned back against the exterior side of the island, nursing a beer as I appreciated the mayhem going down in the middle of the living room.

Taylor Swift blared from the speakers as Raven, Charleigh, and Nolan danced like goofs on the other side of the couch. Their laughter rolled through the house, bouncing off the walls and rattling the windows.

Their smiles infectious as they gave themselves over to the wild moves that Nolan was coercing them into.

"Watch this one, Auntie!" Nolan shouted, and he dropped to the ground, spinning around on his butt like he'd invented an award-winning new move. "You think you can top it? Because I bet my Daddy-O is gonna give it a perfect ten!"

"A ten? No way am I good enough for that!" she teased, reaching out a hand and helping him pop back onto his feet.

"You gotta believe in yourself, Auntie. That's what my uncle Otto always tells me, at least."

Raven sent me an adoring glance. One that I felt spear all the way to the middle of my soul. I tipped her the neck of my beer, hollering, "Come now, Moonflower, show our little dude what you've got."

Raven didn't hesitate. She dropped herself straight to the floor, spinning herself around in that dress, cackling as she did.

God, could anything feel better than this? The sound of her laughter? Our family surrounding us?

"What about you, Momma Dog?" Nolan shouted.

Charleigh giggled. None of us knew where the heck he'd picked that up, but it seemed to have become her permanent moniker.

"I think I'm fine on my feet," she told him, affection rushing out. "See?"

She did some crazy flailing move that made her look like she was having a seizure.

Even though Raven had never left my bed after that fateful day, that Raven and Charleigh had been living apart for all these months, they'd never been closer. Their friendship—their sisterhood—strong and unbreakable.

I'd worried that after Sienna's betrayal, Raven might regress, become filled with distrust, hiding that goodness that wanted to pour from her spirit.

But no, my moonflower had completely bloomed.

She was no longer willing to allow the past to be her guide. No longer willing to allow it to control her decisions and moves.

Raven hopped to her feet, grabbing Nolan's hand and taking him with her, then she grabbed one of Charleigh's.

The three of them started twirling around.

Happiness shined through her expression. It was the only thing that I'd ever wanted to see. Had spent so much time thinking I'd be the one to destroy her that I'd never been brave enough to imagine that I might be a part of putting that joy on her face.

But Raven was brave enough for the both of us. Bold enough to tell me what she wanted and demand what she needed. Good enough to take the time to show me that I didn't have to forfeit this life in favor of the rage. Strong enough to show me that I also deserved the best things in this life.

There was no way to get Haddie back. No way to undo the tragedy and the loss.

The only power we had was in the day. In the moments that were laid out in front of us.

I'd never again be the fool who wasted them.

River chuckled under his breath where he nursed a beer beside me. His affection so stark as he watched his little family dance in the middle of my living room.

"Never is gonna get old, is it?" he mused, gazing at the three of them having a blast.

"Nope," I agreed.

Guessed he and I hadn't ever been closer, either. The things I'd kept like dirty secrets dragged out into the open, given for all of them to see. I should've known my crew would always support me. Should have gotten they'd stand beside me.

We'd always ride together.

No matter what.

All of them were here, enjoying a Sunday afternoon, the way we did each week. All except for Cash who remained secluded in his cabin.

Except today, Kane was all off, sitting by himself at the little table beneath the window, staring out at the lake in the distance as he downed his third tumbler of scotch.

Normally, he was loud and raucous and right in the middle of the mix, but right then, a dark cloud loomed over his head.

I glanced at River who'd noticed it, too, and he hefted a shoulder. "Don't know what's up with him," he grumbled below his breath.

I shrugged, too, though I figured I'd better check it out, so I pushed from the island and meandered over to the table.

I plopped down onto a chair. When he didn't even acknowledge me, I nudged his calf with the toe of my boot, keeping my voice quiet as I asked, "What the hell is up with you, man?"

"Nothin'," he grunted, taking another swig.

"Nothin'? You've been sitting over here acting like a broody fucker for the whole day when you're normally over there instigating the shenanigans." I pointed a finger at the mess out in the middle of the living room.

He roughed an agitated hand through his hair before he turned his head to the side, his throat bobbing heavily as he swallowed.

Then he looked up at me with fear and disbelief written all over his face. "Seems I have a kid. And her mother is dead."

About the
AUTHOR

A.L. Jackson is the *New York Times* & *USA Today* Bestselling author of contemporary romance. She writes emotional, sexy, heart-filled stories about boys who usually like to be a little bit bad.

Her bestselling series include THE REGRET SERIES, CLOSER TO YOU, BLEEDING STARS, FIGHT FOR ME, CONFESSIONS OF THE HEART, FALLING STARS, REDEMPTION HILLS, and TIME RIVER.

If she's not writing, you can find her hanging out by the pool with her family, sipping cocktails with her friends, or of course with her nose buried in a book.

Be sure not to miss new releases and sales from A.L. Jackson - Sign up to receive her newsletter http://smarturl.it/NewsFromALJackson or text "aljackson" to 33222 to receive short but sweet updates on all the important news.

Connect with A.L. Jackson online:

FB Page https://geni.us/ALJacksonFB
A.L. Jackson Bookclub https://geni.us/ALJacksonBookClub
Angels https://geni.us/AmysAngels
Amazon https://geni.us/ALJacksonAmzn
Book Bub https://geni.us/ALJacksonBookbub

Text "aljackson" to 33222 to receive short but sweet
updates on all the important news.

www.ingramcontent.com/pod-product-compliance
Ingram Content Group UK Ltd.
Pitfield, Milton Keynes, MK11 3LW, UK
UKHW041932030225
454602UK00004B/293